THE

GIPSEY'S WARNING;

OR,

LOVE AND RUIN.

AN

ENTIRELY ORIGINAL ROMANCE OF REAL LIFE.

BY

H. J. COPSON.

" Shame, beggary, and imprisonment, unpitied misery; the stings of conscience, and the curses of mankind shall make life hateful to him—till at last his own hand shall end him."— Vide GAMESTER.

LONDON:

PUBLISHED BY J. CLEMENTS, LITTLE PULTENEY STREET.

INDEX

TO

THE GIPSEY'S WARNING.

INDEX.

THE GIPSEY'S WARNING;

OR,

LOVE AND RUIN.

[*See Page 5*]

CHAPTER I.

THE GAMESTERS.

" ' Tis he, 'tis he ;
I know him by the evil eye."

" WELL, Sir Charles, how goes the exchequer by this time ? Have you lost much of late ? A mere trifle, I suppose, eh ?"

" Somewhere about seven hundred pounds," was the reply; " and if I do not make a lucky hit soon, why, I know not what may be the consequence."

" Have you seen Miss Emily Anson of late ?"

" Why," returned the person addressed, who was a young and extravagant spark, and the son of a baronet, " I was there a few days since; but you know that confounded old aunt of her's prevents a fellow from coming to anything like business with her; so I think I must fain give up all thoughts of possessing her fortune, for I positively could not think of marriage."

" Marriage !" reiterated the other with a derisive laugh ; " pshaw ! nonsense, I never entertained any such thought. Marriage ? How do you spell the word ? Ha ! ha !"

" Now listen to me," exclaimed Sir Charles ; " you talk in such a wild, heedless manner. Suppose, now, that I should succeed in carrying off this girl, do

No. 1.

you not remember that her aunt, the only relative she possesses, is now lying upon a bed of sickness; how think you *she* would bear the loss? but I had forgotten, you never expend a thought upon such matters."

" Not I," replied the other; " they are things unworthy of a man of fashion: but nothing can be more easy than to appease the old lady's fury. A few words of repentance and the like will soon quiet her. The girl has a good round sum of money. If you can carry her off, why, as a matter of course the money will be yours. What think you of my plan now ?"

" The same as I have heretofore."

" And pray, my sentimental friend, what may that be ?"

" That it is a villainous plot, and one in which I will take no share, at least for the present."

" What, then, do you intend to do? turn timber-merchant, I suppose; for I see you are having all the timber in your grounds felled to the earth."

" No," replied the other, " I am about to turn pirate."

" What!" exclaimed the gamester, in unfeigned surprise, " *pirate*, did you say? Why, how can you accomplish that? I'm thinking you would make but a queer fish of that sort. Why, if you saw a man struck down in an action by your foe, your chicken heart would instantly cause you to suspend hostilities, the consequence of which would be that your colours would be struck, your craft boarded, yourself placed in confinement, and then—why the business would be concluded by seeing you dangle at the yard-arm to fright away the sea-gulls. Thus would terminate your career as a pirate. My noble friend, Sir Charles, do you not think I speak truly ?"

" So truly," replied the other, " that were it any other but *you*, I should have shewn him my sword. But a truce with this bagatelle; how much money do you now possess? mine runs very low."

" Aye, Sir Charles, and mine is not much better. I have just thirty pounds left out of three hundred."

" Ah! well, 'tis no use to be dejected. Your thirty and my fifteen will make forty-five pounds: this, perhaps, may bring us a cool hundred or two, if we choose to risk the chances this evening. What say you? Do you agree to my plan ?"

" I do," replied Sir Charles; " and we will make an early call at the old damsel's mansion."

" And talk soft nonsense to your prima donna. I am of opinion that you will be glad to accept of my plan after all; however, if you do not, I prophesy that some other generous gallant will spare you the trouble and carry her off in spite of your teeth. That would be *very* pleasant."

" So *pleasant*," replied the baronet, " that I'd tear his libertine heart out of its foul home."

" Like the dog in the fable," rejoined his companion, " you will neither secure the girl yourself, nor permit any one else to do so; that is, I mean, if you can prevent them."

" Emily Anson is an angel," rejoined the baronet in an impassioned tone; " one that is too good, too gentle to be made the common instrument of a libertine's passion. No; I shall still adhere to my old intentions. If I *should* turn roving adventurer, would you join me ?"

" Oh, of course I would," replied the other. " But come, let's be off; I am impatient to behold the lovely Emily."

" Have a care," continued the baronet. " We have ever been as brothers towards each other. Do not, then, give me cause to break those ties—for ever dissolve the friendship I bear towards you. If aught happens of ill consequence to my Emily, to you alone shall I look for satisfaction. Come, I'm for the toilette."

" Poor weak-minded fool !" muttered the libertine, as Sir Charles quitted the apartment; " his conscience he says will not permit him to carry off the girl, even if she should give him an opportunity so to to do. Ah! well, thank heaven and my own free disposition, I have no such scruples. Once possessing the privilege of visiting there, which I will soon acquire, the task will be readily accomplished. Emily Anson and her fortunes shall be mine. I shall then forfeit the friendship of Sir Charles; but what is the friendship of man compared with the society of lovely woman? Though there is one thing, to be sure, I do much admire; Sir Charles will call me out, and whether pistol or sword is the choice, I shall have but little chance of victory. However, I will risk all and every thing to attain the summit of my hopes."

By the foregoing soliloquy the reader may be in some way prepared for the consummate villainy that is to follow. Sir Charles Mortimer was descended from a noble and wealthy family, of which he was the only remaining branch, that is, with the exception of his father, who resided in an elegant mansion, situated near Bentley Heath. At the age of twenty-seven he and his son, Sir Charles, separated. The young baronet was of a free and open disposition. His present companion, one Count Belford, with nothing but his title and the sharpness of his wits to maintain that position in society which was absolutely for the furtherance of his purpose, which was simply, vampire like, to play upon the vitals of the unsuspecting. Sir Charles had first contracted his acquaintance at college. For some considerable time he had been the inmate of the mansion, and enjoyed the first society of the day; but at length Sir Charles began to frequent the gaming-table; large sums of money were lost; the father now began to examine more strictly the conduct of his son, and the result of this was, that he commanded him to discard Belford from his society; the other refused to do this; a quarrel ensued, which ended in the dismissal of Sir Charles from his paternal roof, with a separate allowance of eight hundred pounds per annum, together with the possession of a large estate. This, however, was insufficient to support the many extravagancies in which the young baronet indulged. The greatest annoyance however, was the thought of being separated from and denied the society of his family; for his father had assured him, that until he thought fit to rid himself of Belford, whom he declared to be nothing better than a confirmed swindler, he should not be permitted to enter his presence, while the proud and haughty soul of Sir Charles shrank in disgust from any act that savoured the least of submission; thus promising a lasting enmity between the father and son, which, with insidious caution, Belford strove to strengthen. Among the small circle of his friends, Charles had become acquainted with the beauteous Emily Anson, an orphan placed under the care of her widowed aunt. She was of a good family, and upon coming of age she would possess a fortune of seven thousand pounds. As may be supposed, the knowledge of this, combined with her beauty and great personal accomplishments, procured her many admirers, but under the stern guardianship of her aunt, Emily, even if she had possessed the inclination, would have found it difficult to have lent an attentive ear to their protestations of love and fidelity; as, however, the young heiress had no great desire to change her condition, they seldom spoke upon this subject; but at length the good old lady was attacked with a dangerous indisposition, and believing herself to be upon the bed of death, she summoned Emily to her side.

" My child," she exclaimed, " shortly will you be left alone and unprotected upon the world. Think well upon the imminent danger in which you are placed. While I lived in health, you was secure from all harm; but, I grieve to say, you have a somewhat giddy heart, and the means I can adopt to save you from ruin, is, to place you under the guardianship of Mr. Williams. For years he has been my most intimate friend. Under his eye you will be secure from all temptation. His daughter Clara will be a fitting companion for your innocence. The income I have left for you is sixty-five pounds, in addition to the legacy left by your father, and which you will possess when you arrive at the twenty-first year of your age. Oh, my dear child, remember 'tis your own happiness I seek to promote. Give not your heart to the world, or its vain, giddy pleasures; for a time all may seem fair, and promise well, but rest assured that the end of all such things is trouble and disgrace upon those who follow their baneful course. The wild gallants of fashion possess not a thought of the sorrow they produce in the hearts of those whose generous nature confides too far. Has my Emily any objection to place herself under the protection of Mr. Williams? His holy calling will secure your happiness; and I should then die happy in the conviction of your future safety. Avoid, my Emily, all those vain displays of grandeur called routs or masquerades, where only the most villainous and unprincipled assemble to betray the unsuspecting. Let your whole life, my child, be such that when, as I now am, you are prostrate upon the bed of death, you can, with a mind of calm assurance, call upon your God to take your immortal soul into his sacred keeping."

"My dear aunt," replied Emily, as the pearly tear of sorrow trickled its course down her lovely cheeks, "I am averse to no course which you may think fit to pursue. My dear father, in his dying moments, placed my future tutorship in your own hands; and surely, had he not have imagined you to be fully competent to the task, he would not have entrusted me to your guidance. Shall I, then, act contrary to the wishes of a dear deceased parent? Oh! 'tis many years since I knew a parent's protecting care. How sacred must their counsel be? But you grow faint, my dear aunt; shall I call for assistance? The medical attendant shall be summoned. Surely you are not about to——"

"Lady Flora Mandeville desires to see you, madam," exclaimed the nurse, entering suddenly the chamber of sickness.

"Let her be shewn in instantly," replied Emily.

"With her accustomed good-nature, the Lady Flora comes to bestow comfort upon the wretched," exclaimed the invalid. "Twice before has she visited me; and I now feel that this will be the last time she will behold me with life. Place this Bible upon the table, my dear Emily. Thanks, my dear child, thanks—her ladyship is here."

CHAPTER II.

THE PARSONAGE.

THE Reverend Mr. Williams, together with his daughter Clara, resided at the parsonage-house, situated about three miles west of the house inhabited by Emily and her invalid aunt. For many years they had been resident upon the grounds of Bentley estate, loving and beloved by all. Some three months previous to the date of this, Mr. Williams had appeared before the Romford sessions, in order to prosecute two ruffians who had robbed and nearly murdered one of the neighbouring villagers.

About half-past twelve o'clock on the night succeeding, when all were locked in the arms of sleep, three persons stood before the parsonage-house. Their appearance was unprepossessing in the extreme. One of them, more fierce-looking than the rest, had his features concealed by a large piece of black crape; in his hand he grasped a large pistol, while the others carried large knives.

"Now," exclaimed the foremost, "this drivelling idiot shall pay the forfeit of his honesty. The gold he possesses must be ours; and if he crosses our path, he dies. Now for the door; look quick, or we shall have the morning upon us."

"First," exclaimed the other, "understand that no violence must be offered. No; take the money, but no violence or unnecessary destruction—d'ye hear me?"

"I do," replied the other, "and think with the rest that you have turned very humane of late, what has consideration to do with us? we will have the gold. If he crosses our path, he shall die! Now, have you aught to say against this?"

"So much," replied the man addressed, "that if you dare to break my commands, your own life shall pay the forfeit, therefore beware. Now to business."

The robbers then proceeded to force open the small latticed window, this they accomplished with little or no difficulty. The next thing to be accomplished was the entry. This, too, they effected, and proceeded with cautious tread along the floor of the parlour, the door of which, to their great disadvantage, was secured upon the outer side; the lock, however, was soon forced open, and they ascended the stairs. The first room they entered was that of the man-servant. Observing that he slept soundly, they contented themselves with securing the door and leaving him unguarded. They then entered the chamber where slept the worthy rector, the door of which not being secured, they entered without difficulty. The worthy Mr. Williams was then in a sound slumber. The ruffians paused irresolutely. At length, one of the more impatient hastily drew the curtains aside, and upheld the gleaming blade of a knife. Instantly his arm was arrested by the one who had before cautioned them against using violence. With a fierce glance, he exclaimed, in a deep whisper :—

"Softly, d'ye hear? By hell, if you renew that attempt, myself will soon place it beyond your power to again disobey me. Search the place—see what spoil there is to be found, and then sheer off. Remember this is the last time I shall caution you, so I'd have you remember."

The robbers, with an ill grace, proceeded to obey this man, whom they evidently feared to disobey. The search proved effectual, for in a small bureau they discovered thirty-five sovereigns, besides two hundred and sixty pounds in bank notes. Having possessed themselves of these, the robbers were about to proceed to the adjoining apartments in order to see what else they could carry off, when Mr. Williams suddenly awoke, and started from his bed in alarm, and attempted to raise an outcry. He was instantly seized by the throat, and thrown to the ground. He gazed upon the ruffian who, with a pistol firmly grasped in his upraised hand, prepared to dash out the brains of the prostrate man, should he dare to utter a sound.

"Release me, villains!" vociferated Mr. Williams.

"Silence!" thundered the ruffian, "silence, I say, or you die—dare but to give utterance to a word."

Before he could finish the sentence the reverend man had sprang to his feet. A fierce though brief struggle ensued. Mr. Williams was again thrown to the ground, and would doubtless have been despatched, but for the timely interference of another robber, who, with one tremendous blow, felled the other to the ground. As the fallen man lay in the agonies of death, Mr. Williams gazed upon his features, and with a sudden start, exclaimed in a loud tone of horror, " Oh, God, 'tis my son !"

CHAPTER III.

FATHER AND SON.

His toilette complete, Sir Charles joined his libertine friend, and quitted the mansion, and proceeded in the direction of the house where Emily and her aunt resided. Just as they were turning a corner hastily, Sir Charles encountered the Hon. Sir John Campbell, a most intimate friend of his father. Both seemed equally surprised at the rencounter.

"Ha, Charles, my boy," exclaimed Sir John, " why, you are a perfect stranger. How happens it that you have not honoured us with a call; why, if you and your respected dad think fit to quarrel, it's no reason that you and I, who have always been such very intimate friends should not agree. Come, you must accompany me home; I am just going to luncheon, and we can have a little chat, and discuss the merits of a bottle of Madeira. Come, take my arm, Sir Charles."

Belford looked at the young baronet, then motioned him away.

" I am extremely flattered by your invitation, Sir John, but at the same time must beg leave to decline the same," replied Sir Charles, " and must therefore bid you adieu."

"And why so?" enquired Sir John.

"I have an appointment elsewhere, sir," replied Sir Charles.

The elder baronet, however, would admit of no denial. Accordingly Sir Charles, accompanied by his friend Belford, proceeded with him to his residence, where they remained until about eight o'clock in the evening, when a loud knock was heard at the outer door, and a servant entered and announced Lord Mortimer. Sir Charles arose with a look of confusion, and, bidding his host adieu, together with his friend, quitted the apartment. As they passed through the hall they encountered Mortimer, he started upon beholding his son, who coldly bowed and passed into the street.

"Did your lordship see your son?" enquired Sir John, as Mortimer, with a disturbed air, entered.

"I did," replied his lordship.

"And pray what said you to him?" continued the baronet.

"Nothing," was the reply. "He coldly bowed and passed on, together with his reprobate companion, the Count Belford, whom I perceive, he has not yet rid himself of; but I am determined he shall do so, even though I suspend the payment of his income to effect it, which I will do, if he does not cast that wretch from his confidence."

"Pshaw," exclaimed Sir John, "I think you are a great deal too harsh with your son."

"Perhaps, sir, you will permit me to possess the will and power of controling my own actions," replied Mortimer, proudly, "my son, sir, is leagued with a villain, and until he discards that villain, I consider myself highly justified in withholding my protection, which I shall do."

"Oh, certainly, my lord," returned Sir John, "I hope I have not given any offence by my remark, which was spoken purely out of friendship and good feeling, though I must add that there is much to be feared by this wild-brained young fellow being left entirely to his own discretion; and sooner or later, I fear much harm will come of it."

"How came he here?" enquired Mortimer, not appearing to notice the latter remark.

"I met with him in the street," replied Sir John.

"And that villain with him, I suppose," rejoined Mortimer, pacing the apartment with hurried steps.

"There certainly was an individual with him—and that individual was the same ——"

"Who passed me in the hall," interposed Mortimer; "I know it; why did you permit him, Sir John, to enter your house when you knew that?"

"He was the friend of your son," interrupted Sir John. "I, of course, did not know that he was the villain of whom you so oft have spoken, and even if I had been aware of the fact, politeness would have forbidden my denial of his presence here."

"You will know him then in future," rejoined his lordship, "and if you value my friendship and feelings as a father, you will never again permit him to enter this house; and should I chance to encounter the rascal, he shall, if possessing the smallest possible spark of courage, appoint the time and place for a meeting. I'll goad and insult him to the quick. He must and shall fight. I am determined to rid myself of him at all hazards."

"If you should want a friend, my lord," exclaimed Sir John, with great *non chalence*, "you know, of course, where to apply for one: I am at all times ready and willing to do the honours of the field in person. Will you take a glass of sherry with me, my lord? Cast aside this gloom, and, trust me, your son will one day return to his father."

"Rest assured, sir, he shall return," exclaimed Mortimer, "or, by Heaven, the very source of his existence shall be stopped. I am his father, and as such will teach him that submission is the duty of every son, young or old, to yield submissively to a parent's command. Now, Sir John, did you not ask me to take wine with you?"

"I did," replied the baronet; "come, my lord, come."

Upon quitting the house of Sir John, Charles, and his inseparable companion, Belford, proceeded to the gaming table, which they found to be well attended. For some time they looked on inactive, but at length, a vacancy being made by a young dupe, who had lost his last guinea—and, therefore, was not wanted there—Belford sat down to play, and in a very short time, he rose from his seat a winner of four hundred and twenty-five pounds. So far so well; but, stimulated by his success, Sir Charles accepted a challenge, and sat down to play—his fortune was not so good as his companion's; he soon lost the little he possessed, together with the whole of Belford's winnings—for he borrowed, and the other dared not to refuse him—he then threw the dice with violence from him, and the man who had won his money, chancing to smile at his petulance, he flew into a violent rage, and ended by calling his successful rival, at play, every opprobious term his passion could suggest: To this the other replied not—but continued to smile in silence, at the other's impotent rage.

Goaded nearly to madness by the calm indifference of the man who had deprived him of his last coin, Sir Charles rose from his seat, sprang suddenly forward, and dealt the man a violent blow in the face; the other returned the insult, and a scene of the greatest uproar and confusion ensued. Still, so used were those sparks of fashion to such scenes, that they made no attempt to interfere or produce a cessation of hostilities, until Sir Charles threw his adversary to the ground, when he called out most lustily for assistance. Then, and then only, did Belford interfere, and forcibly drag his pupil from the prostrate gamester.

"Why, man!" he exclaimed, "do you call this fitting behaviour for a man of rank; because a man has had the luck to win a few paltry pounds from you, are you to throttle him?"

"And pray, sir," vociferated Sir Charles, "how dare you to interfere—is it not enough that I am to be deliberately robbed and swindled. Why, then, should I suffer insult from the swindler, after *that* has been accomplished? Release me, sir, I am resolved that either his blood or mine, shall strew the floor this night—release me, I say, or by heaven, yourself shall feel the ill-effects of my anger."

"Sir Charles!" exclaimed Belford, still restraining the enraged baronet; "the wine you drank at Mortimer's, has made you furious."

"Villain!" rejoined Sir Charles, furiously; "repeat that foul lie, and I'll tear you limb from limb. Think you, that I will bear your insolence. No, release me, I command you!"

"My friend," exclaimed another of the gamesters, addressing Sir Charles—"it appears to me, that there is but one way of settling this dispute."

"And that," interrupted Sir Charles, "is by————"

"The field," responded the other, "perhaps you will be pleased to name your time, and place of meeting, with the weapons you would wish to use—that will at once end all farther disputes."

"Agreed," replied Sir Charles. "I *will* do so—*pistols*. And for the time, none that I can appoint, is so fitting as the present moment—while yet the recollection of my insult, is warm within me."

"And the place?" continued the other.

"The spot upon which we now stand," rejoined Sir Charles, "Muzzle to muzzle. Now, I thought some one called me, coward, some few moments since. Now, if he would repeat his assertion, let him come forward and do so—I am prepared to meet him." No person, however, seemed willing to accept this challenge—and Sir Charles, after a moment's pause, exclaimed, "What! is there none here, willing to face the coward, as he was called? Now, where are the pistols? Am I not to have satisfaction for the robbery and insult which have been committed upon me. Though you should one and all protest against it, I demand the pistols be produced instantly."

"They will not, then," replied the other speaker, "this room is not to be made the scene of cold-blooded murder. If you think fit to name your time and place of meeting, I have no doubt, but that my friend will meet you—but you are now incensed, and heated with wine. Now, sir, will you name the time, place, and weapons, in order that this disturbance may be settled with all convenient speed."

"Belford!" exclaimed Sir Charles, turning to that personage. "I leave this business to your decision."

"My friend, Sir Charles Mortimer, will meet you to-morrow, at the hour of four precisely, in the small meadow at the back of Bentley Heath—and if you will now be pleased to name your weapons, all will be settled for this evening, at least.'

"That, sir, I leave entirely to you," replied the other.

"What weapons do you prefer, Sir Charles!" enquired Belford.

"Oh! any," replied the baronet, carelessly; "either swords or pistols, will serve for me, anything, sir."

"Then, we appoint pistols," returned Belford, "and now, for the hour; has that been agreed upon?"

"You mentioned *four*," was the reply.

"Then let four, *be* the hour," rejoined Belford.

"Is there not some other, and more friendly manner of settling this business?" enquired another of the persons present; "surely, there is no necessity for this blood shed, allow me to intercede in this."

"It is useless, sir," replid Belford, "my friend, Sir Charles Mortimer, has received a deep insult; and only one mode of satisfaction presents itself, as I said before therefore, all that you can either say or do in the subject will be perfectly useless"

"What say you sir," continued the intercessor, addressing Sir Charles, who seemed wrapt in gloomy meditation.

"The same as my friend," replied Sir Charles; "that is, if yonder individual now possesses the courage to defend his honour, for I now pronounce him a coward."

"Come, Belford, shall we quit this atmosphere of rascality, and once more inhale the healthful breeze without? We are no longer desirable company here."

"I am of your opinion, Sir Charles," replied Belford, "we will away at once, and await the arrival of the hour, which will convince such of these gentlemen as think fit to be present, that you are not deficient of honour, or an ample share of courage, to protect that honour from being violated by every scurvy knave, in whose company you may have the ill luck to be cast. Now, sir, I am perfectly willing to withdraw."

"And I," replied Sir Charles.

With these words they quitted the room together.

"Why, really, Sir Charles," exclaimed Belford, as they once more gained the street, "I did not give you credit for possessing such courage; it was very impolitic of you to play in such mad indiscretion. Why, you see, I soon cut the dice when I began to win, and ditto if I had have lost; I never win or lose any very great sum, for I am never inclined to trust the fickle goddess too far, or she may perhaps——"

"Suppose I should fall in this duel," exclaimed Sir Charles, interrupting the other, "that would not be a very pleasant recollection, not that I fear death, by-the-bye, though I should like to have my carcase disposed of in a somewhat decent manner."

"And what is to prevent such from being done?" enquired Belford, "are you not of a noble family?"

"Why, I believe so," replied the other; "but as I am upon terms of such enmity with my father, I should very much wish to know who would do it?"

[*See Page* 10.]

"1 would rather than your wish should not be complied with," replied Belford, "but come man, do not speak in this melancholy strain, you are not dead yet, and there is another thing to be considered—being a capital shot, you are not very likely to fall by the hands of such an unpractised fellow as him, with whom you are now about to transact business. But we will now view the opposite side of the question—suppose you should kill him, what then ?"

"Why, in that case, I must fly the country," replied Sir Charles, "in the event of which my income will be suspended, and what the devil I shall do then, I confess, puzzles me."

"Why," returned Belford, "I think it will then be high time to think of the pirate business."

"That, without money, would be impossible."

"How ?" he continued, in astonishment. "I was not aware that a fellow required a capital to start thief—but I suppose the license comes heavy. Ah! I had forgotten that part of the story."

"A truce with this nonsense," rejoined the baronet.

"My meaning is, that should the last extremity demand such a course of proceeding, I would build a frigate from my own timber, be the first to cross her planks, and the last to quit them in the moment of danger—now you know all."

"I do," rejoined Belford, "and a very romantic idea it is, truly ; but stay, in our meditations, I really believe we have passed the mansion—we have too, as I stand here : well, now we are so far, what say you to visiting the meadow, the place I appointed for the meeting, and choose the ground, the exact spot, upon which you would wish to stand, name that, and I will undertake to see it done."

With these words they proceeded to the meadow.

No. 2.

CHAPTER IV.

THE HAUNT.

As may be supposed, the declaration uttered by Mr. Williams, and which was mentioned in the preceding chapter, the robbers were greatly astonished, and looked on in silent amazement. They soon recovered from this, however, and together with their prostrate companion, hastily quitted the parsonage-house, leading their wounded comrade, for the blow dealt by the man to whose timely interference the reverend man owed his life, was heavy and well-directed, and he who had received the same, was rendered thereby incapable of moving without assistance with them, they soon reached their rendezvous, and upon their arrival there, the captain addressed the wounded man:

"What did the clerical humbug mean by calling you son?" he exclaimed. "Do you know anything of him?"

"No," replied the other, doggedly.

"Well, then, it was devilish strange that he should call you his son," replied the other, "but I hope it is so."

"And why?" enquired the wounded robber.

"You must return and solicit his pardon."

"For what purpose?"

"In order that you may get into his good graces, and confidence at the same time, and let us in for the secret where his money may be found."

"I think you have already ascertained that."

"Why, to a certain extent we have," replied the captain; "but I am thoroughly convinced that there is more."

"And for you is the labour of finding the hiding place where it is concealed. Ha! a footstep approaches, who is it?"

"Only Gipsey Meg," replied another of the gang.

"Well!" exclaimed the captain, as Gipsey Meg entered the cavern, for such indeed it was; "what brings you here?"

"The same that brings all other mortals to their destination," rejoined the sybil, who was a finely-formed, handsome-looking woman, whose age perhaps, was about thirty-two years. She was clad in an old tattered silk gown, a small shawl confined the jet-black tresses, which, despite the restraint under which they were thereby placed, here and there were displayed unknown to the possessor.

"You seem in all ill humour, Meg," exclaimed the fellow who had advocated the murder-cause at the parsonage-house.

"And what's that to you if I am?" growled Meg.

"Oh! nothing," replied the fellow; "are you going to prophesy to-night?"

"If I do," replied Meg, "you will profit nothing—it will not detain me very long to prophesy your fate!"

"And pray what is his fate," enquired the captain.

"The gibbet!" grumbled Meg.

"Why, you're always prating about that, Meg."

"I am, indeed, replied the sybil, "and of what else can I speak? what else is pertaining to you? the course you pursue is not fraught with aught else but danger and death; blood and murder produce death—the triple tree, Tyburn, the cart disgrace; infamy, all, all, are before you."

"Once more I ask what has brought you here, Meg?" exclaimed the captain, turning to the sybil.

"What has brought me here?" retorted the Gipsey, "I told you before, the same which brings all poor wretches to their destination; if I was one of your aristocratic, gilded fortune—pampered fools, I should have come here in a carriage, attended by obsequious lacqueys, who would bow and cringe before me, in the hope of securing the possession of their daily bread ; but I—I am a mean Gipsey—at least, so the world think me—but the day may yet arrive when Gipsey Meg, as she is known, and supposed to be, may yet out-rival them all. Once I remember that I fared sumptuously in early and by-gone days—also some indistinct remembrance of a mother's care, but now," and here the Gipsey passed her hand over her brow.

"Come, come, Meg !" cried the captain of the band, crossing to where the sybil stood ; "you are relapsing into your gloomy mood ; cheer up. I and you have known each other in by-gone times, when Dame Fortune was more lavish of her smiles than she at present is ; and often when placed upon the still night guard —for you know that I even share the duty with my men—often I say, when alone in the dark still hour of night, I think upon you, and pause in silence as I contemplate your strange conduct and inexplicable destiny ; but tell me, Meg, do you really believe that your power of predestination is fraught with any probability ? eh, Meg ?"

" Do I think so ?" reiterated the sybil, "in how many cases have I spoken truly ? In the case of Reft Rob, did I not speak rightly ? When the trial commenced, who foretold its issue ?"

" You, Meg ; you," replied the captain, "forgive the question, 'twas a rash one. Come, Meg, your hand."

" There it is," replied the sybil, "and may you never grasp the hand of one who is less faithful to your cause and interest, than Gipsey Meg, I say."

"Amen to your prayer !" returned the captain.

" Now, Meg, will you drain a goblet to our success ?"

" I will wish—nay, more, pray for your welfare," replied the sybil, " but wine I will not taste, 'tis a faithless slave, and has betrayed many men. Look well to your interest, Captain Bond, or it will deal falsely with you. Farewell, I must to my nightly post at the gibbet's foot ; farewell."

" Farewell !" rejoined the captain, "if you are off again ; but I really can't see what there is in that barren waste, and the ugly gibbet, with its bodies swinging to and fro, and the irons creaking in the hollow night breeze."

" There, there will I, while my breath remains, pass the still and silent hours of night ; for twice three years have I sought no other home, the sandy ground has been my pillow, and the skeleton of my murdered boy my companion in sleep."

" Is there nothing that will persuade you into altering your determination Meg ?" enquired the captain.

" No ; Captain Bond," replied the sybil, "nothing that you can offer ; except, indeed, you would instruct me where the blood-hounds, who deprived my son of life, may be found. Oh ! how gladly would I toil ; oh, even until the flesh from my bones should be worn with fatigue, to wreak a mother's vengeance upon the blood-hounds. But hark, the wind howls, and the thunder roars, the lightning too, darts in long vivid flashes upon the lifeless form of my boy, and I—I am here, housed from all ; shame, shame."

With these words the sybil rapidly disappeared.

" Rather a strange customer, that Gipsey Meg !" exclaimed one of the gang, as the wild hysterical laugh was heard above the howling of the blast, and the roaring thunder without.

" Oh ! she is indeed," replied the captain. " Meg, poor creature, has endured her share of sorrow in this world, any how ; and though her nature is most thoroughly changed, and somewhat soured by adversity, still a more kindly heart never yet beat within a human bosom ; she is a dangerous foe, but once your friend, you are secure from all harm ; if danger and concealment be the order of the day ; only place confidence in Gipsey Meg, and my life upon her fidelity and courage."

" You seem to be a great friend to the sybil," exclaimed one of the gang.

" I am what I seem then," replied the captain, " Gipsey Meg has preserved my life upon more than one occasion, and I would now willingly risk that life in her defence."

"You have often promised us that some time or other we should hear the life of this Gipsey," interposed the man, who generally managed business in the absence of Bond, and who was known to the band as Lieutenant Robson.

"I have," returned Bond, "and will now fulfil that promise ;" thus, then, was her history :—

"About twenty-two years since, there stood at the bottom of the hill, which stands to the right of Bentley Heath, a small dilapidated cottage, or hut, which was inhabited by an old man and his daughter; report said that the old man was immensely rich, though how he had accumulated his gold was a question nobody could solve : some gave him credit for being a robber, others for a receiver; however, they one and all agreed, that he was certainly a very suspicious character, and certainly behaved with great cruelty to his daughter. There were also some ugly stories propagated to the effect, that many travellers had at various times halted at the cottage, and never after been heard of. Things went on in this manner, when I (who was then an honest man, possessing a tolerable independence,) chanced to arrive late in the neighbourhood one evening, and the first person I encountered was this girl's father; being, as I afterwards supposed, attracted by my fine dress, he invited me to spend the night at his hovel; I readily took the bait and accepted his invitation. Upon my arrival I was struck by the beauty of his daughter, who seemed greatly moved at my presence; and upon the first opportunity that presented itself she caught me by the arm, and exclaimed, 'Beware of treachery !' I was somewhat startled by this information, and being determined to profit by the same, I watched the movements of her surly father with great activity. After I had passed some little time under his roof, he invited me to partake of a glass with him, while his daughter, by her looks, evidently cautioned me not to do so; it was in vain, however, that I declined ; he continued to importune me, and at last I gave a reluctant consent ; he then opened the door of a small cupboard, and returned with two goblets, one of which he proffered to me; I, of course, took it from him, and was about to swallow off the contents ; before I could accomplish this, however, the girl brushed past, and the goblet fell to the ground; this flashed upon me at once that the wine had been poisoned, and the girl knew it, and thus saved my life. If there had been any doubt as to the truth of this supposition, it would at once have been cleared up by the severity in which the old villain commanded his daughter to retire. After apologising to me for his daughter's apparent clumsiness, he conducted me to my chamber. I was too mistrustful of my host, however, to consign myself to sleep, so I contented myself by throwing my body upon the homely couch, sword-in-hand, fully prepared for the attack I expected would be made upon me. I had fell off into a slight slumber, when a slight tap upon the shoulder aroused me, and upon starting to my feet I beheld the girl. She motioned me to silence, and bid me prepare for the appearance of her father and a ruffianly companion. Scarce had this admonition been given when the sound of their footsteps were audible upon the stairs.

"We both concealed ourselves in a dark corner of the room, and the robbers entered and made repeated stabs at the bed, upon which it was supposed I then lay. Not finding any resistance or outcry they came to a more minute examination, and, of course, could not discover me. I distinctly heard them mutter a few compliments in the way of curses and good wishes for the safety of my soul. They then held a hurried consultation, which terminated by their darting down the stairs at full speed, and starting off in the direction I was supposed to have taken, for they appeared convinced that I had quitted the place. Being once more left to ourselves, my generous preserver bade me make off with all convenient speed. It was in vain I implored her to secure her own safety, by accompanying me. She assured me that her father would gain no knowledge of the part she had taken in my escape. After some time spent in vain solicitation, I quitted the hut. Years passed on, I heard no more of either the old fellow or his daughter ; fortune and I had parted company, and I became what I now am, a common robber. I was one night met near to Epping Forest by a gipsey, in whom I instantly recognised my former preserver. She told me her story, which was a sad one ;—her father was dead—she had married with a man who, after two years, had perished by the law ;—her son, the only fruit of their union, had also, at an early age, perished by the gibbet, though, as his mother to this day declares, he was innocent of the crimes with which he stood charged, and which were those of robbery and murder. Since that time we have been sworn friends, and three times has she preserved my life from the law ; and now, as I have before said, I would risk all to render a service to Gipsey Meg. That is the whole of her history."

"And a very touching one it is, too," replied Robson, " do you not think that her brain is bewildered ?"

" At times I am convinced it is," replied Bond.

" And do you place any faith in her forebodings ?"

" So much," answered the captain, " that I have a real objection to hear her prophesy aught about the gib. She has foretold the fate of many a brave fellow."

" Aye," rejoined the fellow who had received the sybil's fatal prophesy, " and perhaps had a hand in bringing to pass the truth of her foolery."

Bond looked upon the speaker with a fiery gaze, and then in a stern tone exclaimed :—

" If all men possessed the fidelity and courage of Gipsey Meg, the gibbet would want for ornaments. Her son would now be living to gladden her lone hours —I should possess a brother. By Heaven, sir, if you dare to repeat that asser- tion—weak though our numbers may be—I'll send a bullet through your brain with as little ceremony as I would swallow off a goblet of wine."

" Come, captain," interposed Robson, " do not quarrel about Meg—why, if she were here, by Heaven, she'd shame us all by laughing heartily at such folly. Come, be seated—let the goblet pass merrily, and call upon our friend there, Mat Watson, whom the parson called son, for an explanation of his life ; what say you Watson, do you agree to this ?"

" With all my heart," replied Mat, carelessly.

" Not now," interposed Bond, " not now—there is business to be attended to this night, late as it is ; come, lads, prepare for your several stations on the road. You shall have my instructions as we proceed. Now, are you prepared ?"

" We are," simultaneously shouted the robbers.

" Follow me, then," responded Bond.

And with these words he strode from the cavern, accompanied by his lieutenant, and followed by the band.

CHAPTER V.

THE DUEL.

Having completed their observations, Sir Charles Mortimer and his friend Belford returned to the mansion, where the remaining hours of night were spent in gloomy silence. At length the timepiece that stood upon a small tablet of marble proclaimed the hour of two, and interrupted the reigning silence. There is something soul-absorbing and very solemn in the passing of a night before a duel ; thoughts of a very peculiar and unpleasant nature will insist upon rushing unbidden to your recollection, more especially if the insult has been given or taken when you are flushed with wine: then your thoughts wander at random ; you are sensitive upon points which, at any other time, would be passed over, or marked only by a smile of contempt. Nothing is there which tests a man's disposition, and displays indisposition so much as play. We think that man who can sit down to the table, and either win or lose hundreds, nay, thousands of pounds without so much as a single feature being agitated, must indeed possess a more than mortal share of patience and forbearance ; yet we have seen such men, while on the other hand there are those, even within the narrow compass of our acquaintance, who would, like Sir Charles, upon the loss of a few paltry pounds, exhibit the most ungovernable passion. Such persons should never, by any chance, handle a card or dice; for nothing is more ridiculous than to imagine, that simply because any particular person should continue to win he must be playing unfairly, though perhaps such may indeed be the case, we looked upon duels at all times only as a most villainous system of fashionable murder ; but when they result from a gaming table brawl, we certainly must say that a more atrocious insult to the laws of God, man, and humanity could not be perpetrated. What is more piteous than the circumstance of a family, and fond doting wife, being deprived of their natural protector, merely because some sharping scoundrel may have felt the 'truth of a declaration uttered at a moment when the whole passions of the soul are concentrated to one evil intent, and when the speaker is contemplating the utter ruin and disgrace of his family, brought on solely through his folly and indiscretion ?

Sir Charles Mortimer had none of those painful reminiscences, yet he sat buried in the gloomy depths of contemplation, and it was not until Belford had addressed him for the third time that he deigned him an answer.

"Why, I never," exclaimed Belford, after a long pause, "saw any man so gloomy as you, Sir Charles, are this night ; why, one would imagine that you was——"

"Going to execution," interrupted Sir Charles—where, perhaps, such may be the case for aught I know."

"Nothing in the world could be more improbable," rejoined Belford, "why, you are under my protection."

"And pray what if I am !" enquired the baronet.

"Why," replied Belford, "my name is a tower of strength with all those fellows we were among last night."

"And even if such indeed be the case," rejoined Sir Charles, "neither your name or that of a greater man could prevent the bullet from disturbing my brain, providing my adversary does but possess the skill to send it there : am I not correct?"

"You are, indeed, Sir Charles," rejoined Belford ; "but hark ! the clock has just told the hour of three; we have but one hour more, and then——"

"I may be stretched upon the ground a lifeless and disfigured corpse," interrupted Sir Charles.

"My life to a bottle of champagne that you pink the fellow, Sir Charles," rejoined Belford.

"Ah, well," replied the baronet, "perhaps it may be as you say. Reach me down that brace of pistols, will you? the last time I used them it was for a friend."

"And did they do any damage?" enquired Belford, as he handed the duelling case to Sir Charles.

"Only a trifle for him," rejoined the baronet, "they scattered his brains in all directions."

"Then, I presume, he was killed ?" pursued Belford.

"And so do I," returned the baronet, "men seldom live very long after their brains have been distributed. Examine the lock of that pistol, will you ?" he continued, handing one of the above named weapons to Belford, "I think it is a little damaged, if so, I shall not use them, for it might fall to me, and I should like vastly well to have a shot at this fellow."

"I don't think it's anything to speak of," resumed Belford, having ended his examination of the suspected weapon. "'Twas mere fancy, I thi k, Sir Charles."

"Perhaps so,' 'acquiesced the baronet.

The pistols were loaded—both principal and second had swallowed a good stiff glass of brandy, by way of a stimulant, when the latter urged the necessity of preparing for a start. The pistols were then once more consigned to the case, Sir Charles had enshrouded his person beneath the ample folds of a circular cloak, and they then proceeded with noiseless steps from the mansion, closed the door, and threaded the lawn; when they had arrived at the extremity of which, Sir Charles impelled some small object which lay upon the gravel-walk forward with his foot; and, upon stooping to ascertain the nature of the same, he beheld a robin struggling in the agonies of death.

"By Heaven!" he exclaimed, turning to Belford, "if I was inclined to be superstitious, I should look upon this as a warning from Heaven, foretelling my fate; see how the pretty creature flutters; its little heart beats as though it would burst," he continued, as he raised the bird from off the ground.

"Pshaw, Sir Charles!" exclaimed Belford, with gestures of impatience, "throw it away, and let us hasten forward, or, by Heaven, we shall be too late, and then methinks both you and I had better not shew ourselves at the club or table again for some considerable time to come, at least I shall not however."

"And why not?" enquired Sir Charles, laying the bird with care upon a tuft of grass;—"why not?"

"Because," replied Belford, "I have no very particular desire to be branded with the name of coward."

"And who would dare to do so?"

"Each and every one," replied Belford, "and I should certainly consider them justified in so doing, for what else but a feeling of cowardice would induce a man to break an appointment which his honour has been publicly pledged to keep."

"You are perfectly correct," rejoined the baronet, "I was to blame; come, let us hasten forward, and thereby atone for previous delay. I think we shall be there first now."

Sharp walking for the next five minutes brought them to the rendezvous, where the truth of the baronet's statement was fully borne out, no trace of the opposite party presented itself After a few moments of further delay, however, the sound of approaching carriage wheels were distinctly heard; they rapidly approached nearer, and in a few moments afterwards, the party alighted at the distance of about fifty yards. The carriage drove off—the duellist and his friend rapidly drew near. The usual preliminaries were gone through—the men placed—and the word given to fire. The signal was followed by a single report. The seconds rushed forward, when it was discovered that the baronet had not discharged his weapon. An explanation was now demanded, when it was found that the pistol was out of order. He, therefore, insisted upon a second exchange of shots. This measure, however, was violently opposed by the opposite party; but, at length, the decision was found in his favour. Another brace, brought by the others, were now produced; the seconds conferred apart, and the weapons were loaded, the distance measured, for the second time, the signal received, and a simultaneous report followed. Sir Charles dashed his pistol with violence to the ground :—

"Are we children?" he exclaimed, "to be played with thus? there was no ball in those pistols I will not be tricked in this scurvy manner, Belford."

"Here, Sir Charles," replied that personage.

"Is there any possibility of obtaining swords?"

"I have at your service, sir," replied his antagonist; "would you wish to see them?—if you would—"

"I should, sir," replied Sir Charles, bowing coldly.

"Danvers," exclaimed the other, turning to his friend, "will you bring the swords from yonder carriage?"

"Really, sir," rejoined the surgeon, "I cannot permit any such course of proceeding. Why, you have had two exchanges of shots already. Why, instead of having satisfaction, I am now of opinion that it is the life of each other you seek. Mr. Danvers, sir, you will please *not* to produce the desired weapons. I am assured that this affair has already proceeded too far; therefore we will retire."

" We shall do no such thing, sir," replied the baronet. "This vain subterfuge will avail nothing. The last brace of pistols were charged with powder only. I again insist that——"

" Here are the swords, gentlemen," replied Danvers, who had now returned from the carriage with the swords.

" 'Tis well," exclaimed Sir Charles. " Now, perhaps, this business may be settled after a little more delay.

" It may so," replied his adversary, stepping forward. " Now, sir, select your own weapon."

" I will take whichever pleases you. I suppose they are of equal length; and even if they are *not*, I do not object to give you a trifling advantage. Now, prepare."

Sir Charles, as he said this, took the proffered weapon, and fell into the first position. For some moments he contented himself by warding off the thrusts aimed at his breast, which he did with admirable skill and coolness. At length he commenced making thrusts in return. Once, however, his adversary struck the sword from his grasp. The baronet started with astonishment at this; the weapon was instantly replaced in his grasp by Belford, and the next instant was stained with the blood of his opponent. A flesh wound in the right side considerably weakened him; still, however, he would not desist, but recommenced with redoubled fury, and succeeded in wounding Sir Charles slightly through the left arm, and in a moment more he fell, lifeless, and bathed in blood, upon the ground. The baronet's sword had entered his body. In an instant the surgeon was by his side, endeavouring, though in vain, to staunch the blood which flowed copiously; the countenance of the wounded man changed fearfully, his cheeks turned to a pallid hue, his eyes were closed as in death, and pulsation was no longer discernable.

" Great God!" exclaimed the surgeon, " this man is dying."

" Then why not remove him to the carriage, and bear him to his residence without delay?" returned Belford.

" I fear if he was to be removed in his present state of exhaustion, the attempt might be attended by fatal consequences," replied the surgeon. " He is evidently dying."

" If you are convinced of that, sir," continued Belford, " I should say that your most proper course of proceeding would be to convey him from this place with all convenient speed; not let the man die upon the cold earth."

The surgeon paused for some few moments, as if undecided whether he should remove his patient or otherwise, when, contrary to the expectation of all, the wounded duellist slowly opened his eyes, and in a faint tone of voice, enquired for Sir Charles. The baronet was instantly by his side. The dying man extended his hand, exclaiming:—

" I am dying, and rapidly. Hear me all. Bear witness that with my last breath I acquit Sir Charles from all blame in this affair. He was both robbed and insulted. I also accuse his seeming *friend*, Belford, with first introducing the baronet to me as a fitting and easy victim to the swindling practices we have conjointly carried on for years. And you, sir," he continued, addressing the astonished baronet, " if you would escape total ruin avoid that man. He is as an adder in your path, and each day thrusts at your dearest being with more real venom than those you believe to be foes. I speak truly. Do not avoid the counsel of a dying man. I shall live but a few moments longer. Fly—fly quickly, and save yourself, for others will not believe you innocent, as I do, if you a——" The effort made to combat with exhausted nature and give utterance to the conclusion of this sentence proved ineffectual; that unerring messenger and precursor of death's gloomy presence, commonly known as the death rattle, which is a slight gurgle in the throat, was now heard; the surgeon shook his head

[*See Page* 24]

mournfully; Sir Charles Mortimer looked from one to another in mute astonishment; and finally, the dying man, after essaying once or twice to speak, suddenly closed his eyes—and for ever.

The surgeon then placed the body upon its mother earth, and despatched Danvers to prepare the carriage for its reception. This was speedily done; the body was removed, and none but Sir Charles and Belford remained upon the spot.

" Now, Sir Charles," exclaimed Belford, after a lapse of some few moments, "why do you stand so gloomy here; would you be taken upon the spot with arms?"

" No, sir," vociferated the baronet; " I would not be taken with arms nor with life; therefore do not you *attempt* it."

" Me, sir!" reiterated Belford in astonishment.

" Yes, *you*," replied Sir Charles hastily.

" Why, Sir Charles Mortimer," continued Belford, " the death of that cowardly rascal seems to have petrified you."

" No, sir, it has *not*," returned the baronet fiercely; " but his dying words have struck deep into my soul, and convinced me what a treacherous villain I have nurtured."

" Sir Charles!" exclaimed Belford in affected anger, " beware—do not insult me—remember, I wear a sword."

" Aye, sir," rejoined Sir Charles, " and what then?"

" I may convince you that I am not to be insulted with impunity," answered Belford. " I should be loth to quarrel with you; yet if——".

" You possessed the courage to bear the consequences of the same, you would doubtless make the attempt," exclaimed Sir Charles, interrupting him; " but I will not degrade myself by attempting aught like an explanation with you. No, sir; leave me, and remember that from henceforth we are strangers."

" But, surely," rejoined Belford, " you will not give credence to the ridi-

No. 3.

culous statement given utterance to by that dead sharper; really, the idea is ridiculous."

" Ridiculous or not," returned Sir Charles, " my mind is completely resolved. Belford; you and I from this moment have done with each other; therefore you can go your way, while I pursue mine. But, one word of caution at parting.— Attempt not to harm Emily Anson; observe this strictly, and we are friends— Farewell."

With these words the baronet concealed his pistols beneath the ample folds of his cloak, and quitting the late scene of death, proceeded onwards in the direction of his residence, wrapt in gloomy meditation.

" So!" exclaimed Belford, " he has cast me from his confidence, has he? Ah! well, your baronets and men of title have mighty strange whims of their own, and in which they indulge pretty freely; but then *others* may chance to have, aye, and exercise it too. This is devilish awkward, my being cast from such good quarters just now, when town is nearly empty; but he shall repent of this before many hours have elapsed—aye, and dearly too.

CHAPTER VI.

THE HEROINE.

LADY FLORA MANDEVILLE was a beauteous and highly accomplished lady, who had for several years been a resident at Bentley Heath. She was possessed with a very large fortune, left her by an only uncle, who some six years since had died in the East Indies, after having spent nearly the whole of his days there. She lived upon a very large estate, known as Grantley Park, kept a large retinue of servants, costly equipage, a magnificent stud of horses, and was constantly giving large parties; balls, routs, masquerades, and every other description of fashionable amusement was indulged in by the rich and accomplished Lady Mandeville. Notwithstanding her gay and apparent thoughtless disposition, however, Lady Flora seldom forgot, that charity and benevolence to the poor should always form a part of the duty incumbent upon those, who, favoured with the golden gifts of fortune, are thereby possessed with the power, if not the will, to spread happiness and contentment around them. The children of affluence seldom permit the misfortunes of others to possess for a moment the smallest portion of their remembrance, and thought, but think solely how to promote their own temporary happiness. But, as we have before said, Lady Mandeville was a happy exception to the general rule. It is not always that in the moment of sickness or trouble, pecuniary aid alone is needed; no, a kindly word will do more towards comforting the mind than all the vast riches of Peru and Mexico combined. Thus it was with Emily Anson and her invalid aunt. They did not want for riches; and though humbly bestowed now, and generally believed to be of obscure origin, the time had been when the family of Emily Anson and that of her relative might have vied with that of the Lady Flora, to whom alone this knowledge was confined. Yes, the orphan of— but this is anticipation.

" How are you, my dear friend, by this time?" exclaimed Lady Flora, entering the sick chamber, and kindly taking the hand of her invalid friend.

" I grieve to say, my aunt has not been so well, my lady, since you saw her last," exclaimed Emily, in tears.

" Why are you weeping, Emily?" enquired Lady Flora.

" She is somewhat moved by the recent conversation that has passed between us," rejoined the invalid, speaking with great apparent difficulty; " and it is fitting she should be."

" And why so?" resumed Lady Mandeville, stooping nearer to the patient, in order that she might speak with less exertion.

"I have been speaking to her of the world and its snares," was the faint reply. "I feel that my hours are numbered, and that I have very few more to pass in this life; therefore I would willingly pass that few in affording instruction to thoughtless, giddy youth. I have been gently reproving Emily for her partiality to the vain pleasures of this perishable world—cautioned her against committing the folly of what is generally termed 'seeing the world,' which is peopled by creatures whose only boast is in the ruin of the thoughtless and inexperienced. This, my lady, is the cause of her tears."

"Well," responded her ladyship. "I think you speak rather harshly; for I have never seen any impropriety in the conduct of Emily, though I have observed her very closely."

"I rejoice to hear it," rejoined the invalid; "yet when deprived of her natural protector, the only living mortal who will possess the least possible regard for her future welfare, the last of her advisers shall be passed away to the unexplored region of death, who shall then preserve her from temptation's path, and rescue her from dishonour? None: the only shield she will then have must be her own sense of right and wrong. My province, then, has it been, to make that sense as keenly alive to the natural consequences of crime as may be possible. My counsel may sound harshly to other ears, but like the apothecary's drug, which is bitter when administered, its effect, if sowed upon good ground, will be productive of the most salubrious effects."

"You speak truly," replied her ladyship, "but somewhat mournful withal. Come, look more cheerful, and trust me, you will yet recover from your present indisposition; and this doleful conversation will serve as a subject for merriment at the card-table."

"I shall never quit this chamber with life," resumed the invalid, in a solemn tone; "of that I am fully aware—'tis useless to tell me otherwise."

"Then should your words be true," returned Lady Flora, "my care shall it be to protect Emily from all ill. Yes, I will adopt her as my own child; all the care of a——"

"Mother, you would say, Lady Flora," interrupted the invalid. "I thank you for the offer; but Emily is already destined for the family of Mr. Williams. That holy man will of himself be sufficient to keep her from all harm; and knowing her to be placed there, I can die in peace. Still I thank your ladyship."

"Thanks are unneeded," replied her ladyship; "I require them not; though I must say I feel hurt that you will not suffer Emily to share my hours. She should have been to me as a sister. I would have cherished her next my heart, anticipated her most secret wishes; in short, have attended to all those little duties so highly requisite for the future welfare of a young and thoughtless female."

"I again proffer to you my sincere thanks," returned the invalid; "but must maintain my determination. In short, my lady, if I must be more explicit, I think your society too lofty, too much abounding in gaiety and worldly pleasures, for one whose giddy and thoughtless mind is already to be blamed; 'tis that, my lady, that I object to in your establishment."

"And do you not, my dear friend, think that there is often less danger to be incurred in a house where harmless gaiety is maintained, than in many of your mock sanctuaries?" returned Lady Flora.

"Can it be possible," rejoined the invalid, "that you, Lady Mandeville, can revile against the house of God?"

"No," returned her ladyship, "it cannot. But how often, let me ask, has the sacred name of religion been abused, and the sacred name served only as a cloak for crime and iniquity? that, my friend, was my meaning."

"I ask your pardon," returned the other in a faint tone.

"And I," replied her ladyship, "will grant it upon one condition; only remember, if you do not comply with my request——"

"Let me know its nature,' replied the invalid, and then doubtless your ladyship may command obedience."

"It is, then," rejoined Lady Flora, "that should the dear Emily require a protectress—and heaven grant that she may not—you will elect me that happy individual.'

"Since you are so importunate, my lady," answered the patient, "I will decide this important question without farther delay. Emily, my love, under whose care would you rather be placed—that of the Lady Flora Mandeville, or the Reverend Mr. Williams, of the parsonage-house? Speak freely, my child."

"If my dear aunt has no wish to the contrary," rejoined Emily, after a brief pause, "I would rather pass my days with our kind friend and protectress, the Lady Flora."

"There spoke the thoughtlessness of youth," murmured the invalid. "Emily," she continued, "you have not selected the person I had hoped you would; but that you may ever be happy and preserved from all harm, is the earnest wish of your now dying aunt. There is a heavy foreboding which now hangs about my heart ; and though I cannot conceive *why* it is so, yet am I convinced that you are the cause. Oh, my child! if you should ever in an unguarded moment be about to err, and quit the path of virtue, think of my last words—think that my spirit may be hovering o'er your head, weeping to behold your sin, yet deprived of power to warn the evil from you. Lady Flora, your hand; do not shudder, though I grasp you hard! yet, 'tis only the fervency of thought; farewell. Emily, beware of flatterers, the world's vain; miscalled pleasures, and——"

She could not conclude the sentences ; previous exertion had exhausted her weak nature, and she fainted. Restoratives were administered by Emily and Lady Flora ; under the influence of these, the invalid slowly revived ; it was, however, but for a short time—her prophesy proved true ; three days afterwards, the aunt of Emily Anson—her last remaining relative upon earth, had fled to the land of spiritual immortality—and she was left alone, an orphan, possessing wealth, beauty, and all other accomplishments calculated to promote that ruin so fearfully predicted by her relative, upon her death-bed.

Emily now had no bar, no impediment in her path—no warning voice, by which she might be saved from destruction—but like the frail bark cast upon the broad expanse of the ocean, she might be resistlessly borne to the breakers of dissipation, and ruin, until wrecked upon the sharp pointed rock of poignant grief and despair.

CHAPTER VII.

THE MASQUERADE.

Captain Bond, accompanied by his lieutenant, and followed by his men, proceeded onwards in silence, until they arrived at the summit of the heath. Upon reaching this place he came to a halt, which example was of course followed up by his men, still in silence.

"May I enquire for what purpose we are here, my captain ; for the hour is late, and no travellers are likely to——"

"Pass this way to-night," interposed Bond, "I grant you that—but I do not reckon upon *travellers.* No. I have other game in view; in short, to speak more truly, there is a grand carnival to be held at Grantly Hall, to-night. And as it wants now, nearly half an hour before the guests are expected ; why I intend to intercept them on the road, just to ease them of a few superfluous trinkets; nothing more, I can assure you, 'pon my honour."

"If I dare suggest," rejoined the lieutenant, "I could propose a much greater scheme than that, by far."

"Let me know your plan," replied Bond, "and if they are within the compass of practability, rest assured that I shall immediately avail myself of the same."

"It is this, then," returned the lieutenant, "I propose that, instead of robbing, like *common* highwaymen, we return to our rendezvous with all possible speed, select a couple of dresses from our wardrobe, which I'll wager my life against a brass button, is more extensive than that of any nobleman in the land—this done, I would——"

"Join the motley group," interposed the captain.

"Just so," replied the lieutenant, pleased at having his plans anticipated "what think's Captain Bond of the idea—is it worth acting upon, or not?"

"Worth acting upon!" reiterated Bond, "why, Robson, man, I swear 'tis the best concocted plan, and suits my humour and inclination, better than anything thou hast before devised. Come, let's back to our hold, a short time will serve to complete the necessary preparations. And then, hey for mirth!"

"Aye, and for business too," rejoined Robson, "we must not lie idle; the chance afforded, will be a rare one, and must not be suffered to pass on unobserved."

"Right!" exclaimed Bond, "now, let us on."

"Stay," continued the lieutenant, "do you take any of the gang with you, or leave them at the rendezvous?"

"Why, I scarcely know," replied the captain, "what think you?"

"Treachery may, perhaps, follow us," suggested Robson.

"It may so," replied Bond, "but then, our gang is composed of such dare-devil fellows, that I fear, once there, we should find it difficult to keep them under controul. No, Robson, we will not be encumbered with them. A brace of our best pistols, and one of those dress swords, shall protect me from a host. And if you take a similar precaution, we cannot come to much harm, think you we can?"

"Not easily," rejoined the lieutenant, "conspirators do not visit dress balls; therefore, I confess my folly, and am ashamed—nay, absolutely blush at the same."

"Nay," returned Bond, "there is nothing to blush or be ashamed at. Caution and precaution is better in the hour of danger, than the courage of fifty lions, at least, according to my own idea. Now, I think we are fully agreed upon, are we not?"

"I believe so," replied Robson, "now I think we had better lose no time, for the hours fly quickly. Come, follow."

Nerved by the expectation of obtaining a handsome prize in the way of gold watches, trinkets, jewellery, &c., besides some indistinct ideas of pleasure entertained by Captain Bond and his no less daring lieutenant, a very short time served to bring them to the cavern, where the dresses were selected. The two outlaws equipped, and mounting their steeds, they once more quitted the rendezvous.

Bond was habited in a pair of satin fluted inexpressibles, silk stockings cased his legs, and his feet displayed a pair of fancy dress slippers; a dress coat of dark brown velvet, lined throughout with straw-coloured silk, together with a handsome embroidered satin waistcoat, displayed the symmetry of his figure, to the best possible advantage. His head was adorned with a peruke, which was surmounted by a triangular formed hat; a large horseman's cloak concealed his person, and a half mask his features from observation. He had taken the precaution to arm himself, for a brace of exquisitely wrought silver mounted pocket pistols were concealed about his person, and an elegant dress-sword of well tempered steel was suspended from a belt of embroidered silver lace. Thus disguised, it would have been impossible for any person who was not well acquainted with him, to have recognised in the dashing handsome figure before him, Captain Bond, the notorious, fierce, and implacable highwayman, whose exploits had struck terror and consternation into the hearts of many.

Lieutenant Robson, though not attired in so costly a manner, was, nevertheless, equally disguised, and had also taken the same precaution for their mutual safety.

" Well, Robson," exclaimed Bond, as they proceeded; " what think you, man —is it possible that any there will recognise the jay in peacock's feathers ?"

" Not if the peacock does not strut about too much," replied the lieutenant, with a half suppressed smile.

" Why," replied Robson, " in the first place, I must caution Captain Bond, against making too free with the ladies, or he may chance to come in contact with some hot-brained gallant, who will demand satisfaction."

" Which he shall have to his heart's content," rejoined Bond.

" How, let me ask, are you to oblige him," replied Robson.

" Nothing can be more easy," replied Bond, " have I not my favourite little brace of pops, they never yet missed fire."

" True," rejoined the lieutenant ; " but has Captain Bond forgotten, that while giving satisfaction to *others*, he may have the *dis*-satisfaction to be recognised."

" Oh !" exclaimed Bond, " you are such a fellow to foretell things. Why, I should not wonder, that some day we discover you to be a descendant of our friend, Gipsey Meg ; which will fully account for your melancholy forebodings. Tush man, if——"

" You was to be taken," interposed Robson, " I cut the gang directly. No more Bentley Heath exploits for me."

" Why, man," returned Bond, " how foolishly you talk ; if I was to be taken, you, then, would be captain."

" Never," returned Robson. " No, they might disband, for aught I should care. When you leave them, so do I."

" Well, well," replied Bond, " we are neither of us going to do that yet, however. Ha ! see you that file of empty carriages, yonder ? Why, as I live, the guests are all assembled. Spur on your horse, man ; or we shall be too late to join the merry throng—quick !"

They then, by dint of whip and spur, urged their steeds on at the top of their speed and five minutes longer saw them dismount, and their horses taken to the stable by a groom in waiting, while they ascended to the ball-room, the road to which, was by a magnificent flight of broad stone stairs, covered with the most costly description of Turkey carpet, and the choicest of flowers and shrubs, beguiled with their fragrance. The ascent of this object, excited their admiration. They were in a fair way of being lost amid the grandeur of the ball-room, the entrace to which, was through two folding doors, of highly polished, and elaborately carved mahogany; opposite to the doors was placed two large mirrors, encased in the most costly gilded frames, and which, by the aid of three large chandeliers suspended from the roof by stout silken cordage, reflected with the greatest brilliancy upon every object, how minute soever it might be ; those parts of the wall which were not occupied by mirrors, were filled up with magnificent paintings, further adorned with festoons of every hue and description. The farther extremity of this lofty and spacious chamber, opened into a beautiful covered parterre, where wine and refreshments were prepared and laid out in the most tasteful style imaginable. A large aviary of singing birds added new novelty to the scene, as ever and anon the feathered captives fluttered from perch to perch, as if to ascertain why their rest was thus unceremoniously broken in upon, and the broad glare of light substituted for the sable veil of night. To complete the scene, an unseen band of musicians continued to perform the choicest of overtures, quadrilles, and various other dances.

The company present, was numerous and of every description. There was Venus and Adonis, Cupid, Mercury, Ceres, and various other members of the mythological world, together with all the various and indescribable personages of such an assembly.

" By my troth, Robson !" exclaimed Bond, as they entered, and sought the far end of the room ; " I half imagine, that we have wandered into some fairy land, instead of a common ball-room. Why, the women look more like angels, than aught else."

"This Lady Mandeville, has always borne a first-rate character for the display of good taste in such matters as those;" returned Robson, "and well does she deserve the same. Ah! I should like vastly to know who those two are, that have just entered?"

"Which two do you mean?" enquired Bond, in an under tone.

"The lady abbess, and the angelic creature who follows as her attendant nun," rejoined the lieutenant.

"They are a pair of divinity's, truly," replied Bond, "but as to their name or origin, I am as ignorant as yourself—but come, we must not stand inactive here, or we may, perhaps, be observed. Come, man."

They then, confident in their disguises mingled in the group, and continued to take an ample share in their amusements, until the lady abbess summoned them to the refreshment department, towards which, all now flocked simultaneously, and all the seats but two, one on either side of the lady abbess and her attendant nun, were taken possession of—though our hero and his companion had not yet taken their places. Accordingly, Bond was bestowed next to the abbess, while Robson took his seat beside her attendant. Now, all promised well, until one of the lacqueys in waiting, being desired to assist the holy madam to a glass of sherry; when the blockhead clumsily let fall the decanter from the silver salver upon which he had placed it, and in his anxiety to obstruct its descent, caught at it with his hand, but instead of effecting his purpose he made bad worse, and caused it to fall on the shoulder of the lady abbess—who, startled by the pain produced thereby, fell backwards insensible; and, but for the timely assistance of Bond, would have fallen to the ground. In an instant, however, his arm encircled her waist; and her head sank upon his shoulder. As may be supposed, this circumstance produced the greatest confusion. The guests simultaneously rose from the table—all with the exception of Bond, in a state of great anxiety for the lady abbess.

"Do not disturb her," exclaimed Bond, addressing the attendant nun, who appeared very desirous to remove her holy mistress; "the lady has only fainted. A little *sal volatile*, or *eau de Cologne*, will speedily revive her. I have had some experience in these cases—and, therefore, know full well how to treat them."

"Pardon me, sir," returned another gentleman, who was attired as an Italian bravo; "but I think it would be better, if you were to resign the lady abbess to the care of her attendant. She does not appear to recover."

"Nay, sir," answered Robson, "my friend, the Count Bellona, has often practised as a physician—and knows full well how to treat the lady—only leave her in his care for a short time, and my life upon her recovery."

The bravo coldly bowed, and withdrew. A few moments after this, the lady abbess slowly recovered; blushed to find herself in the arms of a dashing, handsome, gallant. And to his solicitations as to her health, informed him with a bewitching smile, that she was more frightened than hurt. The repast was then continued, and after a brief space, the party returned to the ball-room; with the exception of the abbess and her attendant, together with Captain Bond and his lieutenant, Robson. After a few pressing entreaties, the lady abbess articulated a reluctant consent to accompany Bond in a walk through the shrubbery, upon condition only, that her attendant was permitted to accompany her—which she did, being escorted by Robson, in the most gallant manner possible.

They rambled through the walks for some considerable time, during which, neither Bond, or his lieutenant, had neglected to fill the ears of their respective mistresses, with avowals of the most ardent and unchangeable love; which had, of course, completely enslaved their souls. After they had wandered in this way for nearly an hour, the lady abbess proposed that they should return to the ball-room; but Bond implored her in the most impassioned terms, to instruct him how he might obtain an interview on the morrow; and finding that this obdurate fair one would not consent to this, he, as a finale, informed her that he could not permit her return to the ball-room, until she had complied with his request. It was in vain that she implored and protested—he was obdurate—and, at length, she placed in his hand a small card—having first, however, obtained from him an assurance, that he would not look upon the same, until the morrow—to this he readily agreed—and they accordingly, once more returned to the mazzy throng, followed by Robson and the nun. The hilarity was kept up until a late, or rather early hour; when, after having partaken of a cold collation, the party began to disperse. Having bid adieu to the ladies, Bond and Robson withdrew also—obtained possession of their steeds, and enshrouded in the ample folds of their cloaks, intercepted the guests on their road home; and levied contributions from all, but one old gentleman, who, being mounted upon a fleet horse, evaded them with ease. Having seen the last person depart, and one by one, the brilliant lights extinguished within Grantley Hall, Bond and his companion hastened to their rendezvous, thoroughly satisfied with the booty they possessed, and the brilliant conquests they had made.

CHAPTER VIII.

THE DOUBLE ARREST.

Sir Charles Mortimer retraced his steps homeward, entered the doors about half past six. No sooner had he regained his chamber, than throwing his cloak from him, he sank upon his couch and was soon in a sound slumber—from which, he did not awake until the afternoon—when he arose, and ringing the bell, enquired of the waiter who answered his summons, if any person had called, or letters been left for him—having received an answer in the negative, he ordered a slight repast—which he had scarcely sat down to, when the following note was put into his hands by the waiter:—

SIR CHARLES MORTIMER,—You have insulted me—and that grossly—therefore, unless by way of reparation, you forward to my residence the sum of fifty pounds, I shall inform the officers of justice, where you may be found.

COUNT BELFORD.

Such was the astonishment of Mortimer, when he read this sample of villainy, —that for some few moments, he seemed lost in a reverie.

" Is there an answer, sir?" enquired the attendant.

" Is the messenger who brought this note, still in waiting?" rejoined the baronet, not appearing to notice the enquiry.

" He is not," was the reply, " but will return again shortly."

" When he does return," answered Sir Charles, " let him be shown to this apartment, I would see him."

The domestic bowed and departed, and in a short time re-appeared, informing the baronet that the messenger had returned, and then awaited his pleasure.

" 'Tis well," exclaimed Sir Charles, "conduct him hither."

" So, sir," continued the baronet, as a tall mustachio'd fellow, clad in a military undress; " I presume you are from Count Belford, am I not correct in my supposition?"

" You are indeed," replied the other, " I have that honour."

" Were you in my way of thinking," rejoined Sir Charles, " it would soon cease to be an honour. But your business sir, with me—what is the nature of that?"

" Did you not receive a note?" enquired the other, playfully tapping his teeth with the silver-mounted handle of a riding-whip, which he carried in his hand.

[*See page* 29.]

"I did," replied Sir Charles, "and you, I presume, are the messenger who delivered it to my servant?"

The other replied in the affirmative, and Sir Charles with much formality, bade him be seated.

"Now, sir," continued the baronet, "are you aware of——"

"No sir," replied the other, "I am not."

"That declaration has saved you," returned Sir Charles, "for had you answered me yes, instead of no, in all probability, I should have ordered my servant to kick you from the house, for your pains."

"Sir," exclaimed the other, starting to his feet; "if——"

"You are not off in a moment," interrupted the baronet, "I shall be compelled to use force yet."

"May I once more ask, sir; if you will please to explain this most mysterious and ungentlemanly conduct!" rejoined he of the military orders.

"Yes, sir," replied Sir Charles, "you may ask, and I will also condescend to oblige you. Know, then, that your master, friend, or, in short, sir, Count Belford is a rogue, a rascal, and a coward."

"This unlooked for attack upon the honour and courage of my friend," returned the other, "warrants my delivering this to you."

And with these words, the speaker presented Sir Charles with a small note— the seal of which the baronet immediately broke—and having possessed himself of its contents, exclaimed :

"So ho; Mr. Belford has sent me a challenge, has he? Well, I'll accept it. Tell him from me, that I will be there. Now, sir, you are at full liberty to depart."

"Where shall I call upon your friend?" enquired the other.

"No where," replied Sir Charles, "I will settle that business myself. Yes, my friend will accompany me."

No. 4.

The hostile messenger then bowed to the baronet, and took his departure without further delay.

"Now," exclaimed Sir Charles, upon being left alone; " I'll trap this villain in his own toils."

He then sketched a duplicate copy of the challenge, enclosed the same with a note in an envelope, and despatched his servant to the nearest London magistrate, commanding the assistance of a couple of peace-officers.   In a few hours after his departure, the domestic returned, and brought the magistrate's reply with him, wherein, Sir Charles was assured that the men should be at his residence in sufficient time for the meeeting, which Belford had appointed for the following morning, by half-past four; at the same place where the prior duel had been attended with such fatal consequences.   Accordingly, about four o'clock on the appointed morning, Sir Charles—who was in his study— was aroused by a knocking at the outer door : and as his domestics had long since retired to rest, he opened the same, and the officers entered.   A quarter of an hour saw them upon the ground appointed; and in a short time, Belford, and his two friends appeared; in neither of whom, however, did Sir Charles recognise his warlike visitant of the previous day.   A vague suspicion now, for the first time crossed his mind; and as they neared each other, he exclaimed :—

"Officers seize that man in the midst !"

The men instantly sprang forward, and held Belford in safe custody.   Instead of being paralized with astonishment—as Mortimer had anticipated; this accomplished sharper, burst into a hearty laugh.

"Bravo, Sir Charles!" he exclaimed, " Why, you are as cunning as myself; of what am I charged ?"

" With endeavouring to induce this gentleman, whom you call Sir Charles, to commit a breach of the peace by extortion," replied the nearest officer, tightening his hold.

" Well," returned Belford, "you need not hold me so devilish tight; I think I can alter the state of things entirely.   These friends of mine, are officers of the peace, likewise."

" And what do they here ?" enquired the baronet, turning suddenly pale.

" Why, sir, to speak truly," returned Belford, in a sarcastic tone; " they have come to apprehend one Sir Charles Mortimer; whom it was expected would be here—do you know him ?"

" With what is he charged ?" demanded Sir Charles.

" With being engaged as principal in a duel, in which the antagonist was killed," replied Belford.

" Where was the duel fought ?" enquired one of the officers, who had accompanied the baronet.

" On this very spot," continued Belford, " and yonder," he continued, pointing to Sir Charles; "stands the murderer; let him deny the charge if he can.   You see," he resumed, after a brief pause; " he cannot reply to that; officers, seize him !"

The men then, whom Sir Charles had brought to capture his former friend, and inseparable companion, now secured him; the same was observed with regard to Belford ; and in this manner, both were borne off to gaol.

CHAPTER IX.

THE ASSIGNATION.

When Captain Bond and his lieutenant, Robson, met the following morning; the first words the latter gave utterance to, was to enquire who, and what the ladies, with whom they conversed the previous evening were.

"Why," replied Bond, "by my life, I have not yet perused the card she gave me—how thoughtless."

"I should rather say it was thoughtless." rejoined Robson, "why, if you had been a shaveling monk, you could not have been more remiss in your duty. Why, I protest to you, that I have scarce enjoyed a wink of sleep during the whole night, for thinking of them—they were a pair of such charming creatures, truly."

"What!" rejoined Bond, in surprise; "are you too, an admirer of beauty? Pshaw man, I have thought more of the booty we obtained last night, than the girls we flirted with."

"That may be true, certainly," replied Robson, in a tone which served to imply, that he, the lieutenant, entertained a very strong opinion, that it was not; "but really, I thought you was somewhat attentive to your lady abbess, for a man who thinks nothing of women."

"Oh! that may be very possible," returned Bond, in a careless tone; "that, my dear fellow, was merely done to toy away an idle hour or two, nothing more. And, as for loving the girl—pshaw, its perfectly ridiculous. I can't positively imagine, how you can think of any such ridiculous, idle, nonsense."

"For a man, who is an outlaw," replied Robson, " I think, without exception, you possess the most extensive stock of impudence, and personal assurance, of any person whom I may have the honour to be acquainted. Such polished villainy—so refined in your manners, and also——"

"Have done with compliments," exclaimed Bond, interrupting him; "and look upon this card."

"Why, as I live," rejoined the lieutenant, "'tis that of the Lady Flora Mandeville! sure you cannot be in jest. How did you obtain possession of that card?"

"Why, is it not the same that was given me by the lady herself—how else think you, I obtained it—eh?"

"Do not grow so fierce," returned Robson, " I was not about to insinuate that you had stolen it."

"No," rejoined Bond, "I do not imagine that you was—or, if you had done so, it would not have been very fortunate for you; had it have been a gold watch, now, or a well-filled purse—you might have done me the honour—but the idea that a man would rob for a paltry pasteboard card, is not easily to be borne. Now, what is to be done?"

"If I might make bold to propose," replied the lieutenant, "I should most certainly say, pay them another visit, with the least possible delay; in fact, I think 'tis the only measure we can adopt."

"And pray what do you mean by we?" enquired Bond, "surely you cannot possibly imagine——"

"That you will not resign the lady abbess," interrupted Robson, "No, I do not, indeed; but I would here inform Captain Bond, that while he was busily engaged in paying his devoirs to the lady abbess, Robson, his lieutenant, was also actively employed in captivating her attendant nun."

"So, ho," rejoined Bond, "I now find that you had double reason to propose a visit to those bewitching creatures—but tell me, what are your intentions?"

"Towards whom, my captain?"

"Why, your *prima donna*," answered Bond.

"By the same rule, captain," replied Robson, "allow me to ask, what are your's towards the abbess?"

"I am not at liberty to answer," returned Bond.

"Nor I," returned the lieutenant, " Yet, I can give a very shrewd guess, I'm thinking, captain."

"What! you mean to run off with her, I suppose."

"Aye, truly, that is if an opportunity for so doing presents itself. Now, confess captain, are not your designs similar with my own?"

"Well, then, they are," answered Bond, "Now," he continued, "let us prepare fo a start."

"Do you intend to carry any weapons of defence with you, on this occasion?" enquired Robson.

"I think it would be advisable, for we made rather free upon the heath last night; and, if there should chance to be any person there, who might recognise us, a brace of barkers would be anything but incovenient—what say you?"

"I second the motion," replied Robson, "though, at the same time, fervently hope, that no occasion will present itself for their use."

"Now," rejoined Bond, "come and prepare the disguises, after that, to farther ensnare the hearts of the lady abbess, and her attendant nun."

Captain Bond and his lieutenant, then hastened to attire themselves in a suit of black, comprising a pair of fashionable pantaloons and silk stockings of the same sombre hue; their feet were incased in highly polished pumps, (not iron) a waistcoat of satin, and one of those articles, called opera hats, completed the outfit. Their motive for dressing in a style so similar to each other was, that they might appear as brothers.

The toilette complete, they at once started for Grantly Hall; arrived there, a loud knocking at the hall door, speedily brought a powdered footman in scarlet livery—with a nose to match—before them. Of this personage, Bond in a tone of affection, enquired if his mistress was to be seen. The very prompt manner in which the menial answered—would of itself, have assured any person at all versed in the secrets of aristocracy, that the fellow both received excellent pay, and was also well initiated in his duty, as liar in ordinary. Some there may be, who will enquire as to the meaning of this, we will inform them.

If any individual who is not upon the visiting books of our aristocrats, should dare to hazard a visit, it is the duty of the person who answers the door summons to protest, that those they desire to speak with, are from home—indeed, it is, we believe, the morning custom of many, to form a daily list of those, they are desirous of beholding. And if by any chance, the ill-fated domestic should in an unconscious moment fall into an error, his speedy dismissal must inevitably follow. Often when we have made a complimentary visit to a friend residing at the West End, has the domestic appeared confused; and, at length, in a tone of hesitation, replied in the affirmative; this was a clear and distinct proof of his noviciate. Such individuals are held in mingled pity and contempt, by the fraternity.

The man for a moment retired, and re-appeared, requesting Bond and his companion to follow—they did so, and in a moment more, were ushered into a magnificent drawing-room, which was furnished in the most costly style. At the middle window, sat the Lady Flora and her companion of the previous evening.

Upon the entrance of Bond and his lieutenant, they rose simultaneously, and bowed low.

"I trust I find you in excellent health," exclaimed Bond, crossing and imprinting a hasty kiss upon the hand of Lady Flora; "the hours seemed tedious; and since I last saw you, I have chid the tardy progress of time, which has kept me from your beauteous presence."

"You are pleased to flatter me," replied Lady Flora, "but how does your friend?" she continued.

"Charmingly I thank you," replied Robson, who was busily engaged in whispering soft nonsense into the ears of Emily Anson; for she it was, who had personated the attendant nun.

"I have had the greatest difficulty in being enabled to keep my apppointment," rejoined Bond.

"And why so?" enquired the Lady Flora.

" My father has long since, been endeavouring to compel me to'wed with a lady of great rank and fortune – and, because I refused so to do, he has treated me with the greatest possible severity."

" And why do you act in opposition to his wishes ?" enquired Lady Mandeville.

" Because," replied Bond, " she is my aversion ;_and I have fixed my affections upon a more lovely object."

As he spoke the latter words, he fixed a piercing glance upon Lady Flora, who blushed deeply, and cast her eyes upon the ground in evident confusion.

They continued for some time to indulge in *chit-chat and facetia*, when, at length, the domestic entered and presented a note to Lady Flora ; who, having read the same, drew from a satin reticule a small silver pencil-case, and having sketched a few characters upon a scrap of paper, delivered the same to the man in waiting ; and as he withdrew, she turned to Emily, and exclaimed :—

" The note comes from Colonel Stanhope, who has assured me, that his carriage will be here in the course of half an hour, to take us for a morning drive through the parks, it is a delightful morning."

" Surely," exclaimed Bond, " you don't intend to leave us here ; decline this colonel and his offer."

" Oh !" returned Lady Flora, with an arch smile ; " I could not possibly think of that. Why, the colonel has sent me this message for the last three days, and I have disappointed him each time, therefore——"

" The pretext for so doing now, is stronger," interposed Bond, " may I prevail upon you to oblige ?"

" Not for worlds," replied Lady Mandeville, " I never permit any person to prevail upon me."

" Then I must positively leave you," returned Bond, despairingly, and looking melancholy accordingly.

" Yes, sir," you must," replied Lady Flora, " and I now think, that I acted very improper, in permitting you to visit us at all ; more especially, as I now am convinced, that you are designed for another."

" I have already sworn that none but you shall possess my heart," replied Bond, emboldened with being left alone with the lady ; for, finding his presence was irksome to his captain, Robson had prevailed upon Emily to go to the farther end of the apartment, upon pretext of examining the paintings.

" How can it be possible," continued Lady Flora, " that you can be so devotedly attached to one, whom you have seen but twice, and that but for a very short space of time."

" Believe me," rejoined Bond, " when I assure you, that I have on many previous occasions, enjoyed the happiness of your society ; and in secret breathed forth those protestations I feared to declare openly. Oh ! how ardently have I panted for this hour—and now that it has arrived, let me implore of you to——"

" Now," exclaimed Robson, joining them, and followed by Emily ; " have you nearly brought your *téte-à-téte* to a conclusion ? Why, as I live, here comes the carriage of the colonel. Now, Count Ransford !"

These latter words were addressed to Bond—who, hearing a loud knocking at the hall-door, pressed the hand of Lady Flora, bade her hasty adieu, imprinted a kiss upon her delicate hand, and after Robson had performed a similar service for Emily, they simultaneously quitted the apartment, and passing Colonel Stanhope upon the stairs, they then hastened from the place--and having mutually agreed to follow the course of the carriage, made hasty preparations to obtain possession of their steeds.

CHAPTER X.

A FRIEND IN NEED.

SIR Charles Mortimer upon being securely lodged within the narrow confines of a dark gloomy dungeon, had more time and leisure to reflect upon the danger of the position in which he stood; he then, for the first time, began to reflect upon the probable consequences of his incarceration. He knew full well, the villainous disposition of Belford; and he was also fully aware that his anger once provoked, nothing but the ruin and destruction of the offender would serve his purpose. The evidence against him was so clear and unclouded, that upon the trial, there could be no possible doubt entertained as to his guilt. From these gloomy thoughts, he wandered in imagination to the sentence that would follow, death or banishment would surely be the issue. What a blow to the heart of his proud and, haughty parent—what a stain would be upon the escutcheon, which for years—aye, centuries, had remained bright and untarnished. While these racking thoughts haunted his brain, he sank upon the couch of straw, which was placed in an obscure part of the dungeon; and which, in consequence of the almost impenetrable darkness that reigned around, was scarce distinguishable. There he lay a prey to bitter anguish and remorse, until at length,

> "——— Sleep
> That knits up the ravelled sleeve of care
> The death of each day's life,
> Sore labour's balm,"

coming to his aid, he was for a time, buried in happy unconsciousness. On the third day from that of his incarceration, the turnkey entered his dungeon, and informed Sir Charles, that a friend was waiting without, and wished to be admitted into his presence. The fellow disappeared, and the next instant returned, introducing a fashionably dressed personage, who smelt profusely of *Eau de Cologne*, and in whom Sir Charles instantly recognised Sir John Campbell, who with great formality entered the dungeon, and extended his hand to the captive baronet, who looked upon his friend in silent wonder.

"Why, how is this, Sir Charles?" at length exclaimed the baronet. "How have you managed to get here, eh?"

"That is of little consequence," replied Sir Charles pettishly. "Perhaps you can tell me how I can contrive to get away; that is the only information I am at *present* in need of. Can you oblige me in that?"

"Why, no," returned Sir John, "I grieve to say I cannot. But where is your friend, that *he* is not here?"

"I should be pleased if you would oblige me with the name of such a person," answered Mortimer; "friends are scarce, Sir John Campbell; and I do not believe that I am acquainted with one person who really deserves that title—not even a solitary one."

"Indeed," continued the other; "what has befallen your trusty one, Count Belford—him your father requested you to cast off? Surely he has not played you false, Sir Charles. Where is he, my friend?"

"Mention not his name to me," rejoined the captive baronet, "I will not hear him spoken of."

"Why so?" enquired Sir John.

"Because," returned Sir Charles, "he is a villain. It is to his machinations alone I owe my present captivity. He has proved to me a bitter, treacherous foe."

"Then it is all true what I have heard of the duel," pursued the other; and you, Sir Charles, are———"

" A murderer!" interposed the baronet. That is what you would have said—yes, that is indeed true."

" In that case, Sir Charles, your condition is none of the most desirable. Yet you must be released—though how and by what means? I have it; I will call upon your dad; he must and shall assist you."

" I think it will be a useless labour," replied Sir Charles; "for when he knows how and by what means I came here, his rage will know no bounds."

" That I verily believe," returned Sir John. "Yet I will try what he is made of; and if he should *not* consent to assist you, why the next thing will be——"

" That I shall be hanged like a dog," interposed Sir Charles, in a tone of bitterness.

" Not while I have power to prevent it," rejoined the other. " No; if your father deserts his son, I will not. Rest assured, Sir Charles Mortimer, that Campbell will never suffer a friend to be lost, for teaching manners to a dog who has the insolence to——"

" Rob and insult with impunity," once more interrupted Sir Charles; " but if my father should indeed refuse to aid me, how can you, Sir John, effect my liberation? I fear it rests wholly with him."

" Oh, well," continued the other, " perhaps it may be so; but in either case rest fully assured that no exertion shall be spared to effect my purpose; and I dare make bold to bet a thousand, that I do not give up the game until you are a free man." With this comforting assurance the baronet quitted his captive friend, and hastened to the mansion of his father.

We must now plead for the privilege granted to dramatists—shift the scene of our play; and from the cold, damp, dark, miserable dungeon, transport (in idea only) the reader to the magnificent mansion, where jewels supplied the place of chains; the richly-furnished drawing-room, that of the dungeon; sumptuous fare tempted the appetite, instead of coarse bread and filthy water. These—these, are comparisons which rend the heart of misfortune's sons.

Sir John Campbell encountered the father of the imprisoned baronet as he was about to quit the mansion for the carriage. When, however, Sir John informed him of his desire to speak with him, he ushered him into his study.

" Well, Sir John," he exclaimed as the door closed upon them, " what is this important news you have to communicate? I trust you will be speedy."

" I will," replied the other. " What I would say is, that your son Sir Charles is——"

" Well, sir!" exclaimed the other, impatiently interrupting him.

" He is at this moment in confinement."

" What mean you?" enquired the father in haste.

" I mean that he is now securely lodged within a dungeon," replied Sir John, with marked emphasis.

A dark frown now sat upon the fine open features of the elder Mortimer, as he exclaimed, " And pray, Sir John, how can you imagine that the captivity of my reprobate son can concern me? Really, I thought you had something of greater importance to communicate. Why, I shall be too late for luncheon, at my friend Lord Saunter's."

" And can you sit down, surrounded by every luxury life can afford, and know that your son—your only son— is imprisoned in a common gaol?" continued Sir John, in a tone of astonishment.

" Why not, Sir John; why not?" returned the other. " Has not the son proved unworthy of the father? Did he not disgrace his family by leaguing himself with a villain and common sharper, by——"

" Whose means he is in his present disgraceful quarters," interrupted Sir John. " But that is now passed. He is fully aware and sincerely repents of his error; therefore you should endeavour to release him from imprisonment. Do this, and I will willingly stake my life upon his repentance and total reformation. What say you to that?"

"Nothing," replied Mortimer; farther than as he contrived to fall into disgrace and captivity, so he must contrive to effect his release. Now, Sir John, will you take a drive with me this morning to——"

"No, sir!" exclaimed Sir John. "if you so neglect your duty as a father, and willingly consign a son whose only crime—if crime it be—is thoughtless indiscretion, to a disgraceful fate, I from this hour resign your friendship; for the man who can so readily turn a deaf ear to the sacred ties of blood and affection, can have no thought or care for a friend. Good morning to you, sir."

With these words Sir John quitted the presence of his friend, and hastened to propose a new plan to Sir Charles, by which he felt assured that his liberation might easily be effected.

———

CHAPTER XI.

THE RESCUE.

CAPTAIN BOND, together with Lieutenant Robson, were in a very short space of time galloping with their steeds round the park, without gaining any intelligence of the carriage containing Lady Flora, Emily Anson, and their military friend. At length they descried the bright eyes of Lady Mandeville in an open barouche.

"There she goes," exclaimed Bond, addressing his companion. "How happy that fellow must be. By Jove, I would give the finest jewel our store can boast of, to exchange places with him. What say you, Robson?"

"Why," replied the lieutenant, "I don't know whether my dear nun is present also; if she is *not*, why——"

"I suppose you would not care for the ride."

"Not I," replied the lieutenat, moodily.

"I am thinking that we are making a couple of fools of ourselves," continued Bond, "running after a pair of women. Why, I wonder what Gipsey Meg would say if she knew that I, the great woman-hater, had forsaken the interest of my band, and turned to the cause of Cupid. Ha! what was that crash? Look yonder by the water-side—see you anything?"

"I do not," replied Robson; "but let us gallop forward. Assistance may be required, and we too may be enabled to afford it. Come, Captain Bond, forward!"

They then struck spurs into the sides of their steeds, and in a moment afterwards arrived at the scene of action; when it appeared that the barouche, containing Lady Mandeville, Colonel Stanhope, and Emily Anson, had been nearly overturned in consequence of the horses taking fright at some passing object. The sudden start had thrown the Lady Flora from her seat in the vehicle, and precipitated her into the river; while the colonel and Emily were borne off no one knew whither. No sooner did Captain Bond obtain a hurried detail of the above-mentioned facts, than suddenly springing from his horse he plunged into the stream, which was bearing the Lady Flora from the shore. He was an excellent swimmer, and soon reached the drowning lady, whom he held firm with one arm, while with the other he carved a passage through the crystal element, for himself and apparently lifeless charge.

No sooner did Captain Bond regain the shore, than seizing the reins of his steed, he sprang into the saddle, and with the senseless form of the Lady Flora before him soon arrived at Grantley Hall, where her ladyship was consigned to her couch, the medical attendants summoned, and every available means adopted for her recovery.

Immediately upon hearing of the impending fate of Emily Anson, Lieutenant Robson stayed not to ascertain whether the Lady Flora was rescued from the watery element or otherwise. No; he, by a vigorous and continued application of the whip

[*See pages 23 and 24.*]

and spur, proceeded on in the direction by which the infuriated horses had flown, at a tremendous pace. He continued to fly in this manner for nearly half an hour, still no traces of the carriage or its inmates were visible. He at length became by degrees aware of the madness of his search, and with melancholy forebodings slowly retraced his footsteps; and as he proceeded towards the heath, he suddenly remembered Gipsey Meg. Nothing doubting but that he should discover the sybil seated at the gibbet's foot, he, at an improved pace, hastened in the direction of the favoured haunt, where he discovered Meg, seated in a thoughtful attitude, with the body of a man richly attired, lying upon the ground before her.

For some few moments Robson continued to gaze upon her in silence. At length he exclaimed, " Well, Meg, who is it that you have there, eh ?"

" *Where ?*" muttered the gipsey. " Do you mean here ?" she continued, pointing upwards to the gibbet; " or there ?" glancing her sharp penetrating eye upon the senseless form before her.

" I mean," returned Robson, " who is that man lying dead at your feet—him that you are now gazing upon ?"

" He is a rich villain," cried Meg. " He it was who hung my boy. His evidence alone condemned him, when he would have been set at liberty. But when I last saw my son with life, I swore that he should be revenged – that I would avenge him; and fearfully have I kept and fulfilled the vow of blood."

" Surely," exclaimed the lieutenant, " you have not killed him. Speak, quick—why this hesitation ?"

" No," replied the gipsey, " I did not kill him. He was nearly dead when thrown at my feet; but I completed the deed—yes; I it was who *finished* him."

" How came he here ?" demanded Robson.

" A carriage bore him to this spot," replied the gipsey; " and with the fierceness of a tiger I sprang upon him."

No. 5.

" Merciful heaven !" cried Robson, alighting from his horse; " why,'tis Colonel Stanhope."

" Aye," replied Meg, rubbing her hands, " that's his name. Oh, Master Robson, you should have been here before this, it was a brave sight to see him start when he saw who sat by his side; how he prayed too, and implored of me to save his life—but no! I had sworn to revenge the murder of my boy, he knew it—he remembered that as he quitted the hall of justice, I, in a slow and measured tone, breathed my curse into his ear. I gave him but one short moment to remember all his crimes—implore forgiveness for the same—and establish his peace with God. After that, when the brief respite had expired, I placed my right hand about his throat; each instant my grasp grew more firm, his countenance changed —his eyeballs glared fearfully, and appeared as though they were about to quit their natural home—the cold dew of death stood upon his brow—a blackness overspread his features : yet, all this I gazed upon with a smile. Each instant as the torture of the dying wretch increased, with slow though certain measures, I bade him think upon the ghastly mass of bones and putrid flesh that swayed to and fro from the gibbet that was erected by my side. His half-suppressed groans and fearful struggles, however, soon filled even me with terror, and, in pity to him and myself, I despatched the immortal soul that animated this senseless mass at my feet, to the high home of its maker."

" Wretched woman !" exclaimed Robson, " you have committed murder ?"

" A crime," rejoined Meg, " of which Robson has never, by any chance, been guilty. Do I speak truly or not ?"

" I confess that I have," answered the lieutenant, " but mine has been for different motives than your's."

" I know it," retorted the gipsey, " I know it—your purpose was robbery— mine, the revenge of an injured woman. Which, think you, will find the greatest favour in the eyes of Heaven? answer that."

" I know not," rejoined Robson, " but you say that there was a carriage; now, tell me, was there any other than this unfortunate man seated in it; speak quickly, your hesitation to me is madness—answer, or——"

" Hey, dey," cried the gipsey, in astonishment, " what have we here?—you, Robson, in such a rare taking about a petticoat. Why, it was but a few nights since that you railed at me only because I spoke of——"

" Silence, woman," exclaimed Robson, " your words fall like molten lead upon my head. Answer me one question, was there another person in the carriage, or not? now, yes or no; which do you——"

" Well," interrupted the sybil, " there was another."

" And that other was——"

" A female," interposed Meg.

" My worst suspicions are confirmed," muttered Robson. " Now," he con- tinued, turning to the gipsey, " which path did the horses take after they passed you ?"

" The right," answered the gipsey, " they darted—"

Robson stayed to hear no more; but springing into the saddle, struck the spurs deep into the side of his already jaded steed, and was soon lost to view in the maze of distance.

" Some strange alterations have lately been effected in the band of Captain Bond," soliloquised Meg, upon being left alone, " or I am convinced this fellow, Robson, would never have so soon fallen in love with a petticoat; but harm will come of it—I know there will. No captain that admits a woman into his confidence, or suffers any of his men to hold commune with one, can possibly succeed in his career. Women and wine ever have, and ever will be the downfall of all brave men. I have always observed it, for she who has not sufficient virtue to preserve herself untainted by pollution, cannot be alive to the feelings of honour and fidelity : but I will to the cavern, and there endeavour to elucidate the mystery —and, for this," she continued, looking upon the stiffened corpse which lay at her feet, " I will bribe one of the gang to dig his grave—'tis more than the foul miscreant deserved ; but, though I can sit here and endure the worms which fall from the decomposing body of my boy, yet I could not bear the presence of another corpse, and this shall ever be my nightly resting place ;—but, to my plan."

She then arose and slowly proceeded towards the cavern that constituted the haunt of Captain Bond, Lieutenant Robson, and his brave band.

CHAPTER XII.

THE HYPOCRITE.

Upon the re-appearance of Sir John Campbell, the captive baronet eagerly enquired into the success of his mission.

" Why, I grieve to say," returned Sir John, " that all my arguments failed in the desired effect; your father is inexorable—his heart is not easily melted into softness.

" Did I not say it would be useless ?" returned Sir Charles, " I knew that my father would refuse to aid my escape ? My fate is now sealed—a wretched felon's life awaits me."

" Not if I live until the day of trial," pursued Sir John. " I have a little scheme—a plot which I think will turn out completely successful. When does the trial come off ?"

" To-morrow—so the turnkey told me this morning," replied Sir Charles, in a pensive tone.

" To-morrow !" mused Sir John, " not much time to be lost. " Where does this fellow, Belford, reside ?"

" Remember," rejoined the imprisoned Mortimer, I would rather perish than ask my life of such a villain. Let him not imagine that I would for a moment submit to—— By Heaven! I had forgotten ; he also is a prisoner! glorious thought !"

" Not so fast, my friend, with your glorious thoughts !" exclaimed Sir John, " Belford is not a prisoner!"

" How is this ?" returned the other, in surprise. " Why, we were both borne here together; for, as I gave charge of him, he did the same with me ; and that——"

" Is no possible reason why he should be a prisoner !" interposed Sir John.

" But how could he have effected his liberation ?" pursued Mortimer, " has he escaped the prison ?"

" Why, he has, and he has not!" answered the other. " The fact of the matter is, that he was first bailed out upon heavy security, and afterwards admitted as king's evidence against you, of whom he said he had some matters of the most important description to disclose ; therefore, expect a powerful opponent."

" I shall, indeed!" rejoined Sir Charles. " What with his statements, and the friends of the dead man, I shall have but little chance of obtaining an acquittal."

" Silence !" exclaimed Sir John. " As Shakspere says :—

' You'll mar all with this starting !'

I tell you once more that I have a plan which must and shall prove victorious ; defeat them all, only

' —— Look up clear,
To alter favour ever is, to fear.' "

" May I ask for a description of this most rare and excellent plan ?" enquired Mortimer, with a smile.

" Yes," returned Sir John, " you may ask, and that is all. I must now demand to know where this rascal Belford is to be found ; come, out with it."

"Not until I know the cause of your anxious enquiry,' returned Mortimer; "inform me of that, and I may."

"Then refuse," interposed Sir John, "however, you must not. That it is not upon any matter that concerns you, for you are one of very few men that

"Would not serve God if the devil bid you."

After some farther conversation, Mortimer possessed his friend with the required information. He then bade him a hasty adieu, turned from the prison, and in a short time afterwards was ushered into the presence of Belford, whom he found seated in a large arm chair, in a magnificent apartment of the ———— hotel. Upon the baronet's entrance, Belford rose and bowed.

"I presume, sir, you do not recognise me!" exclaimed Sir John, striding into the centre of the apartment.

Belford bowed low, and assured the baronet that he really could not boast the possession of an honour so distinguished, and at the same time motioned the baronet to be seated.

"Thank you," returned Sir John, "I can stand to state the nature of my business. I merely called to ask if you are acquainted with, or know aught of a person bearing the name of Sir Charles Mortimer, a young fellow who is about——."

"Oh yes, sir," rejoined Belford, "I am, that is, I was formerly acquainted with him, but he is——"

"Now in jail," interposed Sir John, "through the connivance of some rascally knave, of whom I am now in search."

"And for what purpose, sir?" enquired Belford.

"in order to inflict upon him a sound thrashing as a fitting reward for his villainy," replied Sir John. "Pray, sir, can you inform me where he is to be found?"

Belford replied in the negative.

"Are you acquainted with him?" pursued the baronet.

"I am most intimately," was the reply. "Why do you ask that question? have you aught of importance to communicate?"

"I have," replied Sir John; "but it is of such great importance that I cannot divulge it to any other than Count Belford in person."

"But really, sir," continued Belford, "you may in safety confide what you have to say to me; it will be the same precisely, because I am——"

"Belford!" suggested the baronet, promptly, "am I not perfectly correct in my supposition? tell me?"

"Well, then," returned Belford, seeing that it was useless to attempt further concealment, "my name is Belford."

"I knew it from the first," returned Sir John. "Now, harkee, sirrah, do you not feel completely disgusted with the disgraceful part you have taken in this most unprincipled transaction?—answer me."

"Really, sir," replied Belford, in evident confusion. "I have not the pleasure of knowing to what you allude, if you will be pleased to explain more——"

"Explain!" reiterated Sir John, "it is from you, sir, I shall presently demand an explanation. Now, tell me, are you not supposed to appear as the principal witness at the trial of Sir Charles Mortimer, to-morrow? that, sir, is my meaning."

Belford stood for some moments busied in reflective silence, apparently fearful of making a reply.

"Now, sir!" exclaimed Sir John, "I am waiting your pleasure."

"I am certainly to appear at the trial," he at length exclaimed, in a tremulous tone.

"And as a witness against Sir Charles," interposed Sir John.

"Yes," returned Belford—"that is, if no previous arrangement could be made to effect my absence."

"What!" rejoined Sir John, "you would suggest the propriety of my cutting your throat upon the spot; but as I am not a professional cut-throat, I have a slight objection, still, if you have any particular desire that it should be done, I will endeavour to oblige you, though it may put me to some inconvenience."

"My dear sir," answered Belford, with marked uneasiness, "you mistake my meaning, greatly; really I have no desire to have such an operation performed upon me."

"Oh! I understand you now," returned the baronet; "you are spelling for a bribe. Well now, as I have a great desire to be liberal, say what sum will be sufficient to detain you from the court? Now, be moderate."

"Well," returned Belford, after a pause, "say a hundred and fifty pounds; that I consider to be a very trifling consideration."

"So don't I," muttered Sir John; "that is a very large sum, sir," he continued, turning to Belford.

"I am aware that it is rather a large sum," returned Belford; "but the business is one that should be well paid for; I am sensible that I am injuring the progress of justice by so doing, but I do not think so much of making a little sacrifice, in order to save a friend; therefore, I intend to devote the money I am to receive from you to charitable services—I shall confer a handsome donation upon the——"

"Gaming table?" suggested Sir John; "but, however, you may of course dispose of the gold as you think fit—only take care not to betray us after you have received the bribe; or, remember, we shall expose you before the whole court; therefore——"

"What an absurd idea," rejoined Belford, "to think, now for a moment, that I should prove false to a friend; though it may be as well to assure you—that if I were so inclined, I could defeat any statement you might think fit to make."

"And pray, how so?" enquired the baronet.

"Why," rejoined the count; "I should first declare that I had not received any money from you, then——"

"But stay a moment," interrupted Sir John, "you appear to have forgotten that both I and Sir Charles Mortimer could swear to the fact."

"True," replied Belford, "I had forgotten that; but even then I should not be defeated; no, I have yet another stratagem, aye, and a thorough good one too."

"May I ask its nature?" enquired the baronet.

"Certainly," replied Belford; "I should then say that you had given it as part liquidation of a debt of honour, which had been one of very long standing."

"Well," rejoined the worthy baronet, shrugging his shoulders; "I must confess that you are not lost for schemes, though they are not fraught with too much honour; however, you shall receive the sum stipulated, and remember that you deal honourably with our cause, or expect to meet——"

"A bullet, I suppose you would say," interrupted Belford. "But you have not yet said how I am to keep from the court, and what excuse I may offer, that will warrant my non-appearance."

"Why!" exclaimed Sir John, "can it be possible that you should ask me for a plan? you, who possess such an abundance of schemes? Impossible!"

"My schemes, sir, are of a very peculiar nature, and only calculated to promote my own personal interests."

"Well, then," returned the baronet; "I have just methought me of an excellent plan. I have a friend, who is now reaping the profit of a very extensive practice as surgeon; now, you must feign to be taken with a sudden fit of indisposition—my friend shall attend you, and notice then be sent to the court, stating your utter inability to attend the trial of Sir Charles Mortimer."

"That may be a very good plan," returned the count; "but it don't seem to come within the compass of probability—that the most sapient judges of Old England are to be thus easily defeated in their projects. If you send them notice that I cannot attend; why, then a deputation will wait upon me here, and take the depositions; therefore we shall be defeated at the very moment when we might imagine success certain.   Now, what have you to oppose to that query?"

"To confess the truth," returned Sir John; "I am of very strong opinion that you are casting every possible objection in the way.   However, leave, and trust all to me; when they arrive, what will be more easy than for you to slumber, or pretend such agony, that you are deprived of your power of speech.   Now, how————"

"If I am to be dumb," rejoined Belford; "I shall expect to receive, at least, an additional sixty pounds."

"Only get us clear through this business," returned the baronet, "and you shall have another hundred."

After some farther controversy, the baronet retired, and speedily joined his friend.   Mortimer informed him of the above detailed circumstances; and both waited with the greatest anxiety, the issue of the morrow.

———

CHAPTER XIII.

CAPTAIN BOND.

LIEUTENANT ROBSON continued to proceed with all the speed his steed could muster, he had traversed a distance of nearly three miles—still without gaining the least possible trace of the carriage-horses—or the object of his search—Emily Anson.   He at length drew up the rein, and for several moments stood irresolutely pausing, not knowing which path to pursue; at length he came to the determination of taking the other road, which lay upon his left hand.   He was about to proceed onwards by his newly-chosen path, when he was startled by the sound of approaching footsteps, mingled with the trampling of horses; he waited in anxious expectation, and in a moment more a postillion appeared, leading a couple of horses, whose jaded appearance, together with the fragments of broken harness that was upon them, left no doubt upon his mind that they were the refractory steeds who had borne Emily, the object of his heart and adoration, he knew not whither.   As the man drew near he thus accosted him—

"From whence did you procure those horses?"

"They have been released from the fragments of a shattered chaise, which appears to have been dashed to pieces—they are a pair of fine creatures though, and————"

"When you arrested the flying course of those horses!" exclaimed Robson, impatiently interrupting him; "did you perceive no person near—no female who——"

"What female!" reiterated the man; "I have not often seen the woman who would venture near a pair of infuriated horses; especially when they are——"

"The person of whom I speak!" impatiently interrupted Robson, "was unfortunately an inmate of the vehicle at the moment when the horses first started."

"Then I should say," returned the postillion, "that by this time she has been smashed to little bones—killed outright.   But I must on."

With these words the man passed Robson, and in a few moments was lost in a cloud of dust.

Robson still proceeded onwards, and made repeated enquiries, but all of no avail; at length he became fully aware of the utter impossibility of meeting with that success he so ardently desired.   He, therefore, came to the determination of returning to the haunt and soliciting the advice of his friend and companion, Captain Bond.

As he passed the gibbet, he as usual, beheld Gipsey Meg seated in gloomy silence at its foot.

"Well, Meg!" he exclaimed, "at your dreary post again; why, the look of you is sufficient to give a fellow the blue devil's, whether he would have them or no."

"Some people," returned the gipsey, "are miserable before they see me; now, speak truly, Lieutenant Robson, are you very happy now? Does not your brain burn, and your heart throb with feverish anxiety, in consequence of a certain individual."

"Silence!" thundered Robson; "or by h—l you shall have ample cause to remember the hour of——"

"Hey day!" interrupted Meg; "why, what's up now? that a body must not speak. But where is the lady you gallop'd after with such violent haste? Why, I thought you was anxious to rescue her from the danger which threatened her life—surely you have not given up searching for her? have you?"

"I have, indeed," returned Robson; "'twas useless to proceed; no clue could be obtained, no person could afford me the slightest information; therefore, it was but a useless waste of time and labour."

"I shall now return to the band, and solicit the advice of Bond; he, perhaps, can afford me some useful information."

"Pshaw!" rejoined Meg; "how think you he is enabled to do as you imagine? from what source can he possibly derive his knowledge? No!" she continued, "the cunning of all is set at defiance; 'tis then a subject, fitting the notice of Gipsey Meg; I wil espouse this cause, and trust me, Lieutenant Robson, I will soon return with intelligence of your lost fair one. Aye, or not behold this spot again. I never yet undertook any project and failed in its completion. Now, lieutenant, farewell!"

"Farewell!" replied Robson; "and here," he continued, offering to her a well-filled purse, "take this as an earnest only of what I will do, should you succeed."

"Now," resumed Meg, taking the proffered treasure; "I will away at once. Farewell! this spot for a brief space will be deprived of its tenant. Once more, adieu!"

The gipsey then drew the tattered cloak more closely around her, and proceeded onwards in the direction by which Robson had returned.

The greatest confusion prevailed at Grantley Hall, upon the appearance of Captain Bond, with his lovely and senseless burthen; the domestics ran to and fro in perfect bewilderment; the housekeeper, a goodly damsel of forty-five, presided at the chamber. At length, when the medical attendant arrived, the most important commands were issued and as quickly countermanded by the mistress of the ceremonies.

At length her ladyship slowly recovered, when the first sentence she gave utterance to, was an enquiry for the safety of Emily. Upon being informed that she was nowhere to be found, the greatest distress was visible in the countenance of the invalid; and she immediately commanded that domestics should be despatched through every avenue of the park in search of her.

In the midst of this universal chaos, Captain Bond had prepared to depart, when he despatched a messenger for the last time, to enquire into the state of recovery in which the object of his care and solicitation was then placed. He had received a favourable reply, and had entered the garden, when he turned, upon the receipt of a light tap upon the shoulder; upon turning to behold the cause, he encountered two mysterious-looking individuals, clad in large shabby coats, their throats were encircled with a couple of dirty-looking handkerchiefs, in their hands they grasped each a thick bludgeon.

"Now, gentlemen, exclaimed Bond, with admirable self-possession, "may I make bold to enquire what the nature of your business may be with me? I am in haste."

"Wery sorry, indeed, to hear that," replied the foremost, "because, you see, we must first trouble you to stop."

"And why so, sir," demanded Bond, who now, for the first time, began to suspect the real character of his interrogators. "Why do you wish me to remain here?"

"Oh! you dosn't know," rejoined the fellow; "how should yer? Oh! how I does pity your wirgin hinnocence. Come, you must go along vith us; so look quick."

"What mean you?" demanded Bond, with feigned astonishment; "this must be some mistake. Good day, gentlemen, good day."

"Stop a minit, my covey," rejoined the officer; "it's no go attempting to come the knowing dodge over us—it won't fit. Your name's James Bond, the robber and outlaw, so now you know all about it. Oh! you needn't look so wery green. Now, are we to put on the ruffles, or will you go quietly? You can have a drag you know, if as how you've got the swag to tip for it. Now, what's it to be?"

"Be!" reiterated Bond, darting upon the nearest man, and seizing the bludgeon from his grap, and flourishing it above his head; "the chance is—that your skull's will either be driven in, or you will make the best of your way from this. My name is Captain Bond, you know my character, rather than surrender, I would perish here upon the spot. Now, begone."

"Wait a little, my daisy," exclaimed the officer, "levelling a pistol; you dosn't sheer off in that ere sort ov vay, so d'ye hear. I charge you to surrender in the king's name; therefore, lay down your arms."

Bond made no reply, but by a well-directed blow struck the weapon of death from the officer's hand, then dealt him a tremendous blow on the head, which laid him prostrate, he then seized the pistol, avoided the uplifted bludgeon of the other officer, suddenly started off at full speed. A small stile impeded his progress, however, he soon bounded over the low structure, and the next instant was lost to view.

CHAPTER XIV.

THE TRAITOR.

Not long after the hour of nine had been proclaimed upon the morning of the trial, Sir John Campbell entered the prison-house of his friend, Sir Charles Mortimer; they were led to the court, and as a matter of course, Count Belford was summoned—he did not appear—a messenger was despatched to his residence, in order that the cause of his non-appearance might be enquired into; the messenger returned, and informed the court that the count was labouring under a fit of indisposition. Once more, however, the man was despatched, and with him too, the brother of him who fell in the duel; and to the horror and consternation of all, shortly re-appeared, together with Belford; both Sir Charles and his friend started with astonishment.

Upon his entrance Belford was ushered into the witness-box—the trial then commenced.

"Now!" exclaimed the judge, "you are commanded to state all you know relative to the duel and death of William Ransford. Now proceed."

"Gentlemen," replied Belford, to whom the above sentence was addressed; "I scarce need add how distressing it must be to my feelings, as a friend to the accused, to stand here and give utterance to words which I know must condemn him irrevocably. But duty to the outraged laws of my country demand that I should unhesitatingly declare before you, the whole and undivided truth; thus then it runs :—

Both Sir Charles and his friend looked aghast upon hearing this new proof of Belford's villainy.

"It appeared," continued the count, "that Sir Charles, who had lost a

[*See Page 26.*]

trifling sum at hazard, grew insane, and in a most disgraceful manner, struck his adversary at play—notwithstanding this glaring insult, the wronged man proffered to Sir Charles his hand, imagining, and rightly too, that he was flushed with wine. To this, however, the baronet would by no means assent; he was averse to any amicable conclusion, and even insisted that pistols should be produced, and a duel fought upon the spot. This, of course, we all exclaimed against, and still Sir Charles indulged in the most ungentlemanly conduct and language; and after repeated insult, he demanded that the time and hour should be appointed for a hostile meeting, and we were literally compelled to accede to this, for Sir Charles spoke in such scurvy terms of our honour. The time approached, we arrived upon the ground, the distance was measured, and the usual ceremonies observed; the word being given to fire, the pistol held by Sir Charles missed fire, and did not even burn the priming; he then insisted upon a second discharge, to this we consented, but charged the weapons with powder only. Upon ascertaining this, the rage of the baronet knew no bounds, and after much abuse from him, a pair of fencing swords were produced, and—the result is already known."

"Why were the foils produced?" enquired the judge, "why were they produced, or even present?"

"It is usual upon such occasions," replied Belford; "that is, when the weapons have not been previously decided upon; though——"

"Pray is it not usual?" again enquired the judge, "to name the weapons when the place of meeting is spoken of? In short, I believe you inferred as much in your own statement?"

"I did so," replied Belford, nothing abashed by this query; "I did say so, "but when gentlemen are in a state of wine and excitement, it sometimes may occur that they forget the prior engagements they may have engaged in; therefore, the swords and pistols are produced upon the ground, that choice may be made by the antagonists."

No. 6.

Further interrogations were made, and at length the trial concluded, by sentence of death being passed upon Sir Charles Mortimer. He was then borne back to his cell, the prey to heart-rending anguish.

The first thing thought upon at the termination of the trial, by the friend of the condemned Mortimer, was the deep double-dyed treachery of Belford, who, amongst the many other acts of villainy, of which we have not made mention, was that concerning the money. When every other point had been cleared up, Sir John, thinking still to confound the witness in his statement, declared that he had absolutely accepted from him, the baronet, a large sum of money. Before, however, he could state any farther particulars, Belford interposed, and assured the judge and others present, that the sum spoken of, was received as part payment of a large debt of honour, long due, thereby fulfilling the declaration made on the previous day.

So thoroughly confounded were both the prisoner and his friend, that neither could offer a word in contradiction to this foul falsehood."

The following morning, however, Sir John arose from a restless pillow at an earlier hour than usual, and determined upon proceeding to the residence of Belford, and expostulate with him upon his unexampled villainy ; he accordingly swallowed a hasty breakfast and departed. The count had just risen, and was seated at his breakfast table, attired in an embroidered dressing gown, and his feet encased in a pair of buff slippers. Upon the entrance of the baronet he arose involuntarily from his seat, and in a faltering voice, demanded to know the nature of the visit. Sir John drew a chair into the centre of the apartment, then, seating himself, cast a penetrating glance upon the count; he thus addressed him :—

"Sir! I have called here for the purpose of demanding an explanation of your foul treachery. Did I not present you with one hundred and fifty pounds, in order that you should not appear against my friend, Sir Charles Mortimer ?"

"You did so," replied Belford, coolly sipping his chocolate. "Now, sir, have you anything more to say ?"

"And pray ?" enquired the enraged baronet ; "pray sir, why did you not act in accordance with our compact ? think you that such conduct is worthy of a gentleman, or a man of honour ? Answer, sir !"

"I grant you," replied Belford, "it is not."

Sir John started from his seat in unfeigned astonishment. "Why !" he exclaimed, after a momentary pause, "you have actually condemned yourself."

"True," rejoined Belford, "I may have done so, but not beyond redemption ; I think you said a few moments since, that I had received the sum of one hundred and fifty pounds, in order that I should not appear at the court yesterday. Did you not?"

"I did, sir," answered the baronet ; "was not such the case? Sir, what means this base subterfuge ?"

"I really think you are correct in your statement," pursued Belford, without appearing to notice the latter remark of Sir John, "but it is now high time to inform you, that from the friend of the murdered man, I absolutely received the sum of two hundred pounds, in order that I should appear. Now, sir, I have informed you of all."

"And could you so basely betray a friend ?" exclaimed Sir John, interrupting him, "after the repeated promises and protestations of fidelity you made to me? Can this indeed be possible ?"

"Possible !" reiterated Belford ; "aye, sir, and probable too, if you had afterwards made me a still greater offer, I should even after that have come over to your cause, and bid defiance to the other in the same manner as I did to you ; that is positively true. But if you will listen to me I can propose a plan by which Sir Charles may be liberated, even now."

The baronet informed his villainous companion that he was all attention, then desired him to proceed.

CHAPTER XV.

A ROBBER SHOT BY HIS LIEUTENANT.

As may be supposed, Captain Bond, upon thus releasing himself from the jeopardy in which his personal safety was placed—lost no time in reaching his rendezvous, where he entered, pale, breathless, and nearly blinded with dust. The men who were seated at the table carousing, simultaneously rose, and eagerly demanded to know the cause of his sudden and discomposed appearance. He answered to their enquiries by commanding them to bring Robson to him.

"That is impossible!" replied one of the men.

"And why so?" demanded Bond.

"Because he is absent," was the reply.

"Where has he started for?" rejoined Bond.

"We know not," was the reply; "he has not returned since he departed from here, in company with yourself; and some fine prizes have been lost through your absence from the gang."

"This is strange!" mused Bond.

"Aye," rejoined the first speaker, "it is strange that both captain and lieutenant should desert the band and its interests for a pair of smooth-tongued, pale-faced petticoats."

"Silence!" thundered Bond, hurling the pistol he had taken from the officer, at the head of the last speaker. "Another word, and I will shoot you upon the spot. D—n, do we govern a band, and not have free will to use and exercise our own unshackled pleasure? Let me have no more of this murmuring, or, curse me, if you don't all suffer. I am now going to retire; and d'ye hear, when Robson returns, tell him to rouse me. I have counsel for his ear, and let's hear no rioting."

"With these words Bond quitted the robbers, in order to seek for that rest of which his agitated mind and fatigued body stood so much in need.

"Our captain is somewhat rough to-night!" exclaimed one of the robbers, "how terrible he looked."

"Aye," returned the fellow, at whose head the pistol had been hurled, "if men were to be alarmed at ugly thieves and fierce words, Captain Bond would kill his share, I'm thinking. I don't like to see a brave set of fellows thus oppressed; what say you, lads? are you willing to make the attempt to wrest the power from this tyrant? he knows not how to use it. A firm heart and steady arm is all that is required. I will lead you on, and—"

"Silence!" exclaimed another of the band; "the captain can overhear your talk; and should he return——"

"Let him do so!" vociferated the former spokesman, "and if he does, my hand shall be the first to strike him to the earth. Now, lads, what say you?"

At this juncture, and before any person could utter a reply to this rebellious traitor, the report of a pistol was heard—the bullet whizzed by the men, and the last speaker fell prostrate upon the ground and expired in dreadful agony."

All looked in the direction from whence this sudden and unexpected messenger of death had proceeded, they beheld Robson standing at the entrance.

He threw the newly discharged weapon with violence to the ground, and striding into the centre of the cavern, he cast a fierce glance upon the group.

"How is this?" he at length exclaimed; "have you no other better manner of disposing of your leisure hours than to be conspiring against that man whose kind indulgence grants the same? Where is Captain Bond; I am anxious to convince him of the sincerity of his band? Where is he, I say?"

"Robson!" exclaimed one of the men, coming forward, "there are none here now who hold one disloyal thought. The only man who dared attempt a mutiny now lies in death upon the ground. We would one and all perish in defence of Captain Bond. Am I not speaking correctly?" he continued, appealing to those assembled. A simultaneous shout succeeded.

The uproar disturbed Bond, who, entering at the same time, demanded to know its cause. The lieutenant stepped forward and explained the whole cause; and, at the same time, directed the attention of Bond towards the body of the deceased robber.

"You have my many thanks," rejoined Bond, shaking Robson warmly by the hand, "you have but anticipated my own actions; and, now that all are assembled, I must tell you all that I expect the speedy arrival of a few visitors in the persons of peace officers or soldiers."

A simultaneous burst of surprise followed.

"'Tis most time," rejoined Bond. "I am in momentary expectation of their appearance."

"And how are they to be received?" interrupted Robson, addressing the men, who simultaneously drew their swords, crossed them, and swore fidelity to Bond.

"You have but acted as I should have expected!" exclaimed the captain; "and to shew you that I fear nothing, believe me when I say that had not this fellow perished by the hand of my brave lieutenant, he should have fallen by my hand; but we must make some preparation for the reception of our friends."

The robbers then proceeded to increase the warlike precautions which were visible to the observer. After which Bond and his lieutenant retired in order to hold a private consultation. The first information Robson required, was concerning the safety of Lady Mandeville. This subject led to others, and Bond came to the detail of his adventure in the garden with the officers, by which the before mentioned expectation was fully explained, to the entire dissatisfaction of Robson.

"I should be much more at rest!" exclaimed Robson, "if these d—d vagabonds were not about to pay us a visit; should we be defeated, the next thing will be —"

"That the whole body are blown into the air like a swarm of invading locusts," rejoined Bond.

"And how is that to be effected?" enquired Robson, with a smile of ill suppressed derision.

"Listen to my plan," replied Bond, "I shall first offer a brave resistance; this failing, I shall blow the cavern, myself, you, and the men into the air. I have some time since secretely deposited beneath the entrance five large barrels of powder, and in the event of a defeat up we go; but do you think those fellows will prove true to our interest, for, in the event of treachery———"

"No fear may be entertained of them," interrupted Robson, "the only traitor we possessed has perished."

"We are not thoroughly convinced of that," replied Bond, "however, we must be prompt and severe in all measures concerning them; but I had forgotten—how fares the young companion of Lady Mandeville? have you seen her since the accident?"

"I have not," was the reply. "I have spent several hours in the pursuit, but all to no purpose. No traces of them could I discover; and now as a last resource, I have despatched Meg upon the scent."

"And my life upon it," returned Bond, "she will prove a faithful bloodhound —but now to make a few preparations for the arrival of our friends."

CHAPTER XV.

GIPSEY MEG.—AN ADVENTURE.

It was several days before the reverend man of the parsonage-house recovered from the ill effects of the blow dealt by one of the robbers, whom, it will be remembered, he recognised as his son. It now remains for us to prove, if indeed, we possess the power so to do, how far his words were correct. The family of Mr. Williams had year by year decreased; death, with his ruthless hand, spares not youth, beauty, age, or innocence—no! all are alike made its victims: like the vapours of a marshy ground we appear and pass from the scene of life, oft times unseen and unknown. No care can ensure the creatures of life from the barbed shaft of destruction. The solemnity of the scene of death is one of soul-absorbing interest; hours have passed—imperceptibly fleeted by—while we have sat absorbed in tears, holding in tender embrace the slender and partially transparent hand of a fond doating sister, who now—God rest her spiritual soul—we trust, is safe, securely lodged in those blessed, pure, and boundless realms of joy eternal, where rest the never dying souls of the true and righteous, while here on earth. Oh, that the heart of man could mould and will itself to the ways and righteous workings of celestial purity and love; then the enemy of life, the foe of mankind, would be compelled to mourn a lasting defeat, and we, happy thought, should ———; but we feel, and keenly too, that the subject upon which we are engaged is of too righteous, too pure a nature, for our polluted soul to hold any converse with: we, therefore, brush a tear occasioned by the recollection—painful as it is—and return to earthly subjects; terrestial thoughts best suit the mortal mind. And now, gentle reader, thy inward wish shall be obeyed, we will not farther transgress upon thy valued moments. About three years antecedent to the date of our production, the wife of Mr. Williams had passed from the world, his eldest son had also, after a serious illness, followed the fate of his mother; and one son and daughter only remained. The daughter still cheered the rector's solitary hours; but the son had joined with a gang of young prodigals, whose wild and extravagant pursuits led them into continual errors, one crime leads to another, and, step by step, the untutored and reckless are led onward to the broad path of destruction until the very verge is reached the fearful precipice is gained, and, with one fatal leap, they are lost, aye, and for ever buried in the depths of crime. The son of Mr. Williams first joined a daring set of poachers: these he quitted—poverty followed—he robbed and murdered a lone traveller upon the highway—fear of detection followed; and, to protect himself from a more dreadful fate, he joined with the band of daring robbers commanded by Bond. This was not all; one night, nerved by wine and desperation, he proposed the plan to rob the parsonage-house, as a revenge upon its reverend owner, who had, upon one occasion, prosecuted a member of their gang, who made an attempt upon his life and property. The plan was eagerly embraced—they entered. The reverend man was aroused, and struck fiercely to the ground by the hand of *his only son!* What a pang of bitterness—what fearful recollections must have haunted the distracted senses of the good man, when, upon recovery, he endured the smarting pain; and, at the moment, remembered that the same had been caused by a child, one on whom he had bestowed years of care and paternal affection. This was a dreadful pang; but, like all others, must be borne; and if our nature is too feeble, the gulph of death presents itself, and the silent grave encloses all that is left of this mortal coil.

Really, authors are beings of a mysterious mould—such contending thoughts—such various reflections are ever present to their fevered brain and imagination; scenes of death, robbery, murder; now, thrilling thoughts of love, and every other passion of nature is developed before them.

Gipsey Meg proceeded upon her journey with the greatest possible caution. No single passenger did she permit to pass without making an enquiry relative to the object of her search, but all of no avail. No one trace could she gain of the lost fair one. And, at length, even Meg began to despair of success. Miles are passed—no person is to be encountered—she rests by the way side, and stops at the door of a small peaceful cottage, and solicits a draught of water. She was immediately ushered within, where a bowl of milk was presented, and Meg gladly accepted the invitation to be seated: and the good woman, who appeared the owner, enquired, in a kindly tone, if she had travelled far, and also the nature of her errand. To all her enquiries Meg gave true and direct answers—and after a brief sojourn, she once more started upon her journey. The next place where she halted, was at a low road side inn. She entered the public room, where was seated some three or four shabbily attired sunburnt men, each of whom carried small packs at their back. Meg ensconsced herself snugly in a corner, and determined to watch their movements narrowly. Something appeared to whisper that by giving attentive observation to these wayfarers, she might solve the mystery which hung upon the object of her search. The men commenced drinking and carousing. At length, setting down an empty bowl, one of the men exclaimed :—

"Rather lucky that we were passing by that road just at the very nick of time; why, it 'ud ha' been a good fifty pounds out of our pockets. I say, how the young chap did fight! why, it was as much as three on us could do to grab him! But, I say, Mike, do you think there will be a reward offered for the recovery of the girl?"

"Why, in course there will," replied the other in a confidential tone; "and if there isn't, why, I shall make her my wife—that's all " ;

"Monster!" involuntarily exclaimed Meg.

"Hollo!" cried one of the men, "who's that calling us ugly names? I should like to know."

"Aye, who is?" chorussed the four simultaneously.

They then rose from their seats, and though Meg shrank into the most gloomy corner, they recognized and addressed her; she, however, did not, or affected not to heed their violent exclamations.

"Why, smash me into dead ducks!" exclaimed one of the four, " if that isn't our old friend and companion, Gipsey Meg."

"Who?" murmured the group in astonishment.

"Gipsey Meg," replied the individual who had expressed a desire to be converted into dead ducks. She sits there as unsociable as a stranger. Come, Meg, lass, join our company, and be as jovial as you once used to be. Come, take a glass."

"Leave me to myself," vociferated Meg, seeing that the speaker was about to advance to where she was seated; "leave me to myself, I say."

"Well, now," rejoined the fellow, "there's no need to appear so very grand, cos nobody in this blessed world cares for you. Besides, you ought to be seized as a deserter from our tribe. The queen told me and every body to happrehend you when——"

"You dare to lay hands upon me," interrupted Meg; "but that you will not do—no, I defy you, one and all."

"Why did you desert the tribe?" enquired another of the men. "You should have stood true to the cause. Why did you desert? I say. Answer me."

"Divest yourself of that bullying accent, and I may perhaps oblige you," returned Meg; "but, as you all should know by this time, I am not to be frightened into your designs; so keep a civil tongue."

"Once for all, I tells you," returned the first speaker, "that you must go with us to the queen of our tribe. Why, she is 'al'us asking for your good-looking self, and offers a large reward to them as brings you back. So, as ve're out upon scent and nearly stumpt out, why I know you'll oblige us—come."

"Stand off!" vociferated Meg, stand off! I warn you. I am desperate, and like yourselves, upon an undertaking of the greatest importance; one, too, that I will pursue with my life; therefore, do not you attempt to molest me."

"But you see," returned the first speaker, "we can't avoid it, cos we must have the swag."

"I came here in peace," rejoined Meg; "met you all as friend should meet friend, and would part as such also. You all know my resolution; once fixed, it is as changeless as the firmament of high heaven. I have sworn an oath that never again with life would I enter the gang of your——"

" And why not?" interrupted one of the men.

" Why not!" reiterated Meg; " because a dear child—an only son—forfeited life in its service."

" Aye," rejoined the first speaker, " and he wouldn't have done that if he had not been a coward."

Meg waited to hear no more; but seizing a large pewter measure, that stood upon the table half filled with liquor, she hurled it with tremendous force at the head of him who had spoken in terms of such disparagement of her deceased son. In an instant the three others started to their feet, and a corresponding number of knives gleamed in the air; still Meg stood undaunted.

" Now," she exclaimed, " let me see the man who will dare repeat this foul statement, and I'll serve him in a similar manner—cause his thick skull to echo to its own music. My son a coward! Did one of the wretches now before me possess but one portion of *his* courage, they would have no cause to fear the gibbet. But look well to yourselves. You have outraged the feelings and raised the displeasure of Gipsey Meg; and look well to it. See that no harm comes of it. I do not threaten, you see; notwithstanding your gross insults, I still caution you as a friend. Mind, then, that you do not neglect that caution; or if you do, and come to harm afterwards, why then, free the gipsey from all blame. Now, I wish to quit this place. Stand from the door there, you, Wat Brandon—stand off, all of you."

" Strike her down, lads!" vociferated one of the men.

" Strike her down, eh?" returned Meg with a contemptuous smile. " Is there one among your tribe possesses sufficient courage to do so? Ha, ha! strike the Gipsey Meg to the ground! Me, who was the first to confront the soldiers when they surprised the tribe by their sudden and unexpected appearance. I killed *six men* then, and shall I now shrink from *four*—such as you, too? No; you appear to have forgotten that Meg is ever prepared for all chances. Look at these," she continued, producing a brace of pistols, which she immediately placed upon full cock; " you see that I am prepared for you. Now, let the most brave coward among you stand forward, and you shall see with what ea-e I'll riddle his brain. What! do you *all* flinch—all tremble before one weak woman? Did your queen but see you now, the noble-minded woman! I am convinced that a rich reward would be your own."

" You may go, if you please," and be d—d," exclaimed one of the men, venturing a glance at the gipsey.

" Thank you for such kind and unexpected condescension," replied Meg in a sarcastic tone; " but I shall use my own free will and pleasure upon that point. Now, as I have succeeded in teaching you good manners, I must know who and what you were speaking of when you entered this room. Now, tell me—quick."

" That—that is a profound secret among ourselves," muttered one of the men in a tremulous tone.

" At this juncture the gipsey's finger was seen to rest upon the trigger of one of the pistols.

" Remove them d—d barkers," rejoined another of the men, as with uneasiness he became aware of the unpleasant consequences that would fall upon his head, should Meg indeed discharge the pistols; " lay down them *fire-irons*, and you shall know all in a very few seconds."

" Thank you for nothing," returned Meg; " but I am unfortunately not inclined to oblige you, Black Muzzle; so, d'ye hear! out with all you have to say, or I shall be compelled to enquire whether you have any brains in that thick-looking skull."

Finding that farther hesitation would be productive of danger to all, and perhaps death to all, they possessed her with the desired information; when being assured that, contrary to her previous expectations, it did not relate to Emily, Gipsey Meg prepared to take her departure. The men did not oppose her; and she had reached the door, when the nearest advanced stealthily behind, and with uplifted knife was about to stab her in the back. His shadow upon the wall betrayed the treacherous villain to the eager eye of the gipsey; who, turning suddenly round, dealt him a tremendous blow in the face with the butt-end of her pistol. Instantly he fell to the ground, blinded with blood and pain. She then discharged both weapons at the three, who were advancing; two fell mortally wounded, and, with a loud laugh of exultation, Gipsey Meg disappeared.

CHAPTER XVI.

THE ADVENTURES OF MEG RESUMED.

Upon quitting the scene of her perilous adventure, Meg hastily gained the exterior of the inn, and pursued her course in moody silence along the broad road that lay stretched on her right. The pistols were concealed beneath her cloak, and she came suddenly to a dead pause, being uncertain which course to pursue. At one moment she had resolved to return and assure Bond of her inability to discover the objects of her search.

"What!" she mentally exclaimed, "shall Gipsey Meg suffer them to say that she failed in accomplishing aught that she had undertaken? No; I will not return until I have discovered them." As she pronounced these words she noticed a child about five or six years of age proceeding towards her with slow, measured steps, and deeply absorbed in tears. This object immediately engrossed her attention.

"What ails thee, girl?" she enquired, as the juvenile weeper approached nearer to her.

"Oh, madam!" rejoined the girl, "my mother, who lies in yonder cottage, and who is now prostrate upon her death-bed, has been levied with a distress upon our humble furniture, and unless the money be paid within the brief space of one hour, the goods will be taken. Oh, madam! if you have the power or means, and would assist a helpless, weak, infirm old woman—in the name of that Power whom we all do serve and adore, afford some speedy assistance, which may serve to avert the ruin with which we are threatened. You stand in thoughtful doubtfulness. Oh! heaven be praised! I see in your sun-burnt, though benevolent countenance, the evidence of sympathy."

"Nay, nay," rejoined Meg, "be not be so profuse in your thanks; I have not yet promised—indeed, I am half inclined to believe that you are deceiving me. Where is your father? Surely he is not the calm and inactive spectator of such a scene of domestic grief and privation as that which you have now described— where is your father?"

"Alas!" replied the still weeping messenger of sorrow, "my father has long since been immured within the dark gloomy confines of a dungeon"

"Then 'twas crime, that first produced the change of fortune, of which you now complain," pursued Meg.

"No, madam," replied the girl, "'tis not for crime but debt, that my father is deprived of Heaven's light and liberty. A few months since, he was in the prosperous path of life—but, alas! repeated reverses so completely overwhelmed him in pecuniary difficulties, that his ruin and imprisonment speedily followed."

"Conduct me to the abode of your mother," pursued Meg, "and I will see how I can best assist your parent in her season of adversity—where is the landlord, now?"

"At the cottage," replied the girl, "busily engaged in taking an inventory of the furniture."

The old woman spoke not farther, but silently motioned the youthful supplicant

(*See Page* 32.)

to precede her to the cottage—she did so, and in a few moments afterwards, Meg was ushered into a neat but homely-looking apartment. The floor was not ornamented with a carpet, but the boards, with their white and spotless surface, told the observer in language, even more eloquent than words could do, that cleanliness was blended with poverty. The small spiral-formed bedstead, too, was hung with coarse, yet clean, linen hangings; an old chest of antique-formed drawers, a large deal table, which stood in the centre of the apartment, together with four highly polished, though somewhat dilapidated chairs, together with one nursing ditto; a few wooden platters, and two spoons, constructed of the same homely unassuming material, constituted the whole stock of household furniture; in short, the whole appearance of the place betokened extreme poverty, blended with honest contentment and cleanliness. Yet, with such a picture as this before him, together with that enfeebled and emaciated form that lay extended before him, upon a bed of sickness—perhaps, death, could the callous-hearted landlord proceed to the most severe extremity allowed by England's law; a law most unjust, one, too, that should not be tolerated, or even permitted to exist in a land where freedom and plenty are said to abound. How many a man, whose life had otherwise have been one continued source of happiness and honest industry, has not by the most unjust decree of his country's laws, been driven from home and friends; his family depending upon him, their natural protector, for support. Clamouring for food—what parent that had a heart, or possessed one atom of affection for those to whom he had given being, could withstand the strong appeal to his maternal feelings, calmly hear their clamourous appeal for food, without making one effort to obtain the necessaries of life; and without which, our very existence upon the broad surface of Nature's face would cease? Thus driven by persecution to seek relief from the cold hand of charity—can we marvel that the otherwise honest victims of persecution, should pursue that course which is ever fraught with shame, ignominy, and punishment? that he should take from the

No. 7.

more wealthy portion of mankind (those who luxuriate in the most refined deli-
cacies produced by bountiful Providence, coupled with their own affluent condition
in society,) that which would sustain exhausted nature, to preserve his destitute
family from the horrors of starvation? For this, the producer—he, by whose
bodily exertions, the commercial portion of the world is kept upon the revolve—is
sentenced to a punishment, the cause of which, is produced by the very persons
who inflict the penalty. But a truce with this moralizing; all we can say will not
produce the desired reformation in the Houses of Parliament, and monuments
may stand in an unfinished state; men may refuse to comply with the demands
of their employers, but it is all in vain; until the aristocracy have less power, and
the working class more sense, the long wished-for amendment never can, or will
be accomplished. Englishmen may truly be likened to the dumb beasts of burden,
whose load is overbearing—they offer a vain attempt at resistance—then, as though
suffiance were the most profitable and available; even though the task should be
doubled—nay, trebled, they still pursue the same unwearied round of dull tyrannous
duty, seeming but too happy that their very life is spared them.

In this, however, we are at fault—for however great the evils of the present
age may be—and great indeed they are—the present time is not fitting, and the
space which should be devoted to the production of that matter—the perusal of
which, would be productive of more gratification to the reader, than the remembrance of those grievances, which, while they bear any visible complaint, are a
source of great personal torture—but to proceed—the old woman gazed around in
an attitude of consideration and thought.

"What!" she at length exclaimed, "and can this be England? A place
where plenty and freedom are said to abound? Impossible, that hearts so callous
to humanity, should a position hold in such refined days of charitable interference.
Shame upon your avaricious soul, which would thus prompt you in spite of all
better feeling, to drive from her humble couch, one, whose head is pillowed thereon,
in the last stage of sickness, and fast approaching death—what is your
demand?"

"Why do you ask?" demanded a diminutive specimen of the sapient repre-
sentatives of England's equitable law!

"Why do you not answer?" demanded the sybil, in a tone wherein was depicted
a feeling of contempt, mingled with an over-conquering desire to give certain
striking proofs of her disapprobation of the whole proceedings.

"Why," rejoined the other, "it is far above your power to discharge."

"And how know you that?" answered Meg.

"Because, if you indeed was possessed of gold, methinks you would soon
exchange apparel, if not for more costly, at least, for one somewhat more respectable."

"So," muttered Meg, "this is your opinion of the world's customs. In your
estimation, none but those who are attired in the gaudy trappings of worldly
splendour, can possess the power, or even the will, to aid the cause of the indigent
and oppressed. I wander the world through in obscurity, and by the discernment
which in God's precious bounty I possess, coupled with this same attire, which
you, in the fulness of deep-rooted ignorance of human nature, are pleased to condemn, I am the better calculated to gain a more complete knowledge of the world
than I otherwise should. But it is ever thus: attired in the most grotesque style of
fashion's advocates. Even the accomplished ruffian can easy access gain to the most
polished circle of society, whose members never entertain a momentary thought as
to the means that have been used to gain possession of the same. No matter how
or by whose industry they have been obtained—suffice it to say, that they have
got them; while the humble producer, clothed in the evidence of his diurnal toil,
is spurned in contempt, by the self-approving unsophisticated multitude."

"Have done with this preaching," exclaimed he of legal consequence; "will
you pay us?"

"When you have informed me of the amount," replied Meg, interrupting
him.

"Well, then, the demand is four pounds four and eightpence, costs included."

"That I suppose will suffice," rejoined Meg, taking from a small leathern bag —produced from the corner of a large pocket-book—four sovereigns and three shillings.

"No, it will not ;" replied the fellow, with a triumphant grin ; "I have told you the amount of my demand ; and not one farthing less then that sum, will suffice."

Without expending time in useless expostulation, Meg immediately produced the remaining portion of the money : then demanded a receipt in full for the same. This was given ; the man then drew forth a well-filled purse—in which, there appeared to be a multiplicity of golden pieces—which Meg observed with a greedy eye. She presented the invalid with three sovereigns, then hastened after the landlord and his satellite whom she met by the door. In a moment more she had confronted them, produced a brace of pistols, which were levelled at their heads with wondrous dispatch—she then, in an authoritative tone, demanded immediate restitution of the sum she had paid him, together with whatever else they might possess.

Thus situated, remonstrance, they rightly judged, would be useless ; they, therefore, with considerable ill grace, submitted to her joint sums to the amount of fifteen pounds, together with a silver watch and appendages ; having possessed herself with these, Meg took her leave—having first intimated the extreme probability of their having to encounter the unpleasant consequence of a brace of bullets each, should they make any attempt to raise a pursuit. Thus ended an adventure, by which she rendered an especial service to a poor and deserving family ; punished their would-be persecutors ; and finally enriched herself—and that to a very considerable extent.

CHAPTER XVII.,

MUST BE READ.

AFTER having listened to the plan, as related by Belford, by which, as he said, the liberation of Sir Charles might be effected, his friend, the baronet, rose to depart, being fully assured of the fallacy of the scheme which we would relate to the reader ; but as it would only tend to prove, if possible, more completely the villainy of Belford, than we have already painted him, we shall refrain, as it would only be a repetition of what may follow. The father of our captive hero had been informed of the somewhat perilous condition in which his son was placed, and instead of expressing any regret, or even concern upon the receipt of the intelligence, he calmly assured Sir John Campbell, who was the messenger, that as the young baronet had thought fit to disobey his injunctions, and follow in the course he had himself chosen, and by that means become involved in the natural consequence of his folly, he must extricate himself as he best could, for that as far he was concerned, no attempt to rescue him from his disgrace might be anticipated It was in vain that the worthy baronet pleaded with all the warm affection of one who took deep interest in the welfare of the young captive ; the other was inexorable, declaring his enmity to be such, that if a word from him would save his son from an ignominous death, he would refrain from giving utterance, though at the same time he enquired when the trial was appointed to come off, and when he had been possessed with the required information upon the subject, he then expressed his intention of being present at the momentous ceremony.

After some farther attempts to produce an alteration in the sentiments of the baronet in favour of his captive son, Sir John returned with a heavy heart, to the dungeon of his friend.

CHAPTER XVIII.

ROBBERY OF A FRENCHMAN.

In the preceding chapter we at first proposed to dwell fully upon the character, future prospects, and other equally important matters, of which Sir Charles, though a captive, would have been the hero. Upon more mature deliberation, we find that there are certain persons who are likewise destined to form a prominent feature in this romance of real life, who in the meantime would have been detained inactive, during the period necessary for such detail; therefore, entertaining as we do, a great abhorrence of any such proceeding, we must request our very numerous and respectable readers to remember the last words spoken by Captain Bond, as to the reception of certain friends (?) in form of peace officers, who were expected to honour them with a visit, but as they were disappointed in their expectations, they, one and all, he among the rest, prepared to consider the whole affair as one complete hoax—accordingly, enjoying this opinion, Bond the following day, accompanied by his trusty lieutenant, quitted their rendezvous, and had not proceeded far, before he declared himself to be in one of those frolicsome moods wherein the thought of danger is swallowed up as it were, in a desire to prove his utter recklessness of whatever might chance to present itself.

"But are you aware of the great personal risk you run, in thus laying yourself open to detection?" exclaimed his trusty adviser.

"I am aware of all," rejoined Bond, in that utter recklessness of manner, which characterized his nature; "I am aware that they may perhaps pounce upon, and unexpectedly secure me."

"The result of which will be——"

"That they have caged a lion!" interrupted Bond, "but in so doing, it is not improbable that he may bite the foremost of his captors."

"That may perhaps be true," replied the other, "but where the utility of that will be, I cannot discern; if you are captured, why, the band must of course dissolve partnership upon the instant, and that for one of my temper would by no means be a pleasant thought."

"'Tis useless for you to attempt to persuade me from my purpose," rejoined Bond; "I shall return free from harm; fear not; these pretty pleaders," he continued, producing a brace of pistols, partially mounted in silver, "will protect their master from all harm, at least they have hitherto extricated me from the many broils in which my professional abilities, coupled with my great personal daring, has from time to time involved me. Farewell, my trusty; dispel the gloom that sits upon your respectable countenance, return to the band, and in my absence console them with the information of my speedy return among them. Adieu!"

Before the lieutenant could offer any comment upon the foregoing sentence, which displeased him marvellously, the captain had disappeared; upon discovering this, he turned suddenly upon his heel, and muttering a few partially inaudible curses upon the obstinate nature of his captain, slowly retraced his steps to the cavern, where the several members of the gang were assembled at a carousal. Upon the entrance of the worthy representative of Captain Bond into the presence of the gang, they simultaneously rose to greet him in a bumper; this partly served to dispel the gloom, which, as we have before said, pervaded his countenance, and he returned them thanks in something like the following address. Though we cannot pledge ourselves that it is strictly correct, inasmuch as at the time of its delivery, we ourselves had indulged in sundry potations, highly calculated to confuse and oppress the brain of man—it ran thus:—

"Gentlemen and gentlemen's sons, I feel great pleasure in having this here opportunity of addressing you, I have been lieutenant of the band for the last six or seven years, during which period I have, and with great pleasure I confess it, had repeated proofs of your individual prowess and bravery. Gentlemen, I could have wished to say much more, but my feelings forbid it—gentlemen, may you all live till you die."

Audible murmurs of applause followed this specimen of outlaw eloquence, and the lieutenant farther won their favour, by pledging one and all in a bumper of wine—this done, he intimated that an innate desire for vocal melody was by him retained.

"Aye, aye, a song!" echoed one of the band—but who is to sing it though, that's the question?"

"Why, the lieutenant," rejoined another whiskerando.

"Gentlemen," returned the individual addressed, "really I——"

"The song, the song!" simultaneously shouted several in a breath.

"Well," rejoined the lieutenant, "if I must, I must, so here goes."

With these words he took a hearty draught of wine and thus commenced a

DRINKING SONG.

I.
With my high mettled steed
Through the mountains I roam,
No danger can ever affright me;
'Tis the darkness of night,
And my wild mountain home,
That in solitude always delight me.

II.
I've a heart free from care,
Aye, and courage to bear,
All the dangers ill-luck can bestow;
Should I linger too late,
And the tree be my fate,
Why, with boldness I'll still meet the blow.

III.
Then away with all care,
While things promise fair;
'Tis true, to be deluged with sorrow,
When trouble they steal
Upon us, we feel
That the heart can't be merry to-morrow.

IV.
With my high mettled steed
O'er the mountains I roam,
No danger can ever affright me;
'Tis the darkness of night,
And my wild mountain home,
That in solitude always delight me.

Leaving them to applaud the foregoing ditty according to their own private opinion of its merits, we shall, for a short space of time, leave the band to themselves, in order to follow the footsteps of Captain Bond, who was proceeding up a narrow lane, fenced on either side with a close impenetrable thickset hedge, which opened into the high road. Suddenly he heard the distant rumbling of carriage wheels ; this brought him to an immediate halt ; the sounds rapidly grew more audible, and he drew his pistols from their resting place, and stood quietly awaiting the issue of the forthcoming adventure. He had not to wait long, the trampling of horses' feet next assailed his ears—this conviction of the speedy arrival of his prey amused him much —in another moment he had arrested the onward progress of a light chaise with yellow body, and wheels to match, which chaise was led, or rather drawn by four horses, two of which were grey, and the others what are generally termed "pieballs," that is to say, their skins presented a kind of "liver and bacon" hue ; besides the glittering harness in which they were attired, the two grey horses, as before mentioned, had the additional honour (?) of bearing two rather antiquated living specimens of the genus "post boys," which boys, by the way, are generally what the majority of worldly persons would style old men, but for some hitherto unassigned reason or motive, post boys never arrive at the age of maturity, in consequence of which, a grey-headed boy, bearing the appellation of grandfather, is an object often to be met with in the equestrian portion of the present age of intellectual improvement.

Upon the arrival of the vehicle near the spot to where our sub hero lay in ambush, he suddenly darted forward, seized the bridle of the off leader, and at the same time presented a pistol to the nearest postillion. Then in a voice of thunder, commanded him to come to an immediate halt, at the same time giving utterance to diver's hints to the effect, that if they, the postillions, did not instantly accede to his demands, certain things in the form of bullets, would most certainly be despatched to their upper regions, in order, if possible, to ascertain the exact quantity of brain contained therein, which threat had the desired effect. But no sooner was the vehicle brought to a halt than the door suddenly flew open, and there issued from the interior, a furious little elderly gentleman, armed with a fancy dress sword, he immediately fell into an attitude of defence.

Bond could not refrain from indulging in a hearty laugh at the grotesque form before him. The individual alluded to was of a very diminutive stature, with a small pig-tail wig ; and in short, that the reader may at once, and without farther delay, indulge in the grin, which even now is in a state of high effervesence. We will conclude the picture by referring him to the "Black Domino" Frenchman, where he will behold the very *beau ideal* of our courageous monsieur.

"Vat you vant wid me, you tam Ainglaise tief?" he exclaimed, flourishing his puny weapon, to the inexpressible delight of Bond ; "I vill transfix you to dat tree, you take youself off."

"I tell you what it is, you French frog" rejoined Bond, "I am, luckily for you, in a most excellent mood for a joke, therefore, will indulge you a little ; put up that skewer, or I shall most certainly be the death of you, I shall, upon my soul, ho, ho, ho."

"You may laugh," vociferated the enraged Frenchman ; "you may laugh, but you are von tam Anglaise robber, and if you grin at me, I shall prick you breast in one little minit ! Vat for you stop my carriage ? Me vish me had you in France, before de commissaire of de police, dey vould teach you de French manners.

"And the guillotine at the same time," interrupted Bond, "but come, you frog eating rascal, shell out, do you hear, eh ?"

"Vat you mean by de shell out ?" enquired monsieur, "dat word is not in de French dictionnaire."

"Oh !" exclaimed Bond, "you don't understand me ; well I'll soon do something towards instructing you. Come," he continued, presenting the pistols, "I know you will not resist these pretty pleaders. Come, look quick, and be d—d to you."

"God dem!" vociferated the enraged Frenchman; "me vish Napoleon had take dis country, he voud have kill all you dam Anglaisemen, and den be should have—"

"Swarmed the country like locusts," interposed Bond, whose ire was somewhat excited; "but as it is, you French-polished vagabonds should not venture among us bull dogs—we have too many of our own countrymen here, and damme, when I meet with a Frenchman like yourself, I'll rob him, if its only out of respect to old England."

Finding, after a momentary pause, that farther reasoning or remonstrance was but a useless waste of time, Bond suddenly darted upon the Frenchman, disarmed him of his puny weapon, then throwing him forcibly to the ground, deprived him of a costly gold repeater watch, together with a massive guard, constructed of the same rare metal, a French silk-netted purse, containing forty-one sovereigns, nine shillings, and several French coins; then, as the ill-fated monsieur insisted upon keeping up a loud and continual clamour, he next took a small piece of iron from his own pocket, gagged and bound his victim, then thrusting him into the carriage, he closed the door, and commanded the postillions to bear their master to his destination, which command they were most anxious to fulfil. Accordingly, a sharp application of the whips and spurs, soon caused the vehicle, together with its hapless occupant, to be borne far from the scene of the late adventure.

Scarce had Bond secured his newly-acquired booty, when the sound of wheels again struck upon his practiced ear.

"Zounds!" he exclaimed, looking to the priming of his pistols; "the fickle goddess, Fortune, is in a merry mood to-day, she is showering her golden opportunities most profusely." Upon reconnoitering, however, his surprise was greatly increased, when he observed a carriage proceeding at a slow and measured pace, followed by two horses, and the shattered remnants of a barouche; a sudden thought flashed upon him, this then must be the colonel and Emily, and his resolution was at once formed, he would follow, and by that means ascertain whether his suspicions were correct. He did so, and the result was, that he beheld the colonel and his female companion descend from the vehicle, and enter the house of a friend; she, who had made such a visible impression upon his heart was then safe and free from danger.

CHAPTER XIX.

THE ACQUITTAL.

Though the father of Sir Charles had firmly declared his intention of seeing his son perish without making one effort to save him, yet the task he had laid upon himself proved too great for him to accomplish. Three days after the trial had elapsed, yet no tidings of mercy or pardon had been hinted at. On the fourth, however, when the captive had long surrendered every hope of life and liberty, the turnkey entered the cell and informed him that his Majesty had most graciously condescended to mitigate his sentence to transportation. Contrary to the expectation of the messenger, Sir Charles received this news in a very sorrowful manner, and after a few moments enquired when the sentence was to be carried into effect, and received answer, that he had been entered in the convicts' books to sail in five days. Having been furnished with this agreeable information, the prisoner was once more left to enjoy the undisturbed possession of his thoughts, which, to judge from his situation, we should be inclined to say were rather of a sombre nature. The next day he was visited by his friend, Sir John, to whom he communicated

the tidings of his disgraceful and altered sentence.   To his great astonishment, however, the baronet burst into a vehement laugh.

Upon demanding, in unfeigned astonishment, as to the cause of this ill-
timed mirth, Sir John informed him that his pardon had been obtained by
his father, who, being anxious that he should suffer all the horrors of
suspense and doubt, had requested that he should not be informed of the
true nature of the reprieve until the time for the supposed execution of the
sentence had arrived.   After conferring various rewards upon several of the
jailors and others, Sir Charles Mortimer and his friend quitted the prison,
his free pardon having been formally announced.   For several days after his
release, the baronet stayed at the house of Sir John, at whose instigation a
meeting between father and son was brought to pass.   The desired obstacle
being removed, and as, of course, Sir Charles would hold no farther intercourse, at least of a friendly nature, with Belford, he was forthwith
reinstated in the good graces of his father, who, happy at the reformation
which he firmly believed the late disgraceful incarceration and public shame
had wrought upon the mind of his son, set no bounds to the indulgences
heaped upon his newly recovered treasure.   Sir Charles was now happy,
once more elevated to a position in society for which his intellectual acquirements, and great personal accomplishments highly qualified him.   Courted,
envied, admired, and flattered, he now looked with loathing upon his former
course of life, and the associates that had been instrumental in first leading
him towards the brink of ruin upon whose tottering precipice he stood, and,
but for the hand of power and parental affection, he wou'd have been plunged
headlong into that gulph which is ever open to receive the erring creature
of sin.

CHAPTER XX.,

IS A SHORT ONE.

WHEN death has removed from us all ties of earthly consequence—when
those whom in life we have loved, are removed from the stage of creation,
and, like a barren plantain upon a desolate and sterile rock, we are left unadvised and without the controul of friendly influence, then that recklessness
of disposition and involuntary abandonment to whatever destiny chance may
propose, which too often leads to an ignominious and inglorious end and death,
invariably follows.   Oh, what a blessing is the possession of parental love ;
how holy and god-like the influence that their counsel inspires over the minds
even of the most youthful and thoughtless.   Parental love is one of the
many joyous treasures of earthly worth, cruel, adverse fate has denied us.
Long, very long is it since the voice of admonition sounded upon our ear. Who
but those that have by fearful experience known its loss, will credit the pangs
of those who, by the Tarquin strides of death's grim minister, have been
deprived, for ever separated, from those by whom they were held most dear,
most precious !   God only knows the dreadful trial the heart endures upon
the decease of those who for whole years have engrossed our thought and
care ; for ever they are removed from the world's care : a shadowless space
is left behind.   Each little endearment and childish act is recalled by the
very absence we mourn, though we may desire to forget them, and bury
in oblivion all care of former regard, and by silence endeavour to jump, as it
were, the life to come ; yet, 'tis impossible.   The very course we follow is
the only means whereby we are again reminded of the loss we have sustained ; the vacant chair betokens volumes of gloomy forebodings ; there is
the empty space, then comes the burial ; we enter the last sad resting place

[See page 30.]

of our earthly remains. There, too, the aperture that is to conceal, for ever shut out, the lovely image of those who have been most dear; with what a mockery is not this solemn ceremony too oft attended—feathers, stately horses, sombre-hued robes floating in awful grandeur, long trains of attendant horses and vehicles filled with, what are too often miscalled, mourners —persons who looked upon such ceremonies as fitting and lawful opportunities for committing those depredations which in times when the mind is most overwhelmed in sorrow, would be more liable to detection; but while we are thus descanting upon the imperfections of the world's creatures, our main object is being neglected. The more immediate subject of our work is most unceremoniously neglected, and thus the patience of our reader tampered with; we, however, trust they will dwell full well upon what we have stated above, that the more youthful portion of those who love to pursue the course of domestic fiction, will dwell fully upon what is there declared. They will also duly appreciate the worth of parental care, and honour the memory and authority of those to whom they owe life. Nay, even more, should this have the effect we desire, our end is accomplished, and our time duly held in secondary consideration, compared with the immense benefit we have been the means of conferring upon the more thoughtless portion of society.

For several days after Captain Bond had discovered the whereabout, and become acquainted with the fate of his favorite, together with her inseparable companion, she was confined to her chamber, through the effects of the late accident to which she had been subjected; not that they had endured any grievous injury, but the fright, coupled with other circumstances incidental to the affair had so worked upon the nervous system that it was deemed expedient by the medical officer who had been summoned, that Lady Flora should confine herself to the solitude and quiet of her couch, the consequence of which was that in four or five days afterwards she had so far

No. 8.

recovered as to be enabled once more to join in the society in which she usually indulged.

Bond, during the interval, had made many calls, in order to inquire into the health of his mistress, without once intimating the ardent desire he entertained to obtain an interview, judging, and wisely too, that when she had so far recovered as to entertain visitors, he should be apprized of the same, without consideration or delay.   Upon ascertaining that she was now in a state to entertain visitors, Bond forwarded his card, and at the same time received the long wished for request ; and he beheld once more the form he had so heroically re-saved from destruction.   The complimentary portion of the dialogue being completed, warm enquiries emanated from the lips of Bond as to her health followed.   These were answered in a manner highly satisfactory.   Then succeeded his declaration of love, to which the Lady Flora listened with all the simplicity of one unused to the artifices of a designing world.   Bond had even appeared to her as one whose whole life had been passed in the most refined and fashionable circles of society ; of a fine, tall, and commanding form, handsome features, and noble deportment ; he presented an appearance highly calculated, in the words of Iago,

> " To make woman false."

This circumstance, coupled with the very romantic manner in which they had become acquainted, all combined to strengthen that love which she really entertained for him.   This he knew full well, and determined to profit by the advantage he had thus acquired over her heart   Upon the termination of their interview, Lady Flora gave a pressing invitation to Bond, the nature of which was that she desired the company of himself and Robson to a dinner party, to be held upon the following evening ; this was precisely what he desired.   Each new opportunity afforded for being in the society of Flora ; he now determined upon appropriating to the furtherance of that scheme he had long held in contemplation, which was that of carrying her off, thereby appropriating the whole of her fortune to his use.   By this measure, though grief and despair would be the lot of her upon whom he practised the deception ; this, however, was with him a secondary consideration, and such is too often proved to be the case, when riches, or even an unrequited passion is the incentive to action.

Upon returning to the cavern, Bond informed Robson of his adventure, and at the same time announced to him the invitation he had received ; this, as may be supposed (at least by that unfortunate portion of mankind who have been involved in love), was very welcome intelligence to the lieutenant, who eagerly enquired of his captain if he purposed accepting the same, and was overjoyed to hear him reply in the affirmative.   Some necessary preparations were made in the form of apparel, and both the robber-chief and his confidant awaited the arrival of the wished-for evening.   At length it did arrive, they started forward, and in due time were ushered into the presence of Lady Flora, Emily, and a goodly assemblage of friends.   What occurred afterwards must be detailed at full, and as it is of somewhat august importance, another chapter shall be the herald of its appearance before our enlightened readers.

CHAPTER XXI.

THE ELOPEMENT.

THE hours flew almost imperceptibly, the hour of two arrived before the guests commenced their departure, both Bond and the lieutenant took a hasty leave of their hostess and her friend; not, however, until they had obtained permission to repeat their call upon the following day. They then hastened to the heath, and levied contributions from many of the guests in their old guise of robbers, then joined the gang, when the remaining portion of the night, or rather morning, was spent in carousing, and it was not until the hour of five that these outlaws retired to rest. The following evening saw the two robbers again in the presence of their respective mistresses. While Bond endeavoured to persuade Lady Flora to consent to a secret marriage, Robson, on the other hand, used all the eloquence of which he was master, to remove the scruples implanted in her bosom by the tuition and virtuous examples of her now deceased protectress, who, for years, had lived only for the comfort and spiritual welfare of her youthful ward. Thus it ever is, those, who by long attention to the admonition of interested devotedness, can with difficulty be persuaded to quit the flowery path of virtue's cause, while those, who in their more youthful days, are left to pursue, unadvised, the bent of their own wild inclination, often, though their very nature may revolt, are seduced into the course of guilt, which invariably leads the misguided criminal, step by step, onwards, to that fate, which is ever the reward of crime. Here we are deviating as usual—insolence unpardonable.

Finding all opportunities in vain, Robson inwardly resolved upon accomplishing his end, and for that purpose determined also to propose a plan of elopement to Bond. Once determined upon this, he felt convinced that his end—namely, the ruination of the orphan would be accomplished.

Much time was spent in attempting to effect the purpose the two robbers had in view, and with different success, for while Emily was, by dint of much flattery and importunity, partially brought to consent to an elopement the Lady Flora, whose long standing in the more aristocratic portion of society, had taught her the utter faithlessness of man's nature, firmly resisted the eloquent appeals made by Bond to her sensitiveness and affection; and the interview at length terminated, by the two bidding adieu to their respective mistresses, one in a most desponding mood, the other elated with sanguine hopes of future consummation. We will follow them a few paces upon their road to the cavern, which, as they rode at a pretty brisk pace, they soon reached; when the following conversation ensued:—

"Well, Robson!" exclaimed Bond, "I fear me that the obdurate nature of our mistresses has for ever rendered the chance or expectation of carrying them off utterly hopeless; therefore, I am of opinion that it would be adviseable to cut the connexion, and seek some more relenting objects."

"Captain Bond," returned Robson, in that tone of mock gravity, which in his more merry mood he was wont to assume, when the subject pleased him; "Captain Bond, speak for yourself in future, and leave my affairs to be settled as their principal shareholder shall think right; you, of course, are at liberty to follow any course you may think fit. But for myself, I must most respectfully decline any change, as I am even now in a very fair way of carrying off my pretty mistress, Emily."

"What!" exclaimed Bond, in a tone that betokened the extremity of surprise; "am I to believe it possible that you have succeeded so well, while I—"

"Am deprived of all thought of success," interposed Robson. "Just so; you have not such a share of fascination and personal beauty, as I possess."

"Now, entertaining, as we do, a decided respect for Lieutenant Robson; we are not disposed, in any way, to doubt the truth of his statement, only we must certainly give vent to our own private feelings, by declaring, and that too, in the most positive manner possible, that if Captain Bond was not so handsome as his subordinate companion, he was certainly the most ugly child of nature ever yet brought upon the surface of the created world; and not wishing that our veracity should be doubted, we will here append a laconic description of his person—first, then, dear 'partners of our toil, our feelings, and our fame;' imagine a man standing somewhere about six feet four inches high, stout and athletic in proportion, of a dark and forbidden aspect, the hue of his countenance well-nigh approaching to a mulatto, small grey eyes, one of which was gifted with that peculiar and rather unenviable expression called a squint, his long raven-hued locks hanging in long matted tresses upon his brawny shoulders.   Thus have we, as faithful biographers delivered to thee, gentle reader, a most faithful description of the personal beauty and accomplishments (?) of Lieutenant Robson.   Now, thou canst judge if the spirit moveth thee; how a lady, and such an one as we have previously described Emily Anson to be, could possibly become enamoured of such a man as he—but, then, according to the old adage, "there is no accounting for taste;" and, from time immemorial, it has been most positively affirmed, that love is blind, in consequence of which declaration there no longer can be any cause or impediment of a true and just nature adduced, to show that Lieutenant Robson should not thrive in his suit of love, as well as the more amiable and fascinating members of society.

We have ever entertained a great veneration for any of those traditional motto's, honoured as they are, by the scythe and venerable form of time; yet in regard to that same god of love and his votaries, we must most respectfully beg leave to state, that blindness is not a constant attendant upon those who are in any way disposed to offer themselves up as a willing sacrifice to the altar of conjugal affection, and in proof of which declaration we here affirm that ourselves have long been following an object, whom, from the inmost recesses of our heart we adore, yet from some cause hitherto undiscovered, we have been unsuccessful, though we neither squint, nor exceed the very reasonable height of five feet six—heigho!   What do we know of Nature and her stock in trade?   Nothing, absolutely nothing.

"Well," answered Bond, after enjoying in an inward chuckle, at the facetious retort of Robson; "I never heard of any commodity that was of such sterling worth to the possessor, as self-conceit and assurance, and you possess a tolerable share of both these qualifications.   So, you really think that I am totally unsuccessful."

"Why," rejoined Robson, "if your own words may be taken as a criterion, you have been most signally defeated.   Why did you not propose beating a retreat?"

"Just so," returned Bond, "but I think, upon second consideration, I shall, most certainly enter the field, and will wager my life to a brass farthing, that I come off victorious, with both the lady and her fortune for my pains."

"Probably you will," responded the lieutenant; "and now let me hear your plan of attack at once."

While they are debating upon this, to them, most important matter, we will accompany the reader to the presence of Lady Flora Mandeville, and our heroine, Emily Anson, who, by the time we are in a position to overhear their conversation, are about to retire for the night—previous to which, however, the following colloquy passed between them, by which much of our plot may be guessed at—

"Well, Emily, commenced Lady Flora; "and what think you of our two lovers? are they not right amiable men?"

"With all due deference to your taste," replied Emily, "I do not think the friend of your admirer is quite so handsome as he might be."

"And yet methinks," pursued Lady Mandeville, "you and he are marvellously amiable."

Emily blushed deeply, and cast her eyes in confusion to the ground.

"Nay, now, do not blush," pursued her ladyship; "he is a very amiable personage, at least," she continued, with marked emphasis, "Emily thinks so, I am sure, speak candidly, do you not?"

A long pause ensued, which was at length broken by Lady Flora.

"My lady," replied Emily, "you befriended and adopted me at a time when my last earthly friend was, by the ruthless hand of death, torn from the stage of life—your bounteous hand, it was that like some ministering angel, stretched forth towards the orphan, who, else, would have been cast forth upon the world, open alike to its temptations and privations. Never shall I forget your kindness and condescension—lady, accept for your generosity, my thanks, and—"

"Nay," interrupted Lady Flora; "there is not so much credit due to me for the adoption as you appear to think. Do you remember that in seeking to win you to my society, I sought for a companion, and one who would beguile the tardy progress of time—and from the first hour of your arrival here, I have had no reason to repent of my selection, you have answered, nay, exceeded my most sanguine expectations—you have converted a dull monotonous life into one of blissful enjoyment, and I am more than doubly repaid for my espousal of your cause."

"Notwithstanding the truth of what you say, my lady," rejoined Emily; "yet I cannot forget that you are my only earthly friend—the only person from whom I might hope to obtain protection or commisseration for my orphan state;" and as these words escaped her lips, tears coursed their pearly course down her fair cheeks, whose hue might vie with the lily and carnation.

"You seem to have forgotten that even when I would have taken you from the home you then possessed, that the good and reverend Mr. Williams most earnestly desired to gain you as a companion for his amiable and lovely daughter, there you would perhaps have been more happy—have met with spirits more congenial with your own. But cease this conversation—the subject of which, by reminding you of former losses and departed friends, causes that depression of spirits, which is as unpleasant to the beholder as yourself. But to the more agreeable portion of our subject, seriously speaking, Emily, I should advise you to think nothing more of that stray gallant—a little flirtation, you know, is sometimes advisable—it serves to beguile the tedious progress of time, only the worst of the men is, that they are not content with being allowed to remain in our company, but must needs attempt to take our hearts prisoner; but neither you nor I will be thus vanquished. No, we will work our pleasure with, and then dispatch them; what say you to that, Emily?"

Poor girl, she gave a faint reply in the affirmative, though she had already lost possession of that treasure, that bears with it the peace of mind, and after happiness of those held in the thraldom of love.

* * * * * * *

The bell of our neighbouring church clock tolled forth in sombre notes, the hour of twelve. Night had spread abroad her sable mantle, the face of Nature was buried in impenetrable darknesss, when a post-chaise, to which was attached a pair of spirited bay horses, appeared. These were drawn up before the garden, fronting the house of Lady Flora Mandeville, a dark, tall figure, enveloped in a huge horseman's cloak, descended from the vehicle, and for several moments moved about with slow and measured steps; at length the door was slowly opened, and a female form issued forth. The man advanced, escorted her to the vehicle—both entered, the door was rapidly closed, and they were driven off at full speed—a pace that rivalled all thought of detection, should any such thought have been entertained.

CHAPTER XXII.

BOND AND HIS BAND RESCUED FROM THE OFFICERS BY GIPSEY MEG.

HAVING effected her purpose upon the avaricious landlord, and bestowed her bounty upon the object of his persecutions, she pursued her way at a tolerable brisk pace, and as it was her intention to rejoin Bond upon the earliest opportunity, she adopted the use of a conveyance, by the aid of which she was enabled to alight at a low hostelrie, situated on the borders of Whitechapel   A brief time after her first starting she was about to proceed onwards, when her attention was attracted towards a group of men, whom she at once suspected to be peace officers; having formed this opinion, her next care was to learn their purpose, of which she more than half suspected was the capture of Bond and his band, and luckily for her, they, after a brief consultation, simultaneously entered the inn, and she followed closely at their heels.   They proceeded into an adjoining room, closely followed by Meg, who took her seat near the door, and in order that her presence might not appear as a premeditated occurrence.   She called for a bottle of strong waters, which was immediately provided by the landlord, a short burly-looking fellow, who also placed a well filled flagon before the other portion of his guests, who conversed for some time in low whispers, which were so inaudible, that she could glean no manner of information.   This annoyed her greatly, more especially as from their extreme caution, she became more firmly convinced of the justice of her suspicion.   At this juncture a loud laugh was heard, at which Meg started suddenly to her feet, this motion was instantly noticed by the foremost of the opposite party, who, in a gruff voice, demanded why she appeared thus disturbed.

Meg replied she knew not wherefore; this, however, was false, the voice heard, she judged, and rightly, was that of Bond.   A few moments afterwards she quitted the presence of her male companions, and entered the room from whence the sounds of merriment had proceeded, and there beheld Bond and several members of the gang; she stole, unobserved, into an obscure corner, when the following conversation ensued:—

" Drink, drink !" exclaimed the foremost, " I hate a fellow that sticks at half measures.   Why, Captain, what the devil makes you so down in the mouth ? I half suspect you are in love."

" Pshaw !" exclaimed another, " you surely havn't such a bad opinion of the captain as that, have you?   Though to be sure, I must acknowledge that there has been a very great alteration in his behaviour of late, though I don't think it's love—oh no, why, I should as soon believe the same of you, who has frequently declared yourself to be a complete woman hater.   But come, isn't it time for us to be off ?"

" Off! no, I should think not," replied another; " why, let's see, what's the hour ?   Nine—oh, then, we've some time to spare yet—after that time————"

" We must away to business," replied Bond.

" I say, Captain," vociferated another, " when do you intend to give the word for a visit to our favourite haunt at *Pol?* I should think the affair has blown over by this time, at all events."

" Leave thinking upon such matters as that to people whose judgment is more sound than your own.   While I am leader of this band, by my directions alone shall its members be guided.   Now, are you answered ?"

" Yes," replied the fellow, but in a devilish queer manner.   " I tell you what it is, Captain Bond; there's three or four of us don't think much of your behaviour.   True, you are our captain; but what of that ?   Can't you give us a civil answer for all that? Then there's the manner in which you have behaved of late. Think you the band is to be kept together, if their leader throws the whole of his time and attention upon masquerades and the pursuit of a petticoat, eh?"

Bond replied not to this, but starting to his feet, threw off the large horseman's cloak in which his person was enveloped, then drawing a brace of huge pistols from the broad leathern belt that encircled his waist, in a furious tone he cried:—

"This is not the first time I have heard of these murmurings. Now, let the man (if he be present) who is dissatisfied with my government say the word, and if he cannot prove just cause for his complaint, I will treat him as all mutinous rascals should be—shoot him through the head. I'm a fellow of few words, and love to act with decision. I've been in this band upwards of fifteen years, as its captain, conducted you all through every danger; shew me one enterprise that has failed. You cannot; your silence at once proves your inability—'tis impossible."

At this moment all further discussion was brought to a premature conclusion by the door being suddenly opened, and a man disguised in a large cloak entered, and after looking around the room he took his seat beside Bond; after a short pause, he exclaimed,

"Shocking affair this murder, ain't it?"

"It is, indeed," acquiesced the captain. "Have they discovered the perpetrators of the dreadful act?"

"No," replied the other, "they have not, that is to say, at present; though I am of opinion that we shall not be very long before we do so."

"Indeed!" rejoined Bond, glancing with a suspicious eye upon the new comer; "have you any idea where they are concealed?"

"Why," answered the stranger, "as for concealment, I do not think they practice much of that—perhaps not sufficient for their own personal safety. I was a very short time since as near to their captain as I am to you. He is a sort of genteel cut-throat kind of fellow. Aye, and I should have secured him too, but he was surrounded by several of his band, just, for instance, as you might now be."

At the termination of the above sentence, Bond cast a meaning glance towards his companion, while his right hand instinctively grasped one of the pistols attached to his girdle, and which was concealed from general observation by his cloak.

"Great heaven! sir," exclaimed the new comer, "you appear greatly alarmed. I trust my presence here has not been productive of uneasiness to you."

"Not in the least, sir," rejoined Bond; "not in the least, I assure you," he continued with assumed composure. "But about this Captain B———. What did you say his name was just now, when you were———"

"Oh," interrupted the other in an apparently careless tone, "I did not mention any name, at least not that I now remember."

"What sort of fellow is this robber?" again enquired Bond, evidently anxious to learn all the information the garrulous nature of his new-found companion might afford.

"From what I have seen of him," replied the other, "I should be inclined to say that he is about your own height, the same complexion, usually wears a large black cloak, and——Zounds, sir, why I begin to think that you are the very man whom I am even now in search of."

"How's this," cried Ned Redfurn, one of the gang, "do you imagine us gentlemen to be———"

"Gentlemen of the road," interposed the other, "oh, most certainly not. I would not insinuate any such thing."

" Then why do you dare to say that our friend there is captain of a band of robbers ?" demanded another.

" I only said I *thought* so," was the reply.

" Well, then, in future you may keep your thoughts till they're called for ; and if you are always mistaking honest men for thieves, why, sir, I'm thinking that 'll be a long time first—what say you, sir ?"

These latter words were addressed to Bond.

" Why," rejoined that personage, " I am of opinion that, like the majority of mankind, he is no better than he should be. Come, let us away at once."

As he said this, Bond pulled his large slouch hat further over his forehead, in order to conceal his features, and drawing his cloak closer about him, arose from his seat and made a movement towards the door. The stranger suddenly started to his feet, threw his cloak suddenly to the ground, and drawing a brace of pistols from his girdle, placed himself with his back to the door, exclaiming as he did so,

" Surrender ! Captain Bond, I charge you in the king's name to——"

" Betrayed !" exclaimed the robbers in a simultaneous tone of surprise ; and in another moment a heterogeneous collection of weapons gleamed in the air.

" I am a peace officer," replied the man. " I have assistance at hand, and therefore resistance is useless. Surrender yourselves quietly, and I promise you no violence shall be offered."

" Well, that's very liberal," replied Bond, " but as we are not disposed to accept the very gentlemanly offer you have made, perhaps you may run the chance of saving your life by standing a little on one side, in order that we may pass. Will you oblige us or not ?"

" Never !" returned the officer, promptly. " I will not."

" Then look to yourself," rejoined Bond, placing his pistols upon full cock. " Now," he continued, turning to his men, " are you ready for the trial ?"

" All right, captain," was the simultaneous reply.

" Once more, will you stand aside ?" demanded Bond of the officer, who still stood by the door.

The man of justice replied not to this interrogation, but instantly drew the triggers of both pistols ; the ball of one entered the opposite wall, without doing any other damage than removing the hat from the head of Bond ; the other only burnt the priming. In an instant, however, these weapons, now comparatively useless, were thrown to the ground, and a broad hanger had been drawn from its scabbard which hung by the officer's side, and he again stood upon the defensive.

Bond now became uneasy, and a vague apprehension of danger stole over him, for the sound of fire-arms had attracted many, and voices were heard, demanding, in clamorous tones, admission from without.

" Now," he exclaimed, " for the last time I command you to stand aside. Then be this your passport to eternity ! Take the reward of your temerity."

With these words he discharged both his pistols ; the contents of one entered the body of the officer, he then rushed forward and aimed a tremendous blow at the head of Bond, the effect of which would have proved fatal, but for Meg, who had until now, been a silent observer of what had passed. She, however, upon observing the immense danger in which, by this new movement, the life of Bond was placed, suddenly rose from her sitting position, and drawing a pistol from beneath the ample folds of her somewhat tattered mantle, presented it at the officer, the bullet entered his brain, and he fell to the ground, blinded with blood.

" What, Meg !" exclaimed the captain, in surprise. " Can it be possible ?

[*See page* 33.]

Do I behold you here, and at such a critical moment? Why, had it not
have been for the friendly service of your bull dog, I should, ere this, have
been at supper with St. Nicholas. Why, you are my guardian angel ; gad,"
he continued, wiping the perspiration from his forehead ; " we have had a
warm task—however, he is done for. How shall we escape ?"

" We shall have to surrender," muttered one of the men, as he noted the
clamour from without.

" The first man that talks of surrendering in my presence," rejoined Meg,
"shall measure his length upon the ground, and that too, with short time
for strife, therefore, if you purpose continuing this conversation, I
should advise a quick remembrance of the sins of which you have been
guilty."

" Whatever we do," suggested another of the band, " must be quickly
decided upon, for the door must give way ; it cannot possibly resist their
attacks much longer, then we shall have no time or opportunity for confer-
ence. Now, captain, what's to be done ?"

" Let every man stand by me," answered Bond, whose coolness and
intrepidity appeared to increase by the danger with which they were threatened. " Stand side by side, here," he continued, taking up his position, so
that when the door was opened nothing but the wounded man was presented
to view. " Now, stand aside, and let them enter."

The men did as he commanded them, and the consequence of which was,
that being deprived of its support from within, the door was soon forced
from without ; and the landlord, armed with a huge blunderbuss, together
with several of the neighbours, each of whom carried something in the way
of weapons, entered the room.

" The villains have escaped !" exclaimed Boniface, glancing timidly
around, " I wonder which way they have gone ?—perhaps—"

No. 9.

A deep groan here interrupted his conjectures.

"Dear me," he continued, in a tremulous tone. "Oh dear! oh dear!" he again exclaimed, chancing to observe the wounded man; "they have killed the officer who came to apprehend them—assist the poor man. They then gathered in a knot around the officer, and while their attention was engrossed with him, the others contrived to steal unobserved from the room; they then darted from the house, and hurried on through Whitechapel, with Bond at their head;—Shoreditch is passed, and they are about to pass the turnpike, and turn into the Hackney-road, when the shouts of persons in their rear, suddenly convinced them, that however adroitly they had effected their escape, still it had been observed. The shouts increased, the pursued fled at a pace that appeared to defy all attempts at capture. Meg now passed them all, and appeared to outstrip the wind; suddenly she slackened her pace, and attracted the attention of Bond towards a post-chaise-and-four, which was proceeding towards them at a slow pace; they neared it, a moment sufficed to bring the postillions from their seats in the saddles, part of the men, together with Meg, entered the vehicle; Bond mounted the near, and one of the men the off-leaders.

"For where are we bound?" shouted the man.

"First for the nearest place of safety, afterwards for Polstead," replied Bond.

They then dashed off at full speed, leaving all pursuit far behind them.

While our friend, Bond, and his companions, are eluding the attempt made to capture them, we will at once undertake the task of explaining to the reader the cause of their having been found at the hostelrie as above mentioned; also, why Meg thought of selecting such a place for a meeting, and farthermore, why, and for what purpose they were about to proceed to Polstead. First, then, three of the band had been a few days, or, rather nights—for that same Oliver (the moon,) is a marvellous friend of your regular highwaymen, engaged in a robbery upon the highway. The object of their depredatory excursion was an aged pedlar, with whom they had chanced to fall into company with, and hearing that he possessed a goodly sum of money, they waylaid and robbed him; he resisted, called lustily for assistance, they ended the adventure by taking his life. This crime, which was committed without the knowledge of Bond, caused a strict enquiry to be made by the official authorities, who, in consequence of some information which was forwarded to them, they discovered, and besieged the robbers' haunt—they escaped, but with great difficulty. This had come to the knowledge of Meg, she knew that the Red Lion, at Whitechapel, was their retreat when any danger threatened, and thus is Meg's presence accounted for.

CHAPTER XXIII.

POLSTEAD.

READER, thou dost remember that in the twenty-first chapter of this work certain indications of an elopement was given thee. Dost thou entertain any suspicion as to who the person or persons therein concerned? Thou dost not—well, now for the information. Notwithstanding all the admonitory conversation of her now deceased aunt, Emily's too susceptible nature had yielded to the hollow flattery and protestations of eternal fidelity uttered by Robson, who, under the guise of a votary of fashion's shrine, had contrived to enslave her heart. At the period when she first embraced the offer made to pass her days in the society of Lady Flora—that lady had been lavish in her attention, and never visited any of her more aristocratic friends, unless accompanied by her orphan *protégé*. But at length her ladyship began to perceive the ill effect of this; among the idle loungers of favoured fortune's sons, were many, whose libertine principles gained new fire upon beholding the beauteous and highly accomplished Emily, and as Lady Mandeville had no desire to lead her ward into any society that might prove prejudicial to her welfare, she forbade to lead her so much into the path of temptation. Emily felt greatly piqued at this apparent coolness, and being naturally of a volatile and cheerful disposition, she could ill brook the solitude that was thus imposed upon her; therefore, while the reflection of this dwelt upon her mind, it is not to be marvelled at, that the blandishments used by Robson, should overpower those virtuous scruples which, by early tuition, had been implanted in her mind. But, advice that savours not of the world's vanities, the errors, and miscalled pleasures of life, is like seed implanted in barren soil; so as the husbandman's labour is then useless, is the friendly admonition administered to the young and thoughtless. Thus it was with Emily; she doated upon the society of her aged relative, and listened with youthful attention to her advice, and at that time entertained no other thought than that of acting in strict accordance to the same. But too true is that proverb which declares that "evil communication corrupts good manners." Her *entrée* into the world had for ever banished all thought of piety; and at length she sealed her after fate, by consenting to an elopement with the lieutenant of a bold and reckless band of highwaymen.

*   *   *   *   *   *   *

Polstead is a village situated upon the borders of Suffolk, it is, or was, when last we passed through it, somewhat small, though extremely picturesque, luxuriant foliage, green leaves, fertile meadows, well-stored granaries, and over-stocked farms, are the most prominent features of this pleasant little place, where the small wickets, latticed windows, and many other symptoms of rural taste, remind us of many happy by-gone days. Now, alas! passed, never to be recalled.

Nearly half-a mile from the village church stood a small neat-looking thatched roof cottage, around which grew the grape-vine and rose-tree in friendly companionship. This abode of humble innocence and happiness was situated at the extremity of a neat garden, in the centre of which stood two tall elms, together with several others, bearing various descriptions of fruit; the other portion of the ground was covered with gooseberry-bushes, vegetables of various kinds, scarlet runners, &c.; a small green-painted wooden wicket opened to the garden, at the bottom of which stood the cottage as we have before stated, which was inhabited by an old cottager, who, for the last twenty years had been an inhabitant of the village. During the period above named, many sad changes had been effected in the good old man's family; he was once the happy father of five beauteous girls and boys, and enjoyed the society of a faithful and affectionate wife. But one of these dear earthly ties of affection had been torn from him by the stern and ruthless hand of death, and now lay in the cold and silent grave. Grave! what volumes does not that simple monosyllable express?—the church, with ivied porch, rustic walls, and merrie bells, together with the usual accompaniment—a church-yard, with its rudely-formed tombs, the receptacle for the last sad earthly remains of those who have for ever quitted life's busy scene and fitful struggle—whose immortal and never-dying spirits, quitting their mortal coil, have passed into the presence of their God—the Father and creator of mankind. In the consecrated ground of Polstead slept many—the rich lord, who, while moving upon the expansive stage of life was followed by crowds of courtly sycophants, all eager to pay their self-interested, mercenary, and sordid-minded attentions,—now, alike unconscious of all, in quiet obscurity lay, coffined, and fast rotting with death's mouldering emblem, side-by-side, with the humble, though honest peasant. In another spot, hard by, perhaps would be deposited the last earthly remains of some holy churchman, whose pious soul in "heaven bestowed," would complete the task of piety, by a kind interference for the general pardon of erring man. Stretching still farther the obscure mist of imaginative power, we can readily imagine, encased within the silent precincts of the tomb, equally humble, the fast withering form of him, who in life was esteemed—looked upon by all as the village oracle—now his last home is trodden—unceremoniously passed—and that too by many, who, upon some former occasion, may have expressed the warmest and most complete approbation at the brilliant wit of him long since forgotten by all, save those whose more reflective nature will cause them to breathe a sigh of regret, or shed a tear of pity as the last sad tribute to the memory of departed worth—then straight pass on, rapt for a time in silent contemplation, and all is again forgotten.

The mellow shades of an autumnal evening reigned around, the pale bright moon shone with refulgent rays upon the sacred pile, as the faint echoes of a light footstep momentarily disturbed the death-like stillness that reigned around. Near to the low rustic stile (where sat the owl, that solitary companion of night), whose monotonous hoot oft serves to startle the passer-by, proclaimed by its presence, night's sable gloom—appeared a female form—a moment, another—it had crossed the stile, the owl had taken alarm and sought the protection of a neighbouring tree. The new comer stood in a passive attitude, looking upon a small flowery bank, around which, in budding beauty, like her who tended them grew the rose and honeysuckle.

For some few moments the maiden moved not, some heart-felt deep-rooted sorrow seemed to have entrap't her reason; the brilliancy of her blue eye was, if possible, by tears, which in quick succession coursed their way down her lonely cheeks; the cause of her grief was sacred, and such as none possessing Nature's soft impulse would dare to interrupt.

Beneath the glossy bank lay entranced in death two persons, side-by-side, engulphed in the gloomy jaws of death, were deposited the corporeal forms, wherein once beat the fond hearts of paternal affection; the parent's offspring—now by death's barb deprived of all care. Orphans cast upon the world's broad surface, possessing no other protector than those acquired by their own virtue and honesty. Suddenly falling upon her knees, and hands piously upraised to Heaven, the maiden, in a solemn tone, exclaimed—"Heaven of purity and love! benign father of mercy! hear thou my humble prayer! Direct me by which means I may best and most effectually accomplish the last earthly desire of my dear departed parents; grant that I may ever follow in the flowery path of virtue's sacred cause, and in pure unsullied innocence pass through life's fleeting hours. And when that terrible hour shall arrive, when the last dead summons shall call before thy awful tribunal all the creatures of life, side-by-side, with my dear parents on thy right hand of celestial power, let me stand. Dear authors of my being, look from the seat of mercy upon thy child, who now, like the fir-tree upon a blighted hill, stands alone and uprotected, with nothing but the shield of virtue to protect her from the manifold temptations with which the world abounds, and—"

She would have said more, but the violence of her emotion prevented any farther soliloquizing—she sank upon the grassy surface of the grave.

The reader will doubtless enquire what connexion the above has with the subject of our work—much, as will presently be seen.

CHAPTER XXIV.

ARREST OF BOND.

Upon discovering the absence of Emily, Lady Flora instituted the most strict enquiries, but all were of no avail, her flight had been as sudden as the motives which prompted it; she had employed no confidante, the servants were one and all in ignorance of her purpose—her absence troubled Lady Mandeville greatly, though she neither knew, nor could even suggest the real cause of her flight, imagining that from the very short period of their acquaintance, no very serious passion could have been engendered, though herself had been somewhat smitten by the blandishments of Bond; but then she was what might be termed a woman of the world, and a flirt withal. Consequently, though a wound might have been inflicted, she was too able a general to permit its interference with her peace of mind, or ordinary pursuits.

While Lady Flora Mandeville pondered in perplexity, upon the sudden and unexpected disappearance of her orphan ward, Bond was equally puzzled to guess at the accident that for the last three months had deprived him of the advice and assistance of his lieutenant, until, in one of his calls on Lady Flora, (for under the disguise of a man of fortune, he still continued to pass short intervals in her society), he accidently chanced to enquire after the health of Emily; he then learned the time and mysterious manner of her disappearance; the thought instantly flashed upon his memory, and without farther delay, he forthwith congratulated himself upon his share of perceptibility, which at once intimated the probability of their having, in his expressive terms, "shot the moon." Knowing, as he well did, by previous experience, the fickle nature of women, he now inwardly resolved to number his visits to the hall, lest Robson should, by deserting his fair companion, involve him and the band in jeopardy; for there never yet lived the woman who, when revenge was substituted for former love, would not provide her discarded lover with a halter, if possible. One thing, however, Bond had also determined upon, and that was—the robbery of Grantley Park. Once resolved upon, nothing now remained but to carry his plan into execution, the time was fixed upon for the next night, that is to say, the night after the plan had been first decided upon. He, therefore, hastened back to Polstead, for since their escape from the officers at Whitechapel, where Meg had so heroically preserved his life—Bond had continued to remain at their country haunt, and had but returned to Bently-heath on the preceding day, to pay a visit to Lady Flora; he, therefore, entered a post-chaise, and made all speed for Polstead, and while he was busily engaged in making preparations for the intended burglary, an unexpected discovery and exposure was made at Grantley Park. About three o'clock on the Thursday, as Bond visited the hall upon the following Monday, a letter was put into his hand by one of the band, this being given at a moment when he was busily engaged in some other matter of importance, he passed it into his pocket and thought no more of it until he assumed the disguise in which he usually visited Lady Flora, when he removed the letter without ascertaining its contents, into the pockets of the coat. When passing through the hall upon his departure, he drew forth a handkerchief and in so doing the letter also accompanied it, and fell to the ground, though, without his being aware of the fact; the second or under footman, chancing to pass through the place, espied the letter, and immediately bore it to the pantry, where a consultation was held as to how the letter was to be disposed of, and after a lengthy discussion it was at last decided by the chief butler that it should be presented to their lady. Accordingly, her ladyship was, a few moments after this had been decided, disturbed by a slight tapping at the drawing-room door; she, in a faint voice, desired the applicant to enter. Upon this, the door was opened, and a tall specimen of well-fed liverymen appeared, bearing in his hand a silver salver, upon which was laid a rather soiled and somewhat oddly-shaped letter, bearing upon it, in unwieldly characters, the name of "*Captain Bond.*" Her ladyship gazed upon it with unfeigned astonishment, and after a momentary pause, enquired of the man from whom he brought it.

"So, please your ladyship," exclaimed the fellow, "we found it in the hall about half-an-hour since."

"Know you not how it came there?" enquired Lady Flora.

"No, my lady," was the laconic reply.

"Well, you may retire," pursued her ladyship.

The man did as he had been desired, and her ladyship was once more alone; she then renewed her inspection of the letter, and was the more perplexed as to who could have been the cause of its being found—being still, however, as it were in the dark, she determined upon dissolving all farther cause of conjecture by bursting the seal, she did so, and judge her astonishment when she read as follows:—

"DEAR CAPTAIN BOND,—

"*You will, I dare say, think it very mysterious, that I should absent myself from you so long, but you will cease all wonder when I tell you that I succeeded in carrying off my young flame, Emily. How do you get on with Lady Flora? have you carried her off yet? Mine is a very angel, but rather grand; bye, bye.*
                                        Yours &c.,
                                           MARTIN, *alias* ROBSON.

"P.S.—I hope to be soon at liberty, and then will pay you a visit at the cavern, my respects to the gang, and assure them that I shall soon accompany you and them upon one of our favourite moonlight trips upon the highway. Steer clear of the traps and avoid matrimony; Emily doats upon, and indeed idolizes me, she, of course; has not as yet discovered who and what I am, nor must she, for we gentlemen of the road, commonly called highwaymen, are not very anxious to give publicity to our very *respectable* and *honourable* calling."

Upon reading this, Lady Flora, for some few moments afterwards, was in doubt, as to whether she could credit the evidence, even of her own eyes. Could it then be possible, that the distinguished fashionable, who had, for such a lengthy period, been paying his constant and apparently sincere *devoirs* to her, was nothing more or less than a common highwayman, an extractor of—not teeth—but purses; one who existed solely by the involuntary donations he received from others—a man whose life was constantly endangered both by the executioner's ardent desire to get him in a line, and the magnanimous existence of those from whom he levied the means of existence. Monstrous! the thought was not to be borne—what was to be done? Should she screen the fact, with which through complete accident she had become possessed, and still encourage his visits, or at once renounce him for a villain? She paused irresolutely, not knowing which course to adopt—her conscience forbade the one, and fear of a public *exposé,* opposed the other. At length, however, her resolution was taken. Bond had appointed to be with her the following evening; and he, within his own mind, had resolved to attempt the burglary—for although that was by highwaymen of the age, considered as being infinitely below their own professional occupation, yet an opportunity like the present, whereby the prospects of realizing so much valuable booty, could not be suffered to pass unnoticed. Lady Flora, upon his entrance, determined that his capture should immediately follow. Accordingly, she penned a note, and 'despatched it to the nearest magistrate, requiring the attendance upon the following evening of four officers of justice, in order to effect the capture of a notorious housebreaker—whom, as her note expressed —would, as she had been informed, attempt to effect a forcible entry into her mansion for the purpose of robbery.

The following evening at length arrived, so did the myrmidons of the law —and they had not been long housed and concealed, when Bond made his appearance. He was shown into the drawing-room, where he found Lady Flora seated upon a sofa, engaged in a volume of Milton—he advanced towards her, and in a tone of affection, enquired as to the state of her health; she replied in a tone of affected coolness, that she imagined it could concern him but little—and in a freezing tone, commanded him to be seated—he unhesitatingly obeyed her—upon which she rung the bell, in a moment afterwards, two out of the four officers entered the apartment. Bond started instinctively to his feet, though he knew not why or wherefore.

" Sir," exclaimed the foremost, addressing him ; " you are my prisoner— and in the king's name, I charge you to surrender immediately."

" What means this? Surrender!" reiterated Bond.

" Yes, sir, surrender," pursued the officer.

" Lady Flora," continued Bond. addressing that personage; " you can, perhaps, best solve this mystery. Who are these men, what is their business with me?"

" These men," answered Lady Flora; " are peace officers. And this," she continued, handing him the before-mentioned letter; " will best convince you of the nature of the business with you."

Bond no sooner beheld the letter, than the whole truth appeared at once to flash before him ; he trembled violently, and let the fatal paper fall from his hand, muttering an inward curse upon his carelessness.

" So, then, my lady," he exclaimed, after a brief pause ; " this is your work. Ah, well! I am not the first Samson that has been betrayed into the hands of the Philistines by a false woman. However, I surrender myself into the hands of justice—that is, if they dare attempt to make good their capture— I am but single, and possess but these good weapons to defend me."

Saying which, he produced a brace of small duelling pistols, which he levied at the officers, who now stood aghast.

" Why, how's this." exclaimed Bond, "do you fear to approach me, man ! Thought you then, that Captain Bond—for such, I now confess my name to be—would suffer himself to be captured without one struggle for that liberty, which we all prize so highly. Now, either advance as men, and complete the capture you desire, or give way and let me pass unmolested—speak, qui how do you decide?"

" Dare not to stir," exclaimed the officer, "or you die upon the motion. In the king's name, I command you to lay down those weapons, and surrender to us.'

" Not until every other chance has failed me," answered Bond, " then, will I sell my life dearly, therefore, beware!"

Finding their repeated commands to surrender, were treated with indifference—and being anxious also, to secure the credit of having made so important a capture, the officers summoned their companions to the scene of action —from which Lady Flora retired, leaving a servant in her stead; for the sight of fire-arms alarmed her greatly—they then, simultaneously advanced towards Bond; who, finding his case becoming more desperate, pulled the triggers of both pistols—one of which only burned priming, the other entered the right arm of the foremost officer—he was now seized, and though disarmed, a desperate struggle ensued—at the end of which, he was overpowered and conveyed into the hall, and a vehicle being already prepared, he was borne direct to a place of confinement—there to await the issue of that trial,

which would in all probability, consign him to the common end of all depre-
dators of his class—*the scaffold!*

———

CHAPTER XXV.

COUNT BELFORD AGAIN.

Count Belford heard with great surprise and even mortification, of the
sudden alteration and improvements of the circumstances of Sir Charles
Mortimer. He knew that by effecting a reconciliation with his father, his
future fortune was secured; and while he enjoyed a life of riches and worldly
pleasures, his sharping acquaintance was beset with difficulties, in the
midst of which, however, he consoled himself with conviction, that notwithstanding his late exposure, and the villainy which caused it, he still felt convinced of his power to once more initiate himself into his confidence—which
should he indeed accomp'ished, he determined that his next step should be to
undo him in his father's estimation, and once more to reduce him to his
former level. Though this plan was formed, and the Count was most
anxious to carry it into effect, yet no opportunity presented itself, by
which he might effect his purpose, until about five or six weeks afterwards ;
when he received an invitation to a masquerade and fancy dress ball, to be
held at the house of Mrs. Major Turnbull, a lady with whom Sir John
Mortimer was on terms of the most intimate acquaintance. This he looked
as a favourable omen, inasmuch, as he felt convinced of meeting with
Sir Charles—when, knowing the nature of his disposition, he doubted
not as to his ability to work a complete change, with reference to himself.
His chief aim, however, was to form a friendly connexion with Sir
John ; this once accomplished, they would then be once more upon an
equal footing. The night arrived, and so did Belford, at the house of
Mrs. Major Turnbull, when he was ushered into the presence of his lady
hostess, by a tall and somewhat antique specimen of African beauty—or,
in other words, by an elderly footman of the Day and Martin school.
Mrs. Major Turnbull, be it known to all, possessed a pair of daughters,
whom she was most anxious to wed with some monied spark ; the younger
one was named Fanny, and was three years the junior of her sister,
who was called Martha. In age, Fanny was twenty-one, of a fine, tall,
and elegant figure, of highly-polished manners, and possessing also, what
would generally be termed a pretty and intelligent countenance – her disposition was also lively and volatile—while her elder sister, Martha, was
deprived of these little embellishments ; her nature was diametrically opposite to that of her sister. Her nature was morose and sullen, her person
was short, and disposition gloomy and thoughtful. Nor were these
variations unnoticed by others, for, while Fanny had a whole host of
admirers, Martha, in all probability, appeared liable to fall upon the unenviable list of old maids. It was for the purpose, as we have before said,
of matching these young ladies to advantageous husbands, that Mrs
Major Turnbull, was in the habitual custom of giving parties—to which
she invariably invited the *élite* of her connexion. And on this particular
occasion, she had outvied all her former efforts at grandeur. Gentlemen
of large fortunes, have been known to fall in love with young ladies at
balls, and even to marry them. And why should not the latter be the
case with regard to the daughters of Mrs. Major Turnbull? However,
that nothing might be wanting to complete the arrangements, and bring
so desirable an occurrence to pass, she determined to make the trial. She
had an immense circle of friends ; and among the same, were several families
of distinction ; to them then, did she issue cards of invitation ; a large

[*See page* 43.]

band of musicians were engaged for the ball-room; which was decorated
in a most tasteful manner; a gallery had been fitted up at one end of
the room for the orchestra, which was hung with green velvet, to which
a profusion of gold tassals and cordage was attached; the walls were
also hung with the same costly material; large chandeliers were suspended
from the ceiling; numerous complicated designs in red chalk, graced the
floor. Nor were these the only outward visible signs that Mrs. Major
Turnbull had inwardly resolved to astonish the natives—that is to say a
few—for an immense oil painting, representing a very stout gentleman
seated upon a remarkable thin and immensely tall horse, in the act of
ascertaining—if possible—the substance and thickness of a skull, possessed
by a very short man in a highland garb—who seemed to be entertaining
serious thoughts of presenting the aforesaid very stout gentleman upon the
very thin and immensely tall horse, with a bullet despatched from the
barrel of a curiously formed pistol; which he, the highlander, held in a
parallel line with his, the very stout gentleman's breast; and, in order if
possible, to prevent the same, the stout gentleman was in the act of letting
fall an immense broad sword; which, at the moment when we observed the
painting, was raised to mid-air—on the head of the said highlander. This
painting, which never saw daylight but upon extraordinary occasions—was,
as Mrs. Major Turnbull informed all those, whose attention might be attracted
or curiosity aroused by its antique appearance, the representation of her
grandfather, Colonel Turnbull, long since deceased, at the siege of ———
   According to her own statements—which were marvellous in the extreme.
This certainly was the most wonderful and supernatural piece of workman-
ship, that ever has, or, indeed, ever will emanate from the hand of mortal
man. For among other relations too numerous to be here set down, would
she inform her guests, how, at the burning of Moscow, (both the picture and

No. 10.

its original being present at that memorable event), after laying for some weeks beneath the ruins of a house, that was a prey to the general conflagration, it was afterwards dug out comparatively uninjured. But the chief curiosity was the frame—which being made or manufactured at a time, when gold-beaters were a race unknown; its maker or makers, had for want of a more economical method, laid on some two or three inches of stout sheet gold—which, although at every dusting (an operation performed upon an average, about once in six months) a considerable portion of the same, eloped from its resting place. Yet, like the equestrian figure it encircled—to get no thinner, indeed, one might almost be led to suppose by these wonderful circumstances, that the purse of Fortunatus, was upon terms of the most intimate acquaintance with the said extraordinary frame—and by some process peculiar to itself, supplied its friend with the means of maintaining an imposing appearance in the pictoral world.

It was not until the evening of the day preceeding that upon which the display was appointed to come off, that Mrs. Major Turnbull recalled to mind, that in order to make all their preparations completely aristocratic, they would be compelled to conform with a custom—which, even in this enlightened age of steam and machinery, is not wholly discontinued—we mean that of converting halls and staircases into flower gardens. The quickest possible notice was accordingly despatched to several florists residing in the immediate vicinity of Hampstead, to be at their residence with all convenient haste; in order that they might form an estimate of the number required, to have (to the infinite honour of all persons of gigantic rotundity) a double row of the largest plants—which they, the nurserymen, possessed—to extend from the interior of the street, to the exterior of the drawing-room doors. The several knights of the spade to whom these orders were issued, arrived in due course, and by the commencement of the succeeding evening, had so far succeeded in the fulfilment of their task, that had not the scene of their labours lacked the presence of the tree of knowledge of good and evil, any individual at all versed in scriptural history, might have fancied himself in the garden of Eden upon a small scale.

Precisely at half-past nine, just half an hour previous to the commencement of the ball; the violin, one flute, a harp, and violincello, marched one abreast (the horticultural productions would allow no more) into the hall; and Mr. Cæsar Bumpor, the before-mentioned ebony footman, who had been elected hall-porter for the occasion, became aware of the presence of the latter instrument and its owner, by the receipt of a severe blow upon the shin-bone, which made him wince again, with the wooden leg or pin, by which the height of these instruments is usually augmented, about a foot and-a-half.

Having divested themselves of their outer garments, an operation which served (it being as the first violin observed, "a reg'lar sokin' evenin',") the purpose of a watering-pot for the flower-bed; by which they were surrounded —which bed now began to assume the very imposing attitude usually adopted by theatrical heroes, when sinking from a mortal wound beneath the left arm —having at length, divested themselves and their instruments of all superfluous attire, the professional gentlemen were, with great secrecy conducted to the place appointed for the exercising of their abilities, where we shall for the present leave them, in order to return to the hostess and her party— who, while we have been absent, are actually seated at the table—where all but Miss Martha, appeared to be perfectly happy. For while she remained almost unnoticed, her sister, Fanny, was seated beside a richly and fashionably attired young gentleman, who appeared to be paying her the most fixed attention—and this to her was agony.

Her victory, however, was at hand; after a lapse of some considerable time passed by Martha in criticising and undervaluing the dresses of their guests, a young gentleman who had before appeared to be secretly devouring her charms, at length requested to be allowed the honour of drinking wine with her; which request being acceded to, the young gentleman aforesaid, proceeded to fill his glass, hand the decanter to Miss Martha, and when that young lady had completed the operation of modestly half filling her glass likewise, she graciously inclined her head and sipped off a small portion of its contents: The young spark spilt one-half of the contents of his own glass down a delicate white shirt and waistcoat to match, and thereby reduced his bumper to the same quantity as that taken by Miss Martha. The ice was now broken, and during the remainder of the evening, the young gentleman with the Bacchanalian shirt and waistcoat, assisted—or offered to assist—the now delighted young lady, to every new delicacy that made its appearance upon the table. Nor did his courtesy end here, for when the company paired off to the ball-room, he, upon the first intimation of the fact, proffered his arm to Miss Martha, and so obtained her hand for the dance.

There was also, another person beside Miss Martha, who felt great delight at the attention shown to her by the young fashionable; this was Mrs. Major Turnbull; she had narrowly watched their proceedings from the commencement—and was overjoyed at having succeeded in matching, at least one daughter, through the medium of the ball. Alas! she had yet to learn, that young gentlemen dance with young ladies, and whisper soft nonsense in their ears, encircle their waists—nay, even presume to meet lips, without once dwelling upon the necessity of anything farther in the shape of courtship and marriage.

As may be supposed, neither Belford or Sir Charles took any considerable share in the festivities. But as the young baronet kept in the near society of his father, Belford could not obtain a chance of entering into conversation with him, as he intended doing. Upon the termination of the ball, however, they withdrew to the supper-table—when chance or design placed the two side by side, and Sir John to the left. Thus situated, the old baronet was compelled to enter into conversation—the supper being removed, they next adjourned to the card-table—when they were by accident elected partners—the game proceeded comfortably for some time; when at length, a dispute arose between Sir Chalres, and the young gentleman upon whom Miss Martha had lavished so much attention; and who was seated at an adjoinging table; Belford instantly interfered, and espoused the cause of Sir Charles most warmly—the other individual with whom the dispute commenced, was clamourous in the extreme, and demanded satisfaction for the insult; which, as he said, had been heaped upon him. Belford strove in vain to appease him, and finding all his attempts to rouse the other's ire—he, at length, as a last resource, rushed forward, and attempted to inflict the disgrace of a blow upon his opponent at play. In this, however, he was foiled; Belford prevented him, —and, at length, as he continued to disturb the comfort of the assemblage, and had long since been proclaimed a nuisance—he was expelled the room and the house—they resumed their seats, but as the general harmony had been disturbed, the whole party a short time afterwards dissolved, and departed to their several homes—not even omitting the young gentleman with the white and scarlet waistcoat.

Upon observing the friendly interest which Belford appeared to evince for his son, Sir John was more than half inclined to alter his opinion respecting him; and when Belford wished them a good evening, he invited him to a luncheon on the following day. This invitation as may be very readily supposed was accepted—and Belford took his departure, inwardly exulting at the triumph he had achieved.

CHAPTER XXVI.

BIRTH OF MARIA MARTIN.

" Tide and Time waits for no man," so says the ancient proverb, which proverb, unlike many others contains an ample share of truth ; however, we may progress. Whether the fond anticipation of former hope has been realized, and we are on the sunny side of fortune, or our every expectation has been blasted, and in old age we are overtaken by the Tarquin strides of poverty, still the progress of time is unceasing. The first twelve months since the flight of Emily from the friendly roof of Lady Flora, imperceptibly glided away, in which interval, Bond had escaped from his thraldom through the machinations of Gipsey Meg. More crimes had been committed, and the minions of what is too often mis-called justice, were again upon his track. The Reverend Mr. Williams, of whom former mention has been made, had passed into the peaceful grave ; while his rebel son, whom long since had suffered an ignominious death, as a reward for being engaged in a poaching expedition—and upon which he had been detected. The clergyman's daughter, of whom we have also spoken, was a few weeks previous to the decease of her father, married to a young and wealthy farmer ; and comfortably settled in the middle circles of life.

Lady Flora Mandeville, after having instituted a strict enquiry as to the whereabout of Emily—after discovering the letter which caused the incarceration of Bond. At length, finding it useless, abandoned her to whatever fate, her own indiscretion might produce.

Emily lived for eight months in perfect harmony with her paramour. At length, however, he grew tired of a life of inactivity, and rejoined the band —at least, that portion of them, who had taken up their quarters at Polstead.

Emily possessed no home, or means of procuring one ; and was, therefore, compelled to accompany him. The course of life pursued by the lawless robbers, however, soon disgusted her gentle nature. And after a sojourn of four months, she one night when Robson, together with several of his companions were absent, contrived to effect her escape.

When she quitted the cavern of the robbers, it was her intention to have pursued her way to the abode of her former friend and protectress. There to supplicate for a renewal of her friendship and confidence ; but much of her former strength and resolution had forsaken her—she expected soon to become a mother—and such was the nature of her constitution, she halted at the cottage spoken of by us in a former chapter. The old man had passed into eternity—the place was now inhabited by a widow and two orphan children—her appeal for a short respite from toil, was answered by a pressing invitation to spend the night.

" My roof is but humble, 'tis true ;" replied the woman, " yet you are welcome, if you think fit to accept my invitation. You are weary, rest will revive you.'

" Thanks, good woman, thanks," answered Emily, " if it will not be placing you at inconvenience, I will gladly accept your kindly offer."

With these words, she entered the cottage, its widowed occupant closed the door. The woman warmed some milk, and a few moments after Emily had drank a portion of it, she felt somewhat revived—and by the advice of her warm hearted hostess, retired to rest. After she had been reposing upon the humble couch for some hours, her groans aroused the woman, who proceeded to enquire as to the cause—when, to her astonishment, she discovered that her newly-arrived guest had been suddenly seized with the pangs of child-birth—a doctor was summoned—and a fine female infant was born—but the mother still grew worse—and early on the following morning, she with great difficulty penned a note—the direction of which, was to Lady Flora informing her as to where she was to be found, and praying that she would immediately visit her—as she feared she was fast approaching her end—the letter was conveyed with all speed to Grantley Park.

Upon the receipt of the letter, her ladyship immediately commanded the carriage to be got ready; and this being done, the messenger and herself entered the vehicle, and in a short time afterwards, were by the side of the now dying orphan. Upon beholding her former friend and protectress, Emily extended her hand, and in a languid tone, begged her forgiveness.

"You, my friend," she exclaimed, in a tone of voice scarcely audible, "little know the many bitter hours of compunction I have passed, since my fatal elopement from beneath your friendly roof—that I loved the man, for whose sake alone I have sacrificed your friendship, honour—nay, even life itself. I feel that my spirit is fast fleeing from this world—soon, very soon, shall I be numbered with the silent dead—secure within the confines of a grave. I have sent for you, as being the only one on earth to whom I could breathe forth my sorrow. Dare I ask for your friendly bounty, now? If I thought, that by your hand, I could be provided with my last earthly resting place. My child too, that dear pledge of an illicit passion—though disgrace be affixed to its name—though its presence be the surety of my dishonor. Yet you will not desert her—remember, 'tis the last appeal of your dying friend. My moments are numbered. Let her name be MARIA MARTIN! that is the name of her father; and when in my days of innocence I tended my dying aunt, she made me promise, that should I ever become a parent, and the child be a female, it's name should accord with hers. Maria—farewell! and may the God whom I have offended hear the orphan's prayer, and preserve you from all danger. My child, thy mother i-s n-o-w——"

Ere the sentence could be completed, a low moan escaped her. One glance at her friend, then all was silent as the grave. The soul of Emily Anson had fled from the troubled sea of life, and entered the celestial abode of her God.

All present were greatly depressed by the scene they had witnessed; and after Lady Flora had seen her now deceased friend laid upon the humble pallet, wrapt in the gear of death, and given orders for her funeral to the neighbouring undertaker; she next entered into an arrangement with the woman, concerning the infant left upon her hands, deprived of its natural protector. Every necessary measure being adopted, whereby respect to the dead, and the welfare of the child could be secured, Lady Flora Mandeville, with spirits much depressed, once more returned to her abode—there to mingle with those, to whom trouble was a stranger and who felt not for the woe of others. Though she was thus once more plunged into the scene of fashionable dissipation in which she usually mixed—though every luxury of life was present before her, yet her ladyship could not forget her deceased friend, whose memory she determined to respect, by lavishing every possible care and attention upon the child. She had already determined upon permitting her to remain with her present guardian, until she should reach the age of five years—at which period, she intended to remove her to a boarding-school, bestow upon her a liberal education, and thus fit her for the highest circles of refined society—even in the very sphere in which she herself moved. This was, indeed, the act of a sincere friend.

Upon the eighth day of her decease, the remains of the ill-fated Emily Anson was borne to its final home—a large family vault, constructed at the expense of Lady Flora, in the following order:—The coffin, which was covered with black cloth closely studded with white nails, was concealed from the public gaze by a white silk covering, called a pall; to each of the handles was attached a white silken cord. These were carried by four maidens clothed in white also, each carried a posey in her left hand. They were followed by Lady Flora, and several of her friends. Then came several of her acquaintance, whom she had formed during her stay at Polstead. In this order they reached the grave; the coffin was lowered—and, after the prayers had been read, the poseys were thrown upon the corpse, and they then returned.

Lady Flora was bedewed with tears during the remainder of the day—and when she was about to return in the evening, she bestowed a present of ten guineas upon the woman, and kissing the child, once more returned to town.

Thus perished one, who, had she not have been led from the path of honour, might have lived long and happy in the society of a loving husband; surrounded too in all probability, by a circle of children. Poor girl! this was but one of the many instances, where confiding woman has too late discovered that she has fallen a victim to a false-hearted villain

---

CHAPTER XXVII.

THE FELON.

The following day, at the appointed time, Belford was at the house of Sir John Mortimer; the baronet gave him a hearty welcome; the luncheon was despatched, and the merits of a bottle of sherry discussed—they then, together with Sir Charles, proceeded to participate in the pleasures of a ride. Belford appeared now, to be as firmly established in the good opinion of Sir John as he was before held in his most complete hatred and contempt. Thus did he, by his own act, forward the very measure he would have retarded— the ruin of his son.

It is needless for us to particularize the many attempts made by Belford, to win over Sir Charles to his own course, suffice it to say, that in an evil hour, he consented to accompany his mis-called friend to a gaming-table; there he for the first two or three visits, appeared only as a spectator. The game, however, too much accorded with his own disposition, to permit him to remain long inactive. Once more was he tempted to handle the fatal die; again had he became a gamester; the first, second, third, and even fourth times of his visits, he was a winner. This, of course, only strengthened his desire to play on the fifth night of his visit; he lost sixty pounds, this he did not heed —again he went, and again became a loser to the amount of two hundred pounds. These repeated sums greatly inconvenienced him, for since his return home, Sir John had allowed him only a somewhat scanty allowance of what is termed pocket-money. Once more plunged into the vortex of dissipation, no bounds could restrain him; his father requested him to defray a couple of bills, the joint amount of which was eighty pounds—this sum, together with twenty pounds of his own private property, he lost at the table the following evening. And this bieng accomplished, he feared to return to his father—and accordingly, consented to a proposition made by Belford, to return to his residence at the hotel. They then lived in companionship with each other for several weeks, visiting the gambling house every evening, sometimes losing, but more frequently winning, for Belford always played with extreme caution—and when he had lost a certain sum, invariably made it a maxim to quit the table, lest they should become too deeply involved.

This course of life was followed for a very considerable time, when the news of his father's death reached Mortimer—he repaired at once to the place where the advertisement which apprised him of the fact directed—and their found his brother had claimed possession of the whole effects and estate; he, however, upon enquiry, discovered that there was a will, which the other had attempted to conceal. Upon being read, it was proved, that by the direction of his deceased father, Sir Charles was to receive the rent of a small estate, which would secure to him, an income of three hundred pounds per annum. Upon learning this, his disappointment and rage was perceptible to all; and his mortification was such, that the following day after the funeral of his father, he mortgaged the property for six hundred; this soon disappeared, and he was now deprived of all hopes of future gain, at least through his family connections. And daily becoming more reckless as to what his fate might be. As time progressed, fortune ceased to smile upon their efforts to gain; penury glared them in the face; and at length, they were so far reduced, that Mortimer sought for, and obtained, a situation as clerk in a merchant's office. The salary he received, was inadequate to his wants, and three months after his first entrance into this new mode of life, he was arrested upon a charge of embezzlement. The case was clearly proved against him, and sentence of death was passed upon him. This, however, was remitted to transportation; and he, who might have been a distinguished *figurante* in the highest circles of aristocracy, was now a convicted felon, and despatched to the hulks.

Belford was exceedingly annoyed at this, though we would not have the reader for one moment to imagine, that he was capable of mourning the misfortune and absence of a friend. No, for he rather exulted in the effect produced by his immediate agency, than grieve at his fall. He was now left unaided and unaccompanied, to pursue his own course of villainy; which, will, doubtless, bring upon him, the vengeance of the law, and expedite that fate, his guilt so well merited. Therefore, with this thought, we shall leave him to proceed as he will, while we follow another and more important portion of this work.

CHAPTER XXVIII.

THE MYSTERIOUS WARNING.

SINCE the period when sanguinary assassins, unrelenting fathers, refractory daughters, sentimental lovers, and occasionally a pert chambermaid were considered as materials of an indispensible nature for the manufacturing of a melo-drama, it has been the custom of their authors to request those under whose immediate notice they came, to imagine a long lapse of time to have passed within the few moments the canvass excludes the performance in question from their view; and such persons as make such unreasonable requests, assign no other cause for so doing than that a "a lapse of years is supposed to take place between the acts," and for why? often to produce a man or woman, that, in the former portion of the production, were nought but children. This we declare to be unnatural, for, though steam is now almost universally adopted, yet it has never been used to promote, or, more properly speaking, to hasten the growth of children. At least, if it has we have as hitherto been insensible to the fact. Therefore, having said thus much to the reader, of course he cannot guess the nature of what is to follow; we have no children to hatch or to grow by steam, or any other but the natural process; no act drops to lower, or such theatrical deceptions, but simply after this circumlocution (used to conceal our modesty), as a most especial favour to request our patrons to read what is about to follow as events which transpired nineteen years after the previous portion of the work.

It was about half past seven upon a beautiful evening in August —— (we must spare dates), that any persons possessing an eye of observation might have noticed if passing by the spot where the cottage was situated, a rather pretty and decidedly interesting female was seated upon a small wooden settle that was fixed at the exterior of the cottage, busily engaged in performing some little task of needle-work, when the garden wicket was slowly opened, and a dark woman clothed in tattered apparel, and bearing upon her left arm a small wicker basket, in which was deposited some glittering trinkets, papers of needles, pins, cottons, tapes, and various other trivial articles of female consumption, appeared. As this strange looking personage proceeded towards her, the young woman had leisure to observe her more closely. She perceived her to be a rather tall woman, of rather brawny features, though somewhat borne down by the weight of age ; a dark complexion, though furrowed by care, exposure to the weather, and the iron hand of time.

" Good evening to you !" she exclaimed, " can I sell you anything in my way ? good tape, sewing cotton, needles, or—"

" No, I thank you," replied the other, interrupting her, " I am not in want of anything at present ; I am sorry that you have taken this trouble, and all to no purpose "

" Think not of that, my child," replied the gipsey, for such she evidently was, " had it not have been for the furtherance of my own purpose, I should not have done so. Will you sell me a draught of milk in exchange for my wares ; the road by which I have travelled is dusty, and I have yet far to go; you shall choose for yourself, my dear."

" Oh no, indeed, I could not do so," was the reply.

" Then I must go away as I came—thirsty," exclaimed the gipsey, in a tone of disappointment.

" No," replied the generous girl, " that was not my meaning ; you shall have the milk, though I will not touch your wares." So saying she hastened into the cottage, and returned with a large brown pitcher filled with the desired beverage, accompanied by a slice of home-made bread, which was also thankfully accepted.

Having taken a hearty draught of the milk, the gipsey returned the pitcher, and as she did so, exclaimed :—

" Well, now, as you will not accept anything in exchange for the milk, suppose you allow me to tell your fortune."

" My fortune," rejoined the other, with a smile, " oh, I am sure there can be no mystery in that, none whatever."

" So, my girl, have many thought before," replied the gipsey, " but it is impossible for you to calculate upon the capability of the human mind, young and inexperienced as you are; much is yet in store before you ; I am convinced much that——"

" Is it so very hard to learn ?" enquired the simple girl.

" Too hard, much too hard for you at present," replied the gipsey, " but why do you not consent to my telling your fortune ?"

" Because I do not think it possible," was the reply. " Why should that God whom we all do serve endow you with more prophetic powers than others ? I cannot consent until you reply to my question."

" You are a shrewd girl," rejoined the woman, " are you in the habit of reading much ?"

" I am—I have read a great deal for my age," was the reply.

" I thought so," half muttered the gipsey, " now," she resumed, turning to the girl, " I'll convince you by theory how it is that I first became possessed with what you are pleased to term my prophetic powers. From the first dawn of infant remembrance, my course of life has been passed in

[See page 47.]

the gipseys camp ; there, joined with the motley tribe, have I experienced many and bitter reverses of fortune—excuse the tear now starting from its hiding place—like the gaunt and hungry wolf prowling o'er the earth when the whole face of nature is hushed in repose. I was once the proud and happy mother of——; but pshaw," she continued, dashing aside the tears that now in quick succession coursed their way down her dark and furrowed cheeks, "this is folly—weakness of which I did not think myself capable. I have been a strict observer of their manners and customs ; from them it was I first learned the art of fortune-telling, in which there is often more truth than persons imagine ; and, in order that you may entertain no unjust prejudice against me for asserting this, I will remind you that there are men of medical fame, who profess their ability to judge of a person's temper, inclination, and disposition, by the formation of their head ; so, then, can we foretel to a certain extent, the future destiny of persons by their countenance, by the lines in the hands, and by cards. Now, are you convinced ?"

" I am not," was the prompt and laconic reply.

"And why so ?" demanded the gipsey.

" Because," rejoined the girl, " you have not as yet put forth any convincing argument. The subject upon which you have spoken is a science called phrenology, and one too that is based upon sound principles."

"And why may not ours be equally substantial and equally scientific ?" demanded the gipsey.

Because it is professed by people of illiterate and uncultivated minds," was the reply—in short, can be termed nothing more than mere vulgar prejudice, promulgated to trap the superstitious and unwary ; and in support of this declaration, grant me leave to ask you one question—do you believe in the existence of a high and Supreme Being ?"

" I do," exclaimed the gipsey.

"And also believe that Being, whom you acknowledge to possess an

No. 11.

unbounded controul over the inclinations, nay, the very actions of his creatures here upon earth, and were created by His agency alone?"

Again the reply was in the affirmative.

"Then," pursued the girl, think you that because my hand may chance to be different in appearance in consequence of the lines, or because my countenance may be set to any particular expression, lastly, because a few coloured pieces of simple pasteboard, may chance to fall together in a manner which you would think peculiar, the Great Ruler of hearts would alter my destiny? Think you because by your prediction I am to be drowned, that should I not visit any spot where the body of water is of sufficient magnitude to cause my death, providing that I were to be immersed, was to be found that rather than your prophecy should go unfulfilled, the being of my adoration would cause a sea to spring from out the solid earth, or if, upon the other hand, you had foretold, or pretended to foretel, that my death should be caused by fire, that such would in reality occur, or even supposing such should, by an unknown chain of circumstances, come to pass, think you that your prophetic influence would have any effect in producing the same? No. 'Tis impossible. Whatever may befal us, 'tis not as many imagine, the fate to which they were previously born, because, when first our infant life is ushered into the world there are many things which may at once terminate our fate and life. We are helpless, and at the mercy of those who nurse our puny limbs; in one moment we might then be dashed to atoms. Thus would all the future hopes and prospects of those from whom life is first given, be for ever blighted. Now, I have, I trust, shewn you the utter absurdity of your profession, by which I grieve to acknowledge, too many of those poor ignorant beings who have by early mischance been torn from those who would have instilled some little knowledge into their minds, have been so often misled."

"All that you have spoken," exclaimed the gipsey, seeing that the other had made a momentary pause, "I believe to be true, and it also clearly proves that your life has been one of the most intense study and research, yet I still protest my ability to anticipate your fortune."

"If, then, this be true; look in my face, and say what will be my destiny—I should like to know that."

"So many have thought before you," replied the woman, "and yet," she continued, with a deep-drawn sigh, "how often and fearfully have they been deceived."

"Is anything dreadful to happen to me?" enquired the girl, fearfully.

"Your face speaks fairly," replied the other "let me see your hand. No, not that one," she continued, as the left was proffered to her, "'tis the right I would see."

The request was promptly complied with.

The gipsey shook her head prophetically.

"Is there aught in my hand to excite alarm?"

Once more the mysterious sybil shook her head.

"Then why look so very sorrowful?" continued the girl—"has aught happened to alarm you?"

A third time this mysterious woman shook her head, and for several succeeding moments appeared to be buried in abstraction. At length suddenly turning to where the girl stood, she exclaimed—"I have taken an undefinable interest in your fate; your hand promises well, fortune and happiness is in store for you, though I fear—"

A cloud once more obscured the fine features of the gipsey.

"Are you alone?" she enquired, after a momentary pause.

"I am," was the prompt and fearless reply.

"Quite?" rejoined the gipsey.

" Not a soul is now within the cottage ; for my mother is gone to the next village to sell some new laid eggs, and will not return until ten o'clock."

" Will you permit me, then, to enter for a short time ?" enquired the sybil. " I have learned sufficient by your hand to make even me curious —if you grant my request the cards shall prove the rest. Say, will you do as I desire ?"

" I will suffer you to enter for a short time," replied the unsuspecting girl, " but you must away before my mother returns, or she might, perhaps, be angry at my having admitted a stranger in her absence."

" I will go, my child, when you request me," rejoined the gipsey.

" Then we had better enter at once," continued the girl.

" Be it so, then," returned the woman.

As they were about to enter, the girl gave utterance to a half suppressed scream, and with a trembling hand seized the arm of the sybil, who, looking around with a cautious eye, exclaimed :—

" What have you seen, my child—tell me what has alarmed you ?"

" I thought," replied the girl, " that I saw the dark figure of a man steal with cautious steps across the garden."

" 'Tis an omen of mischief," muttered the gipsey, in a suppressed tone. " Do not tremble," she continued, turning to the affrighted girl, " 'twas only one of my tribe in search of me ; I have been absent from them longer than usual, and, as is their custom, they have despatched scouts to trace my footsteps, lest I should betray them. Do not tremble so, my girl, trust me, that was the cause of your alarm."

" I thank you for the assurance," replied the girl, " and yet," she continued, " I know not how to describe the sensation that has stole over me ; I tremble like an aspen leaf, and almost fear, though I know not why, to enter the cottage."

" Pshaw," rejoined the sybil, " this is folly ; cheer up my girl."

With these words both entered the cottage, the inside of which was in strict accordance with the exterior. The homely arm chair by the fire side —the blackbird in the large wicker cage—the large family Bible placed upon a small antique chest of drawers—all combined at once to prove the steady and pious disposition of its humble inmates. Though the appearance of the place was homely, yet no indication of poverty was visible ; nay, on the contrary, one would almost have imagined that their means were somewhat above their position. The girl's attire, though humble, was composed of really good materials, and the rich coral necklace that encompassed her neck, whose hue might outvie the lily, also went far to prove that they were what is generally termed well to do in the world. Imagine, reader, how truly bewitching must even the picture of a young and lovely maiden of eighteen appear, her form somewhat above the middle stature, neck and shoulders of alabaster ; of a beautiful and intelligent countenance, full, black laughing eye, long flowing ringlets that for their jet black hue might rival the plumes of the raven, fine taper waist, and, to conclude, a prettily formed foot and ancle. Confess, reader, then, if ye be human, that such as we have now described would call forth thy admiration ; and, if man command your admiration, what then must be the original ? and such an one as her of whom we have now spoken ? a young and guileless girl, possessing all the personal attractions which we have attempted to paint, coupled with a sound understanding and highly intelligent mind. Upon the engaged with the gipsey she was, as we have previously stated, busily appearance of her needle, accustomed as she was to behold rustic beauty in its age of innocence and perfection, the old woman paused to gaze upon the object before her. Her dress was calculated, if possible, to add to the general adornment of the wearer ; her gown was constructed of a superior kind of gingham, hooped up in order to display a neatly chequered cotton petticoat, a white stocking, and black prunella shoe, displayed to the best advantage the exquisitely formed leg and foot, her neck, too, was covered with a snowy white net handkerchief, and her head was surmounted with a small chip hat, or juvenile attempt at a rustic bonnet. By the way, while speaking of these same hats or bonnets (whichever the fair portion of our readers may think fit to style them, for to their superior judgment will we submit) we wish some compassionate young lady would undertake to explain to us why these same hats or bonnets are of such juvenile dimensions that they never, by any possible chance or accident, cover above one fifth part of the head for which they are constructed. What can be their utility we are at a loss to conjecture. They cannot be for warmth, for while they protected one part of the head and kept it in a glow, the other might freeze; and this may chance to be of fatal consequences, for should the part exposed be that upon which the organ of affection is situated, the maiden would grow cold, and neglect to return the love of some swain whose only hope of happiness might be in her smiles; he might be so afflicted at this as to commit suicide—he might succeed, and then what would not the whole bonnet building race have to answer for?

Reader, pull the check-string, and remind us that we are again taxing thy patience by digression—for really, we had almost become insensible of the fact - the subject upon which we spoke, was so truly interesting and agreeable.

The object of our dissertation placed a chair near the table, and after having assisted the gipsey to remove the basket from her arm, they both seated themselves at the table.

The sybil then took from her basket a pack of soiled cards—and selecting the four aces and other court cards, together with a chosen few of the minors —these were, after a great share of shuffling, placed in three rows upon the table—after a somewhat lengthy pause, the gipsey scrutinised them more closely, and exclaimed,

" There is much in store for you—much to be feared from;" here paused, and again pursued the mystic operations; " there will be many contend for the possession of your hand—have you a lover?"

" No," was the hesitating reply.

" It is useless your attempting to deceive me; the cards seem to follow up a very dark man, who, before three days have elapsed will meet you. You will walk with him—nay, more than that, he will kiss you—and while at his earnest request, you will speak fine words—there will be near, one who loves you truly and sincerely; him, you will slight—and by you his very destiny —nay, his very nature will be changed. You it is, that through his agency, will reduce the now innocent though unhappy man, to the lowest grade of vice and infamy—his heart will break—that is not all, by deserting him, you will bring——. But I have already spoken sufficient upon this subject—is there aught more you would wish to know?"

" Nothing," replied the maiden, bursting into tears : " nothing."

" Why do you weep?" demanded the gipsey, " have I pained you?"

" You have indeed," replied the girl, " but do not think of that. My mother will shortly return. See," she continued, pointing to a small metal watch, which hung from a nail over the chimney-piece; " it wants but a quarter to ten."

The gipsey instantly rose and prepared for her departure.

" Should I ever desire to see you again, how am I to find, or seeing, how am I to recognise you?" enquired the maiden.

" I shall always follow your footsteps," returned the sybil, " and when I would warn you, remember me when you hear the word CAUTION, be sure 'tis I, and desist from whatever you were about to follow. If you do not, rest assured that harm will ensue."

" Why this care for a stranger? You never saw me before this evening—

and the very short time you have spent in my company, does not warrant such care."

" My child you mistake," answered the gipsey, " to me, all the circumstances of your birth are known. With me alone, rests the mystery that attained that ever memorable event—trust me, I am not what I seem—nor are you. Our destinies are linked with each other—but even now, I have overstayed my time. Farewell! may Heaven eternally watch over and protect you—farewell."

With these words, the gipsey after having shaken the young cottager warmly by the hand, hastily disappeared through the wicket garden.

Upon being once more left alone, the girl seated herself at the table, and was soon busily engaged with her needle, when she was suddenly startled by a low knocking at the door—she trembled and turned pale, as in a half suppressed whisper, she exclaimed who can that be ? Surely not that terrible dark strange woman again.

The knocking was again repeated.

She rose, and with a trembling hand, essayed to open the door, but her whole frame trembled so violently, that she could not even raise the latch—at this juncture, a well-known voice was heard to pronounce her name.

How truly ridiculous is all this trembling, soliloquised the maiden, gaining new courage, 'tis only Edward Lambourne!

CHAPTER XXIX.

THE ANTIQUARIANS

BEREFT of his companion, Belford, had no other resource, than throughout his circle of acquaintance, to seek for another. One evening, as he was about to quit the gaming table, where he had spent two or three hours, his attention was suddenly attracted towards the opposite extremity of the room, where a great clamour was raised by some two or three of the gamesters, who had for some considerable period, been engaged at play with a stranger of rather elderly appearance ; it appeared that he had lost the whole of the money with which he entered, and which, as he stated, amounted to nearly sixty pounds. The loss of the money, he, however, declared to be with him a secondary consideration ; though he felt assured, that those who now possessed the same, were nothing more or less, than confirmed sharpers : but it was the insult that accompanied the defeat, and which he expressed himself determined to resist. Upon hearing this, the sharpers, one and all rose, as if by common consent, and exclaimed against this insult cast upon them. The old gentleman, however, would not be defeated, or persuaded to alter his opinion—for he thought, and justly, (as we do) that there never yet existed the thief, who, upon any imaginary commentation being made upon his honesty, would not froth up and pretend to be highly indignant at what, in his own mind, he knew to be perfectly just and proper. After some further clamour and disputing, there was a cry from all sides, commanding that the enraged dupe should be thrust *vie et armis* from the room. Upon this, some two or three of the most enraged and determined, stept forward to execute the simultaneous command; and the first that approached within arm and umbrella lengths, received upon their cranium, such convincing evidence of the old gentleman's irrascibility, delivered by a neat bone handle, being part and parcel of an utensil named as above. As some revenge for this insult, the inflictor, notwithstanding his struggles, was seized and would have been ejected, had it not have been for the timely interference of Belford ; at whose solicitation, they after some little hesitation released him. They then quitted the room, in company with each other, and in about half an hour from the time of their quitting the room, the old gentleman halted before the door of his habitation, a rather antiquated mansion, situated at the western portion of Portman Square. The owner of this sombre-looking abode, invited Belford strongly to accompany him to the interior ; and by the time the door was opened by a tall, dull-looking footman, (attired in a suit of clothes, the precise colour of which then perplexed us ; but we have since, through the agency of a sapient friend, discovered that it was cream coloured brown), Belford had become a convert to the cause ; and accordingly, a few moments afterwards, he discovered himself to be ascending a staircase, that, for its width and peculiar formation, might vie with any curiosity now within the precincts of the British Museum.

After they had traversed this modern ladder of Babel, for the space of ten minutes, they halted before a thick and elaborately carved oaken door, which, being opened, discovered a capacious chamber, covered with a costly carpet and hearth-rug ; upon the latter of which, lay a small specimen of the dog kind ; who, by its outer appearance, seemed to claim some near relationship with the one, that, as we are taught, entered the ark of Noah, to escape from the general inundation, that swallowed up the world : probably it was the eldest son of that respected animal.

Upon their entrance he arose from his recumbent position, and having thrice walked the boundarys of the apartment, gave utterance to a low growl which seemed to say, " I wouldn't speak to a bone if I met it," and then resumed his seat.

While the old gentleman divested himself of his superfluous attire, in the form of two coats, and an ample cloak, Belford, had leisure to survey the apartment, the result of which, was, that he came to the firm resolve of setting his guest down as a decided antiquarian.

The furniture was of a somewhat costly description, but of the most ancient make ; the walls were ornamented with numerous valuable paintings encircled by massive frames—and from the centre of the ceiling, was suspended the skin of a stuffed crocodile ; and, in another part, was to be seen that of a wild cat. A large eagle was also to be seen standing with expanded wings in a large glass case ; under its claws was a young sparrow hawk, partly stripped of its plumage, which lay strewn upon the sand which comprised the ground work. Nor was this the only evidence of the decided antique taste of their owner, for numerous other birds and animals of an equally extraordinary nature were placed in different portions of the room. By the time his survey had been brought to a conclusion, the old gentleman requested him to be seated.

He did as he had been desired, and his mysterious guest then agitated a somewhat unwieldly rope which hung from a corner of the ceiling near to the chimney-piece ; this caused a harsh sound, like that proceeding from a cracked iron pot, to be heard, at which sound the before-mentioned domestic made his appearance, and again retired, to return a second time with a small silver salver, upon which was placed a pair of exquisitely-cut decanters, partly filled with port and sherry wines, together with another dish filled with various descriptions of biscuits. After placing these and a brace of glasses upon the table, he retired from the chamber, when a slight hint being given to Belford, he filled the nearest glass with sherry and declared it to be excellent, while his host sipped off a small portion of port, and adverted to the scene as before mentioned, which occurred at the gaming-house, and of which he was the hero. It appeared by his own declaration, that he had never before visited a gambling-table, but having some years since read of a case, wherein a person of respectable standing had, through gaming, reduced himself to the lowest verge of poverty, and from thence descended to crime, the result of which was that he suffered an ignominious death, his curiosity to witness the cause of so much misery increased as time progressed ;

and being at length unable to controul his desire, he had that night resolved to carry his long-premeditated purpose of visiting the nearest h—ll into exe- cution. According to his statement, it appeared that he had not been but a very few moments in the room, when one of the persons present addressed him, and in a persuasive tone enquired if he would try his fortune at a game of hazird; he refused to do so, and the person left him, and proceeded to another part of the room Being desirous of noticing their manners and customs, he enquired of one of them if he could be accommodated with a glass of brandy-and-water. Upon receiving a reply in the affirmative, he re- quested to be furnished with the same. A few moments after the assurance had been given, the required compound was placed before him. He had imbibed very little of the s me, before the man with whom he was afterwards engaged at play (attracted, doubtless, by the odour of the brandy-and-water) accosted him. After a short conversation, he so far conquered the old gen- tleman's prejudices as to induce him to play one game This he was per- mitted to win. They then doubled the stakes and played again; this and the four following games he lost. By this time he was minus forty pounds. Still he had no suspicions as to the honour of his antagonist. They played on, and he now won fifteen pounds. At length, by one stroke, he lost his last coin Still all would have concluded agreeably enough, had not the other added insult to robbery. " Upon learning that he now held possession of my capital," resumed the old gentleman, taking another slight sip at the glass, or the wine it contained, " his insolence knew no bounds. He pre- tended to apologize for having cleaned me out, as he termed it, but with mock civility assured me that if I needed the means of procuring a dinner, he should feel great pleasure in presenting me with the same. These and similar insults so enraged me, that I with great indignation informed him that I was convinced I had been swindled, but having unintentionally entered the company of scoundrels, I must submit This raised their ire, and one of the most insolent threatened to eject me from the room, for what he was pleased to term impertinence to gentlemen and men of honour. I smiled contemptuously at this, and grasped my umbrella more tightly. I then informed this brave ' Bombastes' that if he advanced one step towards the execution of his threat, it was more than probable that some of his bones, together with the flesh appertaining thereto, would suffer, and severely, for his temerity. This led to high and angry words, and had it not have been for your friendly interference, I should doubtless have met with great violence and mal-treatment; therefore I have to offer to you my sincere and heartfelt thanks. But, see, the glasses have been idle all this time; drink, and if you have no objection, let me know under what circumstances you were present amongst the crowd of sharpers with whom you found me, for I do think you are one of their tribe. By-the-bye," he continued, " I have been going to ask you, since the first moment of our acquaintance, if in any of your travels you have met with a fellow called Belford. My motive for enquiring of you is, that the rascal is a confirmed gambler, and therefore invariably to be found at the table, where he stands ready to plunder any fresh caught flat, whom the thought of gain may have lured into the coils which this vulture in human form always sets, in order to fleece them of all they possess."

Had any person, blessed with but an ordinary share of impudence and self assurance been thus attacked, their surprise and confusion—but not so Belford. He looked as calmly and indifferent as if he had never met the individual above named more than twice in his life, and one of that being at a time when he had granted him a loan—*his* modesty prevented his confess- ing the fact.

" Why do you seem so earnest to know more about this Belford?" he en- quired after a pause.

" Because," replied the old gentleman, " I consider him to be a most accomplished villain, and I am somewhat anxious to learn whether he has yet met his just reward."

"And in your estimation what may be the nature of that reward?" enquired the gamester, with great *sang froid.*

"The gallows," replied the old gentleman testily.

"Then you entertain a very exalted opinion of him?"

"So exalted, that I should feel great pleasure in having him now before me; I would not exalt him any more."

"Indeed; and even supposing he were sitting before you, as I now am, what would you then do with him?"

"Why," rejoined the other, "I would treat him to a death peculiar only to myself, and one that he would enjoy."

"And may I make bold to enquire what description of death that might be?" answered Belford.

"Yes, it is this:—in the first instance, I would cause a barrel, or hogshead, of the largest possible dimensions, to be procured; this I would have conveyed to some very sultry spot, then filled with cold water to the brim; he should then be firmly bound and placed in the hogshead, so that his mouth should be about an inch from the surface of the water, but in such a manner, that it would be impossible to imbibe even a tea spoonful; he should be kept in this position until he died of hunger and thirst; and in order, if possible, to augment his sufferings, food of the choicest description should be placed within sight of him. I would then constantly upbraid him with his villainy, and use every possible means of adding to the agony of mind his position would produce."

"Really," replied Belford, "I am of opinion that if this man were to hear you, he would be very thankful for the service you wished to confer upon him. On my *honour,* your intentions are the most humane I have ever had the pleasure of hearing. Do you bear any relationship to the gentle inhabitants of Otaheite? Excuse the liberty, but knowing them to be a very generous and grateful people, I made bold to ask the question."

"You are a wag," exclaimed the old gentleman, "and are quizzing me; but really, do you not think this fellow is a great scamp? Now, speak your mind—I know you do."

If Belford *had* spoken the sentiments of his mind, the old gentleman most certainly would not have been quite so well pleased; as it was, however, he refrained from so doing, for he more than hoped to class his guest among his list of victims, and therefore contented himself with enquiring why he entertained such a great enmity towards a man, who, according to his own statement, he had never beheld, and therefore could not know any ill of him.

"Why," answered the other, "you shall hear. Some years since I read of a case at the Old Bailey, where it appeared that that fellow, Belford, was a sort of companion to a young baronet. Well, they were one evening at the gaming-table, when the baronet quarrelled with some one of the company present. High words were resorted to on both sides, and the tumult terminated by the ground and time for a hostile meeting being appointed, upon which occasion this Belford was present and seconded his friend, whose shot proved fatal to his adversary, who, to the best of my recollection, died upon the ground. However, whether such was the case or otherwise, he died from the effects of the wound received at the duel. His friends were very naturally incensed against his murderer, who was tried for the crime of wilful murder, and but for the evidence of Belford, who, like a villain as he is, accepted a bribe from the adverse side and appeared against his friend, the baronet would have been acquitted; as it was, his sentence was that of the most fearful nature—*death by the hangman!* Now, what think you of the rascal? And besides this, he, at a later period, prompted the same person who, through interest of the most powerful nature, obtained his reprieve, to com-

[*See page* 91].

mit embezzlement upon his employer, and he is now sentenced to transportation, and, indeed, has been in confinement for the last twenty years, though he was not banished from his native land, as his sentence directed."

"But do you not think," resumed Belford, "that when a man has once been deceived by another, he must be greatly in error to place himself a second time within his power, well knowing at the same time the true character of his associate, who, if once criminal, would not easily be led from his course of guilt?"

"There may be many causes for that," rejoined the other, who appeared determined at all hazards to carry off the glory of the argument, if indeed the subject was worthy of any; "the injured man may be of an open, frank disposition, equally a stranger to duplicity and diffidence; the other may make great professions of future friendship, attribute his former villanies to hitherto unknown circumstances over which he had no controul, and which compelled him to act as he had done; these, and similar pleadings, familiar to the imagination of a scoundrel, may cause the reconciliation of which you speak; and he must be a vagabond of the deepest dye that would violate the sacred confidence reposed in him. Now are you answered? Sir, have I defended my cause ably or not?"

"You have, indeed," replied Belford, "and that, too, with the skill of an old practised lawyer, if——"

"Stay," exclaimed the other, interrupting him, "do not class me with the lawyers—those privateers that bear down all before them; fellows who, to enrich themselves, will deprive the widow and orphan of their last mite. They are, if indeed it be possible, more complete robbers than the fellow of whom we have been speaking. I am a friend to justice, and therefore must of necessity detest law and lawyers. I would not hold any communion with them, even if I was convinced that they would enrich me for life."

No. 12.

In conversation like the above nearly two hours were passed, at the end of which an old woman entered, bearing in her hand a china basin, which was filled with a compound, which, to the inexperienced opinion of Belford, appeared to be some ancient description of porridge, but which, according to the same old woman's account, was barley water. This Belford was assured by the old gentleman, to be a sovereign remedy for coughs and colds, and which he imbibed every evening at one hour; this was spoken in the presence of the woman, but upon her disappearance he turned to Belford, and in a suppressed tone of voice, exclaimed—

"You saw that woman that has just left the room?"

"Why?" replied Belford, "seeing that in my estimation it would take exactly three hours for any living mantua-maker to travel round the circumference of her body; I must either have been blind, or granted leave of absence to my eyes, in order that they might enquire into the health of my brains, if I did not—why, she's a regular living specimen of the Brobdignag system; if she was in some countries they would choose her for their queen."

"Indeed!" enquired the other; "and why so?"

"Because she's too fat to run away in time of danger."

The old gentleman smiled at this, and assured Belford that he was a funny fellow.

Belford seeing no possible pretext for contradicting the old gentleman, from that moment believed himself in reality to be a funny fellow.

Now, in proof of what Belford said, we will give just a laconic description of the old dame's general appearance: first, then, we will inform our reader, that she stood about four feet nothing, minus her shoes, that the circumference of her dwarfish body was about two sizes beyond that of the once-celebrated Daniel Lambert, of gigantic rotundity; her countenance was something between the hues of the best Wall's End, and Grimstone's eye-snuff, two small grey eyes, each graced with that peculiar and unenviable expression called squinting; her nose was somewhat about three sizes too large for her face and figure; her head was adorned with locks of "dandy grey russet," and—but this is sufficient for the reader to feel some interest in her welfare, and we will therefore proceed forthwith.

"I would not part from that woman upon any account!" exclaimed the old gentleman, after a pause; "she is the only comfort of my old age—were it not for her I should not live a week—she daily attends upon me, and anticipates my every wish almost before I have myself decided upon my wants."

"Is she your only female servant?" enquired Belford.

"No, she is not; I have three others, but they are wild, giddy, flirting husseys, with a host of lovers. But the good Mrs. Johnson has no lovers, not she, kind soul."

Belford did not reply to this: but in his own private opinion he thought that if Mrs. Johnson had a lover, men's taste and judgment must be at a most alarming discount. This was a theme upon which the old man loved to talk, and he never would have grown tired, had not his auditor informed him that he had a desire to seek the comforts of the pillow. Accordingly, the old gentleman once more summoned the spectral footman into his presence, and then, after bidding Belford repeated adieus, commanded the menial to escort him [to the exterior, the road to which Belford, in an after description of its house and owner, declared that without some assistance he verily believed that he should have been occupied until the last day; the man had now preceded him to the bottom of the stairs, opened the door, and shielding the candle with his left hand from the wind, which blew strongly, he so extended the light, under pretence of holding back the door, that for any person so inclined, there was great facility afforded for dropping any specimen of coin into the said hand, without the least possible inconvenience to the receiver, or difficulty to the donor. Belford, however, did not, or affected not to notice this movement, quickly passed into the street, when the disappointed lacquey shut the door violently, and muttering some indistinct allusions, which bore great resemblance to—fashionable humbug, shabby swell, and many other choice epithets peculiar to himself, and very edifying to others, could they but have heard him. He then proceeded to the apartments from which he had escorted the visitor, and from thence he conducted his master to his chamber, where, with the joint assistance of himself and Mrs. Johnson, the old gentleman was safely anchored in the harbour of Morpheus, where, as his two trusty domestics have quitted him for the same laudible purpose, we shall also leave him to indulge in a slumber, when, doubtless, he will dream of the villainy of Belford, the bravery of his deliverer, the kindness of Mrs. Johnson, and many other little affairs, known only to himself. Therefore, reader, we shall draw the curtains closely around him, and await the return of dawn, when we may perhaps pay another visit to the antiquarian, when seated at his morning meal—commonly called breakfast.

CHAPTER XXX.

CAPTAIN BOND'S DREAM.—HOW HE ESCAPED FROM NEWGATE.

CAPTAIN BOND, during the interval over which we have strode, experienced many reverses of fortune. In an engagement with the soldiers, he lost the greater portion of his men, and with the residue committed those depredations, which were but as a ghost upon his former exploits.

Though his circumstances were altered, and that materially altered, still his spirit was unbroken; the only difference time and adverse fate had worked in him was his temper, which had become more irritable than formerly, when, through the treachery of Lady Flora Mandeville, he was thrown into confinement. On the third night of his imprisonment he dreamt a remarkable dream. As he lay on his pallet of straw, an old woman appeared, and told him that in a few hours he would be drinking wine with his band. On this, he partially awoke; but again fell into another doze, and again dreamed. In this vision, he saw a young woman, of great personal attraction, murdered by her sweetheart, who then buried her in a barn. Bond thought, in his dream, he was himself an inmate of the barn; and, as his dream proceeded, he felt terrified at what he had seen. He now felt himself start up, but was terrified to find himself furiously attacked by four large black cats. The scene had changed to a pleasant cottage parlour; but the cats were still upon him, and one of them was lacerating his forehead, [see engraving]. Again he felt a smart shake by the shoulder, which awoke him, when he found the gaoler standing by his bed of straw, and also discovered that the shock he had felt had in reality proceeded from the patagonian grasp of that sturdy individual. He was informed by the gaoler, that an old woman requested to be admitted to him; this surprised him, he knew full well that the gang were one and all too well known to venture there to visit him, even if they were assured of effecting his own liberation. After a brief pause he declared that he did not wish to be seen by any person.

Upon hearing this the gaoler withdrew, but returned again almost immediately, with the information that she would not quit the place until she had seen him; upon which Bond requested that she should be admitted. He was still at a loss to conjecture who the visitor could be; he felt convinced that none of the band would venture near him, however, he was still in ignorance, and therefore gave up all thought of guessing, and as he did so the gaoler re-appeared, conducting a decrepit old woman into the dungeon, the door of which he secured upon them.

"Now, hag!" exclaimed Bond, in a gruff tone ; "what want you with me ? Come, be speedy, for I am already weary of your company, therefore, if you are not brief, I shall call in the assistance of the gaoler to escort you hence — d'ye hear ?"

The old woman did not appear to take offence at the rather fierce manner in which she had been accosted, but drew from under her cloak, a brace of pistols upon half cock.

Upon beholding them, Bond started back in amazement; they were his favourite weapons with which he had called upon countless passengers to "stand and deliver;" he could select them from a hundred. Yet, how could they have come into the possession of the old woman? this astonished him beyond all comprehension.

"Why, man, how you stare, I have been distracted so of late by the taunts and caprice of a narrow-minded world, that my own eyes play me false? Are you not he whom I seek? are you not Captain Bond ?"

"I am," was the reply, "and you are—"

"Gipsey Meg," replied the sybil, throwing the cloak that disguised her form and features, to the ground.

"What is your purpose here?" enquired Bond.

"To effect your liberation," was the reply.

"Indeed," answered Bond, in a tone of surprise, "and how think you that is to be accomplished, my brave Meg ?"

"Easily," replied the old woman, throwing off her bonnet and gown ; "here, quick, these things by which I entered you can depart in safety ; quick, no time is to be lost."

"What then is to become of you ?"

"Fear not, they cannot detain me; 'tis you they want—you they have offered such rewards to have secured within their power; they have no cause of enmity against me."

"You reason well, Meg," replied Bond, "and could I be brought to believe in what you say, and be convinced of your safety, I would cheerfully act as you advise."

"Fear not," replied the gipsey ; "I shall be safe."

With this assurance Bond quickly donned the disguise, and had scarcely done so when the gaoler re-appeared, and conducted the supposed old woman without the precincts of the prison.

Upon once more gaining his liberty, Bond lost no time in making his way to Whitechapel, where Robson, (or Martin, for that was his rightful name,) together with the few remaining members of the gang were quartered ; hearing them engaged in a low consultation, he placed himself in a position, where unseen, he could listen to the subject of their conversation. He had not been long in this situation when he heard his own name mentioned by the lieutenant; it was evident that they were debating upon their future proceedings ; this, if possible, caused him to listen with more eagerness and profound attention.

"Why," exclaimed one of the men, "our captain is now safely moored in Newgate ; therefore, all we can do in the way of grieving for him will avail nothing ; therefore, my plan is, that instead of wasting our time in thinking of getting him out of the jug, we share the booty and break up the band; that's my advice upon the matter."

"So I perceive," answered the lieutenant ; "and I think, if instead of breaking up the band we were to break your thick head, and make a thoroughfare to your brains, it would only be sparing the hangman a labour : therefore, you may live your time."

"I shall do so, despite your threats," replied the other, "and take care that I do not soon place you all in the same position as Bond now is : therefore, I should advise that you all behave with some degree of civility towards me."

"Civility," reiterated the lieutenant, in a tone of contempt. "Yes, you deserve a great deal of civility from us ; why, your very name would convince anybody of your true disposition."

"Well," replied the other ; "and havn't I brought my share of booty to the gang since I joined it, eh ?"

"Why, yes," replied another of the gang, "we do not pretend to question that ; but, then it's the way in which you do it. Now, for instance, would any one but you have pulled at a watch the other day, and only brought away the seals ?"

"Well," replied the other, whose name was Dingy Bob ; "I 'spose others are liable to mistakes as well as me ; if I did only bring away the seals, didn't I nail a purse yesterday, filled with suv'rins and ten pun flimseys ? That was rather tidy, eh ?"

"Why, yes," answered the lieutenant, "the amount was pretty fair ; but you confessed that it was an old woman nearly eighty years of age, and she couldn't offer much resistance, could she ?"

"No ; but then you appear to forget that she had a servant, and I suppose he took a little trouble, didn't he ?"

"Certainly ; but then the pops would silence him."

"Oh ! you appear to forget that Bob never carries such things with him ; why, the very sight of 'em 'ud make him faint."

Bond listened for some few moments to this bantering, and when order was in some measure restored, he was about to enter, when the voice of Will Huntley, one of the most ferocious and unprincipled of the gang, caused him to pause.

"Well !" exclaimed the ruffian, "you've had a great deal to say about our captain, and Robson appears to advocate his cause very warmly ; perhaps he has just cause for so doing, for we all know that when he deserted the band to follow a petticoat, Captain Bond never once complained of his absence ; one is as bad as the other ; and if the captain hadn't been nabbed by the traps, it was my intention to have peached upon him, as it is, I have been spared the trouble. But, now, lads, if you are all of my disposition, why, you'll leave them to shift for themselves, and after sharing the booty, why, we can each take our own course. As for the captain, why, he'll shortly swing, and I—"

"Shall never live to see it !" exclaimed Bond, suddenly bursting into the room, and felling the last speaker to the ground with the butt-end of his pistol. "Now," he resumed, as the man lay upon the ground, weltering in his blood, "if there's any more such fellows here, let me see and know them, and the reward of their villainy shall soon be administered."

As he spoke these words he looked fiercely round upon the whole assemblage, all of whom appeared to be completely amazed at his sudden and unexpected appearance.

"What, Meg !" exclaimed Robson ; "is it you ? Why, I declare, you are like a guardian angel, always present when least expected and most required— but how came you here !"

"Through the joint assistance of my legs and feet," answered Bond, throwing off his disguise, I am surrounded by a faithful set of men to all appearances, where is Watson ?"

"In the county gaol upon a charge of horse stealing," answered Robson ; "but, tell me, captain, how did you contrive to escape from the jug, and give the cuffins the go by ? did you force your way out ?"

"No," replied Bond, "the doors, or rather gates, were left open for me, and the chief turnkey himself, escorted me to the wicket, when once out of sight I made the best use of my limbs."

"But how was this accomplished ?" again enquired Robson.

Bond then recapitulated the heroic conduct of Meg.

"But, now," he resumed, after a pause; "I have once more accomplished an escape, let us spend the night in revelrie. This carrion," he continued, looking upon the senseless form of Dingy Bob, "may lie here, and rot. Come, lads, let's away, to celebrate my presence here among you."

They then retired to another part of the house, and to a spot secure from the interference of strangers, inasmuch as the locality was known only to themselves, where the wine flowed plentifully. As Bond took his seat at the head of the table, he gave the health of Gipsey Meg, and after the toast had been drank with the usual honours, he exclaimed—

"There is only one thing that now mars my complete happiness."

"And what is that, captain?" enquired Martin.

"The absence of Meg," replied Bond, "would she were here."

"That will not be for many a long day," replied another, "for, depend upon it, as you have escaped, they will, upon making the discovery, take ample vengeance upon Meg."

"Aye," responded another, "the next we hear of Meg will be—"

"That she, among the rest, is here to congratulate the captain upon his escape from the power of his enemies," exclaimed a voice from without.

All started upon hearing this; the next instant the door was thrown open, and Meg entered, attired in the dress of a man; she instantly secured the door, and threw herself into the nearest chair; in a breathless tone, enquired for a goblet of wine, with which she was immediately supplied.

"Why, Meg," exclaimed Bond, "how have you contrived to follow so closely upon my footsteps? have they discharged you upon your own security? or how is it, eh?"

"Why," replied the gipsey, "upon your departure, the gaoler entered, and enquired if I had anything to say to him, as it would be the last time of his visit that night; I endeavoured to maintain silence, but the obstinate fool would insist upon sealing his own fate, by making the discovery before you had sufficient time to secure your safety: I, therefore, rushed upon, and seized him by the throat, he struggled violently, and attempted to cry for assistance. This I at once knew would be fatal to me, I therefore tightened my grasp upon his throat, and soon his struggles became more distant and faint, at length his countenance changed to a black'ning hue, his eyes glared and appeared ready to start from their sockets; this I knew to be the symptoms of strangulation, still I did not relax my hold until he felt stiff—dead—at my feet, I then tore the clothes from the body, and substituting them for those I received from you, walked deliberately from the dungeon, locked the gate, and walked deliberately from the prison, and am now here to warn you, that unless a speedy retreat from this place, accomplished with silence and secrecy, be effected, we shall be a second time captured, and then, my life on't, we shall not escape them so easily."

"Meg," answered Bond, "but think you they have as yet discovered the fate of the turnkey? if so, why, we are indeed surrounded by danger. My appearance here was most providential, I discovered the treachery of one upon whom I placed great reliance; the villain was advising them all to share the booty and dissolve the band, and also openly declared, that had I not have been apprehended, he had intended to peach upon, and secure my capture himself. What think you of that?"

"Think," replied Meg, "why, that the traitor, whoever he may be, is deserving of a death of the worst possible description. But who is the villain, Captain Bond?"

"Dingy Bob," was the reply.

"I always suspected that fellow," muttered the gipsey. "Where is he now? safely confined and unable to escape?"

"He lies in an adjoining room," replied Bond, "dead—weltering in his blood

—I found it impossible to spare him after what I had heard; I therefore struck him to the ground, by dealing a heavy blow with the butt-end of one of my pistols, which, thanks be to your courage and perseverance, I once more gained possession of, and from which I will never more part."

"Now!" exclaimed Meg, "I should once more remind you that we are not in safety here; let's away to Polstead, a place where some of our band cannot go without enduring some of the pangs of conscience," and as the gipsey gave utterance to these latter words, she cast a meaning glance upon Martin, who appeared to wince beneath her penetrating gaze.

"By-the-bye, Robson," rejoined Bond, "what became of the party, through whose indirect agency I became a prisoner? Is she yet living? How came you to part company?"

"The least spoken upon that subject will best please some persons," resumed Meg, "but I wish we were now at Polstead: Captain Bond could there learn more of the fatal consequences brought upon a young and innocent female, whose only weakness and folly was in placing reliance upon the word of an unprincipled villain, whose only desire was to obtain a consummation of his wishes, then abandon the object of his infidelity and falsehood, to shame, disgrace, and even an untimely death. Let those whom it may concern, answer to this accusation if they can, or dare, and if not, acknowledge the justice of my accusation—another look was here cast towards Martin.

———

CHAPTER XXXI.

FULFILMENT OF THE PROPHECY.

HAVING spoken the words with which we concluded the twenty-eighth chapter, the girl opened the door, and a young man entered.

"A good evening to you, Maria!" he exclaimed; "what fear was it that prevented you from sooner giving me admission? Merciful Heaven!" he continued, upon noticing her agitation, which she vainly attempted to conceal. "What has alarmed you?"

"Nothing, Edward, nothing," was the reply.

"I see it all," answered Lambourne, "my presence here offends you; some other and more favoured lover, now enjoys that affection I had once hoped to possess—bitter are the trials for which I am now reserved, a dark cloud now hangs over my destiny; you, Maria, you alone can dispel it, and if you will not do this——"

"Edward!" exclaimed Maria, "you must not talk thus, 'tis improper, you know the strange veil of mystery, with which my birth was attended, and also that I have declared my resolution never to listen to the pleadings of love until that mystery shall be dispelled, therefore—"

"You do not love me," suggested Edward. "Oh! Maria, too well am I convinced of the fatal truth; but farewell, Maria, farewell, I see that my presence is hateful to you, I did not think so once—ah! footsteps approach—'tis your mother."

"Do not let her see you here," returned the girl, "the hour is late."

"Nay, Maria," returned Lambourne, "your mother is too well acquainted with my nature to harbour any unjust suspicion of my honour; she is here, I will open the door to her myself."

"Ah, Edward! you here? This is a late hour for courtship."

This was spoken by the mother of Maria as she entered.

"Mother," interposed Maria, "do not speak again upon that subject."

" And why not, my child ?"

" Because," replied the girl, after some hesitation, " it is a painful one."

" Hey dey," cried the old woman, " what's up now ? have you quarrelled ?"
Maria answered her not.

" Why do you not speak ?" enquired the mother.

" Because," replied Lambourne, " she cannot, but I will for her.   Yes," he
resumed, after a short pause, " for the first time you must know that Maria loves
me not."

" How is this ?" enquired the other in surprise.

" I know not," answered the disappointed lover, " but it is too true ; Maria
does not love me now, nor do I think she ever did so ; but good night, the hour
grows late, and you may want rest."

" Well, good night, Edward," rejoined the old lady, shaking him warmly by
the hand.   " Come, Maria," she continued, addressing her daughter, " light
Edward to the wicket, and in that time perhaps you may contrive to mix up
matters again.   Good night, Edward, good night—there – go along Maria, I
know you lovers are mightily pleased of your own company.   Ah, well, it's
natural ; I remember when I was a girl——"

The old lady was evidently about to commence a lengthy detail of the utmost
importance, which marked her courtship ; but as the young people evinced their
impatience, it was brought to a premature conclusion.   She, therefore, placed
a lighted candle, fixed in a bright metal candlestick, which, in former ages,
might have passed for silver, but now the hue was decidedly copperish.

With this candle Maria preceded Edward to the wicket, at which they had
scarce arrived, when a sudden gust of wind extinguished the light, and at the
same instant Maria half fancied that she could trace the dark outline of the gipsey
as it glided by——

" Maria!" exclaimed Edward, taking her warmly by the hand ; " now
answer me one question, and by that means, either confirm my happiness, or
from this moment make me for ever miserable.   Will you answer me one
question ?"

" I will," replied Maria.   " What is it ?"

" Do you love another ?"

" I do not," was the prompt reply.

" Then, why not, dear Maria, consent to render me the most happy of
men ? why not permit me to indulge in the hope, that we may one day be—"

" Hold !" cried Maria, with sudden energy ; " Edward, you must not question
me, leave me, in pity leave me, and for ever ; 'twill prevent much unhappiness
both to yourself and me."

" What means this ?" cried Edward, in an impassionate tone ; " do you not
hope, Maria, that one day our destiny may yet be joined ? that we may be happy
for ever ?   Will you consent ? say but one little word, 'tis all I require—when
shall we be——"

" Married ?" interrupted Maria.   " Never !" she resumed, in an impressive
tone.

" Caution !" muttered a deep voice, and as the words were borne upon the
air, Maria again fancied she could see the indistinct outline of a human form—she
shuddered slightly.

" What voice was that ?" exclaimed Edward, in surprise.

" I—I—know not," replied Maria.

" Perchance," continued Lambourne, " 'tis some sturdy rogue, who waits but
for silence, and the dark gloom of midnight, to carry into effect his felonious
intentions ; I'll after him, and should my conjectures prove correct, the stocks
shall be—"

" Oh, no—no, you must not stir," cried Maria, forcibly detaining him, as he
was about to dart off in the direction from which the sound appeared to proceed.

[*See Page* 54.]

"More mystery," cried Edward, looking upon Maria; "but 'tis plain—yes, Maria, I have now discovered the real cause of your disquietude at my presence; there is a rival in my path, but I rejoice at the discovery, for now there is an opportunity by which I may illustrate the love I bear you; his claim must, and shall be resigned; yes, Maria, or harm will come of it—aye, his blood or mine. Now, Maria, beware!"

"Edward," rejoined Maria, "you wrong me, and deeply; that was no man who spoke but now—no, as I hope to live."

"Who was it, then?" demanded Edward, impatiently.

"I must not, dare not tell," was the reply.

"And why not?" enquired the other, in astonishment.

"Because," replied the bewildered girl, "because my tongue—my power of utterance is bound—sealed to secrecy by a dreadful tie."

"'Tis useless attempting to deceive me farther by this weak subterfuge," returned Edward; "I will not, cannot believe you, Maria, I am assured 'tis not so —'tis false."

"What!" she cried, in a proud contemptuous tone; "accuse me, Maria, of falsehood! From this moment I command you never again to offend my ears with this hateful subject! Talk not to me of love, I will not hear it from you; turn your thoughts to some less obdurate fair, I am not the only girl in the village."

"I know it, Maria," rejoined Lambourne, in a sorrowful tone; "but you are the only one upon whom my future hope of happiness has long since been raised. To me, those cruel words are death; recal them, Maria, recal them. Upon my knees, I implore of you; the world may then buffet me. Blessed with the sweet smile of my Maria, my every wish will then be consummated."

"Once more, I command you to leave me," exclaimed Maria, as he again

No. 13.

vainly endeavoured to take her hand; "it is now growing late, and my mother is alone—good night."

"Good night," answered Edward, "if, indeed, we must part. So from this hour my nature is altered with my destiny; Maria, farewell."

The youthful pair then separated; Edward to his nightly ramble, and Maria to the presence of her mother.

Three days after the events above related, Maria was hastening to the farm of their landlord, in order to pay the rent due for their humble tenement. She crossed the extremity of a narrow lane, and was hastening onward, when a horse suddenly started before her, and she screamed with alarm; in an instant a young man of rather short stature, and very unprepossessing appearance, was by her side, and in a most tender manner enquired if she had sustained any injury, at the same time apologizing most humbly for the alarm he had caused her, and which he attributed solely to the restive disposition of his steed.

"I thank you, sir," replied Maria, in answer to his solicitations, "but, beyond fright, I do not imagine that the accident has been productive of any ill consequences; but I must on, for I have yet some considerable distance to go, and my mother is awaiting my return."

"Then," replied the horseman, "you shall go to the place of your destination upon the back of my horse, for those lovely feet were never formed for toil, and to tread the hard unyielding earth. Come, I will assist you to mount; you shall take your seat upon the saddle before me."

"I thank you, sir," replied Maria; "but I am a cottager's daughter, and unused to travel in any other manner than as a pedestrian."

"And what is your name, my pretty creature?" enquired the man; "you may think me inquisitive, but——"

"Oh, no, sir," answered the girl, "there is no secret in my name—'tis Maria Martin."

"And mine," rejoined the other, "is William Corder, son to a substantial miller, whose farm is scarce half-a-mile from this. You see I am candid, a further proof I will give you; I am in love."

"That, sir," rejoined Maria, "is a common circumstance."

"It is so," replied Corder, "you speak truly, dear girl, it is a common circumstance for one to be in love, but not with a creature so peerless and lovely as is the object of my adoration. Oh! she is an angelic being, a very Venus, of such exquisite form, such laughing eyes, and red pouting lips, and though her fine expressive features are clouded by a frown—though she may pass in silence by me—yet my very being is centered in her smiles; her presence is bliss to me. No danger is there I would not encounter, or suffering I would not endure to win her heart; yet I have never declared my passion, which, with pure and holy influence enslaves my mind, and in bondage holds my happiness. Oh! could I but snatch from her coral lips, one kiss, the wry world would be as dross to me; but, alas! I fear she loves another, and for me no hope dare be cherished—none."

"Surely, sir," answered the artless girl, blushing deeply, she knew not why, or wherefore. "Surely sir, if you was to declare your love to the lady, she would not, could not, be so cruel as to refuse the boon you would crave of her; or, if she did, then she must be a tyrant, and unworthy of your love. Who is this obdurate fair one, sir? I am impatient to learn her name."

"Caution!" muttered a deep voice, and at the same time the quickset hedge was slightly agitated, and the gipsey glided by. A slight shudder involuntarily passed through the whole frame of Maria.

"Who was it that spoke?" exclaimed Corder, after a pause. "Gracious Heaven!" h resumed, as he looked upon Maria, and observed her countenance to be blanched with fear. "What, dearest girl, has alarmed you? tell me who has dared —and if mortal——"

"Stay," cried Maria, catching his arm, as he moved in the direction taken by the gipsey; "you must not follow."

"Must not!" reiterated Corder, in astonishment; "and why must I not pursue the miscreant who has changed your face of joy to one of fear, and paralized your whole frame? Unhand me, she shall suffer, aye, and severely, for this daring insult; see, yonder she crosses by the copse, I may yet overtake her."

"Pshaw!" rejoined Maria, with a forced smile of gaiety; "what, pursue a wandering beggar. Now, sir," she continued, endeavouring to draw his attention from the gipsey. "May I make bold to enquire who this fair lady may be who has enslaved your heart?"

"You may, sweet girl, you may," replied Corder; "'tis your own dear self! Now, what say you? consent at once to render me the most happy of mortals —refuse, and by your own words, I proclaim you tyrant, and unworthy of my love."

Maria was evidently charmed by the flattering tongue of her admirer, and blushing deeply, she cast her eyes upon the ground.

"What say you, dearest?" rejoined William, after a pause.

"I must not tarry here longer," replied Maria; "I must pursue my journey, or my poor lone mother——"

"No more!" exclaimed Corder, interrupting her; "I will accompany you, stay but a moment, while I deliver my horse to the keeping of yonder aged cottager."

With these words he quitted the side of Maria in order to carry his resolution into effect.

No sooner was Maria alone, than she was startled by some person seizing her forcibly by the arm, and upon turning to discover who had done this, she, to her inexpressible astonishment, encountered the piercing glance of the gipsey, whose fine black penetrating eye was fixed upon her—for a moment both were silent, at length Maria broke the pause by exclaiming—

"Mysterious woman, why are you again here?"

"Have you forgotten what I foretold at the cottage of your mother, upon *that* night; did I not speak truly? Be warned in time. As I crossed yonder copse, I beheld your lover walking alone, dejected, and with folded arms."

"Who mean you?" demanded Maria. "I have no lover."

"No lover?' reiterated the sybil. "Who and what was he who spoke with you at the wicket as I retired? Does he not love you truly and sincerely?"

"I know not," rejoined Maria; "but leave me now."

"I will withdraw," replied the gipsey; "but listen. If you pass but one moment more in the company of him who but an instant since quitted your side, the *Gipsey's Warning* will once more be borne upon the slight breeze that now agitates the ribbon of your bonnet. Well, my child, would it be for you if I speak not in vain. Will you retire with me, and see this man—this prince of flatterers—no more?"

"Flatterer!" reiterated Maria. "How knew you the nature of his conversation? I saw you by the copse full half a mile hence."

"No matter," rejoined the gipsey; "will you accompany me?"

"No!" returned Maria, in a tone of resolution.

The gipsey then suddenly disappeared, and the next instant Maria was joined by Corder, who took her arm.

Here for a moment let us pause, in order, if possible, to meditate upon the mind of woman. We love—dearly love the sex in general; but there is *one* to whom and ourselves the passionate exclamation of Corder is nearly allied. Like him, too, we have loved long and hopelessly. The object of our love, alas! is a giddy, thoughtless maiden, who—but, pshaw! what hast thou to do, reader, with our love? Really, we are taking the most unlimited advantage of thy patience. Woman and her mind is a riddle; let him who may possess more brain than ourselves attempt to solve it. For our part we are content to crowd all sail in pursuit of Corder and Maria, who we find have proceeded full half a mile towards the maiden's abode.

"I must leave you now, sir," exclaimed Maria, as they entered the meadow adjoining the cottage of her mother.

"And why, dearest," replied Corder, passing his arm around her taper waist; "why leave me so soon?"

"I am near my mother's humble roof. See you that ivy-bound cottage through yonder elm-trees?" continued Maria, faintly struggling to disengage herself from him.

"Aye," replied Corder; "What of that?"

"That," rejoined Maria, "is the cottage."

"Before we part," continued Corder, "you must answer me one question. Can you—*will* you love me?"

"Sir!" exclaimed Maria.

"Nay, dearest," he returned, "do not obscure the beauty of those bright eyes by so dark a frown. The question is simple, and the answer should be suited to it. Come, speak; and with one little word, at once seal my happiness or eternal misery."

"I have known you but one short hour," replied Maria.

"And for that reason," rejoined Corder, reproachfully, "you would for ever blast my hopes. Oh, cruel girl! But I see you are impatient to be gone. Some favored lover awaits your coming: but search the world through, and none will you there encounter who can love you with half the true devotion—the smallest possible portion of that pure and undefiled flame that now burns with such unquenchable ardour in my breast. Farewell, and for ever!"

"What shall I do?" soliloquised Maria, as Corder quitted her side. "He surely loves me; yet the gipsey—her mysterious warning speaks the probability of approaching evil. Edward Lambourne, too! Oh, in what fearful mystery are all my future prospects buried!"

"So you would suffer me to quit you without a sigh!" exclaimed Corder, once more returning to the side of Maria. "Oh! how cruel is your sex. But I am now resolved that this moment shall decide my fate for ever. Maria Martin, do you love me? Pause well ere you answer; for should your reply be contrary to my hopes, this moment shall be the last of my stay upon earth."

"What mean you?" enquired Maria, trembling.

"That without your love," answered Corder, "my life would become a burthen too great to be borne. Maria, I love you to distraction; and cannot live to see you the wife of another, as I know you will be if I am rejected; therefore death shall end my sorrows—a suicide's grave shall close me from the world; and for you I die—upon your head rests the crime which I in moments of despair shall commit."

"Oh!" cried Maria, "talk not so: *I am yours for ever!*"

As the maiden unconsciously gave utterance to these words the gipsey's warning struck upon her ear, and like the solemn knell of death was received with terror. She saw that it was too late to recal them; remembered these to be the five words which were to complete the fate of Edward Lambourne. A tremor seized her limbs; her sight grew dizzy. She had fainted, and but for the timely aid of Corder, must have fallen to the earth. He caught her in his arms, and as he gazed upon the lovely and insensible burthen before him, imprinted one soft kiss, the first fond pledge of love and affection, upon her chaste and unresisting lips; this was happiness—bliss extatic!

CHAPTER XXXII.

WHEREIN MORTIMER MEETS WITH HIS DISCHARGE, AND BELFORD RECEIVES NOTICE TO QUIT.

ANY person or persons, who may in the progress of life have had any personal experience as to the ways and customs of an English place of confinement, taking for example the Penitentiary at Milbank, the New Prison, Clerkenwell, Bridewell, or any other such commodious mansions of mobility, may readily picture to their imagination what great changes would be wrought in the personal appearance of any individual who has passed any very lengthy extent of time within their dreary precincts; for to a small and insufficient share of food of the coarsest description, is added either close confinement in the pent-up and unwholesome atmosphere, or hard labour, that of itself is sufficient to reduce the performer to a state of weakness bordering upon childhood. Only one instance of the effects of confinement within a prison has ever come to our knowledge, and that was in the case of a person who had been thrown into the Fleet for debt; this, too, is the only place of confinement we have ever witnessed. What a picture of squalid wretchedness is there! in one corner, perhaps, you may see a man busily engaged in swallowing the contents of a small stone bottle, which has come into his possession a few moments since, through the agency of a kind friend or visitor. In another part you will see a pale, sickly individual seated upon an old ghost of a chair, (which has undergone the amputation of a leg and its bottom,) gnawing his digits, and looking wistfully upon the other, who is sitting opposite to him greedily devouring a scanty supper served up in a dingy, cracked basin, and a dropsical-looking saucer, in the centre of which there is a quaint design, representing a couple of lean and hungry-looking animals of the dog species hotly contending for the possession of a bone, which at present lays in a state of neutrality upon what was meant to represent the ground-work. Passing this spot, your next pause would be to observe a very tall, thin, and somewhat genteel-looking man, who is endeavouring to persuade himself into the belief that he is not in durance vile, but has absolutely commanded his servants not to suffer him to go forth; and by the self-approving manner in which he curls the youthful moustache that is struggling to fix its empire upon his upper lip, we should say that he has succeeded to a certain, or rather, uncertain extent. Look at his sallow cheek, sunken eyes, which have shrunk backwards into the sockets, as if with the intention of forming an immediate acquaintance with his brains. What a tale of dissipation does not his whole appearance bespeak! Look at his white hands and long taper fingers, upon one of which is placed a gaudy ring, the intrinsic value of which would not procure for him even a small portion of that food of which he stands so much in need. When he first became an inmate of his present place of abode, he possessed a suit of clothes, the quality of which was tolerably good, but one by one these soon disappeared, and now his present attire, a pair of threadbare trousers, an old waistcoat to match, and a gaudy dressing-gown, whose colours, through frequent visits to the isle of suds, had quitted their natural resting-place and started upon a voyage of discovery; these, together with an elderly pair of Wellington boots, possessing a very high polish and *low* heel, formed the whole stock of his worldly possessions, not forgetting, however, an old pair of white kid gloves that contained at least half-a-dozen places of entry for the hands of their owner; yet this man appeared happy except at irregular intervals, when he would suddenly come to a pause, pass his hand over his fevered brow, move his parched lips, then start from his gloomy trance, as though his imagination had pictured the approach of some new catchpole, about to present him with the never-to-be-forgotten or sufficiently-appreciated shoulder-tap.

There are instances upon record, where a man upon receiving his discharge, has died from very grief at having been discarded from the only society for which, through long alienation from the world, he was a fitting member. Once confined within the walls, a man is seldom won again into the honest and useful circle of society. The bare thought of his previous disgrace too often proves a barrier to his future welfare; and those who, for some trivial offence, are classed with the common and convicted felon, are by them initiated into the malignant workings of crime, and hence an ignominious sentence and banishment often terminates that career which otherwise would have been marked with honest industry.

How many dreary nights and lonely hours must Mortimer have passed during the long period of his captivity, and what more would he not have endured had the original sentence of transportation been carried into effect; as it was, a settled gloom filled his mind, and after a few years became as it were wedded to his new and somewhat novel mode of life; for though nearly every grade of society have, from time to time, graced the interior of our prison-houses, yet we dare be sworn that the incarceration of a baronet is a somewhat uncommon occurrence. Twenty years had transformed the dashing young advocate of fashion into a care-worn, decrepit old man. Though his age, even then, did not exceed forty, yet the great vicissitudes under which he had laboured had tended greatly to reduce him to a frightful state of debility.

None but those who have been in a similar situation can even imagine the sensation produced upon the mind of Mortimer, when, after a captivity of twenty years, he was one morning presented with a small slip of paper, upon opening which he discovered it to be a written order for his discharge. The paper fell from his hand, and had he not have sank upon a dilapidated chair, which, together with an iron bedstead, formed the only furniture of his dreary apartment, he would have fallen to the ground, such was the effect of this long wished for yet unexpected news; he, however, was not long afterwards before he availed himself of the happy opportunity of quitting a place in which for years he had seen nothing but black walls and stony-hearted gaolers. Accompanying the discharge was a note, requesting him to call at No.`—, Portman-square, which, as the reader will doubtless remember, was the residence of our new-found friend the antiquarian. Mortimer was at a loss as to whom he had to thank for his liberation, or even who was the author of the invitation which accompanied it; thinking, however, that by complying with the instructions contained, some clue might be had to the mystery that at present perplexed him. Upon arriving at the residence of the antiquarian he was immediately ushered into that individual's presence, where, to his utter astonishment, he beheld Belford seated. Immediately upon his entrance that individual rose and shook him warmly by the hand, and complimented him upon his enfranchisement.

" I join with you upon that theme," responded the old man.

" For which accept my warmest thanks," replied Mortimer; " though," he continued, " I am as yet in ignorance as to whom I have to thank for the great and essential service that has been rendered me."

" Did you know who he was," exclaimed the antiquarian, " what would be your first action, if you stood in his presence this moment ?"

" I should consider him as the preserver of my life, and, if possible, find words to express my gratitude for the same."

" That," replied the other, " he would consider to be an insult."

" How is this!" exclaimed Mortimer, in unfeigned astonishment. " Are you, sir, then acquainted with this noble-minded and benevolent person, through whose disinterested friendship I have regained that liberty which is far dearer than life ?"

" I am acquainted intimately with him."

" Indeed; then you, sir, can perhaps inform me of the motives which prompted him to render me so great a service ?"

" I can. Think not that it was the severity of your sentence which prompted him. No; for had its nature have been threefold more harsh, he would have scorned the thought of alleviating that punishment, which, as a firm friend to justice, he would have considered as your just reward. 'Twas not that which caused him to bless the influence he possessed, and by which means alone he was enabled to obtain your discharge. Though criminal in the eyes of the law, he considered you to have been the unsuspecting dupe to the ways and devices of a villain, by whose instrumentality alone you had been first reduced to beggary and disgrace, and afterwards to the commission of that capital offence which led to your incarceration. To rescue an unwilling culprit, one who had as it were involuntarily plunged into the abyss of guilt, was his only thought—the rest is known to yourself."

"There is yet one thing more I would learn," resumed the newly-liberated baronet, "that is, where I may encounter this truly philanthropic individual; but tell me that, and——'

"Have done with protestations; behold him here before you. I am he," said the old man, while a gleam of self-approbation momentarily illumined his furrowed countenance.

Upon learning this, Mortimer would have thrown himself at the feet of his deliverer but the other commanded him, upon pain of his displeasure, to cease all thanks.

"I was once," he said, "a constant attendant at court. I rendered my king an especial service, in return for which he presented me with a jewel from off his royal person, and commanded me, that whenever I might have an important boon to crave, I should present that before him, when it should be immediately granted. I never had occasion to use it for my own necessities, and thus was enabled to reserve it to a good end; and could I but discover the villain who was the cause of your difficulties, the same interest which enabled me to take you *from*, should be used to send him to a gaol. However, time, in its never-varying course, will overtake the rascal, and his punishment will only be made the more severe by long protraction. But, come, sir," he continued, addressing Mortimer, "be seated; in a few moments we shall have the luncheon before us; here, take this chair by me."

Mortimer did as he was desired, and in a few moments afterwards the old man's words were verified, for the man-servant entered, bearing with him the usual paraphernalia of a dinner-table, which being disposed of according to his, the servant's, idea of propriety, he withdrew, and in an instant more returned heavily laden with a large sample of dinner-trays, which was groaning loudly beneath the weight of an heterogeneous collection of boiled pork and rabbit, roasted fowl, onion sauce, potatoes, puddings, tarts, bread, and many other articles of human consumption, which were removed to the table, the plates, &c. arranged for execution. The antiquarian appeared to possess a very sharp appetite, for he partook plentifully of every thing the table afforded, and that largely. Mortimer also took a prominent feature in the affray, and Belford was not far behind. The table was soon cleared, and the wine substituted; the conversation then turned upon the discipline of prisons, and from that Belford's name was brought into mention, though as yet Mortimer knew not of the enmity that was supposed to exist between them.

"By the bye," exclaimed Mortimer, "how long is it since you visited Lady Mandeville, Belford?"

"*Belford!*" exclaimed the antiquarian, dropping the glass he had raised to his mouth; "and can it be possible that I have been induced to keep a moment's acquaintance with that scoundrel! Here, John, Thomas—every body come up here, and assist me to kick this scoundrel from my house." As he said this, the bell-rope was agitated with a violence that threatened to bring it from the place from which it was suspended. A moment afterwards the room was filled with the servants, male and female. Mortimer rose from his seat in astonishment, and looked from one to the other in complete wonder; and, addressing the old gentleman, exclaimed,

" In the name of heaven, sir, what is the meaning of this ?"

" Meaning !" reiterated the other; " why, this is the villain through whose agency an innocent man has been brought into disgrace and suffering.   Out with him !   Kick him from the house !"

Obedient to the commands of their master, the servants simultaneously rushed upon Belford, and bore him to the door; and though he struggled violently against his assailants, still it was useless.   They bore him from the apartment, and thrust him down the stairs; and concluded their very interesting performance by ejecting him with the greatest violence from the house, the door of which was immediately closed upon him.

Shortly afterwards, the antiquarian summoned one of his domestics into his presence, and enquired if his commands had been strictly observed; and receiving an answer in the affirmative, he then charged the man never again to admit Belford within his doors " for," said he, turning to Mortimer, " I verily believe, that though I have thus got clear of him, yet he possesses a sufficient share of impudent assurance to repeat the visit."

Half an hour after the above command had been given, the old gentleman was presented with a note, as follows :—

" OLD ANTIQUITY,—You have thought fit to insult me; therefore, if you do not apologise, I demand the satisfaction of a gentleman and a man of honour. My friend, the bearer of this, will arrange the necessary preliminaries.

                                             " BELFORD."

Having read this epistle, the old gentleman handed it to Mortimer, and then enquired if the man was below, and received an answer in the affirmative.

" Then treat him in a manner precisely the same as you did his friend," was the reply; and for this gentleman, Belford," he continued, " the interior of a dungeon shall cool his courage, and that, too, speedily."

CHAPTER XXXIII.

THE RIVALS.

" *There's a divinity shapes our ends,*
Rough hew them how we will."—SHAKSPERE.

UPON recovering from the fit of insensibility into which she had fallen, Maria Martin proceeded with her new-found lover onwards in the direction of the cottage, and walked on at a slow and measured pace until they arrived in sight of the wicket that opened into her mother's garden.   Maria then paused, and informed Corder that he must leave her.

" And why so, dearest girl," enquired he.

" Because, sir," replied Maria, trembling as she spoke; " because my mother may chance to see you here."

" And even should she do so," returned Corder, " I am here by your own consent, and that circumstance alone must and would silence her murmurings; but I must see the good dame."

" Oh ! no, no," cried Maria, " you must not; my mother would——"

" Why do you raise objections at each new stratagem or proposal I make ?" again interrupted Corder.   " If you——"

" I will tell you," replied Maria.   " My mother would have me wed another; nay, she thinks I shall do so; but I would perish—die, rather than that should come to pass."

" May I ask the name of this favoured one ?" enquired Corder.

" His name," replied Maria, " is *Edward Lambourne.*"

[See Page 61.]

Corder bit his nether lip in evident confusion upon hearing this, and then turning to Maria, exclaimed,

" I have no fear of success, then, if he is my rival in love. Why, Edward Lambourne is but a peasant, a poor needy fellow without a single acre, while I am son to a rich miller; aye, and his only son too: think you, then, that I do not possess a claim to your heart above him?"

" My mother will not think so," rejoined Maria.

" She knows not the superior advantage that will follow," rejoined Corder, she knows not that I am wealthy, and that this Edward Lambourne is but a beggar."

" Even then," rejoined Maria, " her heart would give preference to Edward ; we have been children together, play'd upon the same green together, eaten our daily bread from the same table, learned the first rudiments of scholastic duty from the same book. The children grew to years of maturity ; the friendship of companions changed to the fiery and uncontroulable passion of fierce love on the part of Edward. I strove to return it, but the effort was vain."

" Then what more is required to convince you ?" returned Corder, " you endeavoured to fix your attentions upon that man—you could not succeed, it was contrary to the direct usage of nature—fate had willed it otherwise—this shown to your mother, dear Maria, she must grant an immediate consent to our wishes."

" Never !" rejoined Maria, " my mother has oft assured me, none but Edward Lambourne shall call me wife, even if——"

" Nay," exclaimed Corder, " I think you much wrong your mother's kindly nature—much. I think from your previous statement of her kindness, she loves you too well and strongly. Once convince her that this man is your aversion. and, trust me, she will accede to all : this Edward Lambourne is but a portionless upstart beggar."

" Liar !" vociferated a loud voice, and upon turning to discover the new comer, Corder recognized the object of their conversation standing pale and agitated.

No. 14.

"Now, wretch!" he exclaimed, eyeing the other fiercely, "what have you to say in disparagement to the character and bearing of Edward Lambourne? he is here to defend himself from all the malicious falsehoods which you have promulgated against him.

"Rash beggar," vociferated Corder, "leave us, or by the power that formed us, the consequence will be fatal to one or both. Leave this spot instantly—your presence is unneeded."

"And who, sir, possessed you with the power to tell me that my presence here was unneeded?" demanded Lambourne; "and as for 'beggar,' perhaps if some persons possessed their just and lawful rights, Edward Lambourne might then be enabled to exchange terms with the rich miller's son, who can now boast of the—"

"What and who do you mean?" interrupted Corder.

"William Corder! the man now standing before me," replied Lambourne, "aye, and well does he know to what I allude, or if he does not, perhaps, if the——"

"Silence!" vociferated Corder, in evident agitation. "Dare but [to breathe one word more upon that subject, and I dash out your brains upon the earth: beware then!"

"Pshaw, man," replied the other; "you grow hot and choleric; be cautious, or in one of those fits of rage you will commit some grievous injury—one not to be repaired."

"Take care, then," rejoined the other, "that you are not the first object."

"Me!" reiterated Lambourne, in a slightly sarcastic tone, "you forget in your vauntings, good Master Corder, to whom it is you speak; that there is one before you who is every way your superior both in strength, science, and stature; but I do not wish to quarrel—no, resign Maria to my care—I can resign her into the arms of her mother. The *rash beggar* here possesses a material advantage of the rich miller's son. Come, Maria, I will conduct you within the cottage."

"She quits not my side," retorted Corder, fiercely.

"That," replied Lambourne, mildly, "can be settled in a more friendly and decisive manner; let the girl decide whether she will remain here, exposed to the danger of your villainous arts, or come with me to her mother's hearth. All contention may then be avoided, and the rejected one may retire. Now, Maria, answer me truly; will you accompany me, or remain here in the company of this man, whom until the last hour you knew not? Remember that by consenting to his request you expose yourself to much danger, and deprive yourself of all assistance in case of need; make free prey of your charms to any violence he may be disposed to offer. Once speak the fatal word, and to retract will be impossible, even though you should desire so to do; therefore, speak freely, girl, for though my heart throbs for you alone, still I would not thwart your inclination or desire."

"Nor shall you, sir," interposed Corder, "while I am here to prevent it. Now, Maria, speak freely."

After a momentary pause, Maria was about to comply with the last request when the *Gipsey's Warning* was once more heard by all; but to Maria it fell like a thunderbolt upon the air.

"This is some plan—some villainous scheme," cried Corder, "that voice is meant to intimidate the girl; you, sir," he continued, addressing Lambourne, "you are a scoundrel and a coward."

"William Corder!" vociferated Edward, with forced composure, "I would not willingly harm you; and, for the love of mercy, do not repeat those words; they hiss and scald my throat like molten lead falling upon a surface of water. You know my temper, and I again implore—humbly pray of you not to torture me thus."

"Peace," thundered Corder, "I defy you, coward as you are."

"Nay, then," rejoined Lambourne, "look well to yourself."

With these words he rushed upon Corder, and a fearful struggle ensued; but it was of short duration, the superior skill and strength of Lambourne soon triumphed, and Corder was thrown heavily to the earth: he, however, instantly regained his feet; and unclasping a large knife which he took from his pocket, he was about to plunge the blade into the back of his antagonist, when he received a violent blow upon the head; a cloth was suddenly thrown over his face, and thus he was hurried away. Edward Lambourne was surprised beyond measure at this, and strove in vain to think how this unexpected circumstance, and the unexpected disappearance of his rival had been effected. His astonishment, however, increased when he discovered himself to be alone. Even Maria had vanished !

CHAPTER XXXIV.

BELFORD'S FLIGHT TO FRANCE.

BELFORD's messenger, after having been served with an ejectment, hurried to the residence of his friend, burning with rage, and well nigh exploding with mortification.

"How did they receive my note ?" enquired Belford, as he entered.

"That is a question which I am unable to answer; but I know how I was treated, full well."

"And how was that ?" enquired Belford.

"A forcible ejection from the house," replied the other; but I will be revenged upon the old coward—I'll send him a challenge, and compel him to fight for his life."

"That you are perfectly welcome to do," answered Belford, "but let me have a shot at him first. However, let us have done with this, I am this day going to dine with Mrs. Major Turnbull, by previous appointment; will you accompany me, she has a couple of devilish fine looking daughters, and I have no doubt but that you will mix up matters with one of them : what say you ? shall I have the pleasure of announcing you as an intimate friend? Come, no hesitation, say yes."

Thus importuned the gentleman did say yes, and meant it too; inasmuch as for the three previous weeks a good dinner and himself had not even come in contact; therefore, he looked upon this proposal as a special interposition of Providence; though, if called upon to express our opinion, we should most certainly say that Providence, in general, has very little to do with cooking dinners; however, as that must remain undecided, we will merely proceed to state that both Belford and his friend proceeded forthwith to the residence of Mrs. Major Turnbull and her fair daughters, where, after they had swallowed a hearty dinner, and afterwards discussed the merits of sundry glasses of wine, they withdrew to the gaming table, Belford having previously borrowed the sum of five pounds from Mrs. Major Turnbull for the express purpose of testing his fortune at play—from which alone he now gained the means of sustenance, and indeed all the cash he ever possessed.

Upon their arrival at the table, Belford encountered one of his early dupes, with whom he soon entered into conversation, and shortly afterwards they sat down to play, when Belford, as he usually did, won the whole of his cash, the amount of which was between eight and ten pounds. The other having imbibed more wine than a young gentleman under twenty should do, grew warm, and waxed wrath; the consequence of which was that a quarrel ensued, when Belford, presuming upon his well-known skill and notoriety as a duelist, openly challenged any of the company present to a hostile meeting; his challenge was immediately accepted by one Captain Fletcher, a man who was in every way (villainny not excepted), his equal. The preliminaries were settled upon the spot and four o'clock the following morning was appointed for the time, and an old billiard room above the one in which they then were, for the place of meeting. The room was twenty yards in length, and therefore ample space would be afforded for the use of the small-sword, which were the weapons named. They remained at play until the time had arrived, and then adjourned to the rendezvous where the weapons had been previously placed in readiness for them. For several moments each preserved his first position, they then fell upon guard, and Belford made a plunge at the left side of his opponent, which was skilfully parried, and, instantly recovering his position, his blade made a slight incision in the sword arm of Belford. This irritated him, and they then went more earnestly to work. At length, after much parrying upon both sides, the contest was brought to a termi- nation, by the sword of Belford making an entry at the fore, and an exit at the aft part of his adversary's body. He immediately fell to the ground, a dead man. A surgeon was immediately sent for, and upon his arrival informed them of what they were already aware, viz., that he was dead.

Upon being convinced of this, Belford immediately set about devising some scheme by which he might secure his own personal safety, for he felt well convinced that there were many who would eagerly catch at this opportunity whereby they might

"feed fat the ancient grudge they bore him,"

and surrender him unto the official powers. After much thought and plotting, he determined upon securing an early passage to France; accordingly he hastened to London bridge, and, luckily for him, there was a packet ready to sail at the next high water. He returned home, and packed up a few necessary articles of wearing apparel in a carpet-bag, then returned, and in a short time afterwards he was upon his way to the land of Frogs and French men.

While Belford was contemplating a safe arrival in France, his friend had penned and despatched a challenge to the antiquarian, which challenge that gentleman, by the advice of Mortimer, who, since the period of his enlargement, had been a constant visitant—accepted, and appointed a place and time for meeting, which time, in the due progress of events, arrived; and they, upon their entering the ground, discovered that the opposite party were awaiting their coming.

" Now, sir !" exclaimed the antiquarian, " are you prepared to receive the satis- faction you have desired at my hands ?"

" I am," was the reply, " but as yet I have seen no weapons."

" That has been cared for," rejoined the other, " behold it here in the form of a good stout horse-whip !"

With these words he seized him by the collar and inflicted several severe strokes upon his body, which strokes caused him, after a little vain resistance, to roar most lustily for mercy, and the old gentleman, having exhausted his strength, at length released his hold with one cutting conclusion of the castigation he had inflicted.

" Now !" he exclaimed, " this, I trust, will serve as a warning for you, and prevent you daring to insult gentlemen by presuming to send challenges. Had I thought fit to have met you upon an equality, I could have sent a bullet through your very eye—always know your men before you venture to insult them. Now, if your friend should feel himself insulted, I can supply him with the same satisfaction I have administered to you."

He looked round, but the fellow had vanished. Having now concluded this novel mode of duelling, both he and Mortimer quitted the ground together, leaving the discomfited friend of the fugitive count, to cogitate upon the Hercu- lean strength of his adversary, and the stoutness of his whip. A few moments after they had disappeared, the valorous friend of Belford's friend rejoined him, and they quitted the place in company with each other. Thus terminated the *Antiquarian's Duel!*

CHAPTER XXXV.

WILLIAM CORDER.

UPON quitting the side of Maria, Meg hastened to join Captain Bond, and requested him to accompany her, together with the lieutenant, and some two or three of the men. Bond did not enquire for what service they were required, but instantly proceeded to comply with her request. She led them through the meadow, and, upon perceiving Corder and Maria still engaged in close conversation, she commanded them to retire into the nearest hiding-place; but be prepared to join her upon hearing a preconcerted signal—this they did.

Meg having disposed of them, still followed the footsteps of the others, until the moment when Corder was confronted with Lambourne. Her it was who uttered the watch word that so terrified Maria. Immediately upon the commencement of the quarrel she summoned the highwaymen to her aid, and as Corder was about to strike his rival with the knife, her cloak was thrown over his head—the butt end of one of Bond's pistols dealt him a violent blow—and he was forced off by the band, who bore him nearly half a mile from the spot, then blindfolded and bound him to a tree. While they were thus employed, Meg had also borne Maria away to the cottage of her mother, and there left her with a parting admonition to *caution*.

Since the period when she first became acquainted with Corder, a marked alteration had taken place in the personal appearance of Maria—an alteration that did not escape the observation of her mother, who questioned her closely as to the cause, but without the desired effect: she could glean no satisfactory clue to the mystery which evidently guided the actions and manners of her daughter, for Maria feared to inform her of the attachment that existed between herself and Corder, for she well knew that none but the fond and doting Edward Lambourne would ever gain admittance to the cottage as her suitor; and she had now fixed her heart upon Corder; not that she believed him faultless, or admired his disposition; no, her share of penetration convinced her that Edward was highly superior to the other in personal acquirements, for though Corder was in reality what he boasted himself to be, the son of a rich miller, yet his mind was as uncultivated as the most needy peasant, whose life had been passed at the plough. Like most money-getting men, he was illiterate and ignorant, even to a fault, and possessed, beside, a great share of that unenviable material usually styled low cunning, by which means, however, the possessor can oftimes live in affluence, where a strictly honourable man would perish. This disposition was greatly displayed when he first boasted to Edward of his position in the world—a position which was only acquired in former times in a very equivocal manner.

It was the knowledge of this circumstance that caused Lambourne to allude to the subject of right, and which so enraged the other; and had Corder but have known what was passing in the mind of Maria when the boast was made, he would have surrendered all, could he but have possessed the power of recalling it. She could not but entertain a disgust at the unmanly feelings that prompted Corder to allude in such vaunting terms of the superiority of fortune he possessed over his rival. At that moment Edward Lambourne, though he had been a penniless beggar, was far more estimable in her opinion than the wealthy miller's son, and yet she would suffer him to be insulted—stand by, a passive observer of that scene, which, but for the machinations of the gipsey, must have terminated in the death of Lambourne. As we have stated upon a previous occasion, woman and her mind is a riddle, for, after the admonitory warnings she had received, and her own personal experience of the character of him to whom she so soon and willingly surrendered her heart, one would have been led to imagine that Maria had been so convinced of the superior worth of Lambourne, that by doubling her attention to him, she would have endeavoured to make some recompense for the former agony of mind she had caused. Despite her veneration for the character and disposition of Edward, she yet, through some undefined motive, gave to Corder the preference.

Being unable to obtain any decisive knowledge concerning the cause of her altered daughter's gloom, the mother of Maria resolved when she quitted the cottage, as was her usual custom under pretence of walking through the meadow with Edward, to follow and observe her closely. She did so, and to her unspeakable astonishment, discovered her to be walking and apparently engaged in earnest conversation with a stranger. Upon first seeing this she was at a loss how to act; her first impulse was to confront them, and she had already proceeded towards carrying this design into effect, when, upon more mature deliberation, she altered her determination, and contented herself, for that night at least, with watching their footsteps. She did so, and the result was that she followed them until they reached the RED BARN! here they paused, and a moment afterwards resumed their way towards the cottage. Half an hour afterwards, Maria returned in high spirits and more cheerful than she had been for many previous days. This alteration, however, instead of increasing, greatly depressed her mother's pleasure, for she augured no good from her sudden preference to a stranger whose personal appearance seemed to her Argus eyes to be an index to villainny. Not choosing to question Maria upon the subject, she despatched a note to the residence of Corder (for the whole family were well known to her), requesting him to favour her with a call upon the ensuing evening; and the messenger shortly returned with an answer signifying his promise so to do; and precisely at the time appointed he passed through the wicket and entered the cottage, where he discovered Maria busily engaged with her spinning-wheel Upon his entrance she blushed deeply, and, rising, quitted the room in evident confusion. Corder and her mother were then alone.

"I have sent for you, sir," began the good dame, "in consequence of having seen you and Maria in company with each other. Now that we are alone, I would ask what are your intentions towards her? if anything else but honourable I would have you beware, for though I am both poor and defenceless, yet Maria possesses friends who both have the means and the disposition to punish with the utmost severity any one who shall dare to harm or mislead her; though no other scene than that of humbleness and poverty has marked her progress to the estate of womanhood, yet she will one day be upon an equality with the highest; if, then, you would make her your lawful wife, and she consent, I am willing also; but if, upon the other hand, you are only endeavouring to betray the confidence she may place in you, remember my words, her fall will not be unrevenged!"

"I should merit all the punishment that could be bestowed, aye, and much more," replied Corder, "if I could deal with falsehood when a being of such simplicity and loveliness is concerned. No; I love Maria fervently and truly, and, with your consent, will make her my wife, though I have heard that her heart is already engaged to Edward Lambourne; but then he is poor and portionless."

"And though he should be so," answered the old lady, "yet, in my humble estimation, he is far preferable to many whose more affluent position in society arms with the power to treat with duplicity those whom they imagine are beneath them. Edward Lambourne is a worthy young man, and one, too, who I am convinced would make a good husband."

"Think you not, good dame, that there are others equally worthy? I am as well disposed towards Maria as he can possibly be."

"I rejoice to hear it," replied the other, "if Maria has fixed her heart upon you, and you your's upon her, it would be cruel of me to oppose your love for each other, therefore you are free to visit her here from this moment."

Corder was profuse in his thanks, and Maria was then summoned in by the old lady. She entered, casting a timid glance upon Corder, who advanced to receive her hand.

"Maria!" exclaimed the old lady, "Mr. Corder has openly declared the exact nature of his intentions towards you; I have given my consent to his visiting you; and, since Edward Lambourne can no longer be admitted as your suitor, you had better acquaint him with your preference to another."

"Nay," interposed Corder, "the task is unfitting a maiden's gentle nature; this Lambourne will soon perceive the altered nature of Maria's sentiments towards him; this of itself will be sufficient to convince him that his presence has become irksome, he will then relinquish all thought of her."

"Not so, sir, replied the old lady, "you know but little of the nature and disposition of Edward Lambourne, if you think that he could so soon smother the love he bears towards Maria, and which, to speak in an open and candid manner, I wish she had returned, for though poor, Edward would have rendered her happy: and for money, why that would have been no obstacle; for had Maria been wedded to him, there would have been that forthcoming upon her bridal day, that would have astonished some folks, and have placed her in comfortable circumstances for life. But as the old proverd says—'as she sows so must she reap;' for though I do not intend to act in opposition to her wishes, but, since she has blighted my hopes and expectations, I shall withhold what would have otherwise been her's. You will excuse an old woman's prejudice, sir," she continued, addressing Corder, "but I have so long been accustomed to look upon Edward Lambourne as the destined husband of my child, that I cannot but feel, and keenly, the concern this unexpected disappointment has filled me with; but she has chosen you, take her from my hands, and may she never have cause to repent of this alteration in her destiny."

With these words, the old woman, her eyes filled with tears, joined together in the bonds of love, the hands of William Corder and Maria Martin!

CHAPTER XXXVI.

DEATH OF THE ANTIQUARIAN.

As time progressed, Sir Charles became a more confirmed favourite with the antiquarian, whose health was now rapidly declining. He permitted Mortimer to rule over the house and domestics as absolute lord and master, and all were taught to revere a command once uttered by him as law. In this manner, many months passed away, and, during the interval, the old gentleman's health gradually declined, not through any disease, bodily or otherwise, but through the course of nature, his age being upwards of four score years. At length his debility so increased that he was no longer enabled to quit his bed. While in this state he despatched a letter to Wiltshire, requesting his neice, who was there in the capacity of companion to one of his, the antiquarian's maiden sisters, to return to London, and tend him in his last moments, as he believed himself to be on his death-bed. The result of this letter was that five days afterwards his neice arrived, and in her Mortimer beheld a young and lovely maiden of twenty-one, whose person was above the middle stature, and whose countenance beamed with lovliness and simplicity. Immediately upon her arrival, she was conducted to the chamber were her uncle was confined; and, after the old man had bestowed his blessing upon her, he enquired if she had any lover to share her love and attentions. To this inquiry she immediately and without hesitation replied in the negative.

"Then," rejoined the old gentleman, I shall die happy. "Flora," he resumed, addressing his neice, "you have, of course, observed that gentleman who has just quitted the apartment," (alluding to Mortimer).

" I did, dear uncle," was the reply, " but what of him ?"

" What of him !" reiterated the old man, in a low tone, " listen, Flora, he is the scion of a noble house, but through the villainny of a certain count, for whom he once entertained a regard, he has endured much unmerited, much harsh, and even cruel treatment. He is the son of a baronet, and yet has for twenty years been confined in the society of felons, who have not, however, succeeded in corrupting his noble nature; in short, he has been a victim to the ways and acts of wordly-minded and profligate men."

" But why did he mingle with them ?" mildly suggested Flora, " surely they did not force him to join their company."

" You speak rightly," rejoined the antiquarian, " they did not, but unfortunately, in his more inexperienced age, he became addicted to gaming, an evil propensity which usually carries with it its own punishment ; for those who follow it closely seldom escape from its snares until their ruin is completed This was his case precisely ; he there claimed acquaintance with a man whom his father spurned as a common gamester, and informed his son that he must either forfeit the companionship with his new found accomplice, or abjure his right to enter his paternal home ; and the young baronet being of a proud and haughty spirit, unfortunately held the friendship of a sharper in greater estimation than the society of his father, and was discarded accordingly. A few months served to accomplish his ruin ; he then sank, step by step, from his former position in society ; all his real friends forsook him ; and, at length, he found himself a prisoner in the dull and gloomy interior of Newgate. He is now here as my friend ; 'twas by my influence alone that he obtained his discharge - I am now upon my death-bed, Flora, listen to my last request, will you comply with it ?"

" I will," replied Flora, " if, indeed, it be within the compass of my ability so to do."

" My wish, then, will be complied with, and I shall die happy ; Flora I would see you the lawful wedded wife of that man."

" Uncle !" exclaimed the young lady in evident astonishment, " have you forgotten that we are strangers ; nay, have not as yet exchanged a dozen words with each other : even supposing that I should be inclined to accede to your wishes, you seem to have forgotten that he may be averse to the match ; and you, surely, would not consign your friend to aught against which his will may revolt ; or, if you would do so——"

" I would not," replied the old man, interrupting her, " I will be first convinced of his own idea upon the subject ; but I have now broached the offer to you, being willing to know whether you will obey my request should I make it known in his presence. What say you, my child, will you do as I now solicit ?"

" I have known your friend for so brief a period," replied Flora ; " yet, should I discover in him any of the virtues you have described, I will willingly obey you—that is, if I find it to be his request."

This assurance appeared to satisfy the invalid. He next requested her to agitate the communicator—that is, to pull a large rope that hung by the fire-place, and which led to a young army of cranks, which, in their turn, claimed consanguinity with a few miles of wire, to which was attached a large bell, which bell summoned a dropsical-looking lady—age doubtful ! whose chief propensities was the art of imbibing gin, and converting her nasal organ into a snuff box. This ponderous specimen of woman was designated the nurse. We trust the reader will not imagine her to be the immaculate Mrs. Johnson, for she, since her lord and master had been anchored safe in the harbour of sickness, had been appointed cordial mixer and taster in ordinary. Now, the antiquarian, though different from the majority of mankind in every other particular, perfectly agreed with them upon one subject, and that one happened, unluckily for Mrs. Johnson, to be the idea, that brandy was good in barley-water or porridge—we say this was unluckily for Mrs. Johnson, because there are many envious persons in the world—old women for instance, who may be jealous of her virtues (?) who would be inclined to intimate, that as Mrs. Johnson invariably felt funny, or as some persons would say—fuddled, after tasting and manufacturing the said cordial, that she imbibed large quantities of the same; and they may actually imagine that we are of a corresponding opinion, as we have placed the tasting first, and manufacturing afterwards, which seems to imply that some of the said brandy was purloined first; but this we positively declare to have been impossible, for Mrs. Johnson's sense of right and wrong would prevent her appropriating to herself any portion of the property of her master; for, doubtless, she was equally as honest as the whole race of nurses, who never steal anything (that is placed beyond their reach); therefore, it must have been the intense heat of the fire that obtained an ascendancy over her mental weakness.

The nurse entered the room as the bell replied to the tug by a low tingle, and has actually been standing waiting for orders while we have been applauding her race.

"Let Mr. Mortimer be sent to me!" exclaimed the old gentleman.

The woman curtsied and withdrew. In a moment afterwards Mortimer entered the chamber of the invalid.

"Mortimer!" exclaimed the antiquarian; "I have sent for you here, in order to settle, if possible, a rather tender and somewhat difficult subject. I am now upon my death-bed. Nay, my dearl girl," he resumed, addressing his neice, in whose eye might be traced a solitary tear; "do not grieve for my lot—'tis the fate of all human beings, I shall soon be far from hence; and remember, I now am about to give utterance to my last earthly wish."

"Mortimer, you have long since been my only friend and companion. My neice here, I have summoned from the country, in order that I may propose a plan, which, if carried into execution, will be productive of comfort and happiness to you both. Flora is aware that I have amassed a considerable deal of property, and also have upwards of five thousand pounds in the Bank of England, together with two fifty pound shares in one of the principal coal mines in the North of England. I have no relations to whom I can bequeath it, save my neice, here. You are one of the very few men that, in the course of my earthly experience, I have found to possess a truly honourable and candid disposition; therefore, can appreciate so rare a commodity as honesty when I chance to encounter it. The proposal I have to make is this: my neice is single, and your junior by years, I have long wished to discover some person to whom I could safely confide the happiness of so valuable a charge—you are the man upon whom I have fixed as her future husband. Now say, are you willing to accept her hand, and the property thereunto belonging? remember, you are free to choose, but if my offer is accepted, I shall expect that the conditions of my will be fully carried into effect. Are you prepared to consent or refuse?"

"I, sir, am too grateful for the honour you would confer upon me, by uniting my fate with a being so lovely, to refuse. But does the lady consent to accept me for her husband?"

"That has already been decided," replied the dying antiquarian; "and now, my children, leave me, I am not long for this world, and would fain snatch a few hours of repose ere I quit the scene of life for ever. I have much more to communicate, but will defer it until to-morrow."

"To-morrow! what an ocean of time does that seem to those who await in anxiety its arrival; how soon does it pass when the condemned criminal, though securely lodged within the dark precincts of a gaol, awaits with horrible suspense, the dawn of another day, upon which he is to be brought upon a scaffold—the gaze of thousands—the hours appear to fly with fearful rapidity—they appear to the fevered imagination of the captive—seem condensed into moments, so quickly, and almost imperceptibly, do they glide by; hour after hour disappears in this manner, and at length the hands have but to traverse their proscribed limits once more—and the moment—the awful period arrives, when the corporeal man

No. 15.

is to endure shame and ignominy, while the spiritual soul rushes, unbidden, into the awful presence of offended Majesty—appears before that God whose laws have been violated, whose holy decrees it held in defiance. Oh! what must that man endure, who, having committed any fearful and revolting crime, taking for example, murder, is condemned to die, and yet, a period placed between the commission of the crime and the execution of the sentence, and that period passed in darkness and solitude; each shadow must appear to be the form of his victim, even the echoes of his own breathing picture the presence of the dead. We have been told of men who have been thus situated; have seen one before the crime had been committed, and again upon the morning of execution, and such was the change wrought in his appearance, that we scarce could acknowledge him for the same person. Death, though seen only in the distance, produces fearful revolutions in the mind.

This man, now under sentence of death, was disturbed in his sleep (like Captain Bond) by horrid dreams. He gave us a description of two which particularly related to scenes in his real life, in which he had been the principal tragic actor. [Our artist has endeavoured to delineate, as far as possible, the dreadful visions of the wretched culprit, by two engravings] (See pages 121 and 129). This man had been born of religious parents, reared tenderly, and indulgently; so much so, that he had been allowed too much his own way during his childhood. Our space will not permit us to give a long narrative of his boyish days. On his eighteenth year, he absconded from his home, with all his father possessed in ready cash, which amounted to several hundred pounds, after having broken his mother's heart. His hiding-place was London, that dreadful wen of splendour and misery—of Christianity and crime—of palaces and union workhouses—of churches and gaols—where poverty is a sin, where the poor can never do that which is right, and where the rich can do nought that is wrong. In one of the hells of St. James's, Frank Wayward (that was the culprit's name) lost, in one night, the frugal savings of his heart-broken father's whole life. His next step was to rob on the highway; and in less than two years he became a murderer, and then a condemned criminal in a county gaol: and here it was we visited him. The last time we had seen him was in a place of worship, in his native town, untainted by crime. What an awful change—how haggard his countenance—how deathly pale. Oh, his piercing look of despair, from his sunken eyes, filled us with dismay! And then he confessed to us that he was guilty,—yes, guilty of the unpardonable offence (by God and man) of MURDER—a double MURDER. [We say unpardonable by God and man; for we believe it to be of the most pernicious consequence to hold out a hope to the murderer that God will pardon him, if he repents. The wretches who commit murder always die Christians.] Frank Wayward had waylaid two young females—the one 13 and the other 16 years old—who had been to a market-town to receive some twenty pounds for their father, a small farmer, confined to his bed with a broken leg. Having fallen in with the two girls, as before described, he soon learnt their business and what they possessed. On reaching a very sequestered part of the road, and the evening having set in, he dealt the elder sister, who had the money, a dreadful blow on the head. She fell lifeless. The younger sister took to flight, screaming for help; but in a few seconds Wayward overtook her, stunned her also with his stick,—then cut her throat with a large pocket-knife. Having possessed himself of the money which the elder sister had, he dragged the body to a ploughed field, and then went to the younger sister, who still gave symptoms of life. He told us he then severed her head from her body as the quickest means of dispatching her; and buried both the bodies in the ploughed field above named. The next morning all the neighbours were in alarm for the missing females. Every one who lived near joined in the search after them. But they were indebted to a dog for the discovery. Having arrived near the spot where the murders were committed, one of the men belonging to the father of the murdered females saw the house-dog in the ditch, howling and barking, and scratching the earth. On arriving, he saw what appeared to him a quantity of human blood. In a few minutes several people had arrived, and it was determined to make a general search. The dog still kept howling, barking, and jumping, and at length set off in the direction of the ploughed field, direct to the spot where the murdered victims lay, and where he immediately began scratching with his fore paws, and howling more vehemently than ever. This led to the discovery of the foul deed which had been committed. Fortunately for the ends of justice, the money stolen was in bank-notes; and Wayward having offered one of them for some clothes to a salesman in a neighbouring country fair, he was detained, taken before a magistrate, committed, tried, and convicted. His shoes and the spots of blood on his clothes were damning evidences against him. The shoes were found to correspond exactly with the footmarks in the ploughed field—one, the right foot, had a piece of the iron tip on the heel broken off; this was sufficiently visible in the clay-like soil of the field to have convicted him without other evidence. In the first dream which he described to us, he said, "the KING of TERRORS (his own expression) had appeared to him, and shewed him his victims laying head to foot; but the rays of beautiful light which were reflected from heaven upon them were so vivid—to him so awfully bright, that he could not look on them a second time. The King of Terrors had a crown upon his head, and a fiery meteor in his hand. Again, the King of the Valley of the Shadow of Death appeared to him in a more grisly form! "Oh," said he, "it was a dreadful sight. Here he shewed me the tomb of my murdered victims; and in his right hand, streaming with blood, he held the head which I had cut from the body of one of my innocent victims! Oh, horrible!! horrible!!!"

It will be remembered that we said the antiquarian deferred communicating the remaining portion of his instructions until the morrow. Much has been said concerning the impropriety of deferring anything until the morrow which may be done to day—never was the error more fully proved than in the case of our friend, the antiquarian; for four hours after he had parted from Mortimer and his neice he sank calmly into eternity. Mortimer, as executor, had the conducting of his funeral, which was in every way corresponding with his wealth. Three weeks afterwards the will was opened, and as such a specimen of antiquity is seldom laid before the reading public, we will present them with an exact copy. It ran thus:—

"This is the last Will and Testament of Edmund Wilson, Antiquarian.

"I leave and bequeath to my friend and nurse, Mrs. Johnson, my dog, the blue morrocco bound prayer-book that lies beneath my black wig in the left hand corner of the second drawer, and upon that leaf where the advent collect is printed, she will find a bank note for one pound, and also the knife that was dug twenty-five years ago from No. 5 Mine, by James Pearse. All my other property I bequeath to my neice, Flora, and my friend, Sir Charles Mortimer, upon the following conditions only:—

"*Firstly*. That the said Sir Charles Mortimer do marry my neice, Flora, and settle upon her an annual income of two hundred pounds, to be placed solely at her own private disposal.

"*Secondly*. That he continue to reside in this house, retain all the servants, and give twopence per day to the poor widow and four children who stops before the door, and sings *Rule Britannia* in fits, and *God Save the Queen* in screaming convulsions. He must also let the natural curiosities remain as they are, and above all, never again speak with the rascal, Belford, or, indeed any of his former acquaintances.

(Signed)   EDMUND WILSON.
(Witness)   ROBERT GOUGH."

The above, though eccentric, is a correct copy of his will, the only portion which we were inclined to doubt, was that wherein the songs sang by the widow and her offsprings is mentioned; though that may perhaps bear reference to the peculiar manner in which they were sung. Whether this conjecture, however, is correct, or otherwise, we cannot decide, but each and every one of the conditions contained in the will, were faithfully adhered to; the result of which was, that Mortimer obtained a young and highly-accomplished wife, an immense fortune, and passed the remainder of his days happy, in the society of her he had learned to love.

CHAPTER XXXVII.

THE INTERVIEW.

"What new scheme has Meg got hold of?" exclaimed Bond, as he noticed the effect her communications and hints had upon the countenance of Robson. "Why, Robson," he resumed, "you appear to quail beneath the penetrating black eye of our friend. What's up between you both?"

"Much, Captain Bond, that you are in ignorance of. Where is that justice for which your band was once so famed? The time has been, when, had any man wrought an unjust injury upon another—and you had gained a knowledge of the same, his death would have been the result; now, they are permitted to war, even upon women, with impunity. If this be the justice of Captain Bond, henceforth I relinquish all companionship and intercourse with you, for ever."

"Nay, Meg," rejoined Bond, "that will never do—why, you gone, we should lose our right hand. Besides," he continued, bestowing a good-humoured glance upon the gipsey, "I have the same fear of you as the English Government had of Lord Nelson."

"And what is that?" enquired Meg.

"Why, that you will join the French," answered Bond, "or, in other words, that you may put the officers upon our track."

"Captain Bond!" exclaimed Meg, "you have forgotten how, upon the occasion of our first meeting, I saved your life: even the moment fixed for your death had arrived, and any other hand than mine would have been useless. Was that the act of one who would betray you into the hands of your enemies? and how often, since that time, have I proved to be your friend? Whose hand was it that planned, and effected your escape from that confinement, which would have terminated in your being introduced to a dance upon the tight-rope of eternity?"

"I thank you, Meg, for reminding me, of what, in a moment of careless revelry, I had forgotten. But, now tell me, what is the nature of this sad grievance between you and the lieutenant?"

"Disperse the band," replied Meg, "and all shall be explained."

The word was given, and the trio were alone.

"You, of course, knew the cause of the lieutenant's late absence from the band?" began Meg, "if not, I can inform you. He had allured a poor friendless orphan from her home; first led her from the path of honour, then deserted, shamefully deserted, the victim of his sated passion, who now lies buried in the cold silent grave, fast rotting into decay."

"Dead!" ejaculated both captain and lieutenant in a breath.

"Aye, dead," rejoined Meg; "the last moment of her life was yielded up in giving birth to a daughter—that daughter has now reached the estate of womanhood; her life is threatened by much danger."

"How long is it since her you named became numbered with the dead? how old is the daughter? the cause of her death?" asked Robson.

"The mother died twenty years since," answered the gipsey, "and the child's age corresponds exactly; for I once more repeat that it was in giving birth to that child the mother lost her life."

"Know you where the girl is to be found?" enquired the lieutenant.

"I both know and have conversed with her," replied Meg; "scarce two hundred yards from this spot stands a neat and detatched cottage; 'tis there, under the guidance of the woman in whose arms her mother died, your daughter has been reared—though the money for her support is furnished by some wealthy lady of title, whom it appears, from what I have been enabled to learn, was a particular friend of the mother's. This same lady would have taken the girl away, and introduced her to the higher circles of life, but she preferred rural scenery and a rustic dress to perfumed halls and rustling silk; and, therefore, was suffered to remain with her protectress, whom she imagines in reality to be her mother, and the woman's extreme attachment appears to strengthen the illusion so welcome to both. I again repeat that the life of your child is in danger."

"How? and by what means?" demanded the lieutenant.

"She now listens to the false vows and hollow protestations of one, whom I am convinced means her harm. Sometime since, I, under the disguise of a wandering pedlar, obtained an interview with her, and explained the whole affair as it afterwards fell out. You will, perhaps, enquire how the intelligence came to my ears; it was thus: I overheard this man conversing with one of his giddy companions; the subject upon which they spoke, was your daughter; then it was, that I heard him proclaim his intention of possessing her charms—though, according to his own declaration, marriage would be to speak in his own words, ' Out of the question.' Previous to his introduction to the girl, there was a worthy young fellow, one Edward Lambourne, who paid her the most marked attention; this I also discovered, and warned her not to slight him—but she has done so, and his rival now holds firm possession of her affections, and will continue to do so, until he has accomplished her ruin, and driven her as you did her mother, to a death-bed of shame and remorse."

"If I thought such was to be the fate of my child," exclaimed Robson, with an imprecation; "I would have the villain's life."

"And what would that benefit your child?" enquired Meg, "Nothing," she resumed, "No, if you wish to save her, some measure must be thought on, and speedily too, by which she may be rescued from his power. I have it, what say you; are you willing that she be conducted to the place where her mother resided, when with you? There, at least, she will be safe, until further measures are decided upon. After which, she must be removed with secrecy to——"

"Captain, be on your guard; here are a detachment of soldiers close upon our retreat—and, unless we are well prepared to receive them, our defeat must inevitably follow, should we be compelled to yield."

"The first man that dares talk of surrendering in my presence, I'll shoot through the head," vociferated Bond, starting to his feet, and glancing fiercely upon the man, who in breathless haste, entered to deliver the unwelcome tidings.

"What is to be done, captain?" enquired the man.

"Are all the men under arms?" enquired Bond.

"They are, Captain."

"Then do you away and join them; let my carbine be placed upon the favourite spot, from which I have so often driven those who have sought my destruction—away!"

Obedient to the commands of his captain, the man hastened from the spot, in order to join his comrades, who were impatiently awaiting the arrival of their foes.

"Now!" exclaimed Bond, when they were once more left alone; "we are likely to have some warm and interesting work. To you, my brave friend, Robson, I assign the office of aide-de-camp—you are unknown to them—I, for my part, am such a favourite among them, that they would not suffer me to pass even a yard without exchanging signals with me."

Robson then rose, and quitted the place.

" And, now, my ever faithful Meg, I must again solicit your aid ; how do you advise that I should proceed ? The danger is great, the numbers of the foe nearly treble ours, therefore, extreme caution must be our pass word—you, I suppose, remain here ?"

" There you are in error," answered Meg, " I shall stand by your side—aye, and share the danger of an encounter. Now, why do you stand here inactive— heard you that carbine? Have you forgotten that it is the signal of attack— arouse thee, man, or thy bondage, and thy very life will be endangered."

" I thank you for the hint," answered Bond, in a tone of abstraction ; " I was then meditating upon the strange intelligence you have afforded, respecting that child of Robson's—the death of the mother too, all, all seem but as a dream."

At this moment, a member of the gang entered, and in a hurried tone, informed him that Robson had been captured.

Upon hearing this, Bond started to his feet, and bidding the other follow him, hastened to the scene of action, where he beheld his band and the soldiers in hot contention, and a little more in advance, he noticed the lieutenant in the custody of four of the king's men—he drew a pistol from his belt and fired upon the nearest, who instantly fell to the ground a lifeless corse—the bullet had entered his brain.

Upon beholding their captain, the men fought with redoubled vigour. Once their captain was also in captivity, but a bullet from the weapon held by Meg, soon set him at liberty, and Robson was shortly afterwards rescued. At length the contest ended by the capture of two of the gang, who were immediately borne off and confined in the nearest lock-up.

Lady Flora Mandeville had not as hitherto neglected to forward the sum she had herself named for the support of Maria, since the time of her mother's death —but the money had now become due for several days, and yet had not been received—at length it was despatched by a servant, who bore a note to Maria. The contents of which, ran as follows :—

" If Maria Martin will accompany the bearer of this to the place named by him, she will greatly oblige the writer hereof.   FLORA MANDEVILLE.

Upon the receipt of this communication, Maria was at a loss what to do. She did not personally know the Lady Flora, though she had frequently heard mention made of her name at the cottage, as their benefactor. She, therefore, placed the note in the hands of her mother, who appeared to be highly gratified with its contents, and advised her by all means to comply with the request contained therein ; she, therefore, remedied a few little negligences in her attire, which but made her beauty more lovely, and then accompanied the servant to the end of the walk, where a carriage was waiting their coming—into this Maria was ushered by the servant, the door was closed, and the vehicle proceeded onwards at a speed that at once testified the excellent quality of the horses, and the skill of the coachman. They proceeded onwards in this manner for some considerable time, and, at length, halted before a large garden or lawn ; they then re-conducted her from the carriage, and through the lawn, at the bottom of which, stood a large mansion, into which she was ushered ; a few broad stone stairs covered with a superb carpet, were ascended, and Maria stood in a costly furnished apartment, where, upon an ottoman she beheld a lady richly dressed ; she appeared to be somewhere about forty-two or three, and was, according to Maria's idea of female beauty, somewhat handsome. Upon the maiden's entrance she rose from her seat, and in a soft and mellow tone of voice, thus addressed her :—

" So, Miss, I hear you have a lover."

Maria blushed deeply.'

" Nay," she resumed, " you need not blush, I see no very great crime in that ; though," she continued, in a more grave tone, " I am compelled to hear that he is of very questionable reputation.   Now, I have sent for you, in order that some plan may be adopted, whereby your future welfare and position in society may be secured.   This young man, I hear, is a miller, and though possessed of great property, has no merit attached to him.   This man, too, I hear, is of very intemperate habits. Should you be united to him, a life of misery and privation may be your portion ; and, too late you will bewail your lot   Another consideration too, there is, that has hitherto been forgotten—should he accomplish your ruin, and then, as is too frequently the case, abandon you to shame and misery. Listen to me, I would have you wedded to some one more worthy ; yet, one with whom you can be happy.   You, will, perhaps, say I am much interested in your fate ; at least, too much for the gratification of your own desires ; will you abandon this man, and pass your days here with me ?   See this miller no more."

" Madam," replied Maria, emboldened by the familiarity shewn towards her ; " Madam, I have plighted my love to that man ; and though disgrace, misery, starvation—-nay, even death, were to follow, I would not break faith with him. He is all honour, candour, and integrity ; and though the four winds of heaven, were combined to proclaim him false, still would I risk my own life upon his truth and honour."

The above sentence was spoken in a tone, that fully proved the earnestness of its authoress.

" Well," replied Lady Flora, with a smile ; I find you possess some real spirit ; and since your lover holds such a firm post in your heart, why, it is useless attempting to alter your determination : the consequences of which, will be yours alone, though I could have wished from my heart, you had made some other choice. My opinion of mankind is this, that when once they deviate from the paths of strict honour and integrity, no act of injustice will afterwards be considered as any obstacle to the attainment of their desires—there is much I could reveal to you, much that [you think not of, and which, when related, would cause a complete alteration in your destiny, but it must not be as yet."

" And, why, not, madam ?" enquired Maria, " Oh !" she continued, in an imploring manner ; " if, indeed, there be a mystery attached to me, and one, I am assured there is, why, not, at once, ease this mind of its anxiety, by revealing all to me ; inform me of all without reserve.   My poor mother !"

" What would you say of her ?" interrupted Lady Flora, earnestly ; " you spoke of your mother, surely you have not——"

" Discovered that her, under whose fostering care I have been reared, is not my mother," suggested Maria, " is that what you would have said ?   Oh ! madam," she continued, kneeling at the feet of Lady Flora ; " in pity to a daughter's feelings, let me know who is my mother—for with you alone, I am convinced the dark mystery with which my birth was marked, is known, therefore, if you——"

" Mystery !" interrupted Lady Flora, " how knew you, my child ; how could you imagine that there was a mystery ?"

" It was told to me by a gipsey," answered Maria, " who, even now, follows upon my track.   She, like you, is averse to the object of my affections, and prophecies much affliction from my choice ; this woman it is, who appears as if by supernatural agency, to follow my footsteps—and prophecies my very thoughts before they are known to myself.   She has even appointed a watch word as it were, that by its agency I may be made aware of committing some act, by which my future hopes of happiness—nay, even my very life may be endangered. When first I spoke with Corder, him, of whom you were but now conversing, she then crossed my path, and bade me shun him as I would a raging pestilence ; she it was, who first assured me of the mystery attendant upon my origin ; which mystery, however, I could not prevail upon her to reveal—though at some future period she said, I should know all—and then, by fatal experience, I should remember her words, and the truth contained therein."

" 'Tis singular," mused Lady Flora, " that she should take such an extraordinary interest in your fate. How is this woman to be seen ? or, if seen, recognized ? I should wish much to see her."

" I can at any time bring her to your ladyship," replied Maria ; " that is," she resumed, " if she should be willing to visit you."

" Say to her that I would have my fortune told," rejoined Lady Flora, with a smile. " I suppose she deals in the black art."

" She is a professor, though I do not think a *believer* in the ridiculous art of fortune-telling," replied Maria, " though," she resumed, with something of hesitation in her manner, " nearly all that she foretold to me has come to pass."

" And yet," rejoined her ladyship, " you do not believe in the art."

" No madam, I do not," replied Maria, promptly ; " and my disbelief led to some warm arguments between myself and the gipsey upon the occasion of our first meeting : for while she advocated the cause, I, by virtue of questions founded upon a more rational basis, clearly proved to her the inability of one human being possessed with more prophetic powers than another ; and though I succeeded in convincing, yet I could not *alter* her opinion. Yet how injurious is this supposed art ! What prejudices does it not produce in vulgar and illiterate minds !"

" Indeed !" replied her ladyship ; " perhaps you will entertain me by the detail of some. It may serve as instruction too," she continued. " But surely, child, you have taken a strange fancy into that little obstinate head of yours. Why, I positively declare that you have been standing all this time. Why did you not assist yourself to a chair ? There are plenty of them."

" Because," replied Maria, " you did not invite me so to do."

" Well !" exclaimed Lady Flora, with mock gravity, " you have been reared with a most freezing regard to the etiquette of society."

" Thanks be to your bounty," rejoined Maria, " I trust, your ladyship, I *am* proficient in politeness."

" You absolutely improve upon acquaintance," continued Lady Flora. " When I first conversed with you, I thought I never saw a more self-willed and truly obstinate young lady ; but I now find you to be a creature made up of gratitude ; strong physical courage, mixed with a slight dash of obstinacy."

At this moment a servant entered, and announced the carriage of the Honorable Mrs. Halford, and was desired to " show her ladyship up."

Upon receiving this command the man withdrew, and soon afterwards returned, introducing a tall, meagre-looking lady of sallow countenance, and who was attired in the most ridiculous extreme of fashion. After the first formalities had been gone through, the newly-imported and animated cargo of silk and eau de Cologne looked first at Maria, then at Lady Flora, with a glance that seemed to say " What low-born plebeian rabble have you here ?" when her ladyship, who doubtless interpreted the glance, exclaimed,

" This, Lady Halford, is my young *protegée*, of whom you have heard me speak so often. The young minx has a will of her own, which I have been attempting, though in vain, to thwart."

" That is very wrong of her," interrupted the new comer ; she should learn to always yield in submission to her superiors."

" There, Maria," exclaimed Lady Flora, " you hear that ; now, answer for yourself. Come, defend your own cause ; for I know you to be a very able counsellor."

" Your ladyship is disposed to be merry," replied Maria, evidently piqued at the reproof she had received ; " but I have been taught to look upon all mankind as equal, at least in a spiritual point of view ; and moreover, I do not imagine that the Creator intended that one person *should* be superior, though by the system of unjust monopoly that is now, alas ! too universally practised, has enabled

[See Page 115]

some to possess a superfluity of wealth, while others are absolutely dying from the effects of starvation; though this is too frequently seen, yet in my humble estimation the peasant is upon an equality with the crowned king upon his throne of power; at least, if mankind think not so, their God considers such to be the case. If I have spoken too freely," continued Maria, addressing Lady Flora, "I crave your pardon; but your ladyship will doubtless remember, that 'twas by your license alone I have uttered thus much."

"Oh? there is no offence taken," replied Lady Halford. "Why, surely," she continued, "you must *paint*, child; your cheeks are as red——"

"Paint!" reiterated Maria, indignantly. "No, madam, I do not use what you are pleased to term paint; but you will doubtless remember that I am in no position to indulge in aristocratic idleness. The ruddy evidence of health is gained by honest industry alone. That, madam, is the *paint* used by those who move in the more humble circles of life, and from whom the more wealthy may often learn a profitable lesson."

"And what lesson may that be?" enquired Lady Halford.

"Civility towards their fellow-creatures," was the prompt reply.

Finding her hope of confounding Maria to be abortive, Lady Halford suddenly affected to remember an immediate appointment, till then forgotten; and under that pretence bade a good-day to Lady Flora, and endeavoured to conceal her confusion beneath a hasty retreat from the scene of her discomfiture.

Upon her disappearance Maria burst into tears.

"Why, how have you deceived me!" exclaimed Lady Flora. "There, dry your tears, and do not alarm people by deluding them into the belief that you are troubled with water on the brain. Why, I thought your spirit was far above such weakness. Heigho! there is no accounting for appearances! But, seriously speaking, my dear Maria, I was greatly charmed with the rub you gave her

No. 16.

ladyship. Really, her pride is excessive, and she imagines there is no person living of such profound importance as herself. The woman is a complete nuisance ; and yet I am so situated that I am absolutely afraid to offend her. However, you gave her such a severe rub, that I shall not expect to see her for some considerable time ; therefore, you have involuntarily rendered me a very essential service. Come, dry your eyes, and look up once more cheerfully. She is gone now, and your torment is removed."

A short time after the departure of Lady Halford, Maria also took her leave, and returned to the cottage in the vehicle that had borne her from it.

CHAPTER XXXVIII.

THE ATTEMPTED BURGLARY.

ROBSON debated for some considerable time upon the propriety of Meg's plan with regard to his daughter, whom he was most anxious to obtain possession of, yet feared to venture himself, lest an exposure should be the result, and the girl thus learn to loathe the man whom as a father she had been taught to revere. In one of these moments of brown study he encountered Captain Bond.

" Why, man," exclaimed the robber chief, " what are you meditating upon so intently ? Is it anything of a nature exclusively adapted to your own bosom ; or is it one of those subjects in the knowledge of which all may participate ?"

" Why," rejoined the lieutenant, " I was thinking upon that plan Meg was proposing, by which I might gain possession of the girl. By the bye, what think you of the news Meg brought us ?"

" What news ?" enquired Bond.

" The death of Emily," replied Robson. " Was it not sudden ?"

" So sudden," answerd Bond, " that I have all this time been endeavouring to believe, myself, that it is true, but all to no purpose."

" Can you advise me what disguise to assume for safety ?"

" Why," replied the captain, " there is only one disguise in which you would not be known, but upon that I would stake my life."

" Is it difficult for me to obtain ?" asked Robson.

" Not in the least," answered Bond ; " a few silver pieces will see them yours, and the first tailor's shop you arrive at will be enabled to furnish you with all the requisite articles "

" And you are thoroughly assured that I shall not be recognised ?"

" I am so."

" And what am I to enquire for ?"

" The dress of an honest man, in which you might with safety travel the globe round in perfect security."

" And why should that dress be so superior to all others ?"

" Because they would never imagine that such a complete scoundrel as you would feel comfortable in such attire. But, come ; a truce to this trifling. How do you intend to proceed with regard to the girl ? I think you had better confide wholly in Meg. She will carry the thing into effect more strongly than could either you or I. And while she is contriving that business, you and I will see what is to be done with regard to the commonwealth. Our two friends ought not to be abandoned in their adversity ; and by way of a brightener after our late reverses, what say you to an adventure this evening ? Should you enjoy a little harmless sport ?"

" By all means," replied Robson.

" Then saddle your horse, and accompany me," rejoined Bond. " We will on towards Grantley Park, though not to pay its fair inmate a visit. I have had sufficient experience in the fidelity of women of quality; and as Meg reminded me a few days ago, I should doubtless, but for her kind interference, have been taking the air at Tyburn before this time. But come—to the road."

They then proceeded to prepare themselves for a moonlight trip, and in a few moments rode side by side towards Bentley Heath. They had nearly gained the Heath, when the tramp of horses' hoofs startled them; they simultaneously came to a halt, and concealed themselves beneath some tall wide-spreading trees that providentially stood near. Scarcely had they gained this position, when the sounds, which had rapidly grown more distinct and loud, were augmented into the quick step and loud breathing of a horse, apparently at full speed. No sooner did the wayfarer arrive opposite to the place where they were concealed, than both captain and lieutenant sprang forward, pistol in hand, and commanded the traveller to " stand and deliver." Upon closer inspection, however, the highwaymen discovered the individual before them to be a servant. This discovery caused them to indulge in a hearty laugh as they looked upon the pitiful figure before them. Upon beholding the pistols, the fellow had set himself bolt upright in the saddle, and looked upon them with that expression of countenance peculiar to persons in a fright. After gazing at them until his power of speech, " by fright disturbed," returned, and then, in the most abject terms, he gave breath to a fervent hope that the gentlemen did not mean to murder him, as he was a poor, defenceless young man.

" I am not quite satisfied that we shall not murder you, my fine fellow, by way of example to all courageous servants who endanger the lives of St. Nicholas, by their valorous resistance. First, however, inform us from whence you came, whither you are bound, upon what mission, and lastly, who, and of what dignity your employer; is he man or woman? Ha !rascal, at what do you smile? is it at me?"

" No, sir, I did not laugh at you," answered the fellow; " 'twas only at a slight mistake you made."

" Never think of that, man. Come, who is your employer?"

" A lady, sir."

" And her name is——"

" Lady Flora Mandeville."

" Oh !" muttered Bond, in an under tone to Robson, " now for a plot. Now, sirrah," he resumed, " what valuables have you about your person? because, if you do not instantly resign them, this pistol that you see in my hand, may chance to claim acquaintance with your head, therefore, be speedy."

" I have nothing but an old silver watch," returned the man. " Pray, good gentlemen robbers, do not take that from me, for it is a family relic, and was given to me by my great grandfather's son's uncle's brother's nephew, who was twice transported, and hung after all, through the ill nature of——"

" That devil's imp, the law, I suppose," interrupted Bond. " But, come, the watch, and as I have a very great veneration for antiquities, any day at twelve o'clock, that you may think fit to pass by this road, I will willingly return it to you again, without fee or expense."

" Then, why do you take it from me?" enquired the fellow.

" Why," replied Bond, " because you might meet with some rascally highwayman, and be robbed of your treasure."

" Oh ! then you are not robbers."

" Robbers !" reiterated Bond. " Oh no, we are gentlemen's son's, out upon a roving commission, that is all, I can assure you."

" I am glad of that," replied the other, " for I have a letter in this pocket that I would not lose for the world; indeed, if I lost this letter, I might as well consider myself discharged from my lady's family.

" Indeed," rejoined Bond, glancing at Robson, " then I suppose the letter is of great importance to her ladyship, is it not?"

"Oh, yes, bless your roving gentlemanship's soul, it's of the very greatest importance as any letter could possibly be. You must know that my lady has a cousin who has just arrived from India, where he has been residing for the last thirteen years; they do say that he is immensely rich, and that my mistresss will have all the property at his death—so she wants him to come to Grantley Hall."

"And pray, how long is it since your mistress saw this cousin?"

"Lord bless you, she has never seen him yet."

"Then she does not know him even when he comes?"

"Know him!" reiterated the fellow. "Lord bless you, not from Adam himself; I have been there now to enquire after his health, and he has sent this letter as an answer."

"And when do you expect this rich West Indian cousin to arrive at Grantley Park? Has any time been fixed for his arrival?"

"Oh yes, he comes to-morrow evening at seven o'clock. We knew that a week ago; but may I go now, sir, if you please?"

"Oh yes," answered Bond. "When are you coming for the watch?" he resumed, as the fellow had proceeded some yards onwards.

"At twelve o'clock the day after to-morrow," replied the fellow.

"All right," shouted Bond, "I shall be here with it, waiting for you."

The man turned to thank him for his kindness, but both captain and lieutenant were lost to his view—had vanished. He then stuck spurs into his horse and proceeded onward, at the top of his speed—and upon his arrival at the hall searched for the letter, but to his unspeakable horror and consternation, he discovered that it had vanished. And where could it be gone to? he had not taken it from his pocket—had not halted at any place upon his road home, so that no person could have stolen it; he was completely involved in a labyrinth of wonder. At length he was summoned into the presence of her ladyship, for he had informed her waiting maid, that he bore a letter for her mistress, and she had now communicated the fact to Lady Flora, who was impatiently awaiting the receipt of the same; but, as after a very lengthy search the letter was not to be found, the luckless messenger determined upon putting on a bold front, and concocting a fictitious account of a robbery, in which the letter had, together with other valuables, been taken from him.

"Another long and loud peal of the drawing-room bell caused him to enter the presence of her ladyship.

"Well, sir!" exclaimed Lady Flora, "have you not a letter for me?"

"I had one, your ladyship," was the reply.

"Had one!" reiterated Lady Mandeville; "and pray, sir, have you not got it now?"

"No, my lady," was the laconic reply.

"Then where is it now, sir? have you dared to lose it?"

"No, my lady, I have had it s-t-o-le-n fr-o-m me."

"Stolen, sir? and by whom, pray?"

"The highwaymen, so please you my lady."

"Highwaymen! and how many of them were present?"

"Seventeen, your ladyship! I fought for nearly an hour-and-a-half before they could overpower me, and then they would not have succeeded—but, fortunately for them I——"

"Was afraid to resist longer," suggested Lady Flora. "But tell me," she resumed, "where was this robbery effected? what part of the road?"

"Scarce half-a-mile from this mansion, your ladyship."

Despite the chgarin this intelligence cast upon her, Lady Flora could not be angry with the cause of it. She compressed her nether lip, in order to conceal the visible evolutions which her countenance would otherwise have undergone; and in a tone of affected severity, commanded the man to quit her presence—a command which he very gladly obeyed. Happy at having thus escaped from the ill effects of an accident, which caused dark clouds to obscure his "planetical atmosphere," as purse prophets (fortune teller's) would say.

Having rescued the man from impending disgrace, and seen him once more in company with his fellow-menials, to whom he relates the fictitious adventure, with all the fervour and affected sincerity of truth, we shall now follow Bond and his lieutenant, who, upon the departure of his servant, they both set off at a good round pace for their haunt; and upon following them thither, we find that both are busily engaged in the perusal of a letter, the contents of which ran as follows:—

"My Dear Madam,—I should have done myself the distinguished honour of visiting you to-morrow evening at the appointed time, but a sudden, and at present, very severe fit of indisposition has confined me to my room, but my medical officer assures me that it will be of very short duration; and immediately upon his declaring me to be convalescent, I will, with your permission, make my first call at Grantley Park. Until then, believe me to be,

Madam,

Your friend and cousin,

Oakley Lodge,
Mandeville."

This then must have been the letter missed by the servant—yet how did it come into their possession? surely they did not steal it? Stolen is an awkward word acccording to the testimony of Mr. W. H. Ainsworth. But perhaps they might have "brought it away with them."

"Well!" exclaimed Bond, after a pause; "what's to be done with this fashionable scrawl? shall I avail myself of it?"

"I don't see how that is to be done," answered Robson.

"Wear spectacles," rejoined Bond, "and that may improve your eysight. Why, 'tis as intelligible as the paper before you."

"Then as you are so able a general," returned Robson; "perhaps you will instruct me more fully as to your meaning—what is it?"

"Why," answered Bond, "you, of course, have heard of the treacherous trick this lady played upon me shortly after your disappearance with her young friend, the nun. How, though dropping by ill luck, the letter I had received from you, and which exposed both your plans and my own before they were ripe for execution?"

"I have heard the whole pedigree," answered Robson.

"Well, then, my object is, now, to play her ladyship a game, at which we shall be double or quits. Do you understand?"

"I do—but how is it to be done, captain?"

"Why, I was thinking that if I dressed for this Indian cousin, and you for his *valet de chambre*, we might obtain egress to the mansion, learn where the plate chest was deposited, secure a good round booty, and effect our retreat before the trick could be discovered—that is my plan, and as she has never seen this cousin, there cannot possibly be any fear of detection."

"Not if that portion of the story be true, which I very much doubt," rejoined Robson; "you have no proof to show why that fellow should not have known who we were, and have been carrying on all that flummery in order to mislead us. And should such, in reality, be the true state of affairs, and we go there to-morrow evening, there may chance to be a brace of those ill-mannered, suspicious-looking rascals, known as peace officers."

"And in which case we can present them with the contents of a brace of pretty barkers that never missed fire; and which, upon that most particular occasion, can be as tightly filled to the muzzle, as though prepared for tiger hunting, in which case I think it more than probable, that he'll not live long to tell who hit him. But, even should it be as you say, and he have known us, still it is impossible that harm can come of it—for how are they to know that it is our purpose to come?—the honour of a visit, and also that the other, and original cousin, does not intend being present, therefore, we are perfectly safe. Will you be my valet for the occasion ?"

"I will," replied Robson, "and while you are imposing upon the mistress above stairs, I'll betake me to the lower regions, and there try my hand upon anything of value that is not placed beyond my reach, and not only that, but I'll also sound them in some way about the hiding place of the main treasure, which discovered, our purpose is at once effected."

All the necessary arrangements being completed, Bond, and his lieutenant, joined the gang, and passed the night in carousal.

The highway-captain had made repeated enquiries about Meg; but no person could afford any intelligence of her, she had not been with the band for two days, nor had she during that interval, been seen by any of them, which led Bond to suppose, that they should soon have the benefit of some new discovery made by herself; for she was seldom absent for long periods, without it was upon some secret mission of her own, and, by which, the interest of the band would be promoted; and which, was fraught with danger to herself; for the more difficult and hazardous the nature of an adventure might be, the more ready would it be followed by Gipsey Meg; for she loved danger, and was never so happy as when involved in some scheme, that required her whole stock of prudence and cunning to escape therefrom.

Her great hatred towards all mankind, rendered her even a greater acquisition to the band, than she otherwise would have been; for to betray travellers and other defenceless persons into their hands, was, to her, a source of infinite gratification. In short, she was altogether framed for the society to which she belonged.

Bond was one of the very few men, that called forth her secret admiration; his noble, daring, brave, generous, spirit, served to inspire her with awe; the only blemish she acknowledged, or permitted herself to believe belonged to him, was his temper and disposition; the former though fiery in the extreme, was of a forgiving nature, and would cease to remember any injury, after the pain it caused had vanished; but, upon the contrary, if at the time he came in contact with the injurer, it is more than probable, that his life would pay the forfeit of his temerity —in disposition, he was free and liberal, even to a fault. In no one expedition in which the band, or any portion of its members were engaged, did ever any dispute arise as to the distribution of the booty, for, rather than give any cause for dissatisfaction, he would sacrifice even his own share to them, and thus silence all cause for murmurings. Robson on the contrary, was one of those men, who first look with a greedy eye upon the furtherance of their own interest, and afterwards with a feeling of partiality, proceed to arrange that of others; if they had been engaged in an expedition where but little booty had been the result, his council to Bond, has been to attribute the whole to themselves, though, perhaps, some two or three of the gang had risked their lives in order to secure even that little. But to this, Bond always gave a decided negative; and, seldom at the same time, failing to express his disgust at the bare suggestion of so dishonourable an action.

We have heard much said against highwaymen; but with all their faults, we need not long dwell in the more aristocratic circles of society ere more accomplished and unprincipled robbers appear before the curtain of life—we allude to the fashionable gamesters; those men who coolly sit down at the play-table with those whom they style their friends, ply them with the maddening fumes of brandy, while they sip from the cool and refreshing lemonade, then fleece them of their last guinea—and too often send them home ruined beggars. This is friendship ! Now, we would ask, who is the most criminal? The fashionable gamester, or your bold spirited highwaymen ! When men meet them, 'tis upon terms of open enmity, they can then resist their demands if they think fit—though generally speaking, that would not be a very profitable proceeding, considering that they are fully aware the struggle in which they engage (if resistance be offered) is life for life, and that either one or the other must fall. We know not how it is to be accounted for, but it is invariably seen by the fashionable Newgate Calenders and other sources equally intellectual (?) sources, that a material difference exists between the highwayman and housebreaker; the one is all liberality and honour, the other mean and unprincipled to a fault. There are many other means of distinguishing the highwayman, from the other members of the translating fraternity; but as we have occupied time and space sufficient upon the subject, we leave it for some more able historian.

As the clocks proclaimed the hour of one, and the band were about to separate for the night, when their signal resounded from without, Bond started to his feet, and upon throwing wide the door, Meg entered weary and covered with dust, her hands deeply imbrued with blood, and a gold watch chain hanging from her bosom; upon entering, she threw herself into a seat apparently exhausted from previous exertion.

"Why, Meg," exclaimed Bond, "you appear weary. Where have you been? and upon what errand? that has detained you thus long from our company, which has greatly lacked your presence to-night. Where have you been, my indefatigable friend? I see," he continued, looking upon her crimson-hued hands, "that you have been at your favourite work."

"I have," replied the gipsey, in a spiteful tone; "I have been avenging your wrongs, while you were engaged in drinking and carousal. Thus it is, you see, Captain Bond, to have those about you, who look to your interest more than you yourself do."

"I am thoroughly convinced of your devotion to my interest," replied Bond; "but where have you been, and with whom engaged?"

"Where I have been," rejoined Meg, "is not your business; and for the man with whom I have endured a death struggle; learn that the officer who commanded those by whom we were attacked a few days since, is now no longer living —the spot where formerly the remains of my murdered boy were suspended, is now the scene of slaughter; he is the second victim that has been sacrificed to my revenge. Upon that ground alone, which all I once held dear, perished with ignominy and suffering. Now, your are answered."

"Partly so," replied Bond, "but tell me, good Meg; how did you come in contact with this tinselled tyrant?"

"I was seated at the mouldering remains of the gibbet's foot, for that is all that now remains of that former monument of shame, when I heard the sound of approaching footsteps, accompanied by voices apparently in conversation; as they drew nearer, I discovered in one of the wayfarers, the officer I have named, and with him another man—both were in the dresses they wore when the attack was made. I should have suffered them to pass unmolested, had they not halted before me, and heaped insult upon insult—and when I expostulated with them, I found them to be both intoxicated; the knowledge of this, operated so far above my desire of revenge, that I should have permitted them to rail on, had they not have spoken of the gibbet at which I was seated—this enraged me nearly to madness, I darted forward, and in an instant more my knife was in his breast; he fell bathed in blood—the other then drew a small pistol from his bosom, and presented it at my head. Before he could fire, however, I was upon him, and had wrested the weapon from his grasp; he was then at my mercy, and such clemency as I extend too all mankind when within the compass of my gripe— a moment, and he too fell writhing in the agonies of death. This watch glittered above the ornaments of his dress—'twas tempting in the moonlight—and I brought it with me. Now, you are in possession of every particular. Do you object to the nature of my enterprise?"

"Nay, my brave Meg," replied Bond, "you have accomplished a feat that would have been equal to the most determined member of our band; a deed, that few women can boast the performance of."

"Pshaw," rejoined the gipsey, in a contemptuous tone; "'tis nothing to the acts I have performed when these limbs were younger—but now, I am growing old, my energies are fast receding; but were I weak and feeble as the newly born babe, and any being dared to heap insult upon me, I would resent it, though the effort should cost me life itself. There never yet lived the man who injured me, and lived to tell the deed. Captain Bond, do you intend to pass the night here, or are you about to retire to rest? if so, you must quickly retire, for the night is almost at odds with morning, and I think you have devoted too many hours already to-night, to debauchery and idleness."

"You seem out of sorts, Meg," continued Bond, with a smile.

"I appear then as I am," answered the gipsey, "but don't sit chatting here; make yourselves scarce all of you, I want to have a little serious contemplation —to think upon my deeds of guilt—dwell upon the wrongs I have from time to time endured."

"And, can you not do so, while we remain?" enquired Robson.

"No," replied Meg, gruffly; "I cannot. While I am surrounded by such a host of cut-throat-looking ruffians as you are, my thoughts wander from the point at which I would fix them."

"I say," muttered one of the gang, "let's have little better words Mistress Meg; though you are the favourite with our captain, I see no reason why you should be allowed to talk in this fashion of us all—and to be plain with you I won't stand it. Oh! you need not look over to the captain there, because he must know that it aint pleasant, I'm sure."

"You're sure of nothing," replied Meg, "but a halter for your neck—and that will come to you strong enough before you die. Should you want for a friend to give your legs a tug, I hope you'll not forget old Gipsey Meg, will you?"

"Come, lads," exclaimed Bond, who foresaw that if they remained longer, a quarrel would be the result; "let's away, for the night. Meg here, appears to wish for our absence, and as we all know her meaning to be right, let's indulge her fancy. Good night, Meg, pleasant thoughts to you."

With these words, Captain Bond, followed by the others, rose from off their seats and quitted the place. For some hours after their departure, Meg was buried in a profound reverie, which ended in her sinking into a sound and refreshing slumber.

One hour before the appointed time upon the following evening, saw Bond and his lieutenant equipped for the adventure; the former as a gentleman, and the other as his valet; Bond carried a white cambric handkerchief, ditto kid gloves— smelt profusely of scent, flourished a little gold-headed cane, and displayed various other etceteras, usually sported by a man of fashion; while Robson was attired in a showy livery, and bore in his hand a large (official) stick. A chaise was then hired, and in this manner they proceeded to the mansion of Lady Flora Mandeville; arrived at which, Bond was immediately introduced to Lady Flora as her Indian cousin—and thanks to the large black whiskers, bushy moustachios, and long black ringlet wig, which supplanted the place of his own auburn tresses, her ladyship did not recognise him to be the man whom she had upon a previous occasion despatched to durance vile.

While he was rapidly rising in the favour of his supposed relation in the drawing-room, Robson was not idle below stairs. Upon crossing the servants' hall, he chanced to meet with the fellow from whom they had taken the letter, he immediately entered into conversation with this personage.

"Pray, my good fellow," he exclaimed, "have you been long in this family? Got a pretty good situation I suppose, haven't you?"

"Yes," replied the fellow, "and a very good mistress too. Here, she gave me this sovereign for you"

[*See page* 115.]

As he said this, he handed Robson the coin in question, which the other deposited in his pocket.

"I suppose you have a great deal of property in this house?"

"Oh! yes, pretty fair for that," replied the man.

"Have you ever heard anything of the highwaymen that are supposed to infest this quarter, eh?" enquired Robson.

"You mean those men that are led by a daring fellow, called Captain Bond?" answered the servant.

"I think that is the name," was the reply.

"I'm sure of it," replied the fellow, "and there's a gipsey with them, that fights as well as them; and then, there is a fellow named Robson, that acts as a sort of second captain."

"Are you not afraid that they will pay her ladyship a visit, here?"

"Oh, no; and if they were to do so, we are prepared for them."

"Indeed! and how so?"

"Why, we have secured the plate-chest in the loft, under the roof; don't you think that's safe enough, eh?"

"Oh, yes, to be sure," responded Robson.

The drawing-room bell then summoned the man from the side of Robson, who proceeded to the larder, and when there, endeavoured to find something in the form of silver spoons, forks, or any other trifles that would augment the general stores. Thus he succeeded in accomplishing to the tune of several spoons, and a pair of sugar tongs, which he had scarcely concealed, when the other returned to him, and informed Robson, that his master was invited to remain for the night, and that as he had accepted the invitation, he, Robson, must also prepare to take a part and parcel of his, the servant's, bed; which bed being situated in the pantry, would be warm and comfortable; and, upon Robson's enquiring as to his reasons for

No. 17

sleeping there, he was duly informed, that there was a great portion of the plate therein deposited ; and, that he slept there as guard, in order that if any robbers should find their way into the mansion, he could protect the most valuable portion of the property from being carried off.

This intelligence was precisely what Robson desired to obtain, and he resolved to profit by it—and to a pretty considerable extent. As the evening proceeded onwards, and the hour of twelve drew nigh, Robson rose from the side of the snoring domestic, and noiselessly opened the door, and drawing a small dark lantern from his pocket, he ascended to the hall, where he encountered Bond.

" Well," exclaimed the captain, " what success have you had ?"

" Oh ! the most complete," answered Robson, " her ladyship was in a very liberal mood, for she left a guinea with that fellow that we robbed ; and, as some acknowledgement for the same, I learned from him, the spot where the bulk of the plate is concealed—though a great portion of it is kept in the pantry, and——"

" Quick, man, quick," exclaimed Bond, impatiently interrupting him ; " don't stand idling here, how are we to commence business ? Where is this plate-chest to be found ? If we dally time in this manner, we shall have the morning upon us in a twinkling."

" Make all way for the loft," answered the lieutenant, " under the roof of the house—rather a cunning trick of her ladyship's, wasn't it ? She little thought we should visit it there."

" I suppose not," acquiesced Bond, in a strong whisper.

They then commenced a slow and cautious ascent up the stairs—arrived at the top of which, they discovered to their disappointment that the trap was above seven feet from the ground.

Upon perceiving this obstacle, Robson was for returning, but to this Bond would by no means consent ; the adventure he said, had proceeded too far, and wore too favourable an appearance, for them to abandon it in its birth ; and, after a momentary consideration, he motioned Robson to follow him ; he did so, and the result was, that they, after a brief search, procured a short flight of portable steps, with which they could reach the trap—it was raised—they entered the recess caused thereby, and soon discovered the object of their search—the weight of which was so great, that they, with great difficulty, succeeded in moving it—this was at length accomplished. Another query was now presented—how was it to be lowered ? This puzzled them greatly—a rope being obtained, this difficulty was next surmounted, and they had prepared to descend the stairs with the precious load, when Robson, upon whose shoulders it had been placed, suddenly swerved, and the chest fell from his shoulders, and alighted with a tremendous crash in the hall below.

Here was a position ! the house was alarmed, all the servants, male and female, rushed from their beds in a state of alarm.

Bond held in his breath, and anxiously awaited the result of the accident, which had not only deprived them of a very considerable booty, but placed their very lives in danger.

Lady Flora also hurriedly placed a morning gown over her night gear, and in the greatest alarm, hastened out to discover the cause of such an unexpected confusion.

By this time, Bond and his lieutenant had each placed a brace of pistols upon full cock, and were about to quit the landing, when one of the doors opening thereunto, was seen to revolve upon its hinges—a large head fronted by a young army of curl papers, and surmounted by a three story book muslin night-cap, together with a very brawny pair of naked shoulders, were exposed to view ; and a voice not the most gentle in the world, was heard to vociferate

" Help ! murder ! fire ! thieves ! villains ! help ! help !"

Which words being yelled forth in tones of fear, the door was re-closed with the violence caused by shocked maiden modesty.

Bond and Robson now commenced their ascent from the summit, and upon gaining the hall, they discovered Lady Flora and the servants surrounding the now shattered plate chest, and collecting its late contents. Immediately upon beholding them, her ladyship commanded the servants to seize the robbers; they advanced a few paces, as though about to comply with the orders they had received, but the sight of pistols had a wonderful effect upon their courage, for they immediately commenced a retrogade movement, and by this time the highwayman had gained the door, when the servants gave a still-born imitation of rush number two, but 'twas

"The attempt, not the deed that confounded them."

Again they receded, and our adventurers were about to disappear.

"Lady Mandeville, allow me to return you my most sincere thanks, for the very courteous treatment I have experienced at you hands this evening, as your rich Indian cousin. Ha, ha, ha?"

These words, and the laugh, which were uttered by Bond in his own natural tone of voice, greatly amazed Lady Flora.

"Surely," she exclaimed, "Your voice is familiar to me."

"Probably it may be, madam, do you remember the masquerade?"

"Great Heavens!" ejaculated Lady Flora, "you then are———"

"Captain Bond, madam, at your service."

"And I'm Lieutenant Robson," rejoined that person, removing his hat; "we are both your most obedient servants, adieu, lady, adieu!"

With these words, they suddenly opened the door, retired from the house, and then violently closed it after them.

Thus terminated the visit of Bond, to his former mistress.

CHAPTER XXXIX.

THE SOLDIER'S RETURN.

MEG having once come to the determination of bearing Maria from Corder, and placing her in the safe keeping of her father, at once set about devising the means whereby she could best effect the desired object.

Upon the evening succeeding that upon which Bond and Robson had visited the mansion of Lady Flora Mandeville, as previously detailed by us, she wandered near the cottage where the maiden, together with her mother, resided. She, a short time after her arrival, perceived Maria quit the humble tenement, cross the garden appending thereunto, open and re-close the wicket, then walk briskly up the avenue that inclined a little to the left. She followed closely in her footsteps, and at length perceiving that she was unable to overtake the object of her search, the "gipsey's warning" brought Maria to a pause, and upon turning, she was immediately accosted by Meg.

"Whither in such haste?" she exclaimed, "Have you not one moment to spare for the gipsey? I see you are hastening towards yonder barn; avoid that place, *as you would your grave.*"

"Why should I avoid that more than any other?" rejoined Maria. "Surely there can be no harm arise from an old barn?"

"You speak rightly," replied Meg. "No harm can possibly arise from the *Barn*, but those who visit it may not be equally guileless. You know the moral character of him upon whom you have fixed the standard of your future happiness. He has more than once convicted himself upon matters of no small moment; yet, with all these convictions pressing upon your mind, you abandon yourself to whatever fate his depravity may assign to you. At once defy even fate itself for ever. Accompany me to where those whose only ambition is the premotion of your welfare and happiness are even now awaiting your arrival, and with whom your after life would be one bright scene of happiness and contentment."

"Of whom do you speak?" enquired Maria. "I know of no person, William Corder excepted, that entertains solicitude for my welfare; therefore you have spoken beyond the limits of truth, good gipsey; but leave me now—I am in haste—an appointment——"

"Has been made, and must be broken," interposed Meg. "You must and shall go with me. No harm is intended; and in a short time I will reconduct you to your home myself; but remember, I will receive no denial. If you consent not, I have those at hand who will assist me in my plan, which is wholly for your own benefit and interest. Will you come?"

"I will not," replied Maria, in a tone of fixed resolution.

The gipsey was about to seize her by the arm, when a third person appeared upon the scene. This was Corder. Maria instantly called upon him to rescue her from the importunities of the gipsey. In a fierce tone he demanded of Meg who she was, and also how she dared to molest Maria?

"And pray who are you that dares to question me?" retorted Meg; "though now I gaze upon those ill-proportioned, forbidding features, I know you full well. You are William Corder—the man to whose name there is much crime and infamy attached. And you dare to question me! But proceed in your own course. That path in which you have already trod will one day terminate your earthly career. Now mark well the gipsey's prophesy—*The means of life shall prove your guilt and death*. On, on, doomed one, to thy gloomy fate!"

With these words Meg suddenly disappeared with a glance that, in the language of Hecate, seemed to say,

"This night I'll spend
Unto a dismal, fatal end."

Upon the disappearance of the gipsey, Corder took the arm of Maria, and they both proceeded in this manner towards the *Red Burn*, where after a short consultation they entered, Maria first and Corder afterwards. The door closed upon them; and Meg, who had followed in their track, an hour afterwards wended her way back from whence she came.

*   *   *   *   *   *

[A long interval must necessarily be passed by us, as the circumstances that occurred in the intervening time are by no means fitted for our pages; and indeed have been detailed, in a very minute manner, in the original account of this tragical affair.]

After their first secret interview, Maria and her seducer continued to make the Red Barn the rendezvous for a lengthy period, and at length she disappeared from the cottage of her mother; which was no sooner known than the lonely parent communicated the news to Lady Flora Mandeville, who immediately instituted proceedings calculated to produce some clue as to her whereabouts; but as this proved to be unsuccessful, she left instructions with Mrs. Martin to request Corder, when he next visited her cottage, to pay a visit to her residence, in order that she might question him concerning the flight of Maria. To this, however, he would not consent; and evaded the enquiries put to him by assuring the mother that her daughter was well in health and happiness, and would shortly return to her paternal roof. In this manner a period of three years expired. One fine autumnal evening a soldier halted before the cottage of Mrs. Martin. His brow was wrinkled with care, and upon entering the rustic abode of peace and content he was observed to look wistfully around, as if in search of some object that was not present. At length he enquired of the old woman if her daughter was from home.

"Alas! she replied, the tear appearing upon her furrowed cheek; "alas! sir," she exclaimed, " my poor misguided child has long since quitted this humble roof. She has fled from the society of her lonely and aged mother, to share the hours of a seducer."

" Seducer!" cried the man with a sudden energy, " his name—his name!"

" His name?" reiterated the old woman in surprise.

" Aye, good mother, his name. Do not, in the name of heaven, keep me in this dreadful suspense. 'Tis worse, far worse than death."

" His name," replied the other, " is *William Corder*."

" And she has eloped with that villain! Gone from you—her mother!"

" She has, indeed; and yet I have ever treated her with the greatest possible affection and kindness. But, alas! she has now abandoned me for ever. I have no one now to tend me in my last days; no hand to smooth the pillow upon which my head will soon be laid in sickness; for I daily grow more feeble and infirm. I must now go down in solitude to the grave, with no lineal hand to close these aged eyes, and follow my last earthly remains to their final resting-place in the dark, cold, and silent grave."

" Great God!" exclaimed the young man, sinking into a chair. " And this is Maria! She for whom I have perilled my life—passed through years of toil and hardship. Her upon whom, from the earliest dawn of recollection, I have loved with all the ardour of youthful adoration. She was the empress of my soul, the being of my idolatry. And now I cannot dwell upon her memory with aught but disgust. Oh that men should implant such fickle objects in their hearts; there, like an inveterate canker, to corrode and finally extinguish the flame of life. I am now like a blighted tree amid the fertile grove. My only hope of happiness was centered in that girl, and how has she merited the love I bore towards her? By uniting her fate with that of a villain. May the withering curse of misplaced love light upon and pursue their guilty course. May all the torment of hell fall heavily upon the destroyer of my peace—she——"

" Oh! in pity to a parent's feelings, conclude not your curse," cried the old woman, falling upon her knees, and clinging to the utterer of the above words; " remember, I am her mother."

" And does not the thought of shame and disgrace blister your tongue while you give utterance to the declaration? I know your agony must be intense; but what think you must be the nature of my feelings? Three years since she rejected me because I was poor, and smiled upon my rival, who possessed money and property wrung from its natural owners, and attended by the widow's and orphan's tears of oppression. I quitted my native land, and in a foreign clime, through a field of blood, strove to win that which shall render me equal to my proud rival. I am in some measure successful; return to my native land—return to find her I love, false as hell. And yet the world would say that she is not to blame. They think not of the breaking heart of the disappointed one, whose prospects are for ever blasted. Pardon my ravings, good dame. The sudden surprise caused the outburst; but I am calmer, much calmer now. A draught of milk, good dame, to quench my parched throat. Here is money, for which I have toiled and braved every danger; for the thought of Maria turned every bullet aside; and that Providence that shielded me from every danger, preserved my life while countless numbers fell stricken in death, has reserved me for a fate such as this; and to escape from the remembrance of which death would be a blessing. Has time and the various vicissitudes through which I have passed so changed my outward man, that you, good dame, no longer remember the poor, dejected, and almost heart-broken Edward Lambourne?"

" Edward!" exclaimed the old woman. " Can it be possible! Have you, after so long an absence, returned to share in the general grief that now fills the breasts of those who entertained a thought or feeling of interest towards my poor deluded girl, whom I had always thought possessed too much penetration of soul —too sound an understanding—to be led from the paths of virtue and honour by the flattering assurances of an unprincipled seducer. She has ever been reared in the ways of piety and religious duty; and yet, with all these inducements to continue in the pursuit of rectitude, she must sacrifice all to the interests of a villain. But let me implore of you, Edward, endeavour to banish from your memory one so unworthy of your noble nature. She is my child; yet the knowledge of that does not shut out from my mind the extent of her guilt."

" I have now learned all. A speedy return to those scenes of toil from which I have now returned, shall contribute towards my death. There, on all sides surrounded by danger and the horror of war, I will endeavour to bury in eternal oblivion all thought of the false one that in her days of innocence held my heart captive. Had Maria have listened to my vows, how truly different would have been the fate both of her and myself. She would have lived an honour to those by whom she was surrounded, and have descended to the grave after an exemplary life, respected and lamented by all whose admiration was excited towards an object of meekness and virtue. I, too, should have passed my days in the scene of my more youthful hours. But I must cease to think of this, or Reason, from her tottering seat, will fall, and cause me to sink into the last sad refuge from despair—an idiot's grave. But here, good mother, for by such endearing name I shall ever accost you, though the dear tie that should have confirmed it has not sanctioned our talliance, accept from my hands this leathern purse; in it is the reward of my labours. Do not shrink from it. The sum, though great, has been earned honestly, and hardly purchased with my blood. Take it, good mother; it will preserve you from the fangs of poverty, which may else assail your old age, and make your situation doubly keen. To me, it is as dross; for without Maria, life itself is but a source of sorrow. I will away from the scene of my disgrace and disappointment. Farewell; and may the God of Mercy eternally watch over and protect you from all worldly harm."

And before the sound of these words had died upon the air, Edward Lambourne rushed madly from the cottage that had formerly contained all that was dear to him on earth. He continued to ramble for some considerable time around the adjacent walks, each of which presented some new source of meditation. Here stood a rose-tree, which Maria in days of youthful innocence had with her own fair hands planted in the earth, had tended its budding beauties, and each new day proudly boasted of the success with which her labours were crowned. How like the things she nurtured was the then happy and guiltless maiden—how great, how incomprehensible was the alteration! Then, her step was light and agile as the fawn; her countenance bore the ruddy hue of health and happiness; her disposition was docile in the extreme, yet lively and vivacious. Now, she was changed to the pale, spiritless, and dejected thing, guilt had made her. A few steps farther, and he came in sight of the rustic seat whereon, in years gone by, when childhood's happy age was with them both, they had sat admiring by turns the beauty of the surrounding scenery. Then would their infantine minds expand beyond the level of their years, and they would become entranced by contemplating the wonders of nature, and from thence become absorbed in admiration at the works of the Great Creator. Thus would these two youthful philosophers pass those hours, which others of a similar age would employ in an indulgence of a sport more suited to their years and inclinations. As Edward drew near this spot he sank upon the seat, and buried his face and grief from the eye of casual observation. He had not been long in this position when he heard a light footstep approach; he looked up, and beheld—*Maria!*

To describe the sensations that filled the breasts of those who had formerly entertained such regard for each other, would require an abler pen than that which we can wield. Edward started to his feet, and gazed upon the object of his thoughts with the wild and vacant stare of a madman. Each looked upon the other, as though fearful of breaking the dreadful silence.

Maria was the first to speak, and dissolve the spell.

" Edward!" she exclaimed, sinking upon her knees before him, and bursting into a violent flood of tears that nearly choked her power of utterance: " Edward, can it then be possible that I am fallen so low, am so thoroughly debased, that you, even you, who once loved me so tenderly, refuse to speak—to look upon me ? Oh! this is indeed cruel. All else I *could* have borne; but this—this *is* cruel ?"

" Maria," returned Edward, turning from the prostrate form at his feet, that his emotion might not be visible, " Maria, you cannot judge of the agony of mind under which I now labour. For your sake alone I quitted the scene of my boyhood's days, fled from home and parents, all—all for you. I saw that my poverty was a bar to my hopes, and strove to remove that bar. To do so I sub-jected myself to hardships that must have been endured to be believed. I became a soldier, and subject to the arbitrary commands of those whom supe-riority of fortune had placed in a position above me. Often has my spirit rebelled against their petty tyranny; and once my weapon was half drawn to strike the tinselled monster to the earth, who could thus trample upon the feelings of his fellow-man, but the thought of you stayed my arm, and I forbore to deal that blow, which, by hastening the hour of my death, would have spared me the agony of this meeting, and what is far worse, the knowledge of your disgrace."

" Edward, Edward !" cried Maria, in a supplicating tone, " in mercy spare me. This will break my heart; indeed, indeed it will. I have been criminal, 'tis true, but the heart-rending agony of remorse I have endured has been a fearful punishment. Oh, Edward! did you but know what dreadful privations I have endured since that fatal hour when guilt first stamped its evidence upon my brow; how, hour by hour, I have sat alone, ruminating upon my ruin, one by one the forms of those whose good opinion I have for ever forfeited, appeared before me, and upbraided me for my guilt. Then I thought you was present, and while every other tongue was proclaiming my shame and disgrace, you boldly stood up in defence of the misguided one, and taught the babbling concourse to remember that there never yet was the being who could long withstand temptation; and, that woman was by nature framed to listen and yield to the allurements of man-kind."

" Maria !" exclaimed Edward, you have wrung my heart-strings. For you I had reserved the task of consoling me for the many hardships I had endured. Judge, then, if you can, of my grief when I found you to be no longer worthy of the trust I had reposed in you. Oh, Maria! how could you thus blight our hopes of happiness? But you are now another's, and I must away. And now, Maria, as it may be many a long day before we meet again, one kiss at parting."

" Take it, Edward," rejoined Maria, " and let it be a pledge of the love that in infant days bound us to each other."

These words concluded, a kiss sealed the lips of Edward and Maria. A quick heavy footstep was heard, and the next instant Corder stood before them. Ed-ward started to his feet and looked fiercely upon his more successful rival, who in his turn appeared to be greatly astonished at the presence of Lambourne.

" This, sir, is the second time I have had cause to command your absence. This young woman is my own, and none but me shall hold converse with her; therefore, you will perhaps oblige me by a speedy withdrawal."

" When this young woman shall command me so to do," rejoined Lambourne " I will do so; until then I shall remain."

Upon hearing this, Corder glanced fiercely upon the other, and would doubtless have darted upon him, had not Maria, apprehensive that such would be the case, stood between them.

" Oh! Edward," she cried, " for my sake retire."

With one glance upon the object of his former love he darted from the spot, hastened onward, and in a few hours afterwards was many, many miles from the scene of his disappointment.

Thus terminated the return of Edward Lambourne to his native village, where, full of hope and anticipation, he had sought the presence of her in whom all his hopes were centered, and in whom all confidence was now violated.

CHAPTER XL.

THE GAMBLER'S DESTINY.

BELFORD, for the space of three years and two months, remained securely lodged in France, where he launched freely into every debauchery and extravagance the depraved manners of the country tolerated. His life was one continued and unvarying scene of dissipation. Not an hour of his life, that was not passed in the companionship of Morpheus, but some new species of carnal indulgence was not devised. The gaming-table and his own stock of personal assurance furnished the means necessary for this life of expensive indulgence. Doubtless he would have terminated his earthly career in the French capital, but that he received a letter from his sister, the only remaining remnant of a once large and opulent family, himself excepted. The nature of this letter was to inform him that she, his sister, was then labouring under the ill effects of a violent fever that was then raging in the metropolis; and also that if he, Belford, had any desire to behold her with life, he must return to town without delay.

Upon the receipt of this letter, Belford immediately determined upon the course he intended to pursue. He resolved upon an immediate return to town. Not that he entertained any desire to behold his sister in her dying moments, had he not have felt convinced that she possessed a considerable share of property, which property he hoped to obtain, as she was now upon a bed of death. According to this resolution, he, the day succeeding that upon which he had received the letter, saw him landed at London Bridge; and, calling upon the first hackney carriage he encountered, he directed the driver where to convey the vehicle, and himself included, with the assurance, that if he made the best use of his persuasive powers in propelling his steeds onwards, he should receive two shillings over and above the amount of his legal demand, which in his, the coachman's, estimation, would amount to four shillings, not including an appeal for "summut for luggage."

Instigated by Belford's promise of liberality, the man ascended the old and tottering sides of his vehicle and sank into his seat, resumed the ribbons, and with a preparatory flourish of the whip, requested the consumptive shadows before him to "*kum up*," but they, the consumptive shadows before mentioned, unfortunately having engendered a vague suspicion that they had already "kum'd up" beyond the extent of their physical abilities, refused to move one jot. The whip descended heavily, but in vain. The near horse turned to his companion in misery, as if for the purpose of applauding the stoic indifference with which he endured the castigation inflicted by the enraged knight of the whip. Now, one of the two horses entertained a great propensity for kicking, and this cne had, two years previous to the epoch of which we write, been blinded by a playful young gentleman, son to the stable-keeper. This youthful Solomon, by dint of great exertion, contrived to reach the trough, and then, by the aid and assistance of an iron skewer, did deface and otherwise damage the aforesaid horse's left eye; and being reprimanded for the same, declared that he had made the experiment in order that future ages might be convinced whether or not a "*blind horse could see.*" Since the period of his blindness, the steed in question had entertained a total and supreme contempt for corporeal castigation. The man used both whip and tongue to exhort them to proceed, but in vain. He swore from without, and Belford raved from within; still, however, they were inflexible, feeling convinced, as the blind gentleman silently observed to his companion, that at the end of their journey they would be left to stand, sleep, and devour imaginary fields of hay and clover, while their unlawful and merciless driver was regaling himself with sundry pots of heavy, mingled with a mountain of bread and cheese, or if this be not his ordinary fare, should he be a teetotaller, the interior of a reading-room would receive him, and there he might be seen to imbibe tea and thin bread and butter to an incredible amount.

The appetite of the coachman is as peculiar as his coach and pair. Who ever saw a hackney coach in a hurry? who ever saw a hackney coach horse make a clandestine attempt to run (except backwards), and, lastly, who ever saw a hackney-coachman that did not eat thin bread and butter? We can boldly answer —nobody! We have observed the object of our search enter a coffee-house upon a cold winter's day after having doffed the never-to-be forgotten top-coat, with its multitudinous collection of capes produce an ample supply of beef steak. This was presently re-produced, having during the period of its absence undergone a certain process, known to all persons of culinary celebrity—"grilling." This was flanked by a young regiment of thin-sliced bread and butter on one side, while appearances were kept up-on the opposite one by a slate coloured cup and saucer, filled with a decoction of a Chinese plant known as tea. This, together with milk and four juvenile lumps of loaf-sugar, at eightpence, is placed before the coachman, who speedily despatches the whole (utensils excepted) to the regions of hunger,—intimates his desire to be furnished with a second edition of tea, and thin bread and butter—devours that also—then defrayed the expences incurred thereby—dons the coat, and bustles out to resume his avocation. This is a practice followed even now in this age of omnibus and steam innovation. What they indulged in when the field was their own, and cabs were but the children of some posthumous treatise upon conveyance in general; but, even now, when gaudily painted vehicles with monumental wheels, bright harness, and tall spirited horses, and thin stylish cabman, in a great measure supplant the place of the ancient conveyance—exclude from their ranks the dingy coach with its ponderous body and dropsical coachman, whose very coat would endanger the safety of the flimsy evidence of man's inventive genius before them. Even then we would walk miles rather than encourage such innovation. "Who," says a contemporary, "would ride a mile at full speed for eightpence, when he might

No. 18.

indulge in the slow ricketty motion of a hackney-coach for a shilling?" We speak from personal experience, and say—*nobody!* once more.

After some farther persuasion, the coachman who had the conducting of Belford to his destination hit upon the following plan, which he imagined would prove far more effective than the whip—he descended from his seat, and having emptied the contents of the nose-bags into what is termed the pocket of the coach, he then proceeded to tie the empty receptacles for food before them, and then re-ascended to his throne of power. The effect of this manœuvre soon became apparent. The horses, knowing that they were in the direction of their stables, set off at the top of their speed, and actually did not fall asleep until their task had been completed. Now, doubtless, the reader will enquire how the empty bags could possibly cause the horses to alter their determination? We will inform them. The coachman was in the daily habit of bringing with him upon his morning departure as much provender as, in his experienced opinion, would be requisite for their daily consumption; which, upon his nightly return, was invariably consumed. Considering it was about one fifth portion of what they would require if permitted to indulge in the natural extent of their appetites. Therefore, knowing as they well did, that the bags would, upon returning to the stable, be re-filled they judged, and wisely, that the sooner they arrived there the quicker their hungry cravings would be satisfied; at least, to their usual extent. Propelled by this anticipation, the coachman's end was accomplished, and, in consequence of which, the objects of our debates are once more brought to a stand.

Upon arriving at the bedside of his sister, Belford found her to be in a high state of delirium, produced by the fever under which she then laboured. Upon enquiring of the woman who tended her, he learned she frequently spoke of him in her ravings, and also that her malady, which was then at its height, would soon change either for better or worse; in which case a speedy death or tardy recovery would be the result.

After remaining at the bedside of the invalid, and findidg no chance of her return to consciousness was expected by those who best knew the nature of the disorder under which she laboured, he took his leave, and adjourned to the nearest reading room, where, upon looking over one of the daily journals, the following advertisement met his observation :—

" If the next of kin to Colonel George Turnbull, late in the service of the Honourable East India Company, will apply to Captain Cox, also of the East India Company's service, now residing at No. 10, Argyle-street, Regent-street, they may hear of something greatly to their advantage "

Upon beholding this, Belford immediately repaired to the place mentioned, and there learned that a legacy of four thousand pounds had been bequeathed by the now deceased colonel to his nearest relatives. Possessed with this information, Belford next proceeded to the residence of Mrs Major Turnbull and daughters; and, upon being shown to the drawing-room, he shook hands most cordially with the ladies, who were one and all acquainted with the real cause of his long absence from England. He was more particularly attentive to Miss Martha, the elder of the two, and whom he once thought of leading to the hymenial altar. She was greatly flattered by this renewal of his attentions, which she, of course, endeavoured to persuade herself into the belief of being honourable in the extreme. In this manner three weeks passed imperceptibly away, and at the end of which time, Belford acquainted the old lady with that intelligence which previous to their being put in possession of, he had determined to re-establish himself once more in the good graces of the family, and even make an offer of his hand to Martha.

Immediately upon being acquainted with the welcome tidings, Mrs. Major Turnbull paid a visit to the captain, named in the advertizement, and from him learned that a brother of the late colonel's had applied, and was even now completing the necessary arrangements for obtaining possession of the property assigned to him by the deceased.

Belford's only aim in soliciting the hand of the lady was in order to obtain some portion of the handsome legacy that had thus, as he believed, unexpectedly fallen into their possession, and as it was through his agency alone they had obtained it, he expected something to the amount of about a thousand pounds, by way of a marriage dowry with Martha. Upon learning, however, that the claim of another and nearer relative had obtained the prior advantage, his sentiments towards her, whom he would otherwise have led to the altar, altered very materially, and he, by degrees, became more cool, and at length discontinued his visits altogether.

Now, it so happened that through one of those mysterious and secret channels through which news of a private nature is said to travel, the knowledge of Belford's return to his native land became known to the friends of the deceased man whom three years since, he had slain in a duel; and they in their turn became highly indignant at his assurance, and in proof thereof, placed the officers of justice upon his track. Their first appearance was at the residence of Mrs. Major Turnbull, while the issue of the money affair was unknown to them, and she actually submitted to have the house searched. As may be supposed, Belford not being then upon the premises, coupled with Mrs. Major Turnbull's protestations of ignorance to the place of concealment, satisfied the officers, who withdrew and reported accordingly. Now, however, that Belford had once more deserted them, that lady's sentiments towards him had undergone a very material alteration, and she was now as anxious to promote as she had before been willing to prevent his capture. At length, having, through the subtle agency of her sable footman, the before-mentioned Mr. Cæsar Bumpo, discovered the place of his abode, she forthwith despatched a letter to the nearest magistrates, informing them of the same; upon which a couple of peculiarly intelligent officers, or runners, were selected and despatched to the place mentioned in the note.

The clock of a neighbouring church had proclaimed the hour of twelve upon the morning succeeding that when the news of Belford's whereabout was made known to the officers, and he was about to attire himself for the ensuing evening, when the sound of voices upon the stairs suddenly caused him to start. He instantly equipped himself in his dressing gown, and listened attentively; the result of which was, that the opinion he had previously entertained was now verified, which opinion led to the belief that the persons whose voices he had heard were two catch poles, with whom he had formerly transacted business of a similar nature. Upon being convinced of this he promptly closed the door, and reached a brace of loaded duelling pistols from the shelf that was fixed above his head, and, having primed and cocked them, stood prepared for the intruders. He had not to wait long—a loud knocking was heard at the door.

" Who's there ?" demanded Belford from within.

" Peace hofficers as is come to happrehend Count Belford, who is in this here room," was the reply.

And the words were followed by another vigorous assault upon the door, which now began to give signs of a speedy dissolution.

" Beware !" shouted Belford, " I am armed, and resolved to shoot the first man that passes into this room; beware, I say."

" Werry sorry to trouble you," rejoined the officer from without; " but doty is doty, and must be done; therefore, ve hopes as how you vont be ungenteel, and treat us any vay 'cept that vich von gemman ought to treat another: shoot away —here goes."

As the man uttered these words, they gave one strong and simultaneous thrust and the door fell forward, discovering Belford standing in the centre of the room, with a pistol in each hand, the barrels of which were levelled at the officers, who shrunk backwards, as indeed would any other rationally disposed men who did not entertain any great desire to become an animated target.

"Now !" exclaimed Belford, " these pistols are loaded—my fingers are even now upon the triggers—they might be discharged—the bullets might chance to penetrate your thick skulls, and you might die."

Upon hearing this, the landlord, who in a momentary fit of valour had armed himself with the poker, and a fat old cook, who carried a bristless broom, simultaneously remembered that they had something of the utmost importance to attend to below—stairs we mean—suddenly made a precipitate retreat from the scene of action, leaving the officers and an heroic scullery-maid to withstand the assault.

"Now, your honour!" exclaimed the foremost officer, "vot's the use of all this here nonsense; 'spose you fires them ere pistols, vy, you see they might not hit us—then you see ve should nail you arter all—and 'spose they did hit us, and ve vos to cock our toes, vy then there ud be a lot more come, as ud be sure to nail you—so vot's the odds who does it? You might as vell let us have the credit of the job as any body else; and I'm sure ve von't be hard vith you—not ve indeed. Vy, if you'll only jist consent to come vith us, blow me into bad suv'rins vith a piece out, if I don't pay for the drag—that's vot I'll do, and no gammon about it, and I mean to say that's the vay von gemman ought to treat another: vot do you say, sir, eh?"

"Say," reiterated Belford, "why that if you are not off, I'll send a bullet whizzing through your brain."

"Vell, then, if you von't take the advice of a friend," rejoined the officer, making preparations to rush forward—"you must take the consekvences ov your obstinateness, and——"

A bullet entered his brain—he fell to the ground, dead!

And the next instant Belford had discharged the contents of the remaining weapon through his own head—his brains scattered the wall.

Thus terminated the career of a gambler.

Had Count Belford lived but three days longer he would have enjoyed the possession of eight thousand pounds—the property of his sister, who, in the lucid moments that preceded her death, bequeathed the whole to him; but as he was now deceased, and no other heir appearing to claim the property, by the provisions of the will which so appointed, in the event of his non-appearance, the wealth which would otherwise have been expended in profligacy and dissipation was given towards the support of a public hospital.

We have now completed the history of one of the most accomplished black legs that ever yet moved in the fashionable circles of society.

CHAPTER XLI.

THE DREAM.

Dreams are produced through the exercise of those functions that during the day have been dormant. According to the phrenological system of the head—the faculties—are divided, and are also disposed in regular order throughout the head; and according as they either recede or expand, so are the dispositions, inclinations, and indeed the very actions of mankind, regulated. The common prejudice with regard to dreams, however, is, that they are nothing more or less than warnings from Heaven sent to prepare persons for the fate that awaits them; and in support of this declaration they will assert that upon some such occasion of any tragical event, a former knowledge of the same was produced through a dream. This may in some measure be true; for instance, if any person had a friend or relation who had been long prostrate upon a bed of sickness —what would be more natural than for them to dream of their death? and should such death actually come to pass, they would impute the same to the supernatural influence of dreams. How truly absurd must this appear, for though they may even as it were come to a premature knowledge of the very time, yet can it be possible that it would have been different but for a dream? The thought is ridiculous in the extreme. Dreams arise from several causes besides the one we have just mentioned : any quantity of solid food taken immediately before retiring to rest will prevent the bodily moisture from passing through its proper channel, and thereby disturb the slumberer. Then, again, the system upon which the human frame works is so organized that each faculty of the body is called upon to sustain its portion of action, and should the pursuits of life cause a continual exertion of some, and a total relaxation of others—those which are kept in constant activity naturally become impaired, while the others are thereby compelled to bring themselves into action when the other portion of the system is stationary. There is a great variety in the nature of dreams—some persons will relate in the most minute manner the precise nature of their vision—while others, on the contrary, cannot retain even a particle—others, again, pursue one subject which is as palpably represented before their imagination, as though it were actually in reality—while many are confused and wade through a multitude of subjects which appear gloomy and indistinct. But this is a somewhat shadowy subject, therefore we will quit it upon the instant.

For some considerable time after the departure of Edward Lambourne, Mrs. Martin heard no tidings of her daughter, though she was frequently visited by Corder who always found some new excuse for her non-appearance; at length she became greatly disturbed, and informed Corder that unless he produced her child she should cause proper enquiries to be instituted. This, however, in no way alarmed him, for he immediately produced a letter purporting to be from Maria, who, as he said, was then at Ipswich in a good situation, which he had procured for her. This in some measure quelled her suspicions, and Corder quitted the cottage.

THE VISION.

Three nights afterwards, as the lonely widow was laying upon her pillow vainly endeavouring to snatch from care a brief respite, or in other words seek a short season of repose, when suddenly the cottage seemed to dissolve into air, and she believed herself to be in the interior of the *Red Barn*—a mist was before her, which was suddenly dispelled—the door opened—two persons entered, whom she could not at first recognize. Upon glancing once more towards them, however, in one she recognized Corder, and in the other Maria. As they entered the door was closed, Maria stood near the centre, while Corder receded to a far corner—a brief conversation passed between them—Maria turned from him in apparent anger: a flash, a report, and she fell, bathed in blood. Still life lingered—the murderer drew a knife, and buried it deeply in the body of his victim; then immolated her in an aperture that appeared to have been previously formed for the purpose. The earth was then thrown upon the body, and all evidence of the foul deed was removed.

She started suddenly from her bed and gazed wildly around. The cottage and all stood as usual—the clammy perspiration that stood upon her brow—the maddening thoughts that filled her mind—she had seen a vision, one produced by the thought of what might have befel the child of guilt. She rose and kindled a light, opened the door, and looked around. All was quiet and serene—the moon shone with resplendent brightness, and no sound broke upon the nightingale, whose heavenly notes appeared like the star of happiness sent to chase all care from off the face of Nature. The poor widow re-closed the door, and once more sought her pillow ; but yet she could not sleep, so strongly was the presentiment of evil implanted in her thoughts. She therefore once more arose, and dressing herself, proceeded towards the *Red Barn*, where all appeared tranquil and silent as the grave. In one of his prior visits Corder had, through accidental negligence left the key that opened into this place, which belonged to his father, in the cottage. The lock was presently forced back—the widow entered and twice traversed its limits—then forcing a smile as she thought upon the dream that had caused this minute examination, again quitted the spot, slowly retraced her steps homewards, and as she was about to open the garden wicket, she distinctly beheld the outline of a human form cross the gravelled path. This incident slightly alarmed her. After a momentary pause she traversed the walk that led to the cottage door, which she was about to open, when, as her hand was upon the latch, the ominous hoot of an owl struck upon the ear, and the next instant the nocturnal bird flew slowly over her head. This alarmed the widow more than any previous circumstance had done, for even now the popular prejudice concerning owls and crows runs high among the country folks. The good woman entered the cottage, closed the door, and, filled with dreadful apprehensions of some hidden calamity, impatiently awaited the return of morning, that sweet harbinger of another day, the herald that arouses from slumber the whole face of creation, who rises, as it were, into new life.

CHAPTER XLII.

MEG PRESERVES THE LIFE OF BOND.

FOUR days after the murder of the two officers by Meg, as detailed in a previous number by herself, as she was proceeding by the scene of death she halted, as was her habitual custom, before the gibbet upon which her son had been suspended, when she suddenly became aware of the presence of a second and a third person, by whom she was suddenly secured on both sides; and, upon turning to ascertain the cause. She beheld two ill-looking fellows, one of which was about five feet eight inches in height; his countenance bore fearful evidence of the dissipation that had marked his career, and in his pallid cheek, hollow sunken eye, and pale quivering lips, might be traced the records of villainny; together with whole years of drunkenness and debauchery. The much worn and dilapidated apparel in which he was attired was no less conspicuous than its wearer. His head was encased by a curiously mis-shapen hat, the original colour of which had, perhaps, been brown, at least at some far distant period; but (if we may be permitted to use the term) it was now a dirty no colour at all—that is—time, ill-usage, and the various vicissitudes to which it had been exposed, had so completely served to disguise its original texture, that it would have been a matter of no small difficulty to speak with precision even as to the material of which, in its more pristine days it had been constructed in lieu of a coat. His body was enveloped in the ample folds of a brown coarse-looking garment called (appropriately in the present instance) *brass rascals;* a pair of dirty white cording inexpressibles graced his nether limbs, and —— We were about to conclude the picture, but chancing to remember that a most important part or portion of the attire worn by this *accomplished* gentleman, had been omitted : we pause to inform our readers, his neck (which, by the bye, being short and plump, was most admirably adapted to the hands of the executioner) was protected from the attacks of the weather by the graceful folds of a yellow silk—fogle, we were about to say, but checking ourselves, we remember that the knot or tie had, through some accident, travelled from where it had been originally placed, and halted immediately under the left ear, and being fearful lest the reader should misconstrue this into the hangman's necklace, we exclaimed, handkerchief!

The other, though equally remarkable for the original nature of his attire was somewhat more respectably apparelled, and looked more of the bailiff than his captain, for the first mentioned evidently governed the actions of the second.

"What want you with me ?" demanded Meg, in a savage tone.

"I 'spose you doesn't know me, does yer ? ve have met afore; do you remember the affair at the Inn, when you wos going to shoot us all ? I told you I would be one with you, and I've kept my word."

"I know not what you mean," growled Meg, "for whom do you take me ?"

"Who does ve take you for !" reiterated the fellow, tightening his grasp upon her wrist. "Why, for the mad-headed gipsey as strangles all them as has the ill luck to offend you ; that's who we takes you for."

"Then you are mistaken," returned Meg, promptly.

"In course ve is," acquiesced the fellow, with a knowing wink at his companion, who returned the compliment. "You're not yourself—you're somebody else, isn't you now? Vot a wery cruel thing it ud be if, ven they has hung you up to dry, the real Gipsey Meg vos to come forud. Oh! how I should cry—vorker !"

"There, release your devil's grip upon me," cried Meg, "I feel when within your clutches as though the hangman's cord was about my neck. Let go, do you hear me ?"

"No," replied the fellow, with wink number two, "I'se got bad teeth, and can't hear, 'sides if I could, I has too much respect for my own life to let your devil's claws loose. Hold tight, Bob, or blow me independant if ve shan't go home as dead as mutton—she'll scrag us as ve used to do the poultry upon Westbourne Manor. Come along with you to jail, you she-devil's babby: come away with you."

"I shall not stir hence," replied Meg, "unless you release my hand; why, think you I can escape? Two men! and afraid of one weak woman !"

"Oh, yes," rejoined the fellow, "you're wery weak certainly—"I shouldn't like to trust my neck in your claws, unless I wanted one half of my wind pipe to laugh at the other, and come to a division."

"Then you won't release your hold upon my arms ?"

"No, ve von't."

"Then," replied the gipsey, "here I remain."

As she said this, and before they could prevent her, she had seated herself upon the ground, and turned a deaf ear to their solicitations—the nature of which were to endeavour to prevail upon her to proceed; all their attempts at which, however, proved abortive, and they were at length compelled to comply with her demand. No sooner had she regained full possession of her limbs than she darted suddenly from the side of those who had so lately held her. They followed and quickly overtook the fugitive, who sank upon the earth, as if exhausted by fatigue—the effect of which was that they passed her, and ran several paces beyond the place where she had fallen.

She then started suddenly to her feet, and rushed upon the nearest of the two and endeavoured to wrest the thick bludgeon he carried from his hand. In this she succeeded—a moment more it was raised, and partially descended upon the prostrate ruffian, when a tremendous blow, dealt by his companion, laid Meg senseless and bleeding upon the earth. In this condition she was borne to a place of security, when, upon returning to conscousness, she beheld a medical man standing by her side. Meg, in a fierce tone, enquired his business with her. He then replied that he was there to dress the wounds that had been inflicted upon her head, when, suddenly starting to her feet, she, in an authoritative tone, commanded him to leave her ; and, after some hesitation, she was obeyed.

The following day the prisoner was taken before a magistrate in order to undergo her first examination upon the charge of murder.

"Why am I brought here ?" demanded Meg, as she was escorted into the dock—"look quick and remove me from this place—the air is sultry and perfumed, fitting only for the pampered slaves of fortune."

"Silence !" vociferated the crier of the court, "cease this chattering"

"Then you must knock my teeth down my throat," muttered Meg, "for they will chatter in spite of me—the tap I have received upon my head, and the cold dog hole in which I have passed the night has thrown me slightly out of sorts ; I'm all of a tremble. Can you supply me with a draught of good brandy if I pay you handsomely for it, eh ?"

These words, which were addressed to a rather short and very corporeal individual, clothed in a large blue coat with huge parochial buttons, and beefsteak collar, and cuffs. This was the parish beadle—and to have beheld the expression of his countenance as this inquiry was made, would have been a treat worthy the talents of Hogarth or Cruickshanks. To think of the depravity absolute daring, to ask for brandy in the very presence of his worship—there was only one crime which he, the said beadle, considered to be of equal magnitude, and that was the insolence of paupers.

"Now, you gaping fool, vociferated Meg, "did you hear me speak?"

"Are you aware in whose presence you stand?" enquired the magistrate, addressing the gipsey, mildly.

"I am," replied Meg; "this, if I mistake not, is the miscalled court of justice, and you are the dispenser of its partial mandates—but think not to intimidate me with your false display of legal authority, I am not so easily frightened. But why am I placed here? having been first nearly deprived of life."

"You are here to answer the charge of a double murder, committed upon the bodies of two officers in the service of her Majesty. I am also instructed to promise you an immediate discharge, but upon one condition only."

"Name it," demanded the gipsey.

"You are leagued with a gang of desperate highwaymen."

"Well, what of that?"

"Are you acquainted with their haunt?"

"Should I answer yes—what then?"

"Much," answered the magistrate; "if you will consent to deliver them, together with their captain, into the power of justice, your liberation, accompanied by a magnificent reward, shall immediately follow?"

"And is this the only means by which I may obtain my liberation?"

"It is," answered the magistrate.

"Then, hear me," rejoined Meg; "sooner than consent to your plans—sooner than betray those whose bravery and nobleness of soul is as praiseworthy as your meanness is contemptible; I would make the prison to which your power can consign me, my grave—sooner become immolated from the light of day until death shall remove me beyond the reach of your malice, than betray, into the power of his enemies, so brave a man as Captain Bond."

"And why so?" enquired the magistrate.

"Because," answered Meg, "brave men are scarce, and villains flourish: but had I power they should not, I would nail one against some public wall; and as the others passed by, it would serve to intimidate the bad sort, and transform them to good—but I suppose I may now return from whence I was brought?"

"You may," replied the magistrate, "and there remain until you are removed to a higher court, where you will be tried by twelve jurymen of your country, for the crime of wilful murder, and for which you will doubtless suffer death, unless you will now, and at once, secure your freedom, by affording the required information. Do you still refuse to do so?"

"I do," replied Meg, promptly.

She was then removed from the bar, and borne back to the narrow precincts of the cell in which she had been placed when first brought into custody.

Upon being once more left alone to commune with the damp and loathsome atmosphere of a dungeon, Meg began to meditate upon the critical nature of her situation, and then the thought of the gang, and how Bond, deprived of her aid, would succeed in evading the pursuers that were even then upon his track, employed her mind, and furnished food for meditation. And at length the thought of complying with the request of the magistrate momentarily commanding her consideration, she endeavoured to picture to herself the consternation and rage that would fill his mind upon learning her duplicity. She next considered whether it would be possible to mislead them, and at the same time place Bond upon his guard, lest they should be surprised too suddenly to effect an escape; she determined to carry this measure into effect—pretend to have altered her sen-

[*See pages* 8i *to* 85.]

timents with regard to the band, whom she would lead them to believe it was her intention, to betray into the hands of their enemies. Accordingly, the following morning she informed the turnkey of her desire to speak with the magistrate. This communication was immediately answered by her being conducted to the bar, where she was sworn to deliver the band, or such portion of them as could be traced, into the power of the officers, ten of which, armed with their staves and a brace of pistols each. In this order, and with Meg at their head, they proceeded towards the spot where the band used formerly to meet, but which had long since been deserted by them. Here Meg came to a halt, for she knew not how to proceed; the band were located but the distance of a few hundred yards from the spot where they then stood.

"Why do you hesitate?" enquired one of the officers. "Are you about to play us false? if so——"

"Peace, fool!" exclaimed Meg; "think you that I should have engaged in this business if I had not intended going through with it? If you do not converse in a lower tone we shall have them upon us before we are prepared to meet them— let me have a brace of pistols."

"A brace of pistols!" reiterated the officer, in unfeigned astonishment; "and for what purpose?"

"Question me not," rejoined the gipsey, "either provide me with the weapons or escort me back to the place from whence you brought me; I will have my own way in all, or I refuse to deliver them into your hands, and if I once form the resolution, no power upon earth shall cause me to swerve."

"But you surely will not refuse to assign the cause of your demand for pistols, which are no fitting weapons for the hand of a woman—and should any accident befal you, our project would then fail."

"Pshaw!" cried Meg, in a contemptuous tone; "know you that her to whom you speak has endured more struggles, and received more wounds, in

No. 19.

affrays of life and death, than any of your fraternity have met with in the whole course of their professional career? But those pistols I must and will possess. Say, and quickly, for I am in haste; am I to be supplied with the necessary means of entering their retreat? The passage is of such narrow dimensions that it will only admit of the entrance of one person—and the path is so intricate, that were you to follow me you would become benighted in the thick brushwood in which the road abounds. My plan, therefore, is—that you shall place in my hands a brace of pistols, with these I will enter their haunt, and when you hear one of the weapons discharged, guard well the place from which you see me enter, for it will be the signal for the appearance of the robbers, whom I will lure hither by a false report of booty, then you can capture them at your leisure— this is my plan. What think you, is it not a good one? at least, I know 'twill be successful."

"Here are the pistols, take them, and remember, if you betray us, or in any way attempt to retreat from the compact into which you have voluntarily entered, your own death will be the immediate result; therefore, I would have you beware how you violate the trust which has been reposed in you."

"Fear not for me," rejoined Meg, "I shall act justly, and only betray those who, in my estimation, deserve such treatment; remain you here until my return, and you will then know how to appreciate the conduct of Gipsey Meg. Now, gentlemen, for a short period I must bid you farewell! and believe me, when I say that when next we meet, it will be upon terms widely different to those upon which we now part—adieu! adieu!"

With these words Meg disappeared through the shrubbery.

"I don't know how it is, but I don't half like the parting words of that woman!" exclaimed the second officer, as the gipsey vanished.

"And why not?" enquired the other, "surely you do not think——"

"That she is a traitoress," interposed the other. "By Heaven I do though, and in a few moments I shall expect to see my words verified; I trust she will not prove false, but look well to yourself, Johnson, and if you are prepared to meet treachery, there cannot be any very great harm arise from it, but if not, they make crow's meat of us all; however, you do as you please—you alone command here."

"Well!" exclaimed the other, "I must confess with you, that I do not feel altogether comfortable now that she has vanished; however, we are pretty formidable, and should they descend upon us, why, our bullets will carve a passage through their bodies."

"Ha, ha, ha!" shouted a gruff voice; "now, how fares my noble gentlemen? do they think nobly of Gipsey Meg? what think they now of Captain Bond and his merry men? is he already in their power? have they still the same good opinion of the gipsey, whose confidence they thought to abuse? She still appears the friend of her former associates—see, look upon these weapons—back, back, or you die!"

As these words were spoken they turned to ascertain from whence they came, and perceived Meg standing upon an eminence, with the pistols she had obtained from the officer who commanded them to present the arms they possessed —they did so, the word was given to fire—this command was also obeyed, but ere their contents could reach the place where she stood, the gipsey had once more vanished.

They, however, perceived the path she had taken, and darted after her. Meg, upon descending from her exalted position, rushed off in the direction of the place where Bond, the lieutenant, and band were assembled, and in a few moments afterwards, entered breathless and exhausted, into the place, where luckily they were all assembled.

"What's up now, Meg?" cried Bond; "any new danger afoot?"

"Danger!" reiterated Meg, "the officers are upon us; I have endeavoured to delude them, but in vain—prepare. therefore, to meet them; they are close upon us; therefore, Captain Bond, hasten to meet them—remember, you must be decisive; your lives or theirs; you may see how they have maltreated me. I have been imprisoned, and all for you, therefore, you may think much of your present opportunity, so come, my brave men, prepare to meet your foes, and remember, that if they live to escape, you must not live to confess it. For myself, I shall, with the captain, fight side-by-side, in this glorious struggle, which is now about to commence."

"Nay, nay, Meg," rejoined Bond, as he placed his favourite weapons in his belt, and chip't the flint of an extra pistol. You are now a far more fitting subject for the leech than for an encounter—such as the forthcoming one will be, therefore, take my friendly advice, and remain here in safety till my return."

"So," rejoined Meg, "after having spent the prime, and indeed, nearly the whole of my life among you, I am now to be left here, in time of danger; me, who has always been your beacon-light—me from whom you have always received that information that has treated of the enemy or plunder—me who has ever been your companion in danger; and now that old age has crept upon me, and you think that I am not so able as I before was, I must forsooth remain behind, in order that you may not be encumbered with my useless carcase; however, I will remain."

The tone in which these latter words were spoken, led Bond to believe that Meg had taken a deep-rooted insult at his persuasions, which were spoken, however, with a good meaning. "Why, Meg!" he at length said, after a pause, "I should have been inclined to think that you knew my disposition long before this time—my meaning in endeavouring to persuade you to remain, was the fear that the contest would have been too much for your exhausted frame. Why, you seem to have forgotten your wound."

"Not so," rejoined the gipsey, "'twas the thought of that wound that caused me the more urgently to press upon you the necessity for my being present at, and taking an active part in the conflict, then could I have selected the villain from whom I received the assault; if, indeed, his cowardice would not act as a preventive, and prevent his taking part in the supposed capture of you through my agency."

"Through your agency!" reiterated Bond, gazing upon her with unfeigned astonishment. "And can it be possible that you——"

"Adopted that scheme to save my own life," interposed Meg. "It is, indeed so; if I had not have done so, my exhaltation would speedily have followed; and, therefore, as you now know——"

"The upshot of all your trickery," interposed Robson; "why, now, if Captain Bond was of my opinion, you should share the fate of all traitors, who first obtain the required information of all their secret haunts, then introduce those to whom they are mortal foes."

"Silence!" thundered Bond, "I will not hear Meg thus spoken of in my presence—had she even played us false, as you think; why, even then, I should not have been exempt from the ill consequences."

"Then you appear to think that we are all to suffer from her villainny," muttered Robson; "I, for one, shall most certainly rebel."

"Robson!" exclaimed Bond, "our moments may be few—this hour may be our last—therefore, as we have spent the greater portion of our lives together, I should not like that we should now dispute. Recal those words, or by Heaven harm will come of it."

"Pshaw!" cried Robson, "and does Captain Bond imagine that I am thus to be alarmed by menaces? From this time I hold myself free to act as my own will may dictate."

"Then you mean to infer that we part company," rejoined Bond."

"I do."

"Then be this your passport to eternity," rejoined the captain, and drawing a pistol from his belt, he fired upon the lieutenant, who was about to return the compliment, when Meg fired, and wounded the arm that was raised to the destruction of her friend—the limb dropped, useless, by his side, and the weapon fell to the ground.

Soon as this action had been accomplished Bond was about to give utterance to some observation, when he was attracted by the sound of voices conversing in a subdued tone—he listened, they drew nearer, and in another moment one of the men entered, and informed Bond that the officers had effected an entrance. Upon being made acquainted with this intelligence, Bond commanded the man to follow him—they then rushed from the place, followed by Meg.

Upon being left alone, the enraged robber glanced after them. "So!" he exclaimed, "I am to be thus treated after a servitude of many years, and through the pratling of a woman. Ah! well, no matter, 'tis well for me, for the numbers are now few—the blood hounds once upon the track will not quit the scent, and I absent; they will be deprived of one good hand at least—had not this have occurred I should have been at a loss to devise a cause for my escape. My ideas of life are, ' Every man to himself.' And now that the band is so reduced in numbers that it cannot possibly withstand an attack made upon them by any numbers; I am now free, and my first care shall be to requite the insult I have had heaped upon me—they have managed to disable this limb—let them look to it. My life upon it, that ere long, I will be upon terms of an equal nature; this limb shall be avenged, and deeply—*life for life, and limb for limb!*"

CHAPTER XLIII.

DEATH OF ROBSON.

STRANGE it is, that in the breast of man, those sentiments which, for whole years, perhaps from the earliest dawn of recollection, have been engendered, should suddenly and oft times, by the most trivial circumstances be extinguished. We have known a hate which has been entertained for years become suddenly subdued, and the most warm friendship supply its place. We have also known people whose age, from very childhood, has been one unvaried scene of discontent and horror of some particular object become as suddenly endeared as those who had ever been upon the opposite extremity. There is no accounting for these phenomenæ of nature which are daily presented to the observation of the reflective. Thus it was with Bond and Robson; for a period of nearly twenty-six years, they had been upon terms the most intimate—shared every expedition; their pleasures, pursuits, nay, their very amours were known to each other. In short, no two men could possibly have been upon terms of closer intimacy; when they were upon one occasion merged in an engagement, the life of Bond was endangered by the pistol of an officer, and had not Robson rushed forward and received the bullet in his own side, his death would have been the result. This will be a sufficient illustration in regard of these two men, an incident which fully proves the truth of that proverb, which says that there is even "honour among thieves." And yet these men were now at enmity with each other—at such variance, that they had even attempted the lives of each other—those lives which, in a former period, each would have sacrificed to preserve the other.

Upon quitting the presence of Robson, Meg, Bond, and the man that followed them, hastened to the exterior of their haunt, and no sooner had Bond made his appearance, than he was suddenly seized from behind, and in the succeeding moment Bond beheld some six or seven officers: all carried pistols, and all were held towards the great highway captain.

Thus situated, Bond believed himself to be completely in their power, but the appearances were soon altered, and the situation of the officers was placed at an alarming discount, which circumstance was effected in the following manner:—

"Upon being first seized by the officers, Bond called upon his men to rescue their captain from the captivity with which he was threatened. The late lieutenant at that moment passed by—his wounded arm bleeding profusely, and in the other hand he held a pistol. A thought of their former friendship—a momentary admiration of the noble nature of Bond seemed to flash across his mind; perhaps, too, some spark of the regard they once entertained for each other entered his thoughts. However, without any farther comment upon the reason of such an action, we shall content ourselves by declaring that the right arm of the captive highwayman was suddenly set at large by his agency—the bullet from the weapon carried by the wounded man entered the head of the officer, and he fell prostrate upon the earth, a lifeless corpse."

Being thus suddenly and unexpectedly liberated from his thraldom (at least Bond imagined himself to be free, when he was thus partially rescued from bondage) he turned suddenly upon the one who had advanced to supply the place of his fallen comrade, and seizing the weapon directed at his head, forced the fellow upon his knees, when about to strike, however. another advanced, and aimed a blow at his head, which, had it have taken effect, must have produced instant death. The gang, however, had by this time mustered, and seeing the imminent peril in which their chief was then placed, made a simultaneous rush towards his captors, the result of which was, that the remainder of the officers, who possessed the power so to do, sought their safety in flight—the others, then, having so completely turned the tables upon them, followed, and that too, for some considerable distance, their flying adversaries—but they being somewhat too nimble upon the feet, defied all attempts made to come up with them. Satisfied with the result, they once more joined their captain, whom, together with the gipsey, they found endeavouring to resuscitate one of the band who had fallen in the contest.

Bond had seen the action before spoken of, and through which he had, by the hand of Robson, been released from his captors; and through that, imagined that he had undergone a complete reformation in his sentiments, and also intended to resume his original position among them. He, therefore, enquired if he was within the limits of the haunt.

As he gave utterance to this enquiry, the individual named, stood before him, calm and composed, with his arms folded.

"What would Captain Bond with me?" he enquired.

"Thank you for my life preserved," answered Bond.

"Pshaw!" rejoined Robson, "'twas a trifling service; one, too, that you have often performed for me—is that all?"

"Upon what terms do we meet, Lieutenant Robson?'

"As foes, bearing each towards the other —hate, the most deep and inveterate," replied Robson; "am I at liberty to depart?"

"You are so," answered Bond.

"And ere you go," responded Meg, "listen to my parting words: your victim has long since slept the sleep of death, and the fruits of her illicit attachment is even now paving the path to her own untimely end; I have oft cautioned her as to the danger of her pursuits, but 'twas in vain. You will end your days in an untimely manner, so will your daughter; both are condemned—equally irretrievable."

"Thanks for your blessing, most sapient philosopher," answered Robson, in a sarcastic tone; "though thy prophesy may not prove correct, yet the obligation is the same. Farewell, Captain Bond; Meg, adieu, I shall hope soon to see you mount the scaffold, for 'twill be your just reward—false lying witch, as you are!"

"Lieutenant Robson," vociferated Meg, "if you would quit this place with life, desist from thus insulting me, or—"

"Why, end your threat thus good, gipsey," enquired Robson; "have your say, and then I will commence."

"Preserve a civil tongue," rejoined Meg; "or, 'tis more than probable, that, like a runaway apprentice, you will not serve your original time out — you under-stand."

With these words she withdrew.

"I am sorry, that after so many years of close companionship with you, we should thus dissolve partnership—is there no way by which we can arrange our differences without thus parting, at a time, too, when our joint energies might save us from the hands of the traps," said Bond.

"For that I care not," answered the other, "my life is as free for death at one season as another; and even though it should be the executioner, whose hand performs the last earthly office, it would matter but little to me, though I swear that those through whom my guilt is made known, and with whom I have passed my career of crime, shall not be long in following me to the grave; of this I have long been resolved."

"What mean you?" ejaculuted Bond, in surprise; "was it not your hand that directed the messenger of death to him from whom I should have been passed to a gaol, and from thence to a scaffold—is it possible that you did this, and now talk thus?"

"'Tis true," replied Robson; "I have lived long enough among the various classes of society, to know that the professions of friendship and fidelity are looked upon only as the idle blowing of the wind, and I should be looked upon as an object of curiosity, were I to differ from the generality of mankind."

"Then I am to believe," answered Bond, "that you would deliver me and the band—coolly and deliberately betray us all into the hands of justice, did an opportunity present itself?"

"If I could confer any benefit upon myself by so doing," rejoined Robson; "certainly, some say I am false, what think you?"

"Think!" reiterated Bond; "why, that I have too long nurtured a serpent in my confidence—but now that I am undeceived, a far different course shall be pursued—Robson, consider yourself, from this moment, as my prisoner."

"Prisoner!" responded Robson; "what mean you?"

"Mean?" replied Bond, "that you stir not hence."

"Pshaw!" exclaimed the other, "you grow merry upon the subject—surely, you but jest with me upon that point."

"I am so far in jest," rejoined Bond, "that your life will be in peril if you attempt to quit this place."

"And Captain Bond is of opinion that he possesses power sufficient to detain me here against my inclination"

"At least," replied the other, "it shall be tried."

"Suffer me to pass through that entrance," commanded Robson, producing a pistol from beneath his vest.

"'Tis useless for you to command; remember, I alone am captain here," rejoined Bond.

"Then egress is denied me?"

"It is," was the prompt and laconic reply.

"Then your death shall force a passage."

"Not while this can protect him," exclaimed a voice from behind, and the words were quickly followed by the sharp report of a pistol, at the critical moment when Robson had levelled the pistol at Bond. The sudden start caused by the bullet, which entered the back of the lieutenant, caused him to fire the weapon, and the contents removed the hat from the head of Bond. This clearly proved, that had not the sudden and unexpected surprise of the presence of a third person been felt, the bullets must have penetrated to the brain of Bond, who, as the lieutenant fell to the ground, bathed in blood, beheld Meg, who had suddenly returned upon hearing them conversing in a louder tone than the one in which they had previously adopted; returned, too, at a moment, when the consequence was to Bond, life or death.

" My curse eternally follow, and rest upon you," faintly ejaculated Robson.
" May the ill wish of a dying man for ever haunt your hours of loneliness : a
cowardly blow to strike thus ; the jugglery of hell belongs to that woman ; and,
look well to yourself, or she will betray you as she now has me. I grow more
faint, the purple fountain of life flows fast, soon I shall quit this world for ever—
I quit it, to participate in the torments of that hell to which my crimes will
drive. Farewell, Captain Bond, I grieve that 'twas in such a cause I received
my death wound—but 'tis past now, and—"

He would have said more, but death sealed his lips.

" He is gone to his last account," muttered Meg.

" True," replied Bond, in the same reflective tone ; " and we, Meg, are now
left alone. How many of the band can we now say, alive, are true to us, and fit
for active service ?"

" There are but three," answered the gipsey.

" For many days past," pursued Bond, " I have felt a great depression of
spirits—a sort of presentiment of coming evil – which is as impossible to dispel,
as it is difficult to account for. Robson, my companion and friend, has turned
against me, and paid the forfeit of his infidelity ; I have now no earthly care,
yourself excepted ; the few that now remain of our once formidable band, will
only serve to impede, rather than advance our mutual interest, for we cannot cast
them off, yet place our own lives in jeopardy by keeping so few, who, while they
occupy, will be unable to defend our haunt from the power of the law. I know
not how to act ; for while honour counsels their retention, self-preservation,
which, from time out of mind, has been looked upon as the first law of Nature,
commands that they at once be dismissed."

" If I might council in this case," replied Meg, " I should despatch them, and
that, too, with all possible speed."

" No," rejoined Bond, " though the consequences should prove fatal, even to
myself, still I could not act as you advise—thus desert the men who have fought
and bled for me. No, no, Meg, if we must die, it shall be together. Never
shall it be said that Captain Bond, in order to secure his own safety, abandoned
the partners of his toil and danger. In all else I should be willing to act in accordance with your suggestions ; but in this I cannot ; the stings of conscience would
haunt me for ever after. Still I thank you, even as though I had availed myself
of your counsel, which I have ever found to be sound, and often invaluable in the
moment of peril."

" Gipsey Meg," cried the gipsey, " never yet counselled aught that savoured
of dishonour ; had you have heard my plan to its termination, you would have
entertained a far different opinion."

" If, then, I have not offended too deeply," answered Bond ; " perhaps you
will favour me with the conclusion ?"

" The conclusion is this :" replied Meg. " In your depredatory career much
booty has been amassed ; call the men before you, explain the nature of your
present circumstances, together with your future prospects, which, if you think
fit, you can say have been altered through the reverse of fortune, or my instrumentality—at the same time, assure them of your inability to keep up the
appearance of a band, with your present inadequate numbers—declare your determination of either turning honest, or robbing single-handed. However you decide
upon that point, you must effect their dismissal—but, at the same time, in order
that your sense of honour may not be shocked by such a proceeding, you can
inform them of the amount of booty, in the production of which, they, in common
with others, have taken a part. Offer them a clear share, which, if I mistake
not as to the amount, will be sufficient to maintain them through life, if they are
inclined to cut the profession, which I very much doubt, for I am of opinion
that they have been too long inured to the pleasures of highway excursions, to
resign them for a life of quiet security from the laws they have violated. If
they are men of any consideration they cannot refuse to accede to your terms ;

and should they do so, leave them to reap the fruits of their obstinacy, portionless and destitute."

" Even then I should be in their power," replied Bond ; " for, if brought before the magisterial powers, they would not suffer alone—but, Samson like, involve others in their ruin; then my fall would be more ignoble than if taken prisoner by them in a conflict. Thus, you see, they are enabled to propose their own terms, to which you must either accede, or perish upon a scaffold; therefore, you see, we should then be in a dilemma equally intricate and difficult to escape from ; though I should scarcely imagine, that after obtaining a liberal sum of money, they would betray us."

" I would not trust them," replied Meg; "however, the proposal must be made, and the sooner 'tis done the better for your peace of mind. They are assembled in the adjoining apartment—shall I summon them hither at once ?"

" Do so," replied Bond.

Meg instantly complied with his request, and upon the entrance of the men they enquired the nature of his business with them.

" I have sent for you," replied Bond, " in order to make a proposal, the nature of which will doubtless fill you with surprise. However, you must, of course, be aware of the great alteration which has been effected in my affairs. There, as you may perceive, lies the inanimate form of him, who has for so many years acted as your lieutenant—little now remains for me to say. Yourselves are the only persons now attached to my interests; this is, of course, a great disadvantage to me ; you must also be aware, that if appearances are at all kept up, and we pursue our professional career with any spirit, we shall, of course, be open to the same liabilities as we formerly were when our strength was of sufficient magnitude to enable us to resist the attempted inroads of the law, and yet be dispossessed of the necessary power to defend our liberty. You will perhaps think that I am pursuing a circumlocutory path, which I am; but really the very great and satisfactory evidence I have frequently seen of your skill and bravery, coupled with the lengthy period since we first became acquainted with each other, rivets my tongue, and fills me with sorrow when I deplore the adverse fate that has thus given me cause to address you upon the very unpleasant subject of our meeting. Gentlemen, I must now, to be brief with you, at once pronounce the band of Captain Bond to be for ever broken up, though, as some trifling compensation for your past services, I am now willing to throw open the store-house, when each man will be at free liberty to assist himself, to what, between the honourable estimation of man and man, he considers to be his just due. Are you content with this arrangement ? does it accord with your wishes ?"

" With regard to the money part, yes," replied the foremost man ; " but for the other, no. We have, as you say, served long under your command, and have had no just cause of complaint or murmuring—and think it hard that we should have to part now—that's what we don't approve of."

" And yet," replied Bond, in return. " What is to be done? Can you tell me how to advise ? It is useless placing our necks, as it were, within the very grasp of the executioner, which we most certainly should do by attempting to go on as before, with only one fifth portion of the number we originally possessed. I see no other course open that is fraught with any degree of safety ; and, therefore, however opposite it may be to your feelings—must be adopted, and speedily too, I regret the stern necessity that compels us to part thus, for we have taken part in many adventures, sat down to many a carousal together ; and all this tends to make one man loath to lose another's company. Will you accompany me to the store-house, in order that I may distribute to you your just rights, and after that we will partake of the farewell cup."

" Nay, Captain Bond," answered the former spokesman. " Since you are resolved upon our parting, we have no use for money ; the road can supply our necessities ; and for drinking, why, we have no heart for that now."

"But," pursued Bond, "should either of you come to the jug at last, may I confide in your honour—may I rest assured, that to save his own life, he will not endanger mine, by turning peacher in king's evidence?"

"In that case," answered the man, "I shall only answer for myself, though I think our comrades here are of the same resolution; and rather than breathe a word to injure you—why, damme, I'd be hung first, and transported afterwards."

"That would be a sentence difficult to have carried into effect," rejoined Bond, with a smile.

"Not at all, captain," replied another.

"Indeed, and how so?"

"Why, he wishes that he may be hung round the neck of some pretty lass, and afterwards transported with her favours, and the magnitude of her charms."

This elucidation of what appeared an impossibility, produced a loud and hearty laugh, which, however, the thoughtful visage of the captain ultimately checked—or, in all probability, they would have been laughing until this moment. As it was, however, such an extraordinary phenomenon was prevented, doubtless, to the discomfiture of those who indulge in the pursuit of knowledge under difficulties; for we think it would have been very natural, that after keeping up an incessant laughter for fifteen or twenty years, men would require something in the shape of food, at least, so we should imagine, but then some of our youthful readers may exclaim—

"Ah! you're not everybody!"—"We know it—no more are you."

CHAPTER XLIV

MURDER OF MARIA MARTIN.

"*From rock to rock, from glen to glen,*
From every clime on earth an echo came—
————————— *The last that's left!*"—Vide LAST MAN.

FROM the period when, for the last time, Maria conversed with Edward Lambourne, preparatory to his quitting the land of his birth, never again to return,
No. 20.

Corder's deportment towards the victim of his seductive arts had undergone a visible alteration—the hours of his former absence were now more often converted into whole days. From the mild and loving manner in which he had before addressed her, he assumed that morose and sullen tone that Nature had possessed him with, and strove to be more harsh and disagreeable to the ear of her to whom he had once (kneeling at her feet, and invoking the name of high Heaven, and the saints contained therein,) sworn to love and cherish, even with his life. He had now deprived the rose of its beauty; destroyed, for ever banished its natural hue of loveliness and simplicity. Now he, the despoiler of her happiness, dared to look with an eye of coldness upon the wreck he had made. Oh! how is it, that avenging lightnings descend not from offended Heaven, and bury such wretches in earth's dark centre? and mankind duly punish such villains —spurn them from socie'y, and " place in every honest hand a whip

> To lash the rascals, naked, through the town ?"

Men who can thus abandon those who, for them, have sacrificed home ,friends, honour, and happiness, are, in our own private opinion, more criminal than the guilty wretch, whose hand is imbibed in the life's blood of his fellow-man. For what is woman, deprived of virtue? that pearl, that gem, which, to the possessor, is more precious than gold—far more valuable than the riches of Peru—they are as the drooping lily—a blighted plantain implanted upon a barren rock. This desolation and misery has been produced by man—that being who is supposed to possess more rational sense, more acute discernment of right and wrong, and to entertain the nicest sense of honour.—Honour! oh, how is thy sacred name abused? those who would convert fields into rural slaughter-houses, and get up an assassination upon their own private account, merely because some trifling transaction has occurred, and they thereby consider their honour (?) abused, could, in a moment of calm deliberation, when in possession of every faculty, lead a young, lovely, and innocent female from her home, and the path of rectitude, then abandon her to whatever fate chance may prepare. Out upon such samples of human nature; we cannot, will not, demean the race, by calling them men—such scurvy knaves would disgrace even the hangman's abilities.

Poor girl, she now felt, and bitterly, the effect of her folly; the agony she endured was produced through the confidence she had placed in the object of her adoration, while the heart of him that lived but for her, was well nigh broken by her cruel preference. Corder had ever avoided the subject of marriage when urged by Maria to fulfil his oft-repeated assurances. Now, he absolutely declared his incapability so to do; and more than once when she adverted to the subject, and reminded him of the vow he once voluntarily made, he would tell her how to seek the favoured one of her heart with whom she sat in the place appointed by herself to meet him, Corder. At length he once declared that he knew full well that they had met, and often, at the Red Barn, and challenged her inability to accompany him there at a certain hour of the evening; this, however, she immediately consented to do, which showed him at once, he said, that his suspicions were wholly ungrounded. To describe the change which this voluntary and unexpected accession to his wish produced, would be an impossibility—he flew towards her, embraced and kissed her, called her his own dear Maria, and said that to prove how he repented of his former unjust suspicions, she should appoint her own time for a visit to the Barn upon the following day, as he said he wished her to go, in order to test the nature of improvemen's, which had of late been planned and executed by him.

"I will go to-morrow about six o'clock," answered Maria; "I love to walk at that hour by the Barn."

"Indeed," enquired Corder, "and for why?"

"I have an idea that the hour of six will be, at which, sooner or later, my life will be terminated. Strange, William, is it not, that I should have been so often warned against that Barn and you?"

" And who has dared to warn you ?" demanded Corder.

" An aged gipsey who has ever taken an apparent warm interest in my fate, and prophesied my meeting with you, and the very nature of our first conversation, before I had seen or even knew that such a person existed.

" Is it that gipsey whom I encountered with you, and who was vainly attempting to confront me, and persuade you to accompany her ? Is that the prophetic being who has now warned you of me ?"

" It is," replied Maria.

" But, now," rejoined Corder, " I must away to the Barn, for I have a small alteration which I should wish to have clear for your reception, and to-morrow evening at six. then, you will accompany me to the Barn ?"

" I will." answered Maria.

Corder then withdrew, and the following evening at the appointed time they proceeded towards the Barn

" Strange what a presentiment of coming evil I have upon me this evening."

" 'Tis nothing," resumed Corder, " 'twill all leave you when we reach the Barn, believe me, dearest."

*   *   *   *   *   *   *

' Ah, William ! dear William, do not look so fiercely upon me, your suspicions are ungrounded. Indeed, indeed they are, I never loved any but you—never, as Heaven is my judge ?"

" Liar ! 'tis false as hell—false as your own worthless heart. I loathe, hate you from the deepest depth of my soul."

" Why, have you thus altered your opinion thus quickly ? What have I done ? Of what crime have I been guilty ?"

" The worst to me—outlived my desire."

" Oh ! if that be the crime, leave me, and for ever."

" Hum ! the busy meddling world would call that cruelty ; I shall pursue another course Maria, stand upon your grave—prepare to meet your death."

" William, you surely do not intend to murder me ?"

" I do," dare to raise a cry, and—"

" No, as that God whom I have offended is my judge, no sound or murmur shall escape my lips—here, at your feet will I kneel, and while you deal the blow of death, invoke Heaven's mercy upon your head ; I will not offer any resistance ; if, knowing my love, you can harm the prostrate being before you, strike deep to my heart, and at once end this agony of soul—your only mercy will now be haste.'

" Release your hold upon me." vociferated Corder. " Release me !"

" Never, but with my life !" rejoined Maria ; " if you do intend to murder me, it shall be thus—kneeling at your feet, looking upon you with an eye of fondness—of unalterable love."

Corder struggled furiously to release himself from the grasp of his victim—but in vain. He then drew a small pistol from his pocket, and with the butt-end dealt her a tremendous blow upon that face, which even then was uplifted, beaming with affection ; the poor girl then relaxed her hold, tottered to her feet, and seizing the disengaged hand of her murderer, placed it next her heart, she then fixed her arms about his neck and pressed her lips to his, during this he stood helpless as an infant—his cheek was blanched with horror—the cold clammy evidence of perspiration stood upon his brow, his very lips had turned to a livid hue. He, however, once more gained possession of that stern determination which formed such a prominent feature in his character, and after a brief struggle, threw her from him, she fell heavily to the earth—she essayed to rise, he pulled the trigger of the bloody weapon, and the bullet entered the head of the already dying girl ; even this did not dispatch life from its empire. Maddened by the sight before him, Corder then drew a knife from his pocket, unclasped it, and stabbed her in the side—then with a loud and scarcely audible groan, with one last gaze upon her murderer, the eyes of Maria Martin were for ever closed in the cold and perpetual sleep of death, and her murderer stood transfixed to the scene of his unparellelled cruelty—a prey to all the torments of the damned.

Our very soul sickens as we record such a scene! What were the pangs of the wretch who committed the foul crime, imagination must interpret, for our hand even now trembles as violently as though ourself had been guilty of some such crime; and, therefore, shall bring this painful subject to a conclusion, by merely stating, that in our opinion, the mind of murderers are of different formation to those of other men. Surely their very soul would revolt at the commission of such crimes as are upon record; if in possession of those faculties with which the all-bountiful Providence has supplied mankind, they could not participate in such soul-revolting deeds of blood.

One of the only remaining persons, if we have to speak farther, is the Lady Flora Mandeville, who, upon hearing of the melancholy fate that befel her young *protégée,* immediately caused preparations to be made for her funeral; and, by her agency, the mangled and disfigured corse of Maria was coffin'd, and laid side-by-side, with the other members of the family, in the churchyard of Polstead. Of the wretch by whose hand she fell, nothing need be said, as the reading public have already been made acquainted with his fate through a far different channel.

Our two friends, Meg and Bond, through the importunities of the men, still continued their depredatory career, until at length they, upon one occasion, chanced to stop a Custom-house officer, who was returning to town, through Hounslow, they having removed to that place. He, however, proved no easy prey, and as Meg on one side, and Bond upon the other, commanded him to " stand and deliver," he rose from his seat, and presenting a brace of pistols, fired! Both Bond and Meg fell side-by-side, the bullets had entered their heads, their brains strewed the verdant carpet beneath their feet, and both were dead. Thus, as they had ever accompanied each other through life, so in death were their souls united in those boundless realms, where innocence, purity, and virtue, ever reigns triumphant. That we may, one and all, meet together in those Heavenly regions of joy eternal, when life's faithful struggle shall have concluded—is the ardent wish and prayer of

THE AUTHOR.

www.ingramcontent.com/pod-product-compliance
Lightning Source LLC
Chambersburg PA
CBHW080831250626
47160CB00008B/2900